Touch the Sky

Novels Written by Alison Blasdell

Touch the Sky (Book One of the Touch the Sky Series: Novels of History, Magical Realism, and Romance)

Daughter of the Sky (Book Two)

Power of the Sky (Book Three)

The Confederates' Physician (Book One of The Confederates' Physician Series of History, Adventure, and Romance)

Diary of the Confederates' Physician: Samantha's Legacy (Book Two)

The Assassin's Protégé (A novel of espionage, adventure, and romance)

The Ultimate Target: Code Name Angel (A novel of espionage, adventure, and romance with a twist of the cosmos)

Kassandra: A Tale of Love, War, and One Woman's Destiny (A novel of history, adventure, and romance set in ancient Greece at the height of its glory)

TOUCH THE SKY

Alison Blasdell

Alison Blasdell

Cover designed by Amanda Gardner

This book is a work of fiction. Names, characters, places, and incidents either are products of the author's imagination or are used fictitiously. Any resemblance to actual persons, living or dead, events, or locales is entirely coincidental.

Alison Blasdell

Printed in the United States of America

First Printing: December 2018

ISBN-13 9781730892196

This book is dedicated to:

Girlfriends, who years ago started reading *very* rough drafts of my novels, graciously providing insight and encouragement:

>Jayne Hawe, who was there for the first dream

>Arlene Baggett, who befriended a shy first-grader

>Vallie Gould, who always believed

>Judy Smith, who singularly delighted in chapters

>Sandy Brewer, who was and will always be there

And to: Hubby

Alison Blasdell

PROLOGUE

Beneath her eyelids, closed in sleep, her eyes began to move, darting to the left and then to the right, up into the sky and back down to the ground, searching. Was anyone there? Would anyone see her? Was it safe? Her heart rate increased, the blood moving quickly through her arteries in anticipation, her breathing quickening, her muscles tensing, getting ready. Now!

She breathed in deeply, feeling her lungs expand and stretch, each molecule of air lifting her effortlessly, carrying her upward. She stopped in the top of a tree, its branches hiding her as she crouched down on a limb and scanned the ground. No one. She smiled in her state of REM sleep. Once again, she took a deep breath and let her body unfold. Leaving the security of the tree behind her, she arched her back and soared into the welcoming sky.

CHAPTER 1

"**J**ennifer!"

He caught up with her, stopping her before she could leave, his grip tight, but not tight enough to be noticed by others in the room. "Where are you going?" he asked quietly as he glanced around the room. "The program is about to begin. The others are returning to the table. We should be seated."

"You be s . . . seated," Jennifer retorted.

John's eyes widened. "Good God, you're drunk!"

"I'm not drunk," she countered.

"I beg to differ. Your breath smells of alcohol and you're leaning on me. How many cocktails did you have?" he whispered urgently.

"Not enough. Not nearly enough," she said through clenched teeth as she jerked her arm free of his grasp, the momentum of the movement causing her to stumble backward. John reached for her again, but this time she didn't resist, for she welcomed the pull of his arm, righting her again.

John blinked in surprise. "Of all the times to go beyond your usual two-drink limit. Damn it, Jennifer," he said as he ran his hand through his hair. "Your behavior—"

"*My* behavior?" Jennifer drew back from his grasp. She saw John's eyes narrow as he once again reached for her arm.

"Now is not the time to discuss idle gossip," he hissed close to her ear.

"Dr. Bracken?" a man called as he weaved his way through the tables draped in white linen and fine bone china, circumventing the servers, who were discreetly and quietly clearing away the remains of the luncheon served.

Jennifer saw John relax his face before he turned to their host who had spoken.

"Yes, Mr. Becker?" John replied as the man stopped before them.

Ah, Becker, that was his name. Jennifer had forgotten their host's name, although she had spoken with him several times. Unaccustomed to feeling such anger and hurt, she hadn't been able to concentrate on anything that their host or the other guests had said during the luncheon.

"We'll be beginning shortly. We can't start without one of the guests of honor and his lovely wife," Mr. Becker said as he turned to Jennifer and smiled pleasantly.

"Of course," John said smoothly.

"John," Jennifer interrupted, feeling emboldened by the appearance of their host, "why don't you go back to the table. I'll only be a moment."

Jennifer saw John's jaw tighten imperceptibly, the only imperfection on his perfectly sculpted face—blue eyes, strong jaw, lean, fit body, a sprinkling of gray in his hair that only enhanced his aura of sophistication. At age fifty-six, John was successful, wealthy, and as much as she didn't want to admit it, probably correct as to her current state. She was feeling light-headed and her stomach felt queasy from all she had drunk, but she wasn't *drunk*. At least she didn't think she was, although, having no experience with the inebriated state, she recognized that her self-evaluation was probably not reliable. She straightened her shoulders and smiled at their host. "Mr. Becker, if you would direct me to the ladies' room?"

"Of course, Mrs. Bracken. Just go through that door and turn to your left."

3

Jennifer started to leave, and John reached for her hand. Instantly, he jerked his head up to look at her. His eyes narrowed as he squeezed her left hand.

Jennifer met his gaze. *Yes, and I'm not putting my wedding ring back on, John, until you tell me the truth.*

"Don't take too long, my dear," John said as he released her hand and kissed her chastely on the cheek.

John, always so gracious, so urbane, but Jennifer could see the glint behind his solicitous smile. He was angry. *He was angry!* Shouldn't it be the other way around? Did he have any idea how much his affair, if the rumors were true, and Jennifer was inclined to believe they were, hurt her?

She managed to nod in response, but now that John wasn't holding her hand or arm, she felt off-balanced. As gracefully as she could, she walked toward the door their host had indicated. She pushed through the door and stepped into a wide hallway. To the left, she saw the sign locating the women's restroom, but two women were exiting the restroom and walking toward her. She recognized the women and hastily turned in the opposite direction, hoping they hadn't seen her.

She walked as fast as she dare in her stiletto heels, but she was dizzy. Careful not to let her gaze wander, she focused her vision straight ahead, concentrating on pointing her feet forward and parallel to each other with each step. At the end of the hallway, she turned to the right and walked through another set of double doors.

Jennifer was on the upper level of the British Museum in London. She had toured the famous museum twice—the first time was on her honeymoon eighteen months ago, and the second time was yesterday. She and John had been given a private tour, along with twenty other guests, all part of the museum's efforts to recognize its major corporate donors.

The museum was massive, with countless rooms filled with art and artifacts dating from the beginning of human history, each room dedicated to a particular time period and geographic area of the world. For Jennifer, whose knowledge of world history came from a single class taken her junior year of high school, it had been mind-boggling. Once again, she was aware of her woefully inadequate educational background. Yet, she had enjoyed the tour immensely and was glad the London branch of John's pharmaceutical company had selected the museum as a beneficiary of its charitable endeavors. At the moment, however, she had absolutely no idea where she was in this marvelous museum.

Jennifer turned around. This obviously was not a public area of the museum. The walls were dull gray with black-and-white scratches marring their surfaces. No beautiful Doric columns between display rooms, no subdued lighting to preserve precious tapestries. Utilitarian light bulbs, encased in protective wire mesh, hung from the ceiling. In place of lovely marble floors, her heels clicked on chipped black-and-gray speckled tile.

She walked toward an elevator and pushed the button. As the door rattled open, she stepped inside the elevator, cavernous in size, its walls covered from top to bottom with heavy, brown quilted fabric, torn in places to reveal its metal cage-like structure—a freight elevator, she supposed. No matter. It would surely take her to the lower floor where she could find her way to an exit.

The elevator lurched as it began to descend, causing Jennifer's stomach to heave. She swallowed quickly, a vile liquid burning her throat. She reached for the wall of the elevator as it bounced to a stop and the door opened. Clutching her abdomen in an effort to calm her stomach, she stepped out. She was in a basement, or so it seemed, but she didn't recall the museum having a basement. Maybe she was on the ground floor in a service area?

As the elevator door closed behind her, she leaned against the wall of the hallway. Her stomach continued to rise and fall, as though it hadn't realized she was on stationary footing. She could hear a rushing sound, like the winter wind on Lake Michigan, the wind itself not possessing sound, but everything in its path moaning, cracking, snapping. She shivered, pushing the destructive image out of her mind. Perhaps someone was operating equipment, and that person could direct her to a street-level exit, or maybe the wind was blowing in from a freight door. Either way, it was a means to exit the museum and return to her hotel room.

Jennifer started walking, the sickening vertigo causing her to rest one hand on the wall as she made her way toward the sound. She pushed open a door and stumbled into a room. Harsh, bright lights flooded the room, causing her to blink. She swayed as she tried to focus. The room contained several tables on which were scattered pieces of pottery, stone, metal objects, bottles of clear liquid, artists' brushes, and an assortment of what looked like tweezers of varying sizes.

She suddenly felt hot and could feel the perspiration on her face and neck, the dampness causing her dress to stick to her back. The whirling sound was making her sick. She turned to leave but was so nauseatingly dizzy, she had to reach for a nearby table. Even the table seemed to be trembling in response to the persistent, swirling sound.

She struggled to keep her balance, feeling as though she were in the center of a tornado, the sound deafening. She felt her knees buckle and tried to catch herself as she pitched forward onto the table, hitting a metal object and knocking it onto the floor as she fell. "Ah!" she cried as her head landed on the concrete floor. Rolling onto her side, she touched her forehead, and grimacing, she withdrew her hand to examine her fingers now wet and warmed with blood. As she struggled to push herself up, she spied a metal object laying next to her, the object old, rusted, with a blue-green patina and pointed tip—the blade of an ancient spear. She plunged into a whirlwind of darkness.

* * *

830 B.C. Britain

"Cela," her mother whispered fervently, "you must remain in line."

Cela ignored her mother and, once again, looked beyond the stone circle to the great earthen wall surrounding it. The people were gathered on the wall, their attention fixed upon the hooded figures moving slowly toward the inner sanctuary of the stones. The hooded figures chanted, the sound haunting, causing the people to sway together. And the stones! In the torchlight, they appeared to glow in the dark, their shapes shifting with each flicker of the torch, growing smaller and then mystically enlarging before partially retreating in the shadows again. The smaller stones, six feet in height, were raw and in their natural state. They formed an inner circle. The larger ones, twenty feet high and weighing over twenty tons each, were decorated with the sacred carvings of the People Who Came Before. They formed an imposing outer circle, a boundary separating the common, windy plain, extending for miles from the divine.

At one time, this land was all forest, but the trees had been cleared by the People Who Came Before. These same ancestors built the great stone circles and megalithic formations and pillars that dotted the land from the southern ocean cliffs, to the western plains, to the northern mountains.

"Cela!" her mother called again.

Cela ran over to stand beside her mother. She could see her mother's anger beneath the black hood of the woolen robe she wore. All the priests and priestesses of the Wise Ones who attained the age of thirty wore black robes and were devoid of the bronze-and-gold jewelry worn by the skilled craftsmen of Cela's people. Cela's robe, like those of the Wise Ones who had not reached the age of thirty, was white and also simple, lacking any adornment.

"Cela," her mother scolded, "you are about to be formally initiated as a priestess of the Wise Ones. Conduct yourself as one."

"I'm sorry, Mama," the child answered. "It's just so exciting!"

"It's good to feel the life force flowing through you, my child, for from it comes our power, but you are never to show your emotions before the common people. You know that. You will disgrace us all."

The child's heart sank under her mother's scolding. Cela was a child of the Wise Ones, born into the elite castes of priests and priestesses. She was ten years old, the age all must attain to attend the ceremonies. She had already been schooled in the grave responsibilities that would be hers to share with the other Wise Ones. Cela's young head was filled with all that she had memorized, as was expected of one of the Wise Ones.

She could recite the history of her people and the history of this land. She knew the laws of her people. She understood the power of numbers and computation. She could write, using the symbols known only to the Wise Ones. She had been instructed in the use of herbs and plants.

The Wise Ones were the repository of all the knowledge of Cela's people, from the daily tasks of making pottery, weaving cloth, and planting crops to the mining of copper and tin to make the bronze that was essential for the warrior class of her people. Finally, she comprehended the stars. That was where Cela excelled among the children of the Wise Ones. To be able to track the movement of the earth and consequently predict the seasons was essential for the survival of her people.

Cela glanced up to the sky. Her attention was drawn to the full moon. Clouds blew across it, temporarily covering its luminescence. She had correctly predicted the cycle of the moon, just as she accurately forecast the eclipse.

As the clouds parted, the moon shined down again, surrounded by an eerie penumbra of light. Cela stared at its brightness. Now it would begin. She knew the power of the skies did not lie in the prediction of growing seasons for the grains they planted and harvested, nor did it lie in determining the migration seasons of the animals they hunted for food. The skies were far more than that; the skies were a window to the gods. Were not the People of the Sky messengers of the gods? Cela knew of the People of the Sky—those who had come from the skies long ago to instruct the Wise Ones. All the knowledge of the Wise Ones had come from the People of the Sky.

"Mama," Cela asked, "will the People of the Sky come to us tonight?"

Her mother glanced worriedly toward the High Priest. "You must not ask questions, Cela," her mother answered. Then she leaned close to Cela and whispered, "Perhaps our sacrifices to the gods tonight and tomorrow will bring them to us. Now keep silent."

"Yes, Mama," Cela said as she fell into place with her mother, Ega, and the priests and priestesses.

They entered the stone circle from the northeast side, passing under the ring of lintels erected over sarsen stones and into the double ring of blue stones. The blue stones, powerful and uncut, had been brought, at great sacrifice, from the north by the People Who Came Before.

Cela and her mother chanted with the Wise Ones as they moved toward the inner half circle, their voices in unison, the pitch unvaried, every syllable enunciated clearly, the accent on the third beat, setting up a repetitive rhythm that guided their steps. As their voices grew louder, the High Priest and his attendants entered. Although this was the first ceremony that Cela had been allowed to attend, she knew all that would happen, for some day, as an adult priestess, she would be expected to assist.

"Mama, there's Luc," Cela said.

Luc, Cela's cousin, was older than she. Many believed Luc would be the next High Priest. He had risen rapidly among the Wise Ones, despite his comparative youth of only twenty-eight years. Cela had not spent much time with him, even though they were bound by blood. For some reason, she had always felt an unexplainable discomfort in his presence.

Her attention was drawn back to the High Priest, who began calling upon the gods. She tried to peek out from the white hood of her robe as she moved with the priestesses, walking from the east to the south, as the sun did, in order to complete the circle. She chanted the words evoking the blessings of the gods as the Wise Ones stopped and turned inward, forming a circle around the High Priest.

"Now we will present our gift to the gods," Ega whispered to Cela.

"To the air tonight," Cela said.

Ega smiled at her daughter. "Yes."

The Wise Ones parted as members of the warrior class brought the captives forward. Ten men would be presented to the air tonight. Tomorrow, another ten men would be presented to the water and ten to the earth. The hands of the captives had been bound as they walked forward. Cela saw the blank stares in their eyes. She knew that they had been given a special mixture of crushed berries to drink, dulling their senses. The sacred red berries, with their glossy green leaves, grew on the great oak trees in the winter. The People of the Sky had taught Cela's people their magic.

Cela also noted that, unlike her people, the captives did not shave their facial hair, but rather, had beards that hung down and tangled with the long hair on their heads, creating a wild, dark mass surrounding their pale faces. They were barefoot and naked, some of their bodies still stained with the blood of the day's battle.

The warriors and captives stopped before a large cage constructed of reeds, grasses, and strips of hide. Cela watched as the warriors moved the ten captive men into the giant cage and tied the door shut with rawhide strips. The captives looked dully out of the cage as the High Priest blessed them. Warriors then threw a rope over one of the stone lintels and began to hoist the cage up into the air until it came to rest over a large pile of wood that had been placed on the ground.

Cela's cousin, Luc, brought a torch forward and knelt before the High Priest. The High Priest's eyes bore down upon the sacred torch. Magically, the torch ignited, causing Cela to gasp and step closer to her mother.

The High Priest nodded to Luc. For a second, as Luc looked toward the cage, Cela caught his eye. Involuntarily, she reached for her mother's hand, a shudder running through her. She did not understand the wild look in her cousin's eyes, and it frightened her. Luc turned back to the large woodpile before him and touched the torch to the dried wood. Immediately, the wood erupted in flames, followed by a cheer from the common people, viewing the sacrifices from the circular earthen bank in the distance.

Cela watched as the first flames reached the feet of the naked men in the cage. The chanting was deafening now as the flames leaped higher and higher into the cage. The effects of the drugs given to the captives quickly wore off as the scorching fire licked their skin. Even above the cheers of the common people and the chanting of the Wise Ones, Cela could hear the screams of terror and pain coming from the cage.

"No! Stop!" Cela shrieked, the words wrenched from her throat. "You're hurting them!"

The deafening chanting of the Wise Ones was cut off in mid-beat as they gasped and turned to stare at Cela, their faces a mix of horror and disbelief as she continued to cry. "Mama! They're burning! Help them!"

Already the bodies of the captives were charred, but still the prisoners clawed at the cage. As the flames increased, the bottom of the cage finally gave way, and the bodies began to fall down onto the bonfire, eliciting a deafening cheer from the common people, standing at a distance on the earthen henge.

"The child has defiled the ceremony!" a nearby priest shouted, pointing at Cela.

"She will bring the wrath of the gods down upon us," another accused.

"Mama," Cela cried desperately, impervious to the pandemonium and shouts of condemnation directed at her by the priests and priestesses. She tugged on her mother's arm. "We must help them!"

Ega spun around to her daughter and slapped her face with a force that knocked Cela to the ground. Ega looked frantically about and then motioned to a guard standing near.

"You, Dagga," Ega shouted to the warrior. "Take the priestess back to her lodge."

The warrior jumped forward at being summoned by Ega but then stepped backward as he looked down at Cela.

"Cela, go with the warrior, Dagga," Ega said. "Go!"

"Mama," Cela whimpered as she lay on the ground, her crying causing her to gasp.

"Take her!" Ega ordered the warrior. "Pick her up and carry her to our lodges. Quickly!"

The warrior's eyes widened as he looked down at Cela. He stood still, as though frozen in his stance, incapable of action. Within the circle of sacred stones, the only sound was the crackling of the fire as it nibbled away at the charred flesh and bones of the captives. The High Priest and the Wise Ones gaped in silence, their eyes trained on Cela, Ega, and the warrior. Finally, with a look of resignation and determination, Dagga stepped forward and lifted Cela up into his arms.

Dagga was a battle-hardened warrior who had been posted to the elite guard. It was the greatest honor a warrior could ever expect, for only the strongest and bravest were chosen to guard the Wise Ones.

He had been standing at the edge of the stone circle when, upon hearing a scream, he charged into the forbidden circle, sword drawn, expecting to quickly dispatch an adversary. Perhaps a captive had escaped? The Wise Ones were no match for an enemy warrior, even a dazed one. But instead of a captive warrior, or even a stray wolf, he came upon a child priestess sitting on the ground, her eyes wide in shock, her face a study in horror. The priest and priestesses were all shouting, pointing at the child priestess, their usual calm, steadied voices harsh and accusing.

Dagga, imbued with instinctive intelligence, quickly determined what the child had done to disrupt the Wise Ones' ritual. The child priestess was crying, begging for mercy for the captives. How could that be? Then the Priestess Ega of the Wise Ones had ordered him to remove the child. He would have to carry the child priestess! If he didn't obey the priestess's order, he would be killed immediately, probably tossed upon the fire with the captives. Yet, the order itself was a death sentence for him. The law was clear: no one could touch a priest or priestess of the Wise Ones. The child had sealed his fate. He could die now for disobeying the Priestess Ega's order and suffer a cruel death without dignity, or he could follow her order and hope that his death would be swift and honorable. He made his decision. He had reached down and picked up the whimpering child.

Now, as Dagga carried the young priestess away from the stone circle, the warriors openly gaped at him, but respectfully parted to clear his way. His strong legs carried the child over the earthen henge, crowded with the common people, and off into the night. Eventually, the fervent chanting of the Wise Ones faded so that the only sound was that of Dagga's footsteps as he crossed the rough, knee-length grasses in the night. Even the child priestess was silent.

It took an hour for Dagga to reach the lodgings of the Wise Ones. Their huts were positioned on the top of an intricately constructed round hill that was surrounded by a series of three earthen ramparts. A great wall, twenty feet high and made of tree trunks, protectively circled the entire hill. Entering through the gate in the wall, Dagga climbed the hill of the first rampart to reach the level ground where the laborers of their people lived. He carried the small child past the huts of the metal workers, the pottery makers, the weavers, and the animal caretakers. He walked past the stone fences where the sheep grazed in the night. He ascended the second rampart and descended into its ditch and then up again onto the second level. This was where Dagga lived with the warriors of their tribe. Again, the warriors openly gaped at him as he passed through their quarters and then once again descended into the ditch and started up the last rampart, a full twenty-five feet up to the top of the hill. Two guards stepped in front of him as he arrived at another wooden wall encircling the lodges of the Wise Ones.

"Dagga?" one of them said with surprise, staring at the child priestess in his arms.

Dagga was well known to the warriors and respected among all the elite guard. There was no need for him to explain himself to these men. He ascertained the location of the hut where he might find a priestess who had remained in the lodgings to care for the young of the Wise Ones.

The dwellings of the Wise Ones were no different from those of the people. They lived in round houses made of wood that had been plastered with mud and topped with cone-shaped thatched roofs. Each hut had a fire pit in the middle to provide warmth and light, as well as the heat necessary for cooking.

They were a semi-nomadic people, moving with the seasons to settlements they had built throughout their lands. In the northern mountains, their huts stood on stone foundations placed several feet below the ground, providing shelter from the cold wind and rain prevalent in the mountains. And whereas Cela's people had constructed the massive, three-tiered hill of this southwestern settlement as a formidable buttress against invading enemies, in the north, the mountains themselves provided natural defensive barriers.

As Dagga approached the hut indicated by the guards, a priestess came out. Dagga stopped before her and bowed his head. "The Priestess Ega commanded me to bring the child here," he said.

"She is ill?" the priestess asked with alarm.

Dagga did not answer but reached out with his arms so the priestess could remove the child from him. In that instant, the child priestess cried out and threw her arms around Dagga, clinging to him. The priestess's eyes widened in surprise.

"Why were you commanded to bring the child here?" she asked.

Dagga was silent.

"Answer!"

As Dagga recounted what he had seen, the priestess recoiled.

"The child defiled the sacrifice?" She choked. "If she angered the gods, we could be doomed to destruction," she said with alarm. She stepped backward. "She cannot remain here." The priestess's eyes darted about as she appeared to determine what should be done. "Guard, you will take the child into the forests and wait," the priestess ordered. "Your duty is still to protect the priestess."

"Yes, Priestess."

Dagga bowed and then began the long trek up and down the three ramparts, descending to the final level, passing through the gate and away from the settlement. When he finally reached the forest, he stopped. What was he to do? He was not of these people. He was from a warring tribe that roamed north. He had been captured as a youth. He, himself, should have been sacrificed, as was the practice of these people, but for some reason, he had been spared. A warrior of these people adopted him and eventually trained him to be a warrior. Dagga had fought fearlessly for these people and had the battle scars to prove it. His prowess as a fighter had increased, and eventually, he had been chosen as one of the elite guards.

He looked around as he entered the forest. The night air was cool, and no doubt, wolves roamed the hills in this area. No matter what his fate, his duty was still clear: he was to protect the child priestess.

The child priestess's eyes were shut, and Dagga thought perhaps she had fallen asleep. When he leaned down to place her on the earth, she tightened her hold around him with a strength that surprised him. Cursing under his breath, he awkwardly gathered dry wood and made a small fire, all the while holding the child. His years of training had made him strong and adept, and within minutes, he had unsheathed his sword and was settled before the fire's warmth. He was comfortable, but not so the child. She began to tremble.

Dagga sighed, preferring the field of battle, where he excelled as a master of combat, to caring for a strange child priestess. He separated himself from the child long enough to remove the fur tunic that covered his chest. Then he wrapped it around her small form and settled her on his lap. Wearing only a leather loincloth and the laced hide boots of a warrior, he wrapped his powerful arms around her.

Why had she cried out? She was a child of the Wise Ones, trained from birth as a priestess. Dagga thought about the practices of these people who had become his people. With a shrug, he had to admit that he, a seasoned warrior, did not like their practice of sacrificing people to their gods. It was one thing for a man to die in battle, but another to be ceremoniously killed in the manner that these people used in their sacrifices. Still, it was their way and he did not question it, for he had seen the mysterious power of the Wise Ones.

Dagga's thoughts were interrupted by a movement on his lap. He looked down to see the child staring at him, her face only inches from his own. His first instinct was to push her off his lap, for he had never been this close to one of the Wise Ones.

Suddenly, she scrambled out of his arms. She dropped his fur tunic and walked away from the fire, out from under the canopy of the trees and into the surrounding grasses. Dagga watched as the young priestess stopped and looked up into the night sky. She was eerily quiet as her eyes searched the sky, her slim, child form outlined by the moon shining through her white robe. He stood to follow her, picking up his sword, for she could be attacked by wolves away from the fire. A piece of green wood exploded in the fire, sending flames the colors of a rainbow shooting into the night air. The light from the fire reflected off the child's long, red hair, glowing with an unnatural quality. Then the light died, and only the moonlight illuminated her pale face.

The child turned silently, and Dagga followed her as she walked back to the fire. She sat down and wrapped herself in his fur tunic. Dagga hesitated and then sat down, keeping a respectful distance.

She looked at him. "I am the Priestess Cela," she said. "What are you called?"

"Dagga, Priestess."

"You need not fear for your life, Dagga," Cela said, her child's voice soft but clear.

"I do not fear death, Priestess," Dagga replied.

"No, I know that. You are strong and brave, or you would not have been chosen to guard us. I meant that you need not fear that you will be put to death because of me."

"It is the law, Priestess," Dagga replied. "You are a child of the Wise Ones. To touch a priest or priestess of the Wise Ones is death."

A flash of anger passed over Cela's face. "I know the law! But you will not be killed. I will not allow it."

Dagga was surprisingly touched by the child's statement,

although he doubted that she could prevent his death.

"I am cold," Cela said, her voice barely above a whisper.

"I will build up the fire," he responded, but before he could stand, she stood and hesitantly walked toward him. She knelt before him, and in the firelight, he could see tears in her eyes. "The fire hurt those men," she said, her voice quivering. "It was burning them. They were crying."

In a gesture that surprised Dagga, Cela crawled onto his lap and buried her face in the hardened muscles of his chest. There was an awkward moment when Dagga was uncertain what to do. As her arms clung to him, he gathered the fur tunic she had dropped and wrapped it around her small frame. Then he folded his arms around her, pulling her against him as he stroked her hair, murmuring softly to her.

* * *

Jennifer felt the cold, concrete floor against her face as the images of Cela and Dagga faded from her mind. The night sky of Cela's world was replaced with a glaring, harsh light. There was a vile taste in Jennifer's mouth, and her body was drenched with sweat. The whirling vertigo remained, leaving her feeling nauseated. She could still feel Dagga's hand pressed against Cela's back, and then a shadow crossed her face.

"Miss, can you hear me?" a male voice close to her asked.

Jennifer turned her head slightly.

"You're injured," the man said with concern. She felt strong arms reach underneath her back as she was helped into a sitting position on the floor. He knelt beside her, keeping his arm around her.

"Looks like you've got a cut on your forehead," the man said.

Jennifer watched with detachment as the man reached into the breast pocket of his sport coat and removed a handkerchief. Then she felt it gently pressed against her head.

"It doesn't look too bad," he continued, "although it might require a few stitches and, by the looks of that bronze spear tip, a tetanus shot."

Her teeth were starting to chatter as a chill spread through her. She glanced to the left, and there, laying on the floor, was the ancient spear with her blood staining its tip. Jennifer turned away from the bloody spear and vomited.

"Bloody hell," the man muttered as Jennifer's stomach emptied its contents onto his sport coat.

The man kept his left arm around her back and his handkerchief pressed against her forehead as her stomach once again contracted, the last vestiges of her lunch and accompanying cocktails landing in his lap.

She wanted to leave, to run away from this nightmare, but the vortex was still surrounding her, although its pull was lessening. She was too disoriented and frightened to feel appropriately embarrassed. Her hair had come loose and was falling down past her shoulders, obscuring her face from the man who still held her in his arms. She willed herself to steady her breathing. Her head was pressed against the man's chest, and she wasn't certain if it was his heartbeat she heard or her own. After a minute, he spoke again.

"Are you all right, miss?"

She could feel his breath on her face as he spoke. Oddly, its warmth was comforting for it was, at least, real. So was the smell of her vomit permeating his clothing.

"Y . . . yes," she replied, barely recognizing her own frail voice.

"Well, then," he said as he eased her back from him, "let's see if we can get you cleaned up and secure transportation to the hospital."

Jennifer stiffened.

"You need stitches, and you were unconscious when I came in. You should be examined by a doctor."

She knew he was looking down at her, but she kept her face averted.

"Can you hold this in place while I get help?" he asked.

Jennifer didn't answer, but reached for the handkerchief on her forehead. He moved his fingers aside and then placed his hand over hers as she pressed down on the cloth. A shiver ran through her.

"Don't move. I'll be right back," he said softly.

Jennifer kept her face down until she heard a door open and then close. She couldn't stay here. She wanted to get away from this room. She needed to find John.

Her heart pounded as she reached for the table and pulled herself up from the floor. She glanced down at her linen dress, now stained with vomit and blood. Her steps were uneven as she staggered to the door and opened it. Which way was the elevator? She couldn't remember. She began to run, her steps awkward. There it was. She stepped into the elevator just as the man appeared at the other end of the hallway.

"Miss, wait!" he called and started to run toward her.

She reached for the elevator button, but her hand was shaking so badly, she had to hit it several times before the elevator door responded.

"Stop!" she heard him call, but he was too late as the door closed and the elevator jerked into motion.

CHAPTER 2

"**I** beg your pardon, Mrs. Bracken," the flight attendant said in a crisp, British accent.

Jennifer stirred in her seat in the first-class compartment of the airplane. She hadn't realized she had dozed off during the flight.

"We'll be landing momentarily," the attendant said.

Jennifer sat up. "Thank you," she said.

As the attendant turned to another passenger, Jennifer looked out the small window. She wrinkled her brow in concentration. She didn't know how she had gotten through the day yesterday. Somehow, she had managed to catch a cab outside of the British Museum and return to her hotel. She sent a text message to John, apologizing for her behavior and telling him that she was staying in the hotel room. She didn't have to wait long for him to return.

When John entered the room and saw her forehead and the dried emesis on her dress, he didn't ask her what had happened. Instead, he calmly helped her remove her clothing and step into the shower. When she emerged from the bathroom, he had medical supplies waiting, delivered in response to a single phone call he had made to a London colleague.

John had done a residency in plastic surgery early in his career, and although it had been quite a few years since he had actually practiced medicine, a man like John Bracken demanded nothing short of excellence of himself. Quickly and efficiently, he cleansed the wound, injected a local anesthetic, sutured the skin, and applied a bandage. He then gave Jennifer a glass of water, two antibiotic pills, and put her to bed. When she started crying, he sat quietly on the bed beside her and held her hand.

That evening, they dined in their hotel room. John was kind and attentive, which only made Jennifer feel guilty the next morning when she announced that she didn't want to stay in London for the week, as was their plan, while John conducted his business. Instead, she would like to visit her friend, Nina, in Scotland. She had expected him to be angry, but surprisingly, he had consented. The only tense moment had occurred when he asked her if she was going to wear her wedding ring.

"Are you going to tell me the truth?" she had countered.

"Really, Jennifer, I thought you were above listening to gossip," he had said. "You disappoint me. Go visit your friend, and when you return to Chicago, we'll get on with our lives."

Jennifer looked out the window as the airplane touched down in Aberdeen, Scotland. *Right now, my life is a mess.*

* * *

"Hello?" Harold Rannoch, Earl of Thornhill, spoke into the receiver.

"Father? It's Derek."

"Derek, my boy. It's good to hear from you. How are you, Son?"

"I'm fine, Father. I'm calling to let you know that I'll be home this evening."

"Splendid! Will you be staying a while?"

"For the next six weeks, possibly longer. I thought I

would spend the summer taking some measurements in the northern sectors of the Grampian and catching up on some writing," Derek Rannoch replied.

"Will your schedule permit some shooting and fishing with an aging father?"

Derek laughed. "Why? So my aging father can best me at both?" He heard his father chuckle. "Father, I would like the hunting lodge prepared. My assistant will be joining me occasionally."

"Is she pretty?" Harold Rannoch asked his son.

Derek laughed again. "I'll see you this evening, Father."

"Good-bye, Son."

* * *

Jennifer slowed the car and turned off the road. According to the directions Nina had given her, this had to be the cottage. Jennifer had driven into the small town of Cormara, as Nina had instructed, but became confused about which road she was to take north. Before leaving the town, Jennifer stopped to ask for directions.

"Oh, the American author," a woman had replied. "Yes, dear, she's living in one of the cottages on Thornhill." The friendly woman then proceeded to give Jennifer directions.

Jennifer stopped the car in front of a small gray stone house. The house sat alone, surrounded by rocky green hills. Short stone walls divided the hills into pastures where sheep grazed. Brightly colored purple-and-yellow flowers climbed the twin stone chimneys at each end of the house, balancing and fortifying the small structure, its roof interrupted by two dormers. The door was in the center of the house and flanked by two windows with black panes, the same color as the door. It was neat and tidy, an idyllic

postcard picture. A pathway of pieces of gray flagstone—
the shape of each defined by the moss growing around it—
led up to the door. Jennifer stepped out of the car. She had
been nervous driving on the narrow, mountainous roads
and had not allowed herself to gaze too long at her
surroundings. Now as she stood there, the sheer panoramic
beauty hit her with a force that caused her to gasp. The
surreal moment was broken by a woman's voice.

"Jen! You're here!" Nina Bouvay exclaimed as she ran
down the path to greet Jennifer.

Jennifer smiled at her friend. It had been a year and a
half since she had seen Nina. As Nina threw her arms
around her, Jennifer realized how much she had missed her
oldest and dearest friend.

"Let me look at you!" Nina exclaimed as she stepped
back from Jennifer. "What happened to your head,
McHugh?"

"The name is Bracken, not McHugh, and it's a long
story."

"Can't wait to hear it," Nina laughed. "Still married to
the great Dr. Bracken, huh? Well, you'll always be Jennifer
McHugh to me," Nina said as she linked her arm through
Jennifer's. "Come inside. We'll get your bags later," Nina
said enthusiastically. "Are you hungry?"

Jennifer shrugged her shoulders.

"No matter. Lunch is ready, and then we'll go for a walk
and we can talk. It's so peaceful and beautiful here, Jen.
You're going to love it. Just wait. Two weeks of hearty
Scottish food and good Highland air, and you'll be a new
woman. You'll see!"

Two hours later, Jennifer stopped along the road, her
heart racing and her breathing deep. "When you said a walk,
Nina, I didn't realize it was up a mountain. Can we please
stop?" Jennifer asked, trying to catch her breath after an
hour of walking in the hilly countryside. "Are you trying to

kill me?"

"Okay," Nina laughed. "Over here."

They carefully stepped through the rough, spiny evergreen that covered the ground. Nina explained that it was called "gorse" and was plentiful in the area. She led Jennifer to the stone fencing.

"Up you go, McHugh," Nina said as she sat down on the low stone wall.

"Do you do this every day?" Jennifer asked as she scrambled up next to Nina.

"Just about," Nina answered. "I usually sleep late and then get up and go for a long walk in the hills. It helps me organize my thoughts before I sit down to write."

"Do you write every day?"

"Usually."

"Do you work at your house?"

Nina shrugged her shoulders. "Most of the time, unless I have to go to the university in Edinburgh to do research for a book. I'm a night owl—you know that—so it's easy for me to work late into the night at home."

"I see," Jennifer said with a secret smile. "And do you work alone?" Before Nina could answer, Jennifer continued. "When I called you to see if I could visit, I could have sworn I heard a man's voice," Jennifer said playfully.

Nina smiled. "His name is Shamus MacNeal, like you, McHugh," Nina said.

"The name is Bracken," Jennifer said through clenched teeth.

"We'll return to that subject in a minute. Now, let me tell you about Shamus. You're going to love this, Jen. He's a doctor."

"You're kidding."

"No, but not like John. No big corporation. No big bucks. Shamus is the district doctor assigned to this area. He has an office and house in Cormara, and he's gorgeous. A few years younger than me, but who cares?"

"Oh?" Jennifer said with a smile.

"You'll see," Nina continued. "He's coming to dinner tonight, so you two can meet each other. He's going to love your red hair and perfect complexion, McHugh. If you flirt with him, I'll kill you," Nina added.

"I'm married, Nina. I'm not going to flirt with your Shamus or anyone else," Jennifer replied.

"Maybe you should. God knows if I were married to John Bracken, I'd be looking elsewhere," Nina said.

"Nina—"

"I'm sorry," Nina said quickly. "I shouldn't have said that. Come on, let's go back to the cottage and we can sit on the patio. You can catch your breath and then tell me what's bothering you," Nina said kindly.

"What makes you think something is bothering me?" Jennifer asked.

"I know you, McHugh. Come on," Nina said as she stood up and offered a hand to Jennifer. "We're not that far from the cottage," she said encouragingly.

The sun was low in the afternoon sky as the two women sat in Nina's small garden. Nina had insisted that they enjoy the sunshine, a rare occurrence in the northeast Highlands of Scotland. Gray stones formed a patio that was surrounded by wildflowers and colorful purple heather.

"Do you think John is having an affair?" Nina asked.

Jennifer replaced her teacup on the saucer. "I don't know," she answered. "I overheard some women talking. One asked if John was still paying for call girls every week."

"What?" Nina said with surprise. "Call girls, like prostitutes?"

Jennifer shrugged her shoulders.

"That's ridiculous," Nina said. When Jennifer didn't respond, Nina continued. "It is ridiculous, right, Jen?"

"I don't know," Jennifer said as she blinked tears away. "John works late once or twice a week, not coming home until after midnight. He's done that since we got married."

"Well, have you asked him about it?"

"It was only a few days ago. Just after we arrived in London, I overheard two women in the restroom at a restaurant. They were wives of John's executive officers. Obviously, they didn't know I was in there. When we returned to the hotel room, I told John what I had heard. He became angry and told me to ignore gossip."

Nina sighed. "Jen, I've never been a fan of your husband, but he has a valid point."

"I'm not sure it matters anyway," Jennifer said.

"Of course it matters," Nina countered.

"Okay, it matters," Jennifer admitted. "It hurts," she said quietly. "John and I haven't slept together for a long time."

"How long is a long time?" Nina asked.

Jennifer bit her lip. "We've had separate rooms for the last year."

"What? Jen, why didn't you tell me?"

"From the beginning, John didn't seem to be too interested in that part of our relationship. I used to wonder if it was me. I was a virgin when I married John," Jennifer admitted quietly, "what did I know?"

"When you say separate bedrooms. . . ."

"We haven't had sex in over a year. He lost interest in that part of our relationship shortly after we returned from our honeymoon."

"You've only been married a year and a half! What's wrong with him? He doesn't deserve you, Jen. Get rid of the bastard."

"I think you're biased," Jennifer said as she smiled sadly. "He was good to Mom those last days. I never could have afforded the private care she needed. He helped me through a bad time. He didn't have to do any of that, Nina. We weren't married."

Jennifer paused as a tear escaped down her cheek. "I remember I had gone into the stairwell in the hospital. The neurosurgeon had just told me that there wasn't anything they could do for Mom. I didn't want her to see me crying, so I went out there. It was awful. My mother was dying and I was alone." Jennifer smiled sadly as she continued. "Then John came into the stairwell. I think he was surprised to see a woman sitting on the steps, crying. He introduced himself and asked me what was wrong. The next thing I know, he had taken care of everything. He arranged for Mom's care even when I told him I didn't have the money. He just did it." Jennifer paused. "And the rest you know. We started dating a few weeks later and married two months after that. I don't know what I would have done if he hadn't come along."

Nina thought for a moment. "Okay, I acknowledge that, for whatever reason, John did a very decent thing, and he can be very charming when it serves his purpose. Can I tell you what I think, Jen, and you won't be offended?"

"Go ahead," Jennifer said.

"John was divorced and needed a wife because that is part of being powerful and successful. No doubt there were many women to choose from in his social circle, but you were young—twenty years old—and vulnerable. You had no demands or expectations of him, he already had your adoration and gratitude, and he was what, thirty-five years older than you? But John's not a fool; only the very best can be John Bracken's wife, and he got the very best, Jen. You never have a mean thought for anyone. You're an intelligent and classy lady, Jennifer McHugh, and John Bracken knew it. He still knows it, and my guess is that he's not about to let you go, should it ever come to that."

"Can we talk about this later," Jennifer asked. "I . . . I just can't. . . ."

"It's okay, Jen," Nina said, reaching across the table to take her friend's hand in hers. "I didn't mean to upset you." She squeezed Jennifer's hand and then looked down. "Whoa, Jen, where's your wedding ring?"

"In my purse. I took it off a few days ago when John wouldn't give me a direct answer."

Nina squeezed Jennifer's hand again and then

brightened. "Okay, McHugh, enough talk about John. You're in Scotland now. The Scottish Highlands are one of the most beautiful and dramatic places in the world. I promise you, Jen, we're going to have fun these next two weeks, okay?"

Jennifer smiled at her friend as she wiped the tear away from her eye. "Okay."

"A little more enthusiasm, please," Nina chided.

Jennifer smiled. "Two weeks of fun. Agreed."

"That's more like it. Trust me, McHugh, adventure awaits!"

"Oh, no." Jennifer sighed and looked around. She had spent three days with Nina, but this morning, Nina had business in Edinburgh, so Jennifer, armed with GPS and a map for backup, had set off on her own. Now she sat in the car, frustrated. Once again, she gunned the engine of the car, feeling its wheels spin in protest, unable to extradite themselves from the boggy mud. Sighing again, she turned the motor off and stepped out of the car. Her only recourse was to begin the walk back down the road toward the town.

As the morning wore on, Jennifer again stopped to look at her watch. She had been walking for thirty minutes, the narrow, paved road twisting and curving downward out of the mountain, and not a single vehicle had come her way. She was about to consult her map again when she looked up. She could have sworn she heard a man's voice. That meant a house or farm must be near.

The road was surrounded by small hills, not difficult to walk over, but high enough to prevent her from seeing what was beyond them. Jennifer left the road and started to walk up the hill toward the man's voice. She was glad Nina had loaned her sturdy hiking boots and pants, for the thistle that covered the hill—beautiful as it was with its mauve blooms—tore at her pant legs. And interspersed among the thistle were gray boulders that she had to navigate around.

It took a few minutes for her to reach the top of the hill, and when she did, she was disappointed. There was no house in sight, just another valley between hills. The next hill seemed rockier than this one. If it weren't for the fact that the morning's adventure had made her irritable, she would have enjoyed this view, for it was breathtaking. There was wildness to the land here, and the air was sweet and clear. But she needed to go back to the road. As she turned, she was hit with a violent wave of nausea. The ground spun around her, and a peculiar rushing sound enveloped her. She was aware of her knees hitting the prickly grass as she struggled to stand, the bile rising to her mouth. Then the bright morning sunlight faded from her sight.

＊ ＊ ＊

830 B.C.

Dagga stopped at the entrance to the grove of oak trees. It was forbidden for him to enter the sacred place of the oak where the High Priest and the others of the Wise Ones now waited. He had been instructed to bring the young priestess, Cela, to this place.

Three days had passed since the priestess had disrupted the ceremonies. The others had not returned for her until the morning after the first ceremony and sacrifice, just as Cela had said. Cela's mother, the Priestess Ega, had come, accompanied by several of the priests. Dagga was certain that they were coming for him and that he would be one of the sacrifices to the earth and water that day. Amazingly, they did not take him. Ega had looked at her daughter with concern and fear. Cela was banned from attending the ceremonies of the day. She was to remain outside of the settlement until the priests returned for her in three days. At that time, Cela would appear before the High Priest himself. As Ega started to leave, she reached out and crushed Cela to herself. Then she stood and turned to Dagga.

"You will protect the Priestess Cela with your life, as is expected," Ega said to him. "Food, water, and shelter will be brought to you."

Then she departed with the priests. That afternoon, warriors arrived with bundles of food and animal skins and poles. Dagga constructed a shelter for Cela and began the three-day wait, as ordered. Now, as he stood at the edge of the grove, he did not know what the fate would be of the child or himself.

Cela was nervous as she approached the Wise Ones standing in a circle under the great oak trees. The black-robed priests and priestesses parted, allowing her to walk alone into the center. The circle then closed behind her. She stood quietly as the priests and priestesses moved, circling her from left to right, east to west, following the pattern of the sun. Three times they circled and then came to a quiet halt. The High Priest was directly in front of Cela, although he made no eye contact. Instead, he nodded to another of the hooded priests. The priest stepped forward and lowered his hood. Cela breathed a sigh of relief when she saw him, for he was a kindly man who was one of her teachers. The Wise Ones had many among themselves who were appointed to teach the young of their class. Six more teachers also stepped forward to face her, and the examination began.

For the next four grueling hours, Cela stood straight, answering the questions put to her by her teachers. Her legs were weak and shaking, but she stood fast by tightening and relaxing the muscles of her legs and shifting her weight imperceptibly. She curled and stretched her toes, hidden in her boots made of sheepskin. She systematically contracted and relaxed the muscles of her shoulders, abdomen, and arms—the movements great enough to keep the blood flowing throughout her body but too small to be seen beneath the white robe she wore.

Her teachers began by asking Cela to recite the history of her people and their land. Another teacher questioned her about mathematical calculations of shapes and distances, while still another asked her about the wonders of the plants and herbs used in their healing arts.

She was questioned about the making of bronze: the correct proportion of tin and copper and the means of attaining the high temperature necessary to smelt the copper. For that, Cela's people used small, open-bowl stone furnaces in which the copper was placed. She described in detail the location of the tin and copper mines in the mountains to the west and the technique of lighting fires beneath the mountainous rock to heat it. Then water was poured over the rock to crack it, making it easier to extract the metal.

Cela was asked to explain the methods of butchering game, tanning hides to the appropriate pliancy, the preservation of meat, the making of pottery, and the weaving of wool. Then the questions took a decided turn. Her teachers began to ask her about the mystical aspects of their power. Cela had only recently been introduced to this knowledge, for she was only ten years old. Among Cela's people, a child born to the Wise Ones spent the first thirty years of his or her life learning all that was necessary for the survival of the people—from the most technical craft to the most mundane of labors—all of which a priest or priestess must demonstrate proficiently. Other knowledge belonged to the Wise Ones alone: the healing arts, astronomy, and mysticism.

"Write the method used to follow the stars and predict the solstices and seasons," one of the priests commanded of her.

Cela turned to the priest who had spoken. She shivered slightly when she recognized her cousin, Luc. He stepped forward and thrust a stick into her hands.

"Take it," he said, his cold eyes boring into her. "Write the method," he commanded.

Cela hesitated. "I cannot," she finally answered quietly.

"You do not know, or do you defy me?" Luc sneered.

Cela swallowed. She was afraid of her cousin. What was she to do?

"Cela," another voice cut in.

Cela turned to see one of her teachers step forward.

"Why can't you do as Priest Luc asks?" her teacher questioned.

"Because it is forbidden," Cela answered.

"Explain," her teacher encouraged her.

"To commit our teachings to writing would risk them being discovered by others not born to the Wise Ones," Cela answered. "Only trivial information can be written for others to see."

This was true and one of the reasons it took a lifetime to learn all that the Wise Ones knew. Pleased, the teacher stepped back. Cela took a deep breath, but not before she saw the anger in her cousin's eyes.

At that moment, the High Priest stepped forward, signaling that the questioning was over. Now he would speak with Cela.

"You honor your teachers today, Cela," he began. "You have answered well."

Cela bowed her head in acknowledgment.

"And yet," the High Priest continued, "you defiled the sacrifices. Do you not understand our beliefs?"

Cela swallowed. "I know that the spirit does not die with the body," she began. "The spirit continues and begins life again in yet another body. I understand that sacrifices of this life are the greatest gift we have to offer to the gods." Cela's voice had grown very soft as she finished speaking what had been taught to her.

"Do you believe this?" the High Priest asked.

"Those men were hurting," she said in a childlike voice.

"Step forward," the High Priest commanded. "Look at me."

Cela was trembling as she did as commanded. Would he kill her now? She raised her eyes to his. He was but a foot away from her.

The eyes of the High Priest widened and darkened until they were liquid pools of black. Cela tried to turn away but felt herself pulled toward their darkness. She thought she heard chanting around her but was not certain. After a while, she could hear only his voice. Her body seemed heavy, as though her feet were rooted to the ground like a tree, her arms like broken branches, hanging limply at her side.

"Tell me, Child, what do you see when you sleep?" the High Priest asked.

Under the High Priest's control, Cela did not hesitate but answered clearly and without fear. "I see the sun by day and the stars by night. I move toward them," she said.

"You move toward them?"

"Yes. I leave this place. I go into the sky. I go to other lands."

The gasps from the priests and priestesses momentarily penetrated Cela's consciousness. She had been unaware of everything except the High Priest's eyes. Now she turned to the Wise Ones surrounding her.

"Look at me!" the High Priest commanded. As she turned back to him, she was pulled once again into the murky depths of his eyes. "Tell me more."

Cela involuntarily swallowed. "I see the stars. I see the sun. Sometimes I leave our world and go toward them. I see our stones, but I also see the stones that are not ours. They are on other lands," Cela finished.

"How can you see stones that are not on our lands?" the High Priest asked, his voice eerily soft.

"I see them from the sky. I see them as I move through the sky. I look down upon them."

This time, the explosion from the priests and priestesses

pierced through Cela's hypnotized state. She jerked her gaze away from the High Priest and searched the faces of the Wise Ones. She was confused by the anger she saw and something else. Fear? Yes, fear. Some priests and priestesses had stepped back from her.

"Priestess Cela! How can you move through the sky?" the High Priest thundered. "How?!"

"I don't know," Cela whispered as she returned her gaze to the High Priest.

"What do you do to make yourself move through the sky?" he asked again.

"I don't know. I just do it," she answered, this time louder.

"She lies!" Luc shouted. Other priests and priestesses also raised their voices.

"Silence!" the High Priest commanded and then turned to Luc. "Do you doubt my power over the child?"

Luc bowed his head in respect and stepped back.

Suddenly, a voice pierced the silence. "The child speaks the truth, although she herself does not know it."

All faces turned to see an old woman enter the grove. She wore the black robe of a priestess, the hood obscuring her face. A walking stick in one hand, her back was bent forward as she shuffled into the circle of Wise Ones, forcing them to step back to allow her to pass. She didn't stop until she stood before the High Priest. Then, with hands deformed and knotted with age, she lowered the hood of her robe.

"Sham," she said in greeting, daring to address the High Priest by his personal name. Then she turned to Cela. "Great-granddaughter," the old woman said as she brushed her fingertips lightly down Cela's cheek.

The High Priest's face softened at seeing the old woman before him. "What do you know of this, Mora?" he asked.

"Cela is the child of my child's child. Her mother, Ega, is my granddaughter."

"Yes, I remember now," the High Priest said. "You are

aware of what she did at the ceremony?"

Mora smiled slightly. "I may be too old to participate in the ceremonies of the Wise Ones, but I am still a priestess, and I have not left this life yet, Sham. I know what the child did."

"Her act could bring the displeasure of the gods down upon us," the High Priest said.

"I do not think so."

The High Priest frowned. "You heard what she just said? How can she see from the sky?"

"Because she is not of us. A priest of our people did not start my first child growing within me."

"What are you saying?" the High Priest demanded.

"I was but a young woman then. I had not yet been with a man. I was to be presented at the fertility ceremony. I did not come to that ceremony a virgin. There was another."

The High Priest's face lost all expression.

"He came from the sky," the old woman continued. "My first child was started by him. Cela's mother, Ega, is the child of that man's child. Cela carries his blood in her veins—the blood of the People of the Sky."

The priests and priestesses openly gasped at Mora's revelations.

"He was one of the last of the People of the Sky to have visited us. I have kept this secret all these years. He said a child was his gift to me. He taught me many things that day," Mora said with a gleam in her eyes. "Where did you think I learned all that I taught you and the others?" she said to the High Priest. "He gave me three gifts that day: a child, the knowledge of healing, and a third."

The High Priest looked expectantly at Mora.

"The first two I have shared with my people; the third cannot be shared. It was mine alone, or so I thought." Mora looked at Cela. A smile came to her face. "I used to wonder what kind of child he had started within me. Would my child become one of the People of the Sky? I watched my child closely for the signs of the man from the sky, but I saw nothing. She was just as other children were. Then my child had a child, and again, there was nothing. Then Ega was born. I saw no sign of the man from the sky in my children's children—until now. Now there is this child." Mora turned to the High Priest. "The child's dreams are the third gift. She sees far more in her dreams than I did the day that he took me through the sky with him. Now I have only my memories, but she sees through his eyes."

"Why have you never spoken of this?" the High Priest asked.

"He commanded that I not. Would you have disobeyed one of the People of the Sky?"

Without waiting to be dismissed, Mora turned to leave. Immediately, several of the priestesses came forward to escort the old woman back to her lodge.

The High Priest looked back at the remaining priests and priestesses who were murmuring among themselves, their shock at Mora's revelations clearly evident on their faces. "Silence!" the High Priest commanded. "You will speak of none of this. The child will take her place with the others. You will continue your instruction of her and inform me of her progress. She is to be treated no differently than the other young priests or priestesses."

The High Priest nodded, and the priests and priestesses pulled the hood of their robes over their heads and resumed their positions in the circle. Once again, they began chanting and circling. The High Priest turned his attention back to Cela, his eyes boring into her. She felt herself being pulled into the murky depth of his eyes, their blackness enveloping her, wrapping around her as she slowly crumpled to the ground.

Dagga was waiting. When he saw Cela in her mother's arms, he was certain that they had killed the child. He was surprised at the emotion that welled up in him. He had killed many enemies before, even ones as young as this child priestess. Why should he care what happened to this one?

He waited, expecting an order for his own death to come. When Ega silently passed him and no one followed, he rushed up ahead of her, blocking her path. He looked down at the dead child priestess, her eyes closed, her arms and legs hanging limply at her sides, her neck arched backward with the weight of her head, her hair of fire streaming down, catching the rays of the afternoon sun. He didn't speak but reached out and took the child into his arms. She was surprisingly warm to the touch. He leaned his head down, his ear next to the child's face. Faint, warm air caressed his cheek. He could see it—the slight rise and fall of her chest. She was alive!

* * *

"Watch where you're going! What are you doing?" an angry voice shouted.

Jennifer stumbled, trying to focus her eyes. She could taste the bile in her mouth. She looked around. Where was she? At her feet lay a tripod and electronic equipment in disarray on the ground.

"That's expensive equipment! You've destroyed my measurements!" a male voice shouted. "Where did she come from? Get that woman out of there!"

"I'll take care of it," a woman answered as she ran to where Jennifer was standing.

Jennifer's mind cleared. In horror, she looked around her. "Oh, God, what's happening to me?" she cried, cold terror flowing through her.

"Ma'am?" the young woman said as she reached Jennifer. One look at Jennifer and the young woman stopped. "Are you all right?"

Jennifer focused her eyes on the young woman standing before her—blonde hair in a ponytail, khaki pants, green sweater. *Real.* The woman was real. When Jennifer didn't answer, the woman knelt before her and began to pick up the equipment. Again, the man shouted in the distance.

"Oh, no, this is broken," the woman said as she picked up the pieces of the equipment.

Jennifer looked at the ground. Despite her fear, she tried to calm herself before this stranger. She was trying, with all of her remaining sanity, to quell the sickness she felt.

"I . . . I'm sorry. I wasn't looking where I was going. I was lost," Jennifer said lamely, struggling to make her voice sound normal.

"You're American," the woman said as she continued to work. "Are you hiking? That must be your car on the road over there."

"Where?" Jennifer asked. She felt disoriented, as though her body was turning in circles, or was everything around her spinning? She brought her hand to her mouth as she tasted the bile once again.

"There, between the trees," the woman pointed.

Jennifer looked in the direction the woman indicated. "Oh, thank you. I was lost."

"Bloody hell!" the man shouted as he ran toward the women. He stopped about one hundred feet from them and knelt on the ground to examine the fallen equipment.

"You must excuse my friend," the woman said to Jennifer, "he usually isn't so disagreeable. It's just that we are recording the patterns the sunlight makes on the ground, and sunny days are rare here. That large megalith over there casts a shadow at midday. It stretches out to these rocks over here. We're trying to determine the pattern that is created when the shadow of the stone falls upon this cluster of rocks," she explained. "This laser equipment is very expensive," she added.

Jennifer looked behind her in the direction the woman had indicated. As she did, she froze. There, in the distance, was a tall stone standing alone. She began to tremble as she stared at the stone. From somewhere deep in her mind, images emerged of the stone surrounded by hooded priests and priestesses. She knew this stone, and she knew of its bloody history of human sacrifices. She turned, only wanting to escape the menacing stone, and began to run. She could see her car in the distance, but the air was still swirling around her, slowing her movement. She didn't hear the man until she felt a hand reach out and grab her. As he did, she stumbled to the ground, the man falling down with her. He recovered first and grabbed her shoulders to help her sit. At that moment, the vertigo overtook all her efforts to quell it, and she vomited.

"What the hell!" the man said as the vile liquid landed on his coat.

"Let me go," Jennifer cried, trying to free herself from this grasp.

"Sit still. I'm not going to hurt you," he said. He placed his hand on her chin and turned her face to his. His face showed his surprise. "It's you! The woman at the museum!"

"Let me go," Jennifer said, choking.

"Are you hurt? Are you ill?"

Jennifer jerked free of his grasp and scrambled to her feet, but he was faster. He caught her, turning her to face him, his hands on her shoulders.

"Wait," he said. "What are you doing here? Why did you destroy my equipment?" he asked with more urgency to his voice.

He was tall, with broad shoulders and dark hair that was partially covered by a MacIntosh hat. His clear, green eyes had small creases at the side, suggesting he was a man who spent considerable time outdoors. She didn't sense a threat from him, but she felt a panic arise within her, nonetheless. She looked back at the stone in the distance and the lake next to her.

"You're trembling," he said with concern. "Are you ill?"

"The shadow from the stone divides the lake in half—a

perfect circle—night and day, earth and sky, male and female, life and death. Please," she sobbed openly now, "let me go."

He released her, a look of surprise on his face. Jennifer ran, heedless of the spiny growth underfoot and the bloody patch on the knee of her torn pants. She didn't stop until she reached her car. As she opened the car door, she glanced back. He hadn't pursued her, but stood, staring at her across the moor.

"Why didn't you tell me this before?" Nina asked, her voice full of concern.

"When it happened at the museum, I thought I must have been drunk. That's when I hit my head. I assumed I had passed out from the alcohol or lost consciousness when my head struck the floor. I didn't think it would happen again," Jennifer said.

They were sitting in Nina's small garden. "Nothing like this has ever happened to you before?" she asked.

"No," Jennifer answered. She had her knees tucked beneath her chin, hugging her legs tightly to herself. Tears had dried on her cheeks, but new ones threatened to appear. "I'm scared, Nina."

Nina pulled Jennifer to her. "We'll figure this out, Jen."

"All kinds of things keep going through my head— schizophrenia or a brain tumor. What if it's like Mom? What if I have a brain tumor?"

"Stop that. You're jumping to conclusions."

"What else could it be? The last month Mom was alive, she didn't even know me. She would hallucinate. . . ."

"Listen to me, McHugh. What happened to your mom is not happening to you, and you certainly don't have schizophrenia."

"Then what happened to me?" Jennifer cried.

"I don't know, but whatever it is, we can face it." Nina pulled Jennifer closer. "Together. Okay?" Jennifer didn't answer. "Do you want me to call John?"

"No."

"But, Jen, he's still your husband."

"Not yet. I don't want to talk to him," Jennifer whispered as she started to cry.

"All right, I won't call him, and you can stay with me as long as you like. You know that, but Jen, I think you should see someone. Will you let me call Shamus, please?"

Mutely, Jennifer nodded her head.

"Are you on any medication?"

"No," Jennifer replied.

"No other headaches or visual disturbances?"

"No," Jennifer answered as she looked across the desk at the soft-gray eyes of Shamus MacNeal.

"Dizzy spells?"

"No, just the two times it happened. I felt sick to my stomach and dizzy just before I blacked out. And it was as though the air was swirling around me."

"Any weakness, numbness, or tingling anywhere?"

"No."

"And this has never happened to you before?"

"Never."

"Have you had any accidents or falls the last six months?"

"No, nothing, other than when I fell at the museum last week. I did hit my head when I fell," Jennifer said as she pointed to the almost invisible scar on her forehead.

"Diabetes? Heart or vascular disease?"

"No."

"I've got to ask this, Jennifer. Do you or have you ever used any illegal drugs? Any methamphetamine, marijuana, cocaine, heroin, hallucinogens?"

"No, never. I don't even smoke."

"Alcohol?"

"A glass or two of wine occasionally. Last week at the

museum, I had been drinking, more than usual. I assumed I was drunk when it happened. But I hadn't had anything to drink this last time."

"I'm sorry. I meant no offense." Shamus smiled gently. "Are you taking any prescription medications?"

"No."

"How about non-prescription medications or herbal supplements?"

"No," Jennifer said.

Shamus sat back in his chair. "I didn't find anything abnormal during your exam. You appear to be perfectly healthy. But, as I'm certain you are aware, we can't just stop here. I would suggest other tests."

"What tests?"

"I would recommend a CT or MRI of your head." He paused a moment and then continued. "Nina tells me that your husband is a physician. You should have a complete neurological examination, Jennifer. I can arrange for that here, but unfortunately, there's a sixteen- to twenty-week wait to see a specialist. I can call a colleague in Aberdeen and arrange for an MRI, possibly tomorrow. I wouldn't want you to fly until we have that result."

"You think I have a tumor."

Shamus smiled kindly. "It's premature to say."

"What else could it be?"

"I don't know. I'm not a neurologist. But it's possible that when you hit your head, you might have torn a small blood vessel in the brain. That's why I would want to rule that out before you consider flying home."

Jennifer's lower lip trembled slightly. "Thank you, Shamus, that's very kind of you. I would be most appreciative if you would schedule the MRI."

CHAPTER 3

Jennifer and John were sitting across from each other in the dining room of their home. Jennifer was eating the last bites of her meal when she became aware of John staring at her.

"John, what is it?"

It was a moment before he spoke. "I got the results of your tests today."

There was no emotion on his face, but then, John rarely displayed emotion.

"Is it bad?" Jennifer asked.

"On the contrary. Everything is negative." He stood and walked around to pull her chair out. "Let's go into the study to talk."

Despite his statement, Jennifer was nervous as they walked to the study. Once there, he closed the door, crossed to his desk, and retrieved a folder. "Sit down," he said as he nodded to two chairs in front of the fireplace and then sat in the other one.

"Alex said that the physician in Scotland," John paused as he leafed through the folder, "Dr. MacNeal, was very thorough. However, as you know, Alex repeated the blood work and MRI just to be certain. All of your blood work is completely normal, as is the MRI. No tumor, no cerebral bleed, no structural anomalies." He closed the folder and looked at Jennifer. "There is nothing wrong with you physically, and though your alcohol level may have been elevated when you hit your head at the museum, you said you hadn't had anything to drink the second time it occurred."

"That's right."

"And there is nothing to suggest that, when you fell at the museum, you had any kind of an acute brain injury that might have caused the second episode."

Jennifer breathed an obvious sigh of relief.

"This is very welcome news," he said. "I know you were afraid it might be a tumor," he said kindly.

Jennifer nodded her head in acknowledgment. "Okay, if everything is normal, what happened to me?"

"That is the operant question, isn't it?" John paused.

Jennifer wished she could read him, but John never betrayed emotion. The few months before they married and afterward, while her mother was sick, she had been grateful for his calm, steady, dispassionate demeanor. He took control of everything and made no demands on her. However, after her mother died, Jennifer wanted a husband. She wanted passion and emotion. After a confusing and heart-breaking month or two, she realized her husband was incapable of both.

"Alex asked me if you had been under any unusual stress lately," he said, his gaze direct.

Jennifer felt a deep ache inside of her. "What did you say?"

"I told him the London trip had been difficult for you— that there were issues that were still not resolved."

She looked away, uncomfortable under his scrutiny.

"Jennifer, I have tried to be a good husband to you. You know that, don't you?" Before she could respond, he continued. "I told you before we married that I had certain difficulties. You were, after all, very young. You still are. And a young woman has certain expectations of married life, expectations that I wouldn't be able to fulfill. So I've tried to care for you. I've given you anything you've wanted. You have a limitless credit card, not that you've ever used it," he added. "When you said you wanted to go back to

45

school, I didn't stop you. I just asked that you not let it interfere with our social obligations. I'm quite proud of you and your desire to learn."

He stood up and walked over to the bar. Without asking her, he returned with two glasses of red wine and handed one to her.

"I'm not having an affair," he said, his eyes piercing, "nor will I ever. I respect you as my wife. I think I deserve the same from you."

Jennifer frowned. She knew that John was trying to reassure her, but why did she always feel like he was a parent lecturing an errant child, and she was the child. When she didn't answer, he continued.

"I trust I can take your silence as agreement, and we can put this behind us. Alex asked if I thought you needed something to help you relax. I told him I didn't think so."

Jennifer had the impression that John was expecting an apology from her. When unbidden, the inexplicable image of mistletoe came to her mind.

"Perhaps mistletoe," she whispered, "the berries mixed with . . . I can see the leaves, but I don't know what they're called."

"Jennifer, what are you talking about?"

She didn't answer immediately, frowning as she concentrated. Then she looked at John. "Can mistletoe be used as a tranquilizer?"

"What!"

"Mistletoe. Does it have medicinal properties?"

"How would I know?" John answered, clearly impatient.

"How indeed? How would I know either, John? But *she* knew," Jennifer said.

"Who?" John demanded. "Jennifer, calm down. You're not making any sense."

Jennifer took a deep breath. "How can I find out?"

"Find out what?"

"If mistletoe is or once was used as a medicine."

"Why would you want to know?"

"John, don't you see? She knew. Cela knew. And I remember it from her. The berries have sedative properties when dried and ground up and mixed with the leaves of . . . I don't know what the leaves are called. I can see them. The plant has small purple flowers on it. You have to be very careful, though, for the mistletoe berries can be deadly, too. The leaves are used for stomachaches and can stop vomiting and diarrhea."

"Cela. The girl in your hallucinations," he said.

"Yes. I told you her name was Cela. If I was hallucinating or having some bizarre stress reaction," she added pointedly, "I could hardly dream up accurate facts, information of which I had no previous knowledge."

"If the information is indeed factual," John added. "Everyone who hallucinates believes the images to be real."

Jennifer faltered under his criticism. "That's why I have to find out if this new information is factual. Don't you see?" She paused. "What happened to me was very real and it scares me," she finished softly. For a moment, Jennifer thought she saw something in John's eyes—compassion, concern?

"All the more reason not to obsess over it. Christ, Jennifer, let it go. Get your life back in order." He stood and took both of their wine glasses to the bar. "It's getting late. We should both retire for the night."

If Jennifer had thought that tonight would be any different from all the other nights of their marriage, she was wrong. They did not argue anymore that night, nor did John make any move toward intimacy.

That night, Jennifer's sleep was interrupted by hazy images. In her dreams, she was effortlessly moving through the sky, looking down on the trees and the patterns made by the great stones and earth mounds. It was oddly familiar— and comforting.

The next morning, Jennifer was eating breakfast in the

dining room when John walked into the room. She could see the tension in his body, the clench of his jaw.

"Mrs. Lynch, will you excuse us," John said to the housekeeper. As soon as Mrs. Lynch left the room, John turned on Jennifer. "I saw your suitcases in the foyer. Where do you think you're going?" he demanded.

"I'm going to Scotland."

"I don't think so," he said, gritting his teeth.

Jennifer was silent. She had been so frightened when she had first returned from Scotland. But as each test came back normal, she began to consider other possibilities. If nothing was wrong with her medically, then what had happened to her? She was the same person. Surely if she were losing her mind, she would feel differently. She didn't. With the exception of the dizziness and sickness that she experienced when the images came to her, she was fine. She was in control of her thoughts.

"John, listen to me, please. I didn't just see or hear Cela. I felt what she felt, thought what she thought, knew what she knew. The medicinal use of mistletoe wasn't the only thing I knew when I was with her. Do you know what bronze is?" Jennifer demanded.

"Bronze!"

"Just answer me, please," Jennifer said.

John exhaled loudly, running his hand through his hair. "It's a copper-based alloy."

"John, I don't even know what an alloy is. Before this happened, all I knew about bronze was that it was used in statues and monuments, and I think it turns greenish over the years. Now I can tell you how Cela's people made bronze. They used copper. They mined it and traded for it. First, they would heat it with charcoal to separate the copper from the rock into which it was imbedded. Charcoal. Do you know how to make charcoal?"

"Jennifer—"

"You stack wood in the shape of a cone," she continued, without waiting for his answer. "Then Cela's people would cover the wood with grass turf, leaving an opening at the top and bottom. They would use the opening at the bottom to light the wood on fire. After it burned, instead of wood ashes, there would be charcoal. Isn't that amazing?"

"This is ridiculous," John began.

"After they melted the copper, they mixed it with a small amount of melted tin. Tin! They used nine parts copper to one part tin. Then they poured the hot mixture into clay or stone forms shaped for tools or weapons. How would you explain that?"

"That's easy to explain. Sometime in your schooling, you learned that. You just don't remember."

"No," she said, shaking her head. "I'm certain I never learned any of that. And there is so much more. Ask me about the constellations—northern hemisphere, southern hemisphere, winter sky, summer sky. Do you know that if you remain in one place, the positions of the constellations change and the positions can be used to predict the eclipses? I didn't know any of that, but Cela knew. I also know how to make pottery."

"So what? You probably went to some summer camp as a child and made a silly bowl to give to your mother."

"No," Jennifer said stubbornly, shaking her head from side to side. "You have to dig for the clay, but it's not too difficult because it's close to the surface. You can find various shades of pink, orange, and even red. Cela's people shaped the vessels with their hands and then baked them in stone ovens. The temperature and baking time were important so that the clay could harden but not get too hot, or it would crack.

"I also know how to weave wool—wool from sheared sheep," she emphasized.

"Stop it!" John grabbed her shoulders roughly and pulled her into a standing position. "You're becoming obsessed with this. It doesn't really matter if what you saw was historically accurate. What matters is that you were not rooted in reality. You did, in fact, hallucinate. Do you think that's normal?" John asked, his voice laced with anger as his fingers dug into her flesh.

"You're hurting me," Jennifer cried as she pulled back.

John released her immediately, but Jennifer knew that he was exercising all of his willpower to regain his usual detached self-control.

"I apologize," he said softly. "We will discuss this no more. I expect you to forget this foolishness." He started to turn from her and then stopped. "I shouldn't be late tonight," he said, almost as an afterthought. "Don't forget that tomorrow night, we are hosting a dinner for our new partner. Mrs. Lynch has taken care of the arrangements. You'll want to confer with her, I'm sure." He turned to leave.

Jennifer blinked. She was trembling from the confrontation. She absently rubbed her hands across her shoulders where John had grasped her. She looked at his retreating back. He was dismissing her and everything she had just told him.

"I won't be here tomorrow," Jennifer said.

John stopped in the doorway. "Just how do you plan to finance this trip?" he asked coldly, his back to Jennifer. "Do you plan to use my money? To my knowledge, you have none of your own. I deposit money into your account and pay your credit card bills. The money and cards can be canceled at any time."

Jennifer was stunned by John's words. He turned to face her.

"I'm sorry it had to come to this, Jennifer, but I find your childish behavior unacceptable. I expect you to be here tonight and to be a hostess tomorrow night." Without another word, John left the room, leaving Jennifer speechless.

✳✳✳

"Holy shit!" Nina exclaimed. "Then what happened?"

Jennifer and Nina were sitting outside in Nina's small garden, sipping tea with cream and honey. Jennifer looked across the moors where the sheep grazed.

"I called John from the airport. I've never seen him lose control. I thought the day before I left Chicago was bad, but this was worse. He was furious. I told him that I wished he'd understand. I had to come back here."

Nina shrugged. "That wasn't so bad."

"There's more. John said . . . John said that by nine o'clock Central Time this morning, my checking account would be closed and my credit cards canceled."

"That bastard!"

Jennifer swallowed. "John's not totally at fault, Nina."

"Well, I say forget about him."

Jennifer frowned, fighting back tears. "I feel lost, you know? I've felt that way for a long time."

"Look, McHugh, you can stay with me as long as you want. You can move in, if you'd like to."

Jennifer looked at her friend. "I'm admittedly a little mixed up right now, crazy maybe."

Nina smiled. "You're not crazy, McHugh, and you aren't prone to hysterics. Something very unusual happened to you. In my travels and reading, I have learned that there is a lot that happens in the real world that lacks a rational explanation. Many cultures accept the unexplained as a natural force in this world. Western thought seems to always need to place phenomena in neat little boxes.

"I don't know what happened to you," Nina continued, "but I think you're on the right track, and first thing tomorrow morning, I'll drive you into Edinburgh. We'll start at the library of the University of Edinburgh. There's bound to be someone there who can help us."

"Thanks," Jennifer said gently, "but I can't take you away from your work. You're already behind on a deadline. I can do this alone."

"What do you know about historical research? What are

you going to do, go up to the librarian and tell him that you had this wacky dream and you want to know if any of it happened before? I'll go with you tomorrow to get you started, and then we'll see. You know, Jen, if you're serious about this, you might even have to go to England for a day or two to visit the universities there. You're not going to find the answers overnight."

"I guess I hadn't thought about that."

"Well, one thing I have learned is that you can greatly reduce your research time by talking to the right people. We'll start tomorrow morning."

"Jen," Nina said the next morning as they were sitting in the University of Aberdeen Library, "there's something that's been bothering me."

The University of Aberdeen was the closest university to Cormara. Founded in the late 1700s, its stone, gothic tower contrasted with the glass and stainless-steel modern structures of the campus. The library was a state-of-the-art facility located in the newer buildings.

"Only one thing?" Jennifer asked as she leaned back in the chair. Before her, scattered about on the sleek, modern table were books, papers, and two open laptop computers.

"One for now," Nina answered. "What language did Cela speak?"

Jennifer frowned. She hadn't thought about that.

"Well? Was it English or some other language?" Nina asked.

"I don't know," Jennifer answered softly.

"How can you not know?"

"When I think about what they said, I hear it in English."

Nina sighed loudly. "Jen, from what you have told me, we've determined that Cela and her people lived during the Bronze Age. I can assure you the people living then did not speak English as we know it. I don't know what they spoke, but it sure wasn't English."

Jennifer was discouraged. "So I must have made it all up then. I dreamed it and used words that I knew."

Nina smiled. "You're smart, McHugh, but not that smart. I doubt you ever knew about metallurgy, astronomy, and the medicinal uses of plants. No, Jen, I don't think you made it up, but it sure as hell is strange."

Jennifer was silent a moment. "So where do we go from here?"

Nina stood. "Well, I'm going to the ladies' room. Oh, and here," Nina said as she slid a small piece of paper across the desk, "you take this. The staff knows me, and as a favor, one of the librarians called a secretary in the Archaeology Department at the University of Edinburgh. The secretary has arranged for us to meet a professor of prehistory. I don't have the professor's name, but here is the secretary's name."

"Tomorrow? But don't you have to be somewhere tomorrow?"

"Yes, but we'll figure it out. I'll be back in a few minutes."

"Okay," Jennifer said as she closed one book and reached for another. Absently, she flipped through the pages. There were color photographs of earth mounds and stones, some in circular formations and others standing stark and alone. As she turned the page, a full-color spread seemed to leap out at her. The effect was instantaneous. She swallowed and clutched her abdomen as the acrid taste came into her mouth, the sickening whirlwind assaulting her, pulling her into its depths.

827 B.C.

"Why have your people ventured so far south?" the High Priest asked the captured warrior.

The warrior stood in a trance-like state, his eyes focused on the amulet that hung around the High Priest's neck. "The warmth did not come with the spring. Our land has not recovered from the winter snows. There is little food."

Cela had been summoned with the other Wise Ones. For three days, the warriors of her people had fought the fierce invaders from the northern islands. Now, as the sun set, the meadows were soaked with the blood of hundreds. Cela's attention wavered from the captured warrior to the warriors of her own people. He was standing there in the front, naked except for a loincloth, carrying a heavy sword that still dripped with the blood of battle. His own body was smeared with the blood of those he slew. Still, Cela could not help but notice the strength of his legs, the muscles of his chest. Dagga was taller than the rest of her people, with black, wavy hair, a strong jawbone, and piercing, dark eyes. Once again, he had distinguished himself on the battlefield, proving for all to see that he was a favorite of the gods.

Something was wrong, though. The others were interested in the interrogation of the warrior and did not see the tightening of Dagga's jaw. He stared straight ahead. Cela turned her attention back to the questions of the High Priest.

"Do you have a symbol given to your people by the People of the Sky?"

The warrior nodded his head.

"What is the symbol of your clan?" the High Priest asked.

The warrior knelt down and began to trace a form in the dirt. Even before he completed it, Cela saw it in her mind. She knew the arrangement of the giant stones that marked the lands of these people, although she had never been there herself. With clarity, she looked quickly at Dagga. Dagga knew them also.

Cela waited until the High Priest was finished and the

prisoners were removed. The Wise Ones had much to discuss with the High Priest and the king of Cela's people. There would be a ceremony of victory tonight and more sacrifices to the gods.

As the people started to disperse, Cela stepped away from the other priestesses and walked to where Dagga was standing. "Dagga," she said.

Dagga had been talking with his comrades, recounting the battle, when he heard a feminine voice address him by his name. It had been several years since he had been a guard for the Wise Ones and had carried a child priestess away from the ceremony. He knew the young woman addressing him now was that child.

The other warriors immediately ceased talking and bowed to the Priestess Cela. She ignored them, as it was not necessary for a priestess of the Wise Ones to acknowledge the bows of the common people or warriors. The others backed respectfully away while Dagga bowed his head and waited.

"They were your people," Cela said softly.

He looked away, his face set.

"Did you know those that you killed today?" she asked.

He was surprised by her words, personal words of interest and something else—innocence and sincerity. "No," he finally answered. "I was very young when captured. I remember very little of that clan. These are my people now," he said, gesturing to the warriors and people in the distance.

"Still, you did not like the fighting."

"I am a warrior. I fight."

Cela nodded her head in apparent understanding. "I see a land surrounded by water. Much of the land is covered by marshes. There is, however, the sweet smell of heather throughout the land. Many of the people still live there in the stone houses of the Old Ones. You mark your land like this," Cela said as she began to trace the pattern made by the great stones.

Dagga listened with interest as she continued to describe the island in detail. When she finished, she stood up. They were standing very close.

"You stir my memories, Priestess. How is this? Have you traveled there?"

"No," Cela answered. "I see lands, many lands, here," she said, pointing to her head. "I see places where I have never been. I see them from the sky."

Dagga continued to look at Cela with surprise. It was highly unusual for a priestess of the Wise Ones to take the time to talk to a warrior, and even more unusual for one to disclose this type of information. Boldly, he looked directly in her eyes—a move never made by warriors or common people.

"Do you see people, Priestess?" he asked.

Cela's eyes softened. "No, Dagga, I never see the people, only the land." Cela looked off into the distance. "I don't understand this gift from the gods. None of the others have it." She looked back at Dagga. "The others use their gifts for the good of the people. What am I to do? Others my age have already begun to train with master teachers." Cela sighed. "They all have special gifts that are useful." She looked up at the late afternoon sky. "I read the stars with the others, but while they use the readings to plot the seasons and eclipses, I use them to move through the sky to distant lands. Sometimes the pull of the sky is so strong that I feel like I can almost. . . ." Cela blushed and looked down at the ground.

Dagga studied the priestess before him. He didn't know what to say. He was astounded that she revealed her thoughts to him. She had grown into a beautiful young woman, this child of the Wise Ones whom he had cared for. Hesitantly, he spoke. "I am grateful for the gift you have, Priestess, for it has awakened a memory of my homeland."

"But it has also brought you pain," Cela said with tenderness.

"Cela? Cela, what are you doing?" one of the other priestesses called.

"I must return to the others," Cela said.

Dagga bowed respectfully.

"Cela! We're waiting!" a priestess called.

Cela started to leave and then turned back to Dagga.

"This much I know. You were brought here as a child for a reason, Dagga. The gods did not intend that you die today with the people of your birth. The gods have a plan for you. That is why you are here with us."

"Cela!" another voice called.

"I must go," the young priestess said as she turned and ran toward the waiting priestesses.

* * *

"Jen? Jen, are you all right?"

Nina knelt down beside Jennifer.

Jennifer blinked as the sound of Nina's voice penetrated her consciousness. She was back—back in the library; however, the sickening vertigo still held her, reluctant to return her to the present.

"I'm going to be sick," Jennifer said as she fought the contractions of her stomach.

"You look positively green. Let's see if we can get you to the restroom," Nina said as she reached for Jennifer's arm to help her stand.

Jennifer was alternating between taking deep breaths, gagging, and swallowing the bile in her mouth. Suddenly, she reached for her purse and vomited into it.

"Jen!"

Jennifer felt Nina's arms around her shoulder as she clutched the purse to her, waiting for the nausea to subside. At last her hands stopped trembling and she sat back, still hugging the purse and its vile contents on her lap.

"Take a deep breath," Nina said, one hand on Jennifer's shoulder and the other brushing Jennifer's hair back off her face. "Okay now?" she asked gently.

Jennifer nodded her head as she waited for the vortex to leave her. It left her as quickly as it had come. She took a deep breath and reached for the book in front of her. Hesitantly, she touched the page, her fingers lightly tracing the picture of the megalith.

"The Standing Stones of Callanish," Jennifer said softly as she read the print beneath the picture in the book. "They were built by Dagga's people. It's their symbol. Where's Callanish?"

Nina was confused. "What?"

"This place," Jennifer said, indicating the picture before her, "where is it?"

Nina leaned over the book. "Here," she said, pointing to a sentence in the book. "It's a prehistoric monument located on the Isle of Lewis in the Outer Hebrides."

"Where?"

"The Outer Hebrides. It's a group of islands to the northwest. They're part of Scotland. I've never been there." She frowned. "Look at me, McHugh," Nina said, waiting until she had Jennifer's attention. "When I came in here, I said your name several times. Your head was resting on the table. I thought you had fallen asleep." Nina nodded to the purse. "You weren't asleep, were you?" she asked with a hollow voice.

Jennifer shook her head as tears came to her eyes.

"Okay, McHugh. Can you stand? We need to get you home."

"Yes, I'm okay."

"All right. You pack up the laptops, and I'll empty this," she said as she reached for Jennifer's purse.

As they drove back to Cormara, Jennifer told Nina what she had seen this time during the blackout, or vision, as Nina was beginning to call the episodes. That evening, they poured over their volumes of notes. At one point, Nina interrupted.

"Jen, when this happens to you, do you see it as a third party might? Are you standing aside, watching it all?"

Jennifer thought a moment. "No," she answered. "I see it through Cela's eyes, and 'see it' doesn't really describe it. I feel what she feels. It's as though I am Cela, but not exactly. I don't choose her words or thoughts or actions. It's her life, and when I'm there, it is as real as this is with you," Jennifer concluded.

"Hmmm," Nina mumbled as the phone rang. She left the room and then returned a moment later.

"It's for you. It's John," Nina said.

Jennifer went to the kitchen where the phone was located.

"John?" she answered.

"Hello, Jennifer. Obviously, you arrived safely. Why haven't you answered your cell phone?"

Jennifer hesitated a moment. The reproach in John's voice was barely concealed.

"The reception on my cell is not very good in this area. I'm sorry, John. I should have called you on Nina's landline when I arrived." She paused. "How was the dinner party?"

"It went very well, thanks to my sister. She acted as hostess in your absence."

"How kind of her," Jennifer said, gritting her teeth.

"Your sarcasm is unnecessary. It was kind of her, and you should be grateful."

"I am, John, truly."

There was silence and then John spoke.

"We have several engagements coming up. When might I expect you to return?"

"I don't know. Nina and I spent the day at the university library. I'm going back tomorrow."

"I see. Jennifer, if you don't mind my saying so, the last thing you need now is to have Nina encouraging these fantasies of yours."

"Thanks for your support, John. Is there anything else?"

"Sarcasm doesn't become you, Jennifer."

"I'm sorry, John. I have to go now. I'll call when I know something more specific."

"That's not good enough. I'll expect you—"

"Good-bye, John."

Jennifer hung the phone up and walked back to the living room.

"Well?" Nina said expectantly.

"He wanted to know when I was returning."

"And?"

"I told him I didn't know."

"That's all?"

"He said I was being sarcastic."

"Were you?"

Jennifer shrugged. "Probably. I shouldn't have treated him like that," Jennifer said pensively. "John's starting to bring out the worst in me."

"Oh, I know about that. Maybe the real you is finally coming back," Nina quipped.

Jennifer frowned at her friend.

"Look, McHugh. You haven't been yourself since . . . well . . . since John took over your life."

"Took over my life!"

"Yes. The little girl I met in the first grade and who became my best friend all through school was sweet, kind, with a heart of gold. But she was also as tough as nails with a will of iron underneath that sweet exterior.

"You've had a lot of shitty things happen to you. Growing up—just you and your mom. You worked all through high school and college to help your mom out financially. Then your mom got sick and you quit college to come home and take care of her. That took strength and love." Nina paused. "You were just worn out at the end, Jen, and that's when John appeared. And you weren't even twenty-one yet. I think you're finally recovering," Nina finished.

The next morning, Jennifer stood before the secretary in the Department of Archaeology at the University of Edinburgh.

"You must be Miss Bouvay, the American author?" the secretary asked.

"No, Miss Bouvay regrets she is unable to be here. I'm her assistant."

"Oh, yes," the secretary paused as she consulted her appointment book, "Miss McHugh. Follow me, please," she said as she stood up and walked around her desk. "Professor Rannoch is not in his office at the moment, but he should return shortly." She led Jennifer down a hall and opened a door, motioning for her to enter. "You may wait here. I'm afraid Professor Rannoch has only a few minutes to spare, however. He's not in his office much during the summer months."

"Thank you," Jennifer replied as the secretary left.

Jennifer looked around the small, cramped office. She observed a large oak desk covered with papers, a laptop computer, a small teapot with cup and saucer, books, and a strange, circular object made of stone with two half-moons cut out of its sides and an intricate carving on the surface. Floor-to-ceiling bookcases covered each wall, the shelves overflowing with books and periodicals. Jennifer had to move a stack of books from one of the chairs to sit down. As she did, the door opened and a man entered.

"You!" he said as he stopped in the doorway, regarding Jennifer with surprise.

Jennifer was speechless. She hadn't gotten a good look at him when he found her in the basement of the museum, but she certainly had a few days ago when she stumbled into his equipment in the mountains.

She stood hesitatingly. "You're a professor of archaeology?" she asked.

He raised his eyebrows as though he found something humorous in Jennifer's question. "Derek Rannoch," he said unceremoniously, "and you are Miss McHugh?"

Jennifer hesitated, wondering if she should tell him that her last name was Bracken.

He walked to where she was standing and offered his hand. As Jennifer shook his hand, he frowned.

"Forgive me for asking, Miss McHugh, but you're not going to vomit on me again, are you?"

Jennifer felt the color rise to her face. He didn't wait for a reply, but nodded his head in response to her silence.

"Good, then. It's a pleasure to finally make your acquaintance, Miss McHugh," he said, the hint of a smile in his eyes. "Please sit," he said kindly. "My secretary said that you are an assistant to Miss Bouvay, the American author. How may I be of service?"

"Yes," Jennifer said, still embarrassed about his reference to vomiting, but appreciating his alacrity. "I help Miss Bouvay with the research for some of her books."

"Is that what you were doing up in the mountains?"

"Y . . . yes."

"Might I ask what you were looking for?"

"Nothing in particular," Jennifer lied.

"You made some interesting comments about the stone and the lake. How did you know about that site?" he asked.

"I didn't. I was just out walking."

"And accidentally came upon it?" He frowned. "Not likely. You said the stone was placed there to divide the lake into two halves. How did you know that?"

Jennifer hesitated. "I must have read about it in my research."

"Impossible."

Jennifer cocked her head, a question on her face.

"Nothing has been written about that site as of yet. That rock was only recently dated. We used the potassium-argon method in our laboratories here at the university."

Jennifer wasn't certain what to say. She didn't have the slightest idea what the potassium-argon method was.

"Well, I must have gotten it mixed up with some other place," she said quickly.

"Pretty sloppy thing for a researcher to do."

"I've just recently taken this position. I don't have a lot of experience," Jennifer said in explanation.

"Yet, you told me that the shadow was to divide the lake into two halves—night and day, earth and sky, male and female, life and death. You even told me the shadow would reach the lake in the autumn."

Jennifer was silent. The image of the bloody rock came into her mind, just as Cela had seen it the day before her people went to fight the invaders from the north.

"Well, Miss McHugh? I would say that was very specific information."

"I made it up," Jennifer answered.

"What?" he said, his surprise evident.

"I made it up, all of it. I have no idea if that rock makes a shadow or not. I thought it was something that Nina, Miss Bouvay, could use in her next book."

Rannoch squinted his eyes as he considered what she said and then reached for a paper laying among others on his desk. "The shape of that lake has changed over the centuries. It undoubtedly started out as a peat bog. I had core samples taken from the bottom of it. It dates back to the Stone Age, somewhere in the Neolithic period of 3500 B.C. to 2000 B.C. Oddly enough, the standing stone also dates back to that period." Derek put the paper down.

Stone Age? Cela's people lived during the Bronze Age. Jennifer was certain of that, or at least she thought she was. Her mind was reeling as she struggled to remain calm.

"Any idea what the site was used for?" Derek asked.

Human sacrifices. Jennifer could see the bodies convulsing against the giant rock, blood spurting out of the victims' chests, splattering against gray granite and onto the ground as the priests and priestesses hurried to collect it. She swallowed quickly.

"I have no idea," Jennifer answered.

"I did some calculations. In September and October, the evening shadow created by the stone would reach the far shore of the lake, just as you said. I even conducted extrapolations of the possible size and shape variations of the lake in prehistoric times, taking into account terrain and climate alterations, and there's a high probability that the stone would have cast a similar shadow pattern. That's too much of a coincidence to have come from fantasy; wouldn't you agree, Miss McHugh?"

Jennifer was silent, her mind trying to grasp the dates and time periods he was talking about. She had no answer for him. She didn't know anything about anthropology or archaeology. Her knowledge came from three unexplained experiences she had, and she certainly could not tell him about those.

"Why did you come here today?" he asked.

"I came to ask you some questions. As I told you, I'm doing some research for Miss Bouvay's next book."

"What kind of questions?"

"She wants to know what life was like during the Bronze Age," Jennifer said weakly.

"You don't need me for that. A student would know how to find information to answer that question. Start with Wikipedia," Derek said bluntly.

"No. She needs more specific information than that."

"What do you want to know?"

"Miss Bouvay wants to know about people who possibly lived during the Bronze Age—tribes or clans of people who lived here."

"Here? Could you be more specific?"

"Here in Scotland, in the Grampian Mountains, and in England." Jennifer hesitated. The copper and tin mines of

Cela's people were far to the southwest. "Maybe Wales, too," she added.

"The Bronze Age spans a long period of time," he said. "Scholars disagree on the exact dates, but it can be presumed to be from 2000 B.C. to 600 B.C. Some say that it starts at 3500 B.C. and extends to 1000 B.C. That's because the defining characteristic of that time period is the smelting of copper and tin to make bronze. Some civilizations utilized bronze long before others did. Most certainly, there were civilizations in Britain during that period, although they were not nearly as advanced as those in Egypt and Mesopotamia.

"Greece, Asia Minor, and Egypt were hundreds, if not a thousand, years ahead of the crude civilizations living in Great Britain. Some of the oldest Egyptian pyramids were constructed during the Old and Middle Kingdom periods, roughly 2630-2611 B.C. The Egyptians were molding gold and bronze during this period, while Britain was still in the Stone Age.

"We've carbon dated bronze artifacts found in Britain to as early as 1800 B.C. The British Museum has a large collection of bronze artifacts from this area. I believe you are acquainted with one of our most recent acquisitions, a certain spear tip?"

Jennifer felt the heat rise to her face as he smiled, his gaze direct.

"May I ask why you were in that room, Miss McHugh? It's not open to the public."

"I was, as you say, looking for Bronze Age artifacts. I got lost. I'm sorry. I hope I didn't damage anything."

She was out of her element. Deliberately deceiving or misleading someone was wrong, but she had already started to 'weave a web of lies,' as her mother called it. She could see the humor dancing in his eyes.

"You didn't damage anything, except perhaps your forehead. I see it has healed," he said.

She glanced away. She was embarrassed and needed to

focus her thoughts. Where should she begin? What could she ask? Did Cela and her people actually exist at one time?

"I've read," Jennifer began, "that these people were led by a group of elite whom they called the Wise Ones, and that these Wise Ones were . . . were a repository, of sorts, of all the knowledge of that time: astronomy, mathematics, history, healing. They also led the people in religious ceremonies that involved sacrificing human beings." Jennifer looked expectantly at Derek. "Is this true, Professor Rannoch?"

"What is your background, Miss McHugh?"

Jennifer was surprised by his question. "I have no background. No formal education in archaeology."

Derek frowned. "Tell me more about your recent readings on these Bronze Age people. You are certain they are of the Bronze Age?"

"They used bronze for spears, shields, and tools for planting."

"Did they hammer the metal or melt it?"

"They melted copper and added tin. Why?"

"It helps to place the time that these people lived. Please continue."

Jennifer thought a moment. "They fought with other clans from the north and surrounding areas. Before the battles, the High Priest would conduct a religious ceremony with the other priests and priestesses. They would ask the gods for a victory. After a battle, they again would hold religious ceremonies to thank the gods for their victories. That is when they would sacrifice their prisoners. They also sacrificed people at other religious ceremonies when they would go to the stones marking their clans."

Derek was looking at Jennifer with a peculiar expression.

"Places like Stonehenge and the place where you had your cameras," Jennifer added.

Derek leaned back in his chair, his eyes piercing. "Human sacrifices at Stonehenge?" Then he stood and walked over to a window. With his back to Jennifer, he spoke. "I would be interested in seeing your references."

"My references?"

"Yes, the papers or documents that contain this information."

"I . . . I don't have them with me."

"Perhaps you could bring them by."

"That wouldn't be possible, Professor Rannoch. I have read so much lately that I really don't remember which document contained that information."

"But you're certain it was authentic? Accurate?"

"That's what I came to ask you."

"Well, therein lies the problem, Miss McHugh." Derek turned around. "You see, the people of the Bronze Age who populated the British Isles left no written records. The Hebrews, Egyptians, and Greeks all left some form of writing. We don't even know whether the Bronze Age Britains had a written language. The earliest written records we have of civilizations living in England and Scotland are the reports written by Caesar with the Roman conquest in A.D. 43. You are describing a civilization that existed eight hundred to one thousand years earlier."

"What?" Jennifer gasped.

"I would be most interested in seeing your documents." The softness in Derek's voice belied the intensity in his voice. Jennifer sensed it, though.

"I think I've made a mistake in coming here today," she said.

"What were you really doing in the mountains, Miss McHugh?"

Why was he looking at her like that? Jennifer realized that Derek Rannoch had not believed her story. It was in his eyes. She stood up abruptly.

"I've taken up too much of your time. Thank you for seeing me, professor," Jennifer said, a slight tremble in her voice as she stood.

"Miss McHugh?"

"Good-bye, professor," she said as she exited the door

without turning back to look at him.

"How'd it go?" Nina asked.

"Terribly! Do you remember when I told you about accidentally knocking over some video and computer equipment in the mountains when I had the vision . . . or episode?"

"Yes," Nina answered with suspicion.

"Same man. The man at the museum the first time I had the episode and the man in the mountains the second time it happened. He's the professor."

"What!"

"I could have died when he walked in."

"What happened?"

"He asked me if I was going to vomit on him again."

Nina laughed. "At least he has a sense of humor. Then what?"

"I told him I was working for you, that I was your research assistant."

"And did you ask him the questions?"

"I tried. I told him about some of the things I had seen in these visions, but I said that the information came from some of the research that I had done. He wanted to know what references I used. What was I going to say? I told him I came across some documents. He didn't believe me. He said nothing like that has been written. I don't think we can expect any help from him."

"Who was he? Maybe if I talk to him?"

"Forget it, Nina."

They both were silent a moment.

"I'm sorry, McHugh." Nina sighed. "How about a break from all this?" she asked suddenly.

"A break?"

"How would you like to go to New York with me for a few days? I talked to my publisher. I have some business I have to take care of. It will take several days. I told her I couldn't come now, but I can call her back. We can leave tomorrow. Come on, Jen. It'd be fun!"

Jennifer frowned. "I don't want to go to New York, Nina."

Nina glanced sideways at her friend. "You're right. We should stay here."

"No, you should go. I've kept you away from your work long enough. You go and I'll stay here, that's if you don't mind me staying in your house while you're gone."

"No, I'll stay to help you. I don't want to leave you by yourself, especially now."

"Nina, I'll be fine. I'm not sick, you know."

"But what if you have another vision?"

"What if I do? Whether you're here or not won't matter."

"I'll wait and go next week."

"No, go now. I insist."

Nina smiled. "Are you sure you and this professor didn't hit it off and you're just trying to get rid of me now so you can spend some time with him?"

Jennifer shook her head slowly. "He saw right through me, Nina. He—"

"What?"

"I don't know. Never mind." Jennifer smiled weakly. "I'll help you pack."

* * *

"Yes, professor?" the secretary said as she came into Derek Rannoch's office.

"Have you ever heard of Nina Bouvay? She writes novels."

"Not really. My friend from the library called and said

she was an American author."

"See what you can find out about her—and her assistant, too."

"Of course," the woman said and closed the door behind her. She returned ten minutes later.

"Professor, my friend said that Miss Bouvay is indeed an author. She writes romance novels and is apparently quite successful. She didn't know anything about the assistant, Miss McHugh, but Miss Bouvay moved to Scotland from London six months ago. She's renting a cottage on Thornhill, sir," the secretary said with emphasis.

"Is she now," Derek said, smiling.

CHAPTER 4

Jennifer shivered as she pulled Nina's sweater over her head, anxious to feel the tight weave of the gray Shetland wool warm her flesh. Nina had flown to New York two days ago. She had been reluctant to leave Jennifer alone but had finally agreed, provided Jennifer would allow Shamus to check on her while Nina was away.

It rained all day the day Nina left and the next day, too. Jennifer had spent the two days inside, searching the Internet for information about Bronze Age civilizations of Britain. Shamus, true to his promise, had called Jennifer each morning. Now, as Jennifer finished lacing the sturdy walking boots that she had bought, she stepped outside.

Although it had rained today also, the rain had finally stopped. She looked up at the gray sky, punctuated in the distance by the mountains, also gray, their peaks hidden by the gray clouds. Everywhere a tapestry of gray, with the exception of the trees in the distance and the green of the moors before her, but even the green carpet was interrupted by gray boulders. All rather ominous, but after three days and nights in Nina's cottage, she was restless. In the distance, she could see sheep grazing—large, white sheep with black faces. She would walk in that direction, keeping the cottage in sight.

The grass was tall here, despite the grazing of the sheep. The land had a gentle roll to it, but enough that Jennifer could feel the difference in her legs as she walked up and down the sloping field. Scattered about were boulders that she had to navigate around, but fortunately, the sheep had created paths through the rocky terrain.

She came to a small wall made of stones and climbed over it. Ahead was a stream and trees. She looked back and could no longer see Nina's cottage, although she knew it was just over the small hills behind her. The wind was stronger here, bringing the smell of rain with it. She would have loved to walk over to the trees, but she felt the first drop of rain on her face. She shivered slightly and turned to retrace her steps. At first, she thought the rushing in her ears was the wind picking up its force as it blew through the trees. Not until the familiar nausea assaulted her did she realize what was happening. She started to run, but the wind seemed to reach out, spinning her around, its fingers grabbing her hair, pulling her downward until she hit the rough grass, the rain pelting her face as darkness closed in around her.

* * *

827 B.C.

"The king is awaiting our decision," the High Priest said.

The Wise Ones were gathered among the circular stones, twenty stones total of differing heights, closely placed so that they formed a circular wall with only enough space between them to allow a single person at a time to pass through. Once inside, the stone provided a barrier to sound traveling outside its walls. The High Priest and his council were standing before the other priests and priestesses.

"The winter has come early as we calculated," the High Priest said. "If our predictions hold true, it will be a harsh winter. Our food supplies may not be adequate."

Cela listened carefully to what the council was saying. Her people had moved south recently in order to prepare for the changing season. They had dug pits and buried supplies of wheat, barley, and beans in large pottery containers, but Cela knew that unless they were able to add to their provisions with wild game and more grain, there wouldn't be enough food for all their people.

"Luc, you will soon be my successor. What do you say?" the High Priest asked.

Luc stepped forward. "I say we tell the king to invade. By all reports, Ere is a lush land, blessed by the gods. Their people are few. Our warriors could easily overcome them."

"They can be a fierce adversary. They paint themselves, evoking their gods' protection," a priest of the council offered.

"They are of a small number and possess little intelligence. They know nothing of the gods as we do," Luc countered. "I have seen a victory for our warriors."

"Soon it will be time for me to go to the next life," the High Priest said. "I am old in this lifetime, and my visions are not as clear as yours, Luc. I am unable to determine the will of the gods in this venture. That is why I have asked all of you to speak freely."

The council priests all looked down at their recent sacrifice. His body lay still now, the convulsions long ago ended. Cela had not watched the sacrifice, even though she understood its importance.

"The people of Ere do not have priests to lead them. How could they win?" Luc asked.

Cela watched as he spoke confidently to the others. *Soon he will be the High Priest.* The thought made her shudder. She was watching Luc when something that one of the priests asked caught her attention.

"And can the waters be easily crossed?" the priest asked.

"Yes," Luc said. "We will not need to send a large force, for they are a simple people. They lack the wisdom of this council."

"Mama," Cela whispered urgently, "that land is not a simple land."

"What are you saying, Cela?" her mother asked.

"The land that they speak of—across the waters to the west. It is not a simple land, and they are not simple people."

"How do you know this?" Ega asked.

"You wish to speak?" the High Priest asked.

Ega and Cela looked up in alarm. The High Priest was addressing them.

"Priestess Ega, have you had a vision that we should know about?"

Ega hesitated. "No," she finally said as she bowed her head slightly. "I have seen nothing."

There was silence. Cela timidly stepped forward.

"The people of Ere are not a simple people," she said softly.

All faces turned toward Cela.

"Come forward," the High Priest motioned.

Cela walked cautiously, careful to avoid the bloody body of the enemy just sacrificed.

"You may speak freely, Priestess Cela," the High Priest said.

"The people in the land of Ere also know the gods."

"How would you know that?" Luc challenged. "You do not even divine from the sacrifices, do you cousin? And yet you dare to contradict me?"

The High Priest frowned at Luc. "Let us hear what the Priestess Cela has to say," he said to Luc and then turned to Cela. "Priestess, why do you say what you say?" he asked.

"I see the land Ere across the narrow waters."

"Liar!" Luc shouted.

The High Priest glanced sharply in Luc's direction. Luc's eyes were boring into Cela, and he did not see the reproach of the High Priest.

"I will hear what the priestess has to say," the High Priest thundered.

Although the High Priest was old and frail now, his voice still carried authority. Luc reluctantly stepped back as all faces turned to Cela.

"Speak, Priestess Cela," the High Priest commanded.

"I see the land of Ere. They, too, are people who know the People of the Sky," Cela began.

"How do you know that?"

"I see their clan symbols. They set their great stones as we do, but their stones are far more numerous than ours."

The council priests inhaled sharply.

"How can this be?" the High Priest asked.

"I see them from the sky," Cela answered. "The land is green and lush. The animals are plentiful, but the clan symbols are also many. Their stone symbols are throughout the land."

"But that means that they know the People of the Sky," a council priest said with alarm.

"Then they have the council of the gods," another said.

"If what Priestess Cela says is true, our warriors could be destroyed with such an invasion."

"How do we know what she says is true?" Luc countered. "None of us have seen this. I, myself, have seen a victory for our warriors," Luc argued.

"Silence! It is my decision that we wait," the High Priest said, his strong voice belying his weak body. "We must be certain of the will of the gods. Tonight, we will make sacrifices to the water and earth. Surely the will of the gods will be revealed to us then."

The High Priest nodded his head, dismissing the council. Cela turned to rejoin her mother. As the others slowly filtered back to their lodgings, Ega looked at her daughter with concern, silently cautioning her against speaking. Only when they were inside their hut did Ega speak.

"Cela, I fear for you."

"Mama?"

"Luc will be High Priest soon. You must be cautious. Your open challenge of him in front of the others has caused him great anger and embarrassment."

"I do not like Luc."

"He is powerful, Cela."

"But he is wrong about the land of Ere."

Ega looked at her daughter. "Tell me about your visions, Cela. Do you still move through the sky to distant lands?"

"Yes, Mama, and sometimes the visions are so clear, so strong, it feels like they are pulling me away with them."

"What do you mean?"

"I want to go, Mama. I want to go where my mind goes. I want to fly through the sky."

Luc could not conceal his shock when the High Priest had finished talking. They were alone in the lodgings of the High Priest. Jealousy ripped through him. He and Cela were cousins, although he was not descended from the old woman, Mora, who had recently died. Cela was the granddaughter of the old woman, and if it was true, Cela was descended from the People of the Sky.

"You will soon succeed me, Luc," the High Priest said. "Cela's gift could be very valuable to our people. She is still young, however. As High Priest, you should help her develop her abilities."

Luc was trying to control his anger. "You are certain she sees what she says?"

"Yes. I believe it is a gift from one of the People of the Sky, just as her grandmother, Priestess Mora, said."

There was silence between them.

"Luc, you must never put your own feelings above the good of our people," the High Priest admonished him.

Luc looked away.

"Do not try to hide your thoughts from me. You cannot. I know of your thirst for power. Up until now, I thought it would actually help. Our numbers are increasing, and the people will need the Wise Ones to maintain order among them. Neighboring clans are warring more. That will require strong leadership. Now, however, I'm not certain that you are the correct choice."

"But—"

"No, there is nothing that you can say. I will look to the gods for the answer. If you are chosen, remember this: the Priestess Cela is a link to the People of the Sky. We desperately need them to return to us. It has been too long. I fear for the fate of our people if the People of the Sky do not return. Cela must be guided and helped. I believe the blood of the People of the Sky runs strong in her, but what do we know of their powers? I do not know how to help Cela discover them."

By the time Luc left the High Priest, his hatred for his cousin Cela had intensified beyond his control. Because of her, the High Priest was actually reconsidering his choice of Luc as his successor. He was considering one of the older priests of his council. Luc knew his young cousin feared him. He could see it in her eyes when he looked at her. He would not let her prevent him from becoming the next High Priest of the Wise Ones.

That evening, just before the sun set, the Wise Ones assembled in one of their most sacred circles. Built by the Old Ones, their ancestors—and at the instruction of the People of the Sky—it consisted of some seven hundred rough-hewn stones set in three rings. Three was a sacred number to them. The outer circle was surrounded by an earth rampart and ditch that was sixty feet deep. It was the largest of the stone places that the people had ever created. It was also the site where the People of the Sky appeared most often.

The common people and warriors stood at a distance while the Wise Ones moved within the circles. A large fire had been erected in the center. It cast an eerie glow as it reflected off the stones at sunset. The priests and priestesses began to circle, chanting as they did. Soon, the sacrifices to the earth would be made. Tomorrow they would move to a nearby grove of sacred oak trees where a small body of water lay. There, they would make their sacrifices to water, seeking the gods' permission to cross the waters to attack Ere.

Cela circled with the priestesses as the chanting increased. They had formed three rings: the priests in the center, the priestesses in the middle, and the younger priests and priestesses, who had only recently been initiated, forming the outer ring. Just beyond them were the elite warriors who guarded the Wise Ones. Dagga was once more among that group.

The High Priest signaled that those chosen for sacrifice were to be brought forward. Two posts had been erected near the fire. One man at a time would be tied up between the posts. As the soldiers placed the prisoner in position, Luc approached with the ceremonial knife that would be used. Two priestesses accompanied Luc, each holding a bowl that would be used to collect the blood and heart of the sacrificed man. As the two priestesses started to kneel, each on a side of the struggling victim, Luc halted one of them. He reached out and took the bowl from her, motioning for her to join the other priestesses. Then, he turned. His eyes found her immediately. With slow, deliberate steps, he passed through the circle of priests and stopped before Cela. All turned to watch as he held the bowl out in front of her.

Cela gasped in horror. She stood motionless, rooted in fear.

"Do you refuse?" Luc dared.

No! How could he do this to her! Cela knew that she could not refuse. The priests and priestesses would not tolerate another breach of ceremony. Besides, she was no longer a child. Any other priestess would consider this a great honor. To all present, Luc had just honored his young cousin.

Slowly, Cela reached out and took the bowl from Luc's

hand. She had no choice but to follow him. Her walk was not that of the graceful, young woman that she was; it was, instead, the walk of one in great pain.

The chanting resumed, and Cela knelt next to the body that was restrained between the two poles. The chanting was deafening now. The High Priest approached but did not remove the knife from Luc. Luc would perform the sacrifices.

Cela wanted to close her eyes to the sight before her, but she knew she could not keep her eyes closed and hold the bowl as was expected. She stood, her hands shaking as Luc plunged the knife into the victim's chest. The restrained man screamed in pain. Only Luc saw the tears streaming freely down Cela's face. A malevolent smile danced in his eyes as he prolonged the prisoner's agony by slowing pulling the knife back and forth, twisting as he thrust.

It seemed as though the nightmare would never end. Cela caught the flowing blood as was expected. She offered it to Luc and then picked up another bowl to fill it with the fluid of life. She could hardly see through her tears as she held the bowl against the gaping wound in the prisoner's chest, the flow decreasing now as life drained out of the man, bringing an end to his screams of pain. Her hands were shaking so badly that she spilled some of the blood as she once again offered the bowl of warm, dark liquid to Luc. She stepped back, the prisoner's blood soaking through her white robe and clinging to her skin, the blood still warm.

Finally, the dead body was removed and another tied between the posts. Two new priestesses stepped forward with bowls. Luc was chanting with the priests again. Cela saw her opportunity to escape. She must leave before Luc noticed her, for she knew that he intended to again dismiss one of the priestesses and force her to assist him.

As calmly as she could, she pulled the hood of her robe around her face. Looking down, she walked back to the inner circle. She had to force her feet to walk slowly, for she wanted to run. As soon as she reached the priestesses, they began to circle again. Cela did not follow them, but turned and walked through the outer circle of young priests and priestesses and past the outer ring of stones. Her vision was blurred by her tears, and she felt her stomach contract violently. She swallowed the bile that came to her mouth repeatedly as she continued to walk. She reached the elite warrior guard but kept her face down, her hair covered by the hood of her robe, and continued to walk.

At last she reached the ditch. Her legs were shaking as she began to descend. Again, she forced herself to swallow the vile contents of her stomach as they came up into her tightly clenched mouth. Finally, she reached the bottom. Normally, climbing the ditch would have been easy for her, but as she began the ascent, she struggled. Her legs were weak, trembling instead of strongly moving forward. Her refusal to vomit was burning her throat, causing a pain to spread through her abdomen. She would disgrace herself for the last and final time if the Wise Ones saw that she was sick.

Dagga had instantly recognized the small form of the priestess who walked past the guards. Several of the guards turned, their eyes following her. They looked at each other questioningly. Should one of them accompany the lone priestess?

"I will go," Dagga said quickly before the others could discuss it.

He knew something was wrong. It took him no time at all to descend the sixty-foot ditch and reach Priestess Cela as she stumbled, trying to climb up the hill. Without a thought of himself, he picked her up, as though she was once again the small child she had been four years earlier.

Cela's eyes widened as she felt Dagga's arms go around her, but she did not resist as he carried her up the hill and out of the glow of the fire. Dagga did not stop until he was far beyond the people and the chanting. He found a small grove of trees and gently placed Cela's feet upon the ground. She immediately collapsed, retching violently. Dagga pulled Cela's long, red hair out of her face. Then he placed his hand upon her forehead and supported her until, at last, the violent contraction ceased. He took his own cloak and wiped her face. She did not resist as he sat down and enfolded her in his arms.

* * *

Derek Rannoch looked up as, once again, his two Irish wolfhounds barked. Both were pawing at the door, their massive feet striking the ancient, unyielding oak portal. He was sitting before a fire, reading. "What is it?" he asked as he stood and walked over to the dogs. They both turned in circles, waiting for their master to open the door. Derek frowned. "What's got you two so worked up?" he asked as he reached down and petted the mammoth dogs. The female dog began to whine and then pawed at the door again. Derek reached for the latch and opened the door. He watched curiously as both dogs bolted out into the rain.

"All right, let's see what we have," he said as he removed his jacket from where it hung by the door. It was a common garment in Scotland, dark green and water resistant. He also pulled on a pair of green wading boots and stepped out into the rain. The late afternoon sky was dark gray as he squinted in the distance, searching for the dogs whose gray coats were blending into the rain. He called to them once and immediately heard their response, giving him direction in the storm. He followed the sound into the surrounding woods.

Jennifer shivered. She tried to stand but her legs were weak, and she fell back onto the wet undergrowth. The cold rain stung her face as the wind whipped her hair about, obscuring her view of the surroundings. She tried to brush her hair out of her face, but her hands were trembling so that she was only able to push a strand or two back behind her ears. Her fingers burned with the cold. She awkwardly tucked them under her arms for warmth, but the rain had even penetrated the thick Shetland sweater she wore.

It had happened again, but this time Jennifer didn't feel the vertigo or nausea that she had experienced on the previous occasions. Perhaps it was because of her current physical state—she was freezing. Once again, she tried to push herself up to a standing position. Her teeth were chattering and her arms and legs were shaking so badly, she only got as far as one knee when the fierce wind pushed against her and the weight of the wet sweater pulled her back to the ground.

She lay there a few seconds, gathering her strength for another attempt, when she heard the distinct barking of dogs. She gasped as she saw the great beasts, their shape barely discernable in the pelting rain, come bounding out of the trees. She was about to scream when they stopped before her. Jennifer felt the rough, warm tongue of one of the dogs as it licked her face. The other pranced around her, occasionally stopping and facing back in the direction of the trees as it barked. Now that she had determined that the great beasts were indeed dogs and didn't seem to be a threat, she tried to push them away, but to no avail.

"What the devil?" Jennifer heard a man exclaim. Then she saw the man emerge from the woods and run toward the dogs. "Back," he commanded, and the dogs stepped away from Jennifer. The man knelt down beside her. "Miss McHugh!" he said with surprise. "Are you hurt?" he asked as he reached down to her.

Jennifer's teeth were chattering so much she could hardly

speak. "N . . . no."

He put his arm around her waist and lifted her so she could stand. Her knees buckled. Instantly, he caught her and lifted her into his arms.

"Put me down," Jennifer said. "I can walk."

"You're half frozen, woman! What the hell are you doing out here?" he shouted into the rain as he carried her.

Jennifer tried to protest, but her words were lost in the wind. In the end, she curled into the warmth of his arms, grateful for the protection from the pelting rain. When she felt his steps slow, she opened her eyes to see a gray stone house. He carried her inside, with the dogs following close behind.

"Can you stand?" he asked, his face close to hers.

"Yes, I can stand," she said with embarrassment.

He put her down but kept his hands around her waist, his touch gentle but steady, until he was certain she wouldn't fall. Then he nodded his head and released her. Jennifer watched as he closed the heavy door and removed his coat.

"You've got to get out of those wet clothes. Come over here," he said as he led her over to the fireplace, the water dripping off with each step, leaving a wet trail behind her. "I'll see what I can find for you to wear."

She watched as he crossed the room and opened a door. She noted that he had to duck his head as he entered the other room. He was tall, yes, but she suspected that this was a very old house, the doorjambs originally made to accommodate generations of shorter statured inhabitants long ago. Just how old the stone house was, she couldn't guess. She took the opportunity to examine her surroundings. The walls were gray stone, covered with portraits and tapestries. Notched into the stone walls were spaces occupied by iron candelabras.

The walls rose up two full stories with enormous, dark beams supporting the ceiling. The floor was gray slate, its color the same as the stone walls. The massive fireplace, with its large, open hearth, dominated the room and warmed the stone walls surrounding her. A black leather sofa faced the fireplace, winged by two matching leather chairs angled toward the fireplace. Each chair had a small end table, one with a pile of books and the other a decanter of golden-brown liquid. The room was warm and comfortable, and Jennifer had the sense that it had been here a long time.

She turned as she heard the professor approach behind her.

"Here," he said as he handed her a shirt, sweater, and some socks. "Sorry, I don't have anything else." He reached for a thick plaid blanket of woven cloth. "You can wrap up in this."

Jennifer stood there, staring at him.

"Miss McHugh, isn't it?"

"Yes, Professor Rannoch, I can explain. I was—"

"Later. If we don't get you out of those wet clothes, you're going to be sick."

Jennifer clutched the clothes he gave her but didn't move. The professor smiled slightly.

"I'll see if I can find something for you to drink to warm you. You can just leave your wet clothes there on the floor."

He didn't give Jennifer a chance to respond but turned and walked out of the room. She stood there a moment. This was the last place she wanted to be now, but he was right. She was feeling weak as she stood there shivering. Already the floor was wet beneath her where the water was dripping off her clothes. She reached for the sweater she was wearing, but it felt as though it weighed a hundred pounds as she tried to pull it over her head. Her entire body was shaking, her teeth chattering, and she struggled with the wet wool for several minutes. When the professor returned, she was still trying to remove it.

"Here, let me lend a hand," he said as he laid some towels down on a table.

He pulled the garment off, his grip on the sweater

causing more water to cascade down onto the floor.

"You're soaked all the way through," he said, noticing her wet shirt. "Here," he said as he reached for the towels. "Remove your clothes and dry yourself."

What? She remained frozen where she stood. Surely he didn't expect her to. . . .

"Do you need assistance, Miss McHugh?"

"No, I don't need your assistance," Jennifer replied quickly.

Again, a smile appeared in his eyes. "Very well, I'll bring something for you to drink."

Despite her shivering, Jennifer undressed quickly as soon as he left the room. The shirt and sweater that he had provided reached the middle of her thighs. The socks were too big, but warm. She hastily grabbed the plaid blanket and wrapped it about herself, concealing her legs. She had just finished when the professor returned, carrying two cups. He put them on the table and turned to her.

"Sit," he commanded.

As Jennifer sat on the large, black leather sofa by the fire, he removed her wet garments that were laying on the floor, pausing a moment as he picked up her underwear and bundled it with her pants and sweater. She flushed as she saw him smile briefly. He then dried the floor and removed the wet towels and clothing. Finally, he returned and handed her one of the steaming cups. He settled himself into a chair next to her.

"Drink it. It will help."

Jennifer took one sip and coughed as the warm, fire-like liquid went down her throat. She frowned. "That's awful."

"Drink it all. It will warm you quickly."

"What's in it?"

"It's an old Highland remedy—a little whisky, a little warmed cream, and a few other things."

Derek raised his own cup and drank deeply. When he finished, he eyed her challengingly.

Jennifer swallowed and raised the cup to her lips. Taking

a deep breath, she again drank from the cup and grimaced.

"Professor Rannoch—"

"Finish it," he said.

"What?"

He nodded to the drink. "Then you can explain."

Jennifer took another sip, her taste buds growing accustomed to the fiery brew. "I should call someone to come get me."

"Miss Bouvay? You said you were her assistant; you are staying with her, aren't you?" he asked.

"Yes. She is also my friend. She's renting a cottage on the Thornhill Estate. Do you know where it is?"

He smiled slightly. "Yes. That cottage is only a few miles from here."

"Where is here? I'm afraid I'm lost," she said as she took another drink.

"You seem to have a penchant for that."

"Well, only recently," Jennifer said softly.

"This lodge also belongs to the Earl of Thornhill. It used to be a hunting lodge."

"Oh."

"Would you like to call Miss Bouvay?"

"She's in New York for a few days. If you wouldn't mind, I could call Dr. Shamus MacNeal. He's a friend of Nina—Miss Bouvay. He's been checking in on me while she's away." Jennifer was shivering so badly that her teeth banged against the cup as she took another drink.

"You're still cold."

"A little," Jennifer admitted.

"Keep drinking."

He got up and placed two more logs on the fire. As he returned to his chair, he looked at one of his dogs lying on the floor in front of Jennifer.

"She knew you were out there," he said, nodding to the dog. "She found you."

Jennifer looked down at the dog. "I've never been around dogs much," she said.

"They're Irish wolfhounds."

"What's her name?"

"This is Isabella of Mar and that is Robert the Bruce."

Jennifer lifted an eyebrow.

"Thirteenth-century Scottish history," Derek said in explanation. "Issy and Bruce."

"I'm afraid I don't know very much about Scotland's history," Jennifer answered. Again she shivered. The professor stood and took the cup from her hands. He returned a moment later with it filled again.

For the next few minutes, they sat in silence as Jennifer huddled in the blanket and drank the warm brew that he had prepared. Even though she didn't like the taste of it, she had to admit that she was feeling better. The drink and the roaring fire at last had their effect upon her. Her shivering ceased, and she actually loosened the plaid blanket that she had wrapped around her.

The professor stood, and Jennifer watched as he walked to a wall and flipped a switch. The black iron candelabras on the stone walls came to life, the electric bulbs flickering like candlelight. Again, she had the sense that this room had warmed its inhabitants for centuries, and for the moment, at least, she was glad to have been included. Still, she had imposed upon the professor enough.

"Are you hungry?" he asked, interrupting her thoughts.

"I have inconvenienced you enough, Professor Rannoch. May I call Dr. MacNeal now?"

"Of course," he said, "but you need to eat and so do I. We'll have dinner, and then I'll drive you back to Miss Bouvay's cottage."

"I shouldn't stay here," Jennifer said, suddenly nervous despite the professor's kindness. She wasn't afraid; on the contrary, she felt safe, warm, and at peace. And that was precisely *why* she was nervous. This unnatural level of comfort was strange. "You've been very nice—especially after the trouble I've caused you—but I don't even know you," she said as she pulled the blanket tighter around her.

"The phone is in the kitchen," he said kindly. "Old-fashioned," he added in explanation. "Mobile phone reception is not reliable in this area, especially when it rains, which is often."

Jennifer followed him into the kitchen, taking the large blanket with her. The kitchen had a low beamed ceiling that had various pots hanging from it. There was a large, solid oak table situated in front of a stone fireplace. Jennifer realized that it was the same fireplace that was in the other room; it had two openings in it, making the kitchen as warm and comfortable as the living room had been. But on this side of it, there was an iron roasting spit and several hooks with black pots that could swing into the hearth. To the side of the hearth was a stone opening that Jennifer assumed had once been an oven, similar to ones she had seen in pictures of American colonial settlements.

The professor indicated the chair closest to the fireplace and then pulled the phone over to the table. He found Shamus MacNeal's number in the directory and dialed the number.

"This is Derek Rannoch," Jennifer heard him say. "Might I speak to Dr. MacNeal?" There was a pause and then Derek spoke again. "Dr. MacNeal? This is Derek Rannoch. An acquaintance of yours is here with me, Miss Jennifer McHugh. She got caught in the rain and found her way to the hunting lodge on Thornhill. I have suggested that she have dinner with me, and then I will drive her back to Miss Bouvay's cottage. Perhaps you would vouch for my character and assure the lady that she is safe in my company."

Jennifer blushed as he handed the phone to her without waiting for a reply from Shamus. He seemed to find something amusing in what he had just said to Shamus, for his mouth curved up slightly and his eyes danced. She took the phone and the professor turned. He was a tall man, athletic in build, but he had a relaxed, easy walk. She waited until he reached the refrigerator and began removing food.

"Shamus?" she said into the receiver.

"Jennifer? Are you all right?"

"Yes, Shamus. I thought I could go for a short walk before it started raining again, but I got lost. Professor Rannoch found me. I'm afraid I was completely soaked through, but I am fine now. I'm sorry to bother you."

"I'm glad you called, Jennifer. Do you want me to come get you? I have a few more patients to see, but I could be there in about an hour."

Jennifer watched as the professor worked in the kitchen. She hadn't had time to think about this latest loss of consciousness. Had she walked during the blackout? How long had it lasted this time? It was even more important that she understand what was happening to her now, and Derek Rannoch might be able to help.

"No, Shamus, thank you, but that won't be necessary. Professor Rannoch has offered to drive me back to Nina's house."

"All right, but if you need anything, just call me."

"I will. Thank you."

Jennifer hung up the phone. The professor stopped what he was doing and walked over to her. As he picked the phone up to place it back on a smaller table, he looked at her. "Are you more comfortable now, Miss McHugh?"

Jennifer blushed again. She started to speak, but he spoke first.

"You have nothing to fear. Besides, Issy seems to have appointed herself your protector," he said as he motioned to the dog. For the first time, Jennifer noticed that the female dog had followed her into the kitchen and now lay at her feet. "There's very little that could get past her," he added in a manner Jennifer was certain was to reassure her.

The professor returned to his work. He seemed to have no need for conversation while he prepared the meal. After a while, Jennifer accepted the silence and settled into the chair by the fire. She let her mind drift back to the events of an hour ago. The details of Cela's world were clear in her mind. She could see the crude, round lodgings made of wood and thatch, as well as the woven wool robes that the Wise Ones wore and the tunics and skins that the common people wore. And the bloody sacrifices. She shuddered and tried to direct her mind away from those sights. Each time she experienced Cela's world, Jennifer became more convinced that it was not a world conceived by her own wild imaginings. That might have been more acceptable, for modern psychiatry could treat that phenomenon. But this? She was staring at the fire, when suddenly, the flames appeared to swirl around, driven by an unseen vortex. She pulled the plaid blanket around her, holding it close as she felt the familiar knot begin in her stomach.

✳ ✳ ✳

827 B.C.

"Why?" Cela whispered.

Dagga frowned. Cela had not moved from his lap since he had carried her from the sacrifices. Her body had finally quieted after the despair that had torn through her, but she had remained ensconced in his arms. He was shocked at such familiarity; she was no longer a child, but a young woman and a priestess of the Wise Ones. She looked up at him.

"Why do the gods ask that of us? Why do they demand that we sacrifice life to them? Why do they thirst for blood?" Cela asked.

Cela seemed to expect Dagga to answer. When he did not, she looked away. Dagga felt that he had somehow failed her. How could she expect him to answer such a question? He had been trained to fight; he had not been trained to talk with the gods, as the Wise Ones were.

"I do not know the answers to your questions," he began

awkwardly. Cela had settled herself back against him, her head resting upon his chest. It moved gently up and down as Dagga breathed. "You are a priestess of the Wise Ones. Your ways are unknown to us. We depend on you to tell us the will of the gods. Can you not divine the answer to your own question?"

"How?" Cela asked as she sat forward. "By observing the convulsions of a man as his heart is pierced and removed? By noting the movement of his eyes as the air is choked out of him? By watching the flow of his blood after he is garroted and placed face down in the water? I see nothing of the gods there. Nothing. The others do, but I do not. Do you understand?" she asked, her voice strained with emotion. "Perhaps I have not learned well enough. Perhaps I am not fit to be a priestess," she finished as new tears formed in her eyes.

Dagga held her. When she finally quieted, he spoke softly. "Priestess, I was trained as all warriors are trained, but I do not fight as my fellow warriors do. We are taught how to hold the sword and shield and how to strike when the enemy attacks, but there are times when I move in a different way. I strike in another way. I defend myself in my own way. Perhaps that is why I have lived through so many battles. Priestess, I was not taught to fight the way I do. I fight in a way that is natural to me. Do you not also know the will of the gods in your own way? Do you not also speak with the gods in your own way? Are your dreams not your own and different from the others of the Wise Ones?"

Dagga had no way of knowing how provocative his last words were. He was startled when she bolted up, her eyes glowing, the wind whipping her hair about her face, her body tense, ready to spring.

"That's it! Yes! Come, there is little time!" she said excitedly.

Dagga sat there, confused. Cela reached out with her hand.

"You are wise, Dagga, very wise. Let's go. I must do this

before the others finish and come looking for me. We must travel quickly."

"Where are we going, Priestess?"

She rapidly made the calculations. Could they travel that distance before the sun rose the next morning? She was young and healthy. Dagga was a strong warrior.

"Come. We must walk most of the night."

Cela set a fast pace as they moved across the plains, keeping among the trees as much as possible. Once, Dagga became concerned, fearing that they were off their course.

"Priestess, you do not check the stars. Are you certain of our path?"

"I am certain. It is not necessary to plot the stars. I see this land from the sky—as you said, from my *dreams*. I know my way."

They stopped every hour for a brief rest. The last star was fading from the sky when they crossed the final hill range and approached the great monument. Dagga's first reaction was to stop as he approached the great circular earth work, but Cela motioned him forward. The great megalithic circles loomed above. Cela entered from the east, Dagga behind her. The stone circles seemed unnaturally quiet with only the two of them present.

Cela passed through the outer ring made of the gray sandstone blocks with lintels topping and connecting each. She walked through the inner circle of blue stones and motioned for Dagga to come no farther.

"You must not interfere," she said as she turned to him. "No matter what happens, you must not interfere. Wait here."

Dagga wanted to ask questions, although he knew it was not his place to do so. He stood, as commanded by the priestess. Was it just three years ago that he had carried the child priestess away from these very circles?

Cela began to walk, starting in the east and moving toward the south. She continued the movement until she had completed a circle three times. Then she stopped and reverently removed the robe of a priestess. Next, she took off her remaining garments and shoes until she stood naked. Dagga watched in amazement as she withdrew a small piece of mistletoe. He wanted to move closer, but dared not. Even at this distance, there was no mistaking the small dagger that she placed in her hand.

Slowly, Cela entered the half circle of trilithons and approached the flat stone at the very center of the circles. Ceremoniously, she lifted the mistletoe into the air as the sun began to crest upon the new day. Dagga watched as she raised the dagger into the air and held it against the mistletoe. She was chanting, her words difficult for him to understand. Then, just as the rays of the sun broke forth upon the circle, Cela stopped. For a second, the reflection of the sunlight against her red hair blinded Dagga, and then he heard her call out to the sky.

"Hear me! I am Cela, daughter of the People of the Sky, priestess of the Wise Ones of our people, and your servant. I have been instructed in the ways of the Wise Ones and have offered sacrifices to you as commanded. Why?" she shouted to the sky. "You are the life force. Why do you demand death? Hear me! I am Cela, your daughter. No more will I end life for you. No more will I offer you the blood of my people. No more will I offer you the blood of our enemies. If it is blood that you demand, then you shall take mine, for never again will I offer the blood of another to you."

Dagga heard every word, and he watched in horror as Cela pulled her long, flaming hair to the side, exposing her neck. She raised the knife once more into the air and then slashed out across her own neck. By the time Dagga reached her, she lie on the ground, lifeless, the blood flowing out of her neck.

Dagga was a seasoned warrior. Knife wounds were nothing new to him. Although the wounds of the surviving warriors were always treated by the Wise Ones skilled in the healing arts, Dagga had learned much from observation. He reached for Cela's white robe and pressed the coarse fabric against her neck to stop the flow of blood. His quick assessment told him that he needed some way to hold the severed skin of her neck together so that the bleeding would stop.

Dagga had seen the Wise Ones sew the skin, but he had neither the fine bronze needle nor the strands of gut made from sheep entrails. He had also seen them apply a mixture that pulled the skin together. What was it they used? He had never seen them mix it, and he was not privy to their secrets. But he had heard the Wise Ones talking among themselves. One ingredient was a yellow powder that had a distinct smell. He didn't know where to find that, but he did know where to find the other ingredient. He would have to carry Cela, though, all the while keeping pressure on her neck. She was lying so still on the ground.

He shifted his weight and lifted her into his arms. The robe hung down as he pressed it against the wound and began walking out of the circles. He broke into a run, maintaining pressure on the wound. For thirty minutes he ran, clutching Cela's lifeless body to his chest, his own heart pounding, the beginning of sweat appearing on his brow. When he reached the trees, he slowed his pace, moving into the deep underbrush. At last, he found what he was looking for.

Gently, he lowered Cela to the ground. He would need to remove his hand from her neck, but he would work quickly. He reached up and pulled the large web down, disturbing the spider that had ceased its work as the sun rose. The sticky substance clung to his fingers. Kneeling by Cela, he wiped away the newly formed blood on her neck. He pinched the red line together and then began to dab the sticky web onto it. Next, he grabbed the spider and pushed its end onto the wound, squeezing the sticky fluid out of the spider. When the entire length of the wound was covered, he tossed the spider aside and pulled Cela's robe between his knees. Removing his own knife, he tore a small piece of the robe and placed it on the wound, applying a steady pressure, sealing the cloth against the sticky web and the wound.

Satisfied, Dagga repositioned himself under the shade of the tree and placed Cela's head on his lap, still pressing against the wound. With his other hand, he covered her naked body with her robe. He could not bring himself to burn the delicate flesh of Cela's neck. However, if the spider's web and cloth failed to stop the flow of blood, he would heat his knife and lay it on her neck. She had told him not to interfere. Well, her gods be damned! She would not die while under his protection.

Dagga sat under the shade of the giant oaks until well past midday before he felt a stirring from Cela. In all those hours, he had released his pressure upon her neck only to hastily apply it with the other hand. Now, as Cela began to turn, he quickly reached out with his other hand to prevent her head from moving. Cela winced against the restriction and opened her eyes.

"Priestess?" Dagga spoke softly.

Cela frowned at the sound of a human voice. She moved her eyes toward the face above her.

"Do not move your head. The wound is still fresh," he cautioned.

Cela nodded her head slightly in understanding.

"You will live, Priestess. You are lucky that the wound was not deeper, or there would have been nothing I could have done to save you. You would have been a sacrifice to the gods whom you defied today."

A slight smile appeared on Cela's face. "I am a priestess of the Wise Ones," she whispered with effort, "trained in the art of human sacrifice. I did not make the cut so deep that the blood would pulse out rapidly and bring a quick death. I made it close to the surface to allow for a slow death to give the gods time to reconsider my sacrifice."

Dagga smiled. "You are a very unusual woman, Priestess, even among the Wise Ones. You should rest now. This evening, we will see if the wound holds."

Cela closed her eyes. "You were right, Dagga," she whispered. "The gods do not speak to me as they do to the others. They do not speak to me in death. I see them in the life force that surrounds me. I hear their voices in the wind. I feel them in the warmth of the sunlight and in the glow of the moonlight. They call to me from the sky."

Dagga watched Cela's breathing become slow and steady as she fell into sleep. He maintained a steady pressure on her wound.

✻ ✻ ✻

"Miss McHugh? Miss McHugh?"

Jennifer looked up, startled. She blinked as she turned and surveyed the table before her. The vertigo made it difficult to focus. The professor had set the table and placed plates of food before her. She hadn't even heard him do it. He was staring at her now. How long had he been watching her? She was aware of the large dog pawing her lap and whining softly.

"I thought you had fallen asleep before the fire, but when Issy began to bark and you didn't stir, I became concerned. You're very pale." He reached for her forehead. "No fever," he said to himself.

She unconsciously swallowed the vile contents that came up into her mouth and drew the blanket tightly against her abdomen, trying to ease the cramping of her stomach. She was going to be sick in front of Professor Rannoch!

"You're trembling," he said. He knelt down on one knee beside her and wrapped the blanket tighter about her. Then he put his arm around her and held her close. She accepted his warmth and let her head rest on his shoulder. His touch surprised Jennifer, for it seemed to ease the swirling vortex and her stomach quieted. She felt comforted by the presence of this man she barely knew. "Perhaps I should call Dr. MacNeal," he said.

"No," Jennifer said. "I'm fine." She hesitated. "I guess that drenching took more out of me than I realized. I was feeling exhausted, and the fire was so inviting. I did fall asleep. I'm all right now," she said softly, hesitant to leave the security of his arms.

She felt him shift and separate himself from her, although he did leave one arm around her. She arched her neck up to see a look of doubt on Derek's face.

"Please, I'm embarrassed enough to be sitting here like this," she said, indicating his clothing and the blanket. He withdrew his arm from about her, and for a fraction of a second, Jennifer felt a profound sense of loss. The deep-seated emotion surprised her.

"Very well," he said as he stood. "Do you feel like eating?"

"Yes, I do." Jennifer was surprised, but her appetite had returned. "How many people have you invited to dinner?" she asked as she surveyed the abundance of food set out before her.

"Ah, only you, milady," he said with a smile as he helped Jennifer pull her chair to the table. "Good. You've stopped trembling and your color is back." He walked around to the other side and sat down across from her. "Would you like whiskey or do you prefer wine?" he asked as he held up two bottles. "I also can offer you water, and I might be able to find a soda."

"Wine, please, professor," Jennifer replied. "Your malt whiskey is a bit strong for my tastes." Her stomach had indeed calmed down, and she felt herself relax. She sighed inwardly, grateful that she had not gotten sick.

The professor poured a deep-red wine into Jennifer's glass and then motioned to the steaming bowl of soup before her. "You should eat before it gets cold," he said. "And as we are about to become dinner companions and you're wearing my shirt, I think we can dispense with the formality. I'm Derek," he said.

Jennifer felt herself blush. "I'm Jennifer."

"It's a pleasure to make your acquaintance, Jennifer."

The barley soup was tasty, and by the time Jennifer had finished it, she felt warm and relaxed. The soup was followed by one of the tenderest cuts of beef that Jennifer had ever tasted. There were also potatoes, scones, and several cheeses.

The professor proved to be a charming conversationalist throughout dinner. His questions were polite but not probing. He laughed easily and quickly put her at ease. It was not until the dinner was concluded and the table cleared that his mood signaled a change. He sat across from Jennifer, content to sit quietly and sip a glass of whiskey. Finally, Jennifer broke the silence.

"You're waiting for an explanation of why I was wandering about, practically in your front yard, on a day like this."

Derek raised his eyebrows but said nothing.

"Nina, my friend, has been away for three days, and all I have done is remain inside while it's rained. I was feeling cooped up. I guess it wasn't the best time for a walk."

Still, Derek remained quiet.

"I intended to stay near Nina's cottage, but I guess I started daydreaming, and by the time it started to rain again, I could no longer see the cottage. I was lost."

Jennifer looked down at the remaining wine in her glass. She might as well say it.

"Professor Rannoch—Derek, I need your help."

"How can I assist you?" Derek asked.

"As I told you in your office, I have come across some information and I want to know if it's accurate. I have no background in this area, and as you correctly surmised, I have no experience in archaeology or anything related to it. But I have this information, and I need help understanding it. That's why I came to you."

"And this information is relating to a civilization that existed during the Bronze Age?"

"Yes."

"And you believe this civilization existed here?"

"Yes, in Scotland, Wales, and England." Jennifer thought for a moment. She recalled Luc's desire to invade the island. "Perhaps Ireland, also."

"How is it that you have come across this information? Are you in possession of artifacts, documents?"

"I can't tell you that."

"Then how do you expect me to validate this information?" Derek asked.

"By what I tell you about the civilization."

Derek shook his head. "That's impossible. It doesn't work that way."

"Why? I will tell you all I have learned. I just can't tell you how I learned it."

"And what do you expect me to do?"

"Help me to find the truth. I'm not hiding some valuable ancient document or artifact. I promise. What I have come upon has only recently been written down," Jennifer said out of desperation.

"So you just want to tell me about what you have read, and you expect me then to validate it for you."

"Yes," Jennifer said.

"I don't think so," Derek said as he stood and walked over to the kitchen cabinet. He removed the bottle of Scotch whiskey.

Jennifer twisted in her seat. "You must help me."

"No," Derek replied, his back to her as he poured himself another drink.

"Why not?"

Derek turned to look at her. "You know nothing about archaeological research," he accused. "Even with the documents in hand, authenticating their contents could take months—years. It's a slow, methodical process, everything cross-checked against volumes of other data." Derek returned to the table and sat down. "For all I know, this could be the fantasy of your writing friend," he said as he slowly took a sip from his glass. "I'm not about to waste my time on fiction."

Jennifer was frustrated. "Nina did not make any of this up, and neither did I."

"So prove it then. Give me the papers or documents."

"I can't."

"Then I can't help you."

Jennifer looked down at the table. She had to know if Cela and her people had once lived. Cela. God, what Cela had just done. She was not yet fourteen years old, and she had defied her gods and the Wise Ones because she was sickened by the human sacrifices of her people. She had been willing to give herself to her bloodthirsty gods rather than participate in the sacrifice of one more living person.

Nina was right. Jennifer had been living in a cocoon the last eighteen months—no thoughts of her own, no goals, no desires. She *did* feel different since coming to Scotland, and she felt emboldened by Cela's courage. She took a deep drink of her wine and looked across the table, meeting his gaze.

"Aren't you just a little curious? You can't tell me that, as a scientist, you aren't interested in what I might have to say."

He leaned back in his chair, a smile dancing in his eyes. "Why should I be?" Derek countered. "As I said, it could be fantasy. I don't waste my time on such."

"But what if it isn't? I can tell you what these people wore, what they ate, what their lodgings looked like. I can describe what weapons they used in battle, how they treated their wounds, how they studied the stars, and how they indulged in human sacrifice to appease their gods. You said little was known of the people of that era. Well, I can tell you a lot," Jennifer finished.

Derek calmly studied the woman before him. In his years of working all over the world, he frequently interviewed the local inhabitants of an area. From them, he gleaned an oral history that often provided the clues he needed for discovery. He had an uncanny ability to discern if a person was telling him the truth or simply trying to ingratiate himself to the foreign archaeology team. All of his instincts told him that Jennifer was telling the truth—at least as she knew it to be. There was something else, too. Yes, she was right about his curiosity. He had deliberately baited her by telling her initially that he would not assist her. He had hoped to press her to the point where she would share her documents with him in order to get his help. He still wanted those documents—and he would get them eventually—but they could wait for the moment. Derek was a man who combined logic and reason with strong instinct, and right now, his instinct was heightened. He had a gut feeling about this woman. He made up his mind.

"The coffee is in the cabinet," he indicated, "and the pot is on the stove. I'll see if your clothes are dry."

"Where do I start?" Jennifer asked.

They were sitting at the kitchen table, a pot of coffee before them. Derek held a pencil, poised before an open notebook.

"Before we begin, I must ask you two important questions, and I must insist on a truthful answer. Do you understand?" he asked.

He sounded so serious. Jennifer swallowed and nodded her head in agreement.

"Are you in possession of any artifact or object that the UK might have a legal proprietary interest in?"

Jennifer was surprised by his question. "No, as I told you—"

He held up his hand to stop her. "Yes or no?"

"No."

"Have you seen any such object in the possession of another, or do you know the location of any such object?"

"No, absolutely not."

He stared at her for what seemed a long time and then nodded his head. "Very well, let's begin. Tell me about your documents. You said they were only recently written?"

"Yes."

"When did you first come across the documents?"

"Several weeks ago."

"Can you tell me what it is that you have or where you found it?"

"No. We agreed that I would tell you what I know, but not about the source of the information."

Derek sat back in his chair, eyeing Jennifer. "Very well. Tell me what you read."

"There was a young girl," Jennifer began slowly. "She was a member of an elite class of people who were called the Wise Ones. They were the lawmakers and priests of this civilization."

As the hours went by, Derek periodically refilled their cups and resumed writing in his notebook. He interrupted occasionally to ask for clarification on something that she had said and then asked her to continue. It was early in the morning when Jennifer concluded. "That was the first time—the first paper that I read," she added hastily. Her voice was hoarse from talking.

Derek looked up with surprise. "The first paper? How many are there?"

Jennifer thought quickly. She had four blackouts, no, five, including the most recent one that occurred at this table while Derek prepared dinner.

"I've read five of them," she answered.

"You've read five. Are there others that you haven't read?"

Jennifer hesitated. "Yes," she answered. There was no way to know if these would continue, but she needed to allow for that possibility.

"How many more are there?"

"I don't know."

Derek sat back in his chair. "Very well; I'll accept that for now." He looked down at his notes. "Tell me more about what the people wore."

"The Wise Ones wore black, hooded robes made of wool, except for the younger priests and priestesses. Their robes were white." Jennifer frowned. "When they were in the northern settlements, they added layers of woolen robes for warmth and wrapped themselves in animal pelts. They sewed boots of pelt, lined with fur for warmth."

"Sewed?"

"Yes, they used thin strands of sheep gut for the thread and bronze needles, similar to today's needles."

"Did these people migrate? Did they establish multiple settlements?" Derek asked.

"Yes. I don't know how many, but they lived in the southern plains, the western mountains—where the mines were located—and in the far northern mountains. They moved with the seasons and the animals they hunted. They had settlements, like small villages, in multiple locations."

"All right. We'll come back to their housing. Continue with their clothing," Derek instructed.

"The common people wore knee-length shirts and tunics made of wool. They had round, woolen hats. Not much color, though. Some, like the skilled metal workers, wore jewelry made of gold or bronze—neckpieces and bracelets, mostly."

"That's helpful," Derek said. "Fashioning jewelry and weaving wool helps to date your civilization."

For the next hour, Jennifer answered Derek's questions about the dress, lodgings, and food of the people. He insisted on fine details. When she felt that she could go on no longer, he pushed for more.

"I want to hear about the sacrifices made at the young girl's initiation," he said as he shuffled through the volumes of notes that he had made while Jennifer talked. "Tell me exactly what was done."

"I already told you about those," Jennifer answered.

"No, you skimmed over them, omitting the details. You said that they made the girl sick. I need to know exactly how they sacrificed their victims."

"What does it matter? It was very gruesome."

Derek laid his pen down and looked at Jennifer. "It matters a great deal. Every detail is significant. Almost since the beginning of civilization, human beings have been sacrificing other human beings in an effort to appease the gods that they created for themselves. Patterns are important. They all had their own particular rituals and techniques. Sacrifices had to be done in a certain way. It was all part of their religion. My guess is that it was the same way for your people, wasn't it?"

"*My* people?"

"Yes, the ones that you are describing. Sacrifices were not haphazardly done, were they? There was a meaning behind everything."

Jennifer thought for a moment. Derek was right. Cela had been expected to know the proper way to make the sacrifices to each of the gods.

"What do you need to know?" Jennifer asked with resignation.

"Details," Derek said casually as he picked up his pen and waited.

"The first sacrifice that I read about," Jennifer began, "was made to the air. Ten men were chosen. Ten and three were important numbers to the Wise Ones."

For the next half hour, Jennifer tried to recall the sacrifices. The visions brought waves of nausea to her, and she spoke slowly and in a monotone voice to control the emotions she was feeling. It was as though she were feeling Cela's pain and sickness as the grisly visions came into sharp focus. She could see it happening all over again. "I can't talk about this anymore," Jennifer said, her voice cracking.

Derek looked up and frowned. Then he put his pen

down and his expression relaxed. "Perhaps it's time to quit," he said kindly. He stood and walked around to where she was sitting, stopping in front of her. "My apologies. I'm afraid I've been insensitive. I can easily get lost in my work. This has been exhausting for you, and you need to sleep. Come this way," he said as he turned. "You can stay here for the night."

"What!"

Derek looked at his watch. "It's almost three in the morning. There's no need to drive to your friend's place. You can sleep here." He started walking toward the door of the kitchen.

"I can't stay here."

Derek turned, frowning. "Why not?"

"I don't even know you. We're practically strangers."

"Jennifer, you need to understand something," Derek said. "You have asked for my help, and I have agreed. That will mean working closely together for long hours. If you are not willing to do that, then tell me now, and we won't waste any more of each other's time."

Jennifer stood there, dumbfounded. He had not spoken unkindly, but his straightforwardness surprised her. Did she understand him correctly?

"N . . . no," she finally stammered. "Professor, I asked for your help to determine if what I read could possibly have happened at some time in history. I want your help and have agreed to tell you what I know—however long it takes—but that is all I agreed to."

Derek frowned. Then the frown faded as he hid the smile that threatened to appear. "You appear to have misunderstood me. Due to the lateness of the hour, I have invited you to stay the night. I have not invited you to share my bed. Now, it is getting later by the minute. You can have the bedroom upstairs. It's this way," he indicated with his hand.

She was certain her face was bright red. "Oh, I thought you. . . ." She looked down at the floor to avoid his gaze.

"I'm so embarrassed."

He smiled. "I can see that," he said as he nodded to her flushed face and neck, "but there's no need to feel embarrassed. It's late and you're tired. Follow me, please."

"Why don't you just throw me back out in the rain," Jennifer said as she started to follow him out of the kitchen.

Derek laughed as they returned to the living room. His laughter was warm as it echoed off the stone walls. They walked past the great stone fireplace, where she had initially warmed herself, to the stairway located by the entrance door. As she followed him up the stairs, made of gray stone like the rest of the lodge, she looked at the enormous coat of arms hanging above the mantle on the stone fireplace. It was at least eight feet tall, a colorful shield at the base, a helmet above, and a red lion perched on top.

"Professor, what is that?" Jennifer asked, stopping midway on the stairs.

Derek stopped and turned to face her. "As long as you're spending the night with me, as it were," he said with a grin, "do you think you can call me Derek? And that is the coat of arms of the Earl of Thornhill. The family is descended from Stuart, Marquis of Bute." Derek's grin was infectious.

"Okay, Derek," she said shyly, "what does it say?"

"Nobilis est ira leonis," Derek quoted. "Noble is the wrath of a lion." Derek looked out across the room. "The fourth Earl of Thornhill built several of these small hunting lodges, scattering them about his estate. He deliberately kept them small so he could enjoy his privacy and escape the demands of his position. He supposedly married a fiery Scottish girl of the Campbell clan. The story is that she wasn't much to look at and was not of royal blood, but she brought the loyalty of one of the strongest clans in Scottish history to the earl."

They reached the top of the stairs. Before them was an ancient, wooden door, solid oak, five inches thick, its iron hinges creaking in protest as Derek pushed it open. He walked over to a table and turned on a lamp.

The room was surprisingly large. Dominating the room was a magnificent canopy bed, draped in a plaid of red, green, and white. Hanging above the pillows was a smaller version of the earl's Coat of Arms. The furniture was heavy and dark, undoubtedly crafted from the same English Oak that was evident throughout the lodge.

"Electricity was installed the early part of the twentieth century, and a bathroom and closet are through there," Derek said as he motioned to a room off to the side. "Most of the furniture has been here for centuries. The plaid is the official tartan of the Stewarts of Bute." A wicked smile came to Derek's lips. "The past earls used to bring their mistresses here for some privacy. It is said that many an illegitimate child had been sired by the succeeding earls in this lodge, probably right here in this bed."

Jennifer turned around sharply.

Derek laughed. "Oh, you have nothing to fear. The present Earl of Thornhill is almost sixty years old and very devoted to the memory of his wife, who died ten years ago. I think you'll find everything you need," he said as he walked over to the stone fireplace opposite the foot of the bed. "Despite the central heat, it can still get damp in here," he said as he reached for some matches. Jennifer stood, her arms folded across her chest as she looked around the room. In no time at all, Derek had a fire burning and stood to leave.

"Well then, I bid you good night, Jennifer. I'll see you in the morning," he said and, nodding his head to her, walked out of the room without another word. Jennifer was still standing in the same position when Issy, the great Irish wolfhound, came bounding into the room. Jennifer jumped back and watched as the dog settled herself on a rug next to the bed.

"Professor," Jennifer called, walking to the door, "uh, Derek?" She turned back to the dog. "Go on," she said, "go back to wherever you came from." She tried to motion with her hands, but the dog just lay there, its head resting on its massive paws. "Go on. Go sleep somewhere else." Still the dog remained. Jennifer sighed and turned back to the door. She reached out with both hands to close the door, but it didn't move. Again she tried, straining against the ancient wood. Still, the heavy door resisted. Jennifer thought about calling Derek for help but changed her mind. Resigned, she turned back to the bed.

"So what do I do now?" she said to the dog. "I'm in a strange house with a man I hardly know and a dog that looks like a small pony." She looked around the room—a castle room with its ancient, gray stone edifice, its upper floor of hardened oak planks, a heavy oak door that she was certain was original, and an archer's window that at some time had leaded glass added to it. It was with awe that she contemplated its age. Such history it had witnessed. She smiled ruefully. *Illegitimate children, indeed.* Derek had not said what happened to the children or to the long line of mistresses who had come to this lodge to meet with the earls over the centuries, if indeed the story was even true. Still, looking at it, Jennifer could imagine it. This bedroom and the lodge itself were warm and intimate.

She walked over to the lamp and turned it off. The room was immediately immersed in darkness, lit only by the crackling fire. She turned back to the bed. She was so tired. Recalling the first episode for the professor had been exhausting. Maybe she wasn't demonstrating good sense, but at this late hour, she didn't care. She eased onto the bed, careful not to step on the sleeping dog. She would just slip under the top blanket, leaving her clothes on. As she lay down and settled her head on the pillow, she thought about the professor. He was ruggedly handsome, every bit the personification of the outdoor adventurer, yet there was no mistaking the keen intelligence in his eyes. He possessed a vast amount of knowledge and was very perceptive. She surmised that he was not easily fooled, and she would have to be careful.

John would be shocked at her behavior. *John.* Why had

she thought of him? Guilt spread through her, for she had not thought about John since she returned to Scotland several days ago. If John were here . . . no, Jennifer could not picture John here. He didn't belong here—not in Scotland and not in this room. She felt like the room welcomed her. It would not welcome John. Images of John quickly faded from her consciousness as she relaxed in the comfort and protection she felt in this place. In a matter of minutes, she was breathing deeply as sleep overcame her.

CHAPTER 5

Jennifer awoke from a deep sleep, surprised to see sunlight filtering through the window. Issy was standing at the bedroom door, alternating between a bark and a deep, throaty growl. Jennifer threw back the blanket and walked over to the dog. Cautiously, she stepped out of the room and to the top of the stairs, the dog beside her.

"Professor Rannoch? Derek?" Jennifer called. The lodge was silent, allowing Issy's barks to echo in the great room. Suddenly, Issy bounded down the stairs and stopped in front of the door, growling.

"Professor Rannoch?" Jennifer called again, just as there was a knock at the door. She hurried down the steps, taking care on the centuries-old, uneven stones, and over to the door where Issy stood barking. She reached for the latch and opened the door a few inches. "Yes?" she asked, peering out.

"Jennifer?"

Jennifer opened the door. "Shamus!"

Shamus MacNeal stepped back suddenly as Issy placed herself between Jennifer and himself. "Will she bite?" Shamus asked.

"Uh . . . Issy . . . come back here," Jennifer said awkwardly to the dog. "It's okay."

The dog responded to Jennifer's voice and stepped back, placing herself next to Jennifer. She ceased barking but kept Shamus in her sight.

"The dog belongs to Professor Rannoch," Jennifer said apologetically. She looked back into the lodge. "I don't know where he is."

"I was concerned when you didn't answer your cell phone this morning," Shamus said.

"Oh! I'm sorry. Come in, Shamus," Jennifer said. "I haven't had very good reception on my cell phone since I came to Scotland."

Jennifer stepped back, the dog beside her. Shamus cautiously entered the room, his eyes darting to the dog.

"She's a beautiful dog," he commented. "I have dogs myself. They can be quite protective. I'll just keep my distance until she sees that I'm no threat to you." He smiled.

"Thanks for your concern. I'm sorry about the phone call this morning. I should have called you, but I just woke up."

"Oh?"

Jennifer smiled weakly and shook her head. "It was a long night. Professor Rannoch has agreed to help me, Shamus. I told him about the first vision."

"You did?"

"Yes, only I didn't tell him that I actually 'saw' it. I told him that I came across some documents and that I read all of it."

"And he accepted that?" Shamus asked with surprise.

"No, not at all, but he agreed to at least listen to what I had to say. I'm hoping that when I finish, he'll tell me that these people did exist at one time. I need to know that I'm not crazy."

Shamus smiled gently. "You're not crazy, Jennifer. What has been happening to you may be crazy, but you're not. Derek Rannoch has a reputation for being a leading scholar in his field. If anyone can discern the accuracy of your visions, he can." Shamus paused. "Have you thought about what you will do then? I surmise that you're hoping that what you have experienced is some sort of time travel." He frowned. "No. If I understand you correctly, it's not time travel as usually perceived. You're not Jennifer thrust into the past. It's more like a window letting you see the past through the eyes of someone else. And if it is, then what?"

Jennifer shook her head. "I don't know, Shamus." She looked up at him. "For an educated man, you seem very comfortable with all of this. I would have thought that you, a man of medicine, would have immediately rejected a 'window to the past,' as you say."

"I had a grandmother who always knew when some misfortune was going to strike the family before it actually happened. It's in our Scottish blood."

Jennifer smiled. "I appreciate your kindness. You and Nina are the only people who believe me. Professor Rannoch would probably refuse to listen to me if I told him the truth. We talked, or I talked, until three o'clock this morning. That's when he suggested that I stay here rather than drive back to Nina's." Jennifer looked around. "I don't know where he is now. Let me check the kitchen."

Jennifer, accompanied by Issy, left Shamus standing in the living room while she went to the kitchen to look for Derek. The kitchen was empty, but there was a hand-written note laying on the table.

"Shamus," Jennifer called as she returned to the living room. "Professor Rannoch left a note. He had to go out this morning. Would it be too much trouble to ask you to drop me off at Nina's on the way to your office?"

"Not at all."

"Great. I'll just get my shoes. They're upstairs."

A few minutes later, Jennifer was seated next to Shamus in his Land Rover, heading back to Nina's. She had left a hastily scrawled note for Derek. It had been a struggle to get out of the door without the dog. She finally escaped, leaving Issy barking on the other side of the door.

Jennifer glanced at her watch. "I'm supposed to pick up Nina at the airport this morning."

"That was my other reason for coming to find you. Nina

called last night to say that she would be delayed another few days, possibly a week. She tried to call you."

"Another few days?"

"Yes. She was really excited. They're talking about making a movie out of one of her books."

"You're kidding! That's great!"

"She'll tell you all about it. I think she's also feeling badly about leaving you alone in Scotland. I think she would like it if you could join her in New York."

"I can't. I'll explain it to her when she calls."

Shamus drove Jennifer to Nina's cottage and then left, insisting that Jennifer call him if she needed anything while Nina was in New York. Jennifer wasted no time peeling off the clothes she had slept in and climbing into a tub of hot water. Her long hair was a mass of tangled curls. She washed her hair and then let herself settle into the warm water. She was relaxing, leaning her head against the back of the tub, letting the water cover her, when there was a knock at the door. Almost immediately, it was followed by the barking of dogs.

Jennifer stepped out of the tub and hastily dried herself. She wrapped herself in a thick terry robe and padded barefoot to the door.

"Who is it?" she asked, not surprised to hear Derek's voice. She opened the door slightly and then suddenly jumped back as Issy and Bruce came bounding into the room. Derek stood at the entrance, taking in Jennifer's appearance.

"It appears I'm interrupting," he said smoothly, the hint of a smile on his lips.

Jennifer crossed her arms in front of her. "I was just finishing a bath."

"You left without having breakfast."

"Shamus came over to check on me. He woke me up," she said sheepishly. "He drove me over here and then went on to his office."

"May I come in? We have some matters to discuss," Derek said.

"Oh, of course," Jennifer replied, stepping to the side. "Wait here and I'll get dressed."

"That's partly what I wanted to discuss with you."

"Excuse me?" Jennifer said, frowning.

"While you are dressing, why don't you pack some clothes for the next few days? This is Wednesday. We could work the next three days. My assistant is coming up Saturday evening. She and I have some other matters to work on this weekend. I'll bring you back Saturday. Then we can start again Monday morning."

His suggestion surprised her. This was something she had not anticipated. "I don't think that's possible."

"Why not?"

"My friend will be returning. I'll need to be here."

"Your friend, Miss Bouvay?"

"Yes."

Derek stared at Jennifer a moment before speaking. "Does Miss Bouvay have an interest in the documents?"

Jennifer sighed. "No, as I told you last night, Nina is my friend. When I met you in your office, I thought you might be more inclined to help me if I told you I was doing research for her, a recognized author."

"Does she know about the documents?"

"Yes, she knows about them, but she hasn't seen them. I told her about them."

"So she is aware of their contents?"

"Not all of them, but the first ones."

"Who else knows about them?"

"Shamus MacNeal. He and Nina are . . . good friends. He was here when I told Nina about them."

"Anyone else?"

Jennifer hesitated. For some reason, she did not want to mention John. He was not a part of this. "One other person—a man in Chicago where I live." Jennifer shrugged her shoulders. "He didn't believe me."

"An archaeologist or historian?"

"Neither," Jennifer said quickly. "It's personal."

Derek knitted his brows together. "Then the only thing preventing you from working with me the next several days is a desire to spend time with your friend. When do you expect her back?"

"I don't know for certain. A few days . . . a week?"

"Then I suggest you call Miss Bouvay or leave a note for her explaining the circumstances. She can contact you when she returns."

In the end, Jennifer was persuaded. She emerged from the bedroom, dressed and carrying a small suitcase.

* * *

"Dr. Bracken?"

"Yes, Margaret, what is it?" John Bracken asked as his secretary entered his office.

"There still isn't any answer at the number you gave me. Is there another number where Mrs. Bracken might be reached?" Margaret asked.

John Bracken threw the file that he was looking at down on his desk. "No, that's Nina Bouvay's number as Jennifer gave it to me. And Jennifer's still not answering her cell phone?"

"No, sir."

"Keep trying!"

"Yes, sir," Margaret said as she backed out of the office.

"Have you lost little Jennifer?" a female voice asked.

John turned around to see his sister breeze into his office.

"I'm very busy, Hillary. What do you want?"

Hillary smiled. "So where is she?"

"I'm sure that she and her friend have just gone sightseeing."

"Really?" Hillary said. "Interesting. Just how long have you been trying to get in touch with her?"

John glared at his sister. "What do you want, Hillary?"

"I had lunch with Jane Satler today. She said that your annual company garden party is coming up, and that no one has started the planning. She was wondering why Jennifer hadn't called. She said that usually they have most of the arrangements made by now."

John swore.

"My, my, John, I don't think I've ever heard you raise your voice in such a manner," Hillary purred. "You're losing some of that self-control you're so famous for."

John turned an icy gaze on his sister. "Was there anything else you wanted, Hillary?"

"Excuse me, Dr. Bracken," Margaret said as she knocked and then entered John's office.

"Did she answer?" John asked.

"No, sir, but your father is on the line."

"I'll leave you to your phone call," his sister said as she followed Margaret out of the office.

John swore again and then picked up the phone. "Dad?" he said.

"Did Jennifer leave you?" John's father demanded.

"Of course not. She's visiting her friend in Scotland," John answered angrily.

"Huh," his father grumbled. "Hillary said Jennifer hasn't taken your calls and has missed some social functions."

"Hillary can go to hell."

"Are you still whoring around? Did Jennifer find out about your sick, perverted appetites?" his father grounded out.

"I am not having this conversation with you, Dad. I have work to do."

"I told you what I would do if you cost this company money for another divorce," his father shouted. "You fix this with Jennifer!"

* * *

"That's the last of it?" Derek asked.

They were sitting at the old oak table in the kitchen. Jennifer raised her head off the table where she had been resting with her arms folded on the table, her eyes closed.

"Yes. That's all I know," Jennifer mumbled.

It was Friday night. They had been working for three days, usually into the early morning hours.

"If you ask me one more thing, I swear I'll scream," Jennifer said.

Derek laughed good-naturedly. Jennifer closed her eyes again and put her head back on the table.

"Do you always work like this?" she asked.

"Sometimes, not always," he answered.

"Some life," Jennifer mumbled.

"One more thing," Derek said as he sifted through his papers, "and then we're finished for the night."

"No more," Jennifer said in a muffled voice as she yawned, her head still resting on her arms on the table, her eyes closed.

"I've drawn a sketch of Stonehenge, as you described it, and Avebury," Derek said.

"What . . . bury?" she asked without moving or opening her eyes.

Derek laughed. "Avebury. I think it is the other megalithic site that you said the people used. It is approximately the distance from Stonehenge that you estimated."

"Umm," Jennifer said sleepily.

"Here. Just look at them and tell me how accurate they are."

"Okay," Jennifer mumbled again, not moving.

"Jennifer?"

"Just leave them here on the table. Leave me here. I'll sleep here and look at them in the morning."

"All right," he said with a laugh. "You can look at the sketches in the morning. This way, milady. Your chambers await," he said in a mocking, heavy Scottish brogue.

"No. I'll sleep here. I'm too tired to climb the stairs."

"Come along, Jenny," he said softly. Derek gently moved her hair aside with his fingertips. It was a simple gesture, but Jennifer was instantly awake. His fingers brushed upon her neck, and she was shocked at the warmth that spread throughout her body. She was very much aware of the closeness of his hand and the quickening of her heart. He moved his hands to the back of her chair to pull it out as she stood.

"If the lady will allow me?" he said with a questioning lilt to his voice.

Jennifer accepted Derek's arm as he guided her around the table and toward the kitchen door. She allowed him to walk her across the living room and to the stairs. Issy came bounding up beside them and ran ahead.

"Sleep as late as you like in the morning," Derek said. "When you get up, we can talk about the next step. Then I'll take you back to your friend's, and you can have two complete days without me questioning you. How does that sound?"

They had reached the bedroom, and still Derek had Jennifer's arm.

"I think I'll sleep the next two days," Jennifer said. Derek had lit the fire earlier, bathing the room in a soft glow.

"Do you need anything else?" he asked.

"No," Jennifer said, stepping away from the touch of his hand on her arm. "I'll just turn on the lamp."

She started to take a step forward, unaware that Issy had already found her spot on the rug next to the bed. Jennifer stumbled as her foot hit the massive dog. She automatically reached out for the bed as she started to fall. Derek was there, his arms coming around her, catching her.

"I'm sorry," she said. She felt the warmth of Derek's body against hers and looked away.

He reached up with one hand and gently moved her hair back, letting his fingers trail across her neck. Jennifer felt his fingers touch her chin and carefully turn her head until she was looking at him. He did not remove his hand but let his fingers linger.

"Jenny?" he whispered softly, his eyes searching.

Jennifer held her breath. Derek's arm rested lightly against her chest, his fingers still upon her chin. Slowly, he moved his fingers across her cheek and to her hair. Once again, he brushed her hair back and then lowered his head. When Jennifer felt his lips upon her neck, she shuddered, surprised at the intense desire that radiated through her. She put her arms around his neck and instinctively pushed into him. When he kissed her, she wasn't even certain how to return his kiss; she just knew that she craved his touch, his closeness.

"Jenny?" His voice was deep and questioning as he pulled his head back to look at her.

"I've never done this," she whispered, her body in a state of arousal that she had never experienced before.

Derek frowned. Jennifer understood the question on his face.

"I . . . I mean that it has been a very long time since I was with a man." Jennifer's voice trailed away.

"Are you afraid of me?" Derek asked gently.

"No," Jennifer answered honestly. "Perhaps that's the strangest thing of all. I hardly know you and yet I. . . ."

Derek was watching her closely. His arms were still around her, and then he surprised her by releasing her and stepping back. "I think I should go," he said softly. "For the most part, I am a bit of a rogue, Jenny, with your hair like fire," he said as he ran his hand through her long hair.

"Allow me to be a gentleman tonight," he whispered.

Jennifer, for all her confusion, noted that his voice had slipped into a Scottish brogue as he spoke.

He brought her hand up to his lips. "Good night, milady," he said and then turned and walked out of the room, leaving Jennifer standing there, bewildered.

It was several minutes before she moved. In a daze, she undressed and crawled under the blankets. The fire cast shadows that danced across the canopy of the bed. She wanted to scream as she lie there, her body demanding something that was not to be. She rolled over onto her side, burying her head in the pillow as tears formed in her eyes. It was a long time before her body quieted and even longer before sleep came. In all the time with John—including the beginning when she thought she was in love and that he loved her—she had never experienced anything close to what she had felt tonight when Derek had touched her.

Derek sat at the kitchen table, a glass of Talisker Scotch whiskey in his hand. He swore under his breath as he set the glass down. Jennifer had not been the only one aroused in the bedroom upstairs. He knew that he could have easily maneuvered her into the large bed, but something stopped him. He didn't think that Jennifer was a woman who could casually sleep with a man. He wondered how experienced she was. There was an innocence about her; he had sensed that when she was recounting the information in her documents.

That was another thing that bothered him. Most of the time, she told him about the people of her documents in an objective, collective sense, whether telling him about the warriors, the Wise Ones, or the common people. But every once in a while, she would interject information of a personal nature, usually when talking about a young priestess. Her tone of voice would change then. Derek doubted if she was even aware that she had given the young priestess a name while talking with him.

What kind of document would discuss a prehistoric civilization so specific as to identify several individuals by name? Egyptian, Greek, Mesopotamian, Sumerian—yes, those civilizations left artifacts, architectural structures, paintings, and, most importantly, writings. From these, specific names, usually kings or queens or note-worthy individuals, could be gleaned. But Britain's Bronze Age civilizations were crude by comparison—hundreds, if not a thousand years behind.

Derek ran his hand through his hair. Maybe she was just unconsciously adding her own interpretation to what she had read. She obviously had emotional feelings about the documents.

The image of Jennifer formed in his mind, and he looked up at the ceiling in the direction of the bedroom. He swore again and took another drink from his glass. "Face it, Derek, my boy," he said in a heavy brogue, "you would like to bed the lady."

Issy's barking woke Jennifer. She was surprised to see daylight filtering through the window. She looked at her watch. It was eleven o'clock! She couldn't believe she had slept that late, although she hadn't fallen asleep until about five o'clock in the morning. It had been difficult. She'd been so confused. Finally, sheer exhaustion had consumed her, and she fell into a deep sleep in the ancient bed.

Jennifer heard Bruce barking downstairs, and then she thought she heard Derek call to the dog. She jumped out of bed and grabbed her pants and sweater that were laying where she had hastily thrown them last night. She pulled on her socks and shoes and stepped out of the bedroom door, Issy by her side, just as Derek crossed the living room below. He glanced up at her, smiled, and then walked to the door. Jennifer watched as he opened it.

"Linda!" Derek said with surprise.

A young woman with blonde hair breezed through the door. Jennifer recognized her as the woman who had been by the lake with Derek the day that Jennifer had accidentally knocked down his equipment.

"Surprise!" she said gleefully. "I left early."

Derek stepped back to allow the woman to enter. She walked several feet into the living room and then dropped a small suitcase on the floor.

"I couldn't take it anymore," she said. "You owe me, love. Do you know how boring it is, cataloging all that data you left me? That's all I have done for the past week. But," she said with a sly smile, "it's nothing that twenty-four hours of great sex can't cure."

Derek's assistant was wearing a light blazer, pants, and a blouse. She reached up and quickly unbuttoned the blouse and began to remove it and the blazer in one movement.

"Linda," Derek said, stopping her movements, "we have a guest."

Linda froze and followed the direction of Derek's eyes. She saw Jennifer standing on the landing above. "Oh," she said with obvious embarrassment. She turned her back to Jennifer and buttoned her blouse. When she finished, she turned to Derek, a challenge in her eyes. "Well?" she said to him.

"I don't believe you two have been introduced," Derek said. "Linda, this is Jennifer McHugh. Miss McHugh has been staying here for the last few days while we have been working on a project." Derek looked up at Jennifer. "Jenny, this is my assistant, Linda Bensen."

Linda looked back at Jennifer, recognition dawning on her. "You were at the lake site." She turned back to Derek. "But I thought you said you didn't know her."

"I didn't. Miss McHugh came to my office in Edinburgh and asked for my help."

Jennifer descended the steps. "I was leaving this morning," she said. When she reached the bottom of the steps, she glanced at Derek. "May I call Dr. MacNeal? I'm sure he will come get me," she said, trying to keep her voice steady. She could feel the tears threatening in her eyes.

"That won't be necessary. I told you I would drive you back to your friend's cottage when we finished," Derek said, his eyes penetrating but not showing the least bit of concern over what she perceived to be an awkward moment.

"We *are* finished, professor," she said, a touch of anger in her voice. "I've told you all I know, and I would prefer to call Dr. MacNeal." She looked to Derek's assistant. "It's nice to meet you, Miss Bensen. If you will excuse me, though, I will make arrangements for someone to pick me up."

Jennifer turned and walked into the kitchen, her thoughts in a turmoil as she reached for the phone.

"I will drive you," Derek said as he caught up with her and placed his hand over hers on the phone.

Jennifer was mortified. She knew he could feel her shaking. Last night, Derek had kissed her. Jennifer swallowed when she thought of what else she had almost done last night; she'd almost slept with him. She had wanted to, and he knew it. He was the one who'd left. Now Linda Bensen was here—a young woman who was obviously more than just Derek's assistant.

Jennifer couldn't look at Derek. She wanted to get away from him as quickly as possible without creating a scene.

"All right, I'll get my things," she said, her voice strained. She pulled her hand away and walked past him and up to the bedroom upstairs. She hastily packed her clothes and returned to the living room where Derek and his assistant were waiting. By the look on their faces and the raised voices she had heard while upstairs, they had been arguing.

Linda Bensen spoke first. "It was a pleasure meeting you, Miss McHugh," she said when Jennifer reached the bottom. "I'm sorry about the way I came in."

"No, I'm the one who was intruding," Jennifer offered. "Good-bye," she said as she walked toward the door.

There was an awkward moment when Derek reached to

take the suitcase from Jennifer's hand. His fingers touched hers, and Jennifer released the suitcase immediately, letting it hit the floor. She was surprised at the warmth that spread through her in response to his touch, embarrassed and angry at herself for being such a naïve fool. Derek retrieved the suitcase easily, though, and walked beside her to his vehicle. Jennifer was silent as he opened the door of his Land Rover for her and as he walked around to the other side. She tried to focus her eyes on the road ahead as he pulled away from the hunting lodge.

They had driven only a few minutes when Derek spoke. "I apologize for Linda's entrance," he began.

"When will you be able to give me your opinion about my documents?" she asked curtly. "We've talked for several days now. I would appreciate your thoughts about this civilization."

Derek sighed. "There are already some interesting parallels with other civilizations," he said, watching Jennifer from the corner of his eye. "I would like to go to the sites that you mentioned. I made some sketches, but it would be better if we went to them together."

"What" Jennifer said, turning sharply to face him.

"I thought that next week we would go to Stonehenge and Avebury and on to the Isle of Lewis."

"You're kidding, right? I'm not going to those places with you."

All she wanted was to get away from Derek Rannoch. She was confused, angry, and hurt. Even now, sitting next to him, her heart was racing. How could he have that effect on her?

Derek's eyes narrowed slightly, but he tried once again. "It's essential that we go together," he said with emphasis. "We must look for links, connections."

"You're unbelievable," Jennifer said angrily, opening the door of the Land Rover before Derek came to a complete stop in front of Nina's cottage. She started running toward the door of the cottage, but Derek caught her arm and turned her to face him.

"Jenny, I'm sorry. Last night when we—"

"I don't care about last night," Jennifer said forcefully.

Derek's gaze was penetrating, once again giving her the impression that he knew what she was thinking, what she was feeling. "What are you afraid of, Jenny?" Derek asked softly.

Jennifer gasped. "I'm not afraid of anything, and I'd rather not see you again," she said, knowing she was close to tears, the ultimate humiliation, and knowing he was aware of it.

"Jenny," he began, "I—"

"And," she said, "I'm also not going to be one more of your assistants who does research with you during the day and sleeps with you during the night." Jennifer stopped, surprised at the vehemence of her own words.

Derek's eyes narrowed perceptively. When he spoke, his voice was cool. "I don't recall asking you to."

The air was thick between them as they stared at each other, she feeling humiliated by his remark, and Derek?

"As you wish, then," he said with restrained formality. "I don't believe we have anything more to discuss. Good day, Miss McHugh."

She watched him walk away from her. "You're not the only one who knows something about Bronze Age civilizations. I'll find someone else to help me," she replied churlishly to Derek's back as he got into his vehicle and left.

Jennifer barely closed the cottage door behind her when she erupted in tears. She knew that she had just behaved abominably, like an ill-mannered child. How could she have said those things to him?

Derek was right, of course; he was very perceptive. She was afraid. The reason that she didn't want to travel to England with him was because of what had happened—or almost happened—last night. If he hadn't left her room

125

when he had, she would have slept with him. But he obviously had a relationship with Linda Bensen.

"Damn you, Derek Rannoch," she shouted through her tears.

She was thinking how he had no right to have held her in his arms and kissed her if he already had a girlfriend. How could he do that? She stopped suddenly. She was standing, facing the closed door. She squeezed her eyes shut and turned around, letting herself slide down against the door until she was sitting on the floor. She rested her head on her knees and let the tears fall.

What right did she have to judge him? *She* was the one who was married, not Derek Rannoch. *She* was the one who was being disloyal. Whatever his relationship was with his assistant, Derek was still single. She, Jennifer, on the other hand, was married. And as long as she was being honest with herself, she had done nothing to correct his mistaken impression that she was single.

She didn't know how long she sat on the floor, alternating between self-criticism, anger, disappointment, and—longing. How could Derek Rannoch have affected her in such a way? How was it possible that, even now, she wished she was sitting at the table with him at the hunting lodge? Her thoughts were interrupted by the phone ringing. She dried her eyes with the sleeve of her shirt, pushed herself off the wall, stood up, and walked into the kitchen.

"Hello?" Jennifer answered.

"Mrs. Bracken?"

"Yes."

"Oh, I'm so glad we finally caught you. This is Mrs. Lynch. Hold on, please. Dr. Bracken wishes to speak with you."

Jennifer heard Irene Lynch, their housekeeper, put the phone down. In a moment, John's voice came on the line.

"Jennifer? Where have you been?" John demanded.

Jennifer took a deep breath to calm herself. "I've been doing some sightseeing," she said.

There was silence, and then John spoke again. "When are you coming home?"

"I don't know," Jennifer answered.

"Jennifer, I have tried to be patient and have indulged this fantasy of yours long enough. You will need to come home immediately."

Jennifer gritted her teeth. "Why, John?"

"What do you mean? I should think that would be obvious."

"John, I don't want to argue about this. I'm not finished here."

"So you're still chasing after your hallucination."

John's words hurt, but Jennifer was silent.

"You have responsibilities, one of which is the annual company garden party," John continued.

"Oh, shit," Jennifer said under her breath. She had forgotten all about it.

"Jennifer!"

"Sorry, John," Jennifer apologized. She knew how John hated vulgar language of any kind. He considered it to be a bourgeois trait.

"I can have Mrs. Lynch book you a Monday morning flight," John offered.

"I'm not sure I can make that," Jennifer said hesitantly.

"Make it, Jennifer! We'll talk about all of this when you get home. I'll see you then."

The phone line went dead. Jennifer carefully replaced the phone and almost immediately, it rang again.

"Hello, Jennifer? It's Shamus."

"Hi, Shamus," Jennifer said, breathing a sigh that it was not John again.

"I talked to Nina last night. She's returning Monday afternoon."

"I'm glad to hear that. Do you want me to pick her up?"

Shamus gave Jennifer the flight number and arrival time.

"Would you like to go out for dinner tonight?" he asked.

"That's very kind of you, Shamus, but I'm very tired. I'm

afraid Professor Rannoch didn't allow me much sleep the past few days. I think I'll just go to bed early."

"How did it go with the professor?"

"Not as well as I'd hoped. I told him all about the episodes that I've had, although he thinks that I read it all in some documents that I found. I couldn't tell him the truth. He asked a lot of questions, took a lot of notes. He wants me to accompany him to Stonehenge and some of the other sites. I told him I couldn't. He wasn't too pleased."

"You don't sound too happy, either. Are you certain you wouldn't like me to pick you up for dinner?"

"No thank you, Shamus. I appreciate the offer, though. I think a quiet evening alone is what I need tonight."

"All right. Call me if you change your mind."

"I will. Thank you."

Jennifer stepped outside. It was midafternoon on Sunday. Nina would be back tomorrow. Jennifer had already decided that she was not going to fly back to Chicago. She would have to call John and explain.

The afternoon sun was warm. She was wearing a comfortable pair of jeans and a linen shirt. She closed her eyes and lifted her head up, letting the sun warm her face. It felt wonderful. She had already deduced that sunshine was a rare occurrence in this part of The Highlands. She had debated about going for a walk, fearing that the visions would recur. In the end, she couldn't stay in the house any longer.

She set off across the meadow, walking in the opposite direction of where she thought the hunting lodge was. She didn't pretend to know how to navigate; however, she was walking parallel to a low stone fence and toward the afternoon sun. She had her cell phone with her, not that she'd had much luck getting reception in the Grampian Mountains. Still, she felt comfortable, warmed by the sun and the beauty of the area.

The landscape was truly breathtaking—highland mountains surrounding her with wide valleys of green, occasional areas of forest, and large patches of thick, spiny evergreen shrubs with yellow flowers. Purple heather grew around the occasional rock boulders scattered about the green meadow grass of the foothills. So much of this part of Scotland was rocky, making this patch of grass all the more pleasant. She smiled to herself as she walked. Photographs couldn't do justice to the Scottish Highlands; photos couldn't capture the *feeling* of The Highlands—fierce beauty that pulled at the soul.

She was still walking parallel to the low stone fence when she climbed up a small ridge. The sight below her caused her to draw in her breath. There, standing in the center, surrounded by the foothills, was the most magnificent house she had ever seen. No, it wasn't a house; it was a castle. Complete with towers! It was rectangular in shape, a massive structure of gray stone. All four corners had square towers, complete with T-shaped slits used by archers in the Middle Ages. The stone walls had windows that looked out over the expanse of the Scottish countryside, the windows probably being an addition in later centuries when defense was no longer necessary. Even at this distance, looking at the windows set back into the walls, she could see that the walls were easily eight or ten feet thick. Below her, next to the castle, was a walled-in garden, its green hedges and shrubs laid out in a pattern. Flowers seemed to overflow from everywhere within its confines. It was the most beautiful sight she had ever seen.

For a second, she felt guilty, realizing that she probably shouldn't be here. It could be a public building, but she had the feeling that it wasn't, and she was undoubtedly trespassing. She reluctantly started to turn to leave but felt compelled to stop. A sense of warmth and peace came over her as she looked down upon the castle. After a while, she couldn't remove her gaze from it. A myriad of emotions flooded her consciousness, the primary of which was that she never wanted to leave. The image of the massive, gray structure consumed her. She didn't know how long she stood there, basking in contentment, when suddenly, she was startled by a voice.

"Rather formidable, isn't it?"

Jennifer turned to see a man standing behind her. He was dressed in beige-colored pants and a tweed jacket. He was very handsome with his gray hair, and although he held a walking stick, he gave the impression of robust health as he stood there, smiling at her. He walked up next to her, and motioning to the castle below, spoke again.

"What do you think? Do you agree?"

Jennifer hesitated a moment. The man had such gentle eyes. She smiled at him and returned her gaze to the castle.

"Formidable? No." She paused. "Warm. Peaceful."

"Really? It's quite old. Most people find it to be cold and stark."

"They're wrong," Jennifer said with certainty, gazing at the building. "It's solid. Protective. Soothing. Caring."

"A life of its own?" the man asked.

Jennifer turned and smiled shyly. Just then, she heard barking and howling, and a mass of hounds came over the hill. They were all large and gray, just like Derek's dogs. There must have been at least eight of them. They charged toward her, causing Jennifer to gasp and step back. She was about to scream for help from the man, when the dogs parted within a few feet of her and formed a complete circle around her. Jennifer was so shocked, she failed to notice the startled expression on the man's face.

Another man appeared over the hill, running over to where the dogs were. He looked like he was in his mid-thirties, dressed in corduroy pants and a black turtleneck shirt. He stopped abruptly at seeing the dogs. "Lord Harold?" the younger man said, a startled expression on his face as he looked at the dogs and back to the older man without acknowledging Jennifer.

"I can't explain it," the older man answered. "They just

ran toward her and. . . ." He didn't finish his sentence but pointed to the now silent dogs, still encircling Jennifer. "Brandon, perhaps you should take them back to the house."

"Of course, sir," the younger man said.

The older man turned back to the dogs. Jennifer heard him make a guttural sound, but the dogs remained where they were. He looked puzzled and repeated the command, motioning with his arm. This time, they responded and bounded down the hill with the younger man.

He turned back to Jennifer. "My apologies," he said in a dignified voice. "I've never seen them do that before. I hope they didn't frighten you. I assure you they would not have harmed you. However, my deepest apologies," he said as he bowed slightly.

Jennifer hesitated. "I think I'm the one who should apologize. I believe I've trespassed. He called you Lord Harold. This is yours?" she asked, motioning to the castle below.

The man smiled kindly. "Thornhill," he said. "And yes, I am the Thirteenth Earl of Thornhill, Harold Rannoch."

"I'm sorry," Jennifer said quickly. "I'm Jennifer . . . McHugh," she said, offering her hand.

"It is a pleasure to make your acquaintance, Miss McHugh." He released her hand and turned back toward the castle. "Do you garden, Miss McHugh?"

"No, I don't."

"Neither do I, but my late wife did. The garden was a frightful mess when we first married. My parents had neglected it, but Maggie did wonders with it. It was her passion."

"It's beautiful."

"You are American?"

"Yes. I'm visiting my friend, Nina Bouvay. She is currently renting one of the cottages on your estate."

"Of course, the American writer. And have you enjoyed your visit to Scotland?" he asked pleasantly.

Jennifer's brow creased. "A lot has happened since I arrived." Jennifer cursed herself inwardly. Why did she say that? She should have just answered "yes."

Harold Rannoch's face registered surprise, but he continued smoothly. "I'm curious about your impressions of the house."

"Oh," Jennifer said self-consciously.

"Please, I would like to hear more," he encouraged.

Jennifer shrugged her shoulders and smiled slightly. "It was just a feeling I had when I saw it—strong, loyal, fiercely protective of its inhabitants, but also calm, peaceful, soothing. It's timeless. I couldn't take my eyes off it."

He smiled. "Would you like to see the inside?"

Jennifer looked at him with surprise.

"It's almost time for tea. Would you care to join me, Miss McHugh?" he asked pleasantly.

"I can't impose any more than I already have."

"It's not an imposition," Harold Rannoch said. "It would be my pleasure. This way," he said, motioning with his hand.

Jennifer smiled. "Thank you."

"You are right about the house," he said as they walked. "There are parts of it that date back to the twelfth century. This was a wild country then. Most of the house was rebuilt in the seventeenth century, though. Generation after generation has found solace within its walls."

Harold Rannoch talked until they reached the entrance. "I think we will have tea first, and then I will show you around."

They entered into a large foyer with walls made of gray blocks. Tapestries hung everywhere on the walls, and thick carpets were scattered about the slate floor.

"Clara," Harold Rannoch said as a woman approached. "We have a guest for tea."

The woman bobbed and smiled. "I'll bring it right in, and Lord Harold, your son is here."

"Wonderful! Miss McHugh, I would like you to meet my

son."

Harold Rannoch indicated the way, and Jennifer walked beside him. Ahead of them was a wide hall with a magnificent staircase winding upward several stories. Lord Harold turned to the right and opened a door next to the stairs. He paused to let Jennifer enter first. Expansive windows with glazed panes and leaded glass opened out onto the garden beyond. The walls themselves were paneled in rich, dark wood. Large, overstuffed chairs, with their floral chintz covers mimicking the garden, were arranged in the middle of the room. As they entered, a man rose from one of the chairs and turned around. Seeing him, Jennifer suppressed a startled gasp and stood still.

"Derek! It's good to see you, Son," Lord Harold said as he walked over and embraced Derek. "I would like you to meet someone." He turned to Jennifer. "Miss McHugh, this is my son, Derek. Derek, this is Miss Jennifer McHugh. She is an American visiting Scotland for the first time."

Derek's jaw tightened, his eyes narrowing. "Miss McHugh and I have met, Father," he said, his gaze coldly assessing Jennifer.

Harold Rannoch raised his eyebrows, obviously surprised at his son's animosity. He glanced at Jennifer and then, frowning, returned his gaze to his son.

Just then, Clara entered, carrying a tray. "Excuse me," she said as she placed it on a low table that sat before a brightly covered sofa. "Lord Harold," she said, turning, "there is a call for you from a Mr. Broderbound in London."

"I'll take it in the library," Harold Rannoch said and then turned to Jennifer. "Will you please excuse me, Miss McHugh? This shouldn't take long. Derek, perhaps you could see to it that our guest is comfortable."

Derek waited until his father had closed the door and then spoke. "What are you doing here?" he asked. Before Jennifer could answer, he stepped toward her. "Did you think my father would help you with your project?"

"What? No!" Jennifer retorted, surprised at the anger she saw in his eyes. "I didn't even know he was your father."

"All of Scotland knows who the Earl of Thornhill is and that I am most certainly his son. We share the same surname, in case you hadn't noticed."

"Well, I didn't know who he was, and I didn't connect the last name. My mind was elsewhere," she said in defense. She recalled the powerful effect Thornhill had on her when she first saw it and the fear she felt when the dogs charged toward her. She focused her attention back on Derek. "And you, you may recall, happened to omit mentioning that you were the earl's son, even when you were telling me about the lodge and the coat of arms. How was I to know that you were related? I thought that you were renting the lodge just like my friend is renting a cottage."

"And you just happened to come to Thornhill?"

"I was out walking—"

"And got conveniently lost again," he said sardonically. "Am I correct?"

Jennifer gritted her teeth. "I think I have lost my appetite for tea. Please give your father my apologies." Jennifer turned to leave.

"You've managed to get an invitation to tea. How can I explain your absence when he returns?" Derek asked, irritation in his voice.

Jennifer hesitated. "Your father seems like a very kind man. Please thank him for me."

"Thank me for what?" Harold Rannoch asked as he entered the room.

Jennifer blushed.

"I'm sorry," she said as she glanced at her watch. "I hadn't realized how late it is. I know this is terribly rude of me, but I'm afraid that I can't stay."

"Oh?" Harold Rannoch glanced quickly at his son.

"You've been very kind," Jennifer added.

"Well, I shall miss your company, my dear. Shall I have you driven back to your friend's?"

"No, thank you. I'll enjoy the walk."

"Then let me see you to the door. I do hope that you can visit me again," Lord Harold said pleasantly.

Jennifer tried to control her steps as she climbed the hill leading away from Thornhill. Her heart was pounding—not from the climb, but because of her unexpected meeting with Derek. She had just reached the top of the hill when she broke into a sweat, her palms clammy, her skin tingling. Her stomach contracted, the familiar vertigo overwhelming her. She reached for a tree, leaning against its trunk for support as the sickening vortex claimed her again.

* * *

827 B.C.

They were standing in a grove of trees. The High Priest, his health failing, and the council of the Wise Ones had all assembled. Cela stood before them.

"Child," the High Priest said, addressing her, "do you doubt our teachings?"

"No," Cela answered. "As surely as the air moves into my body, I know of the continuance of life. The life force can neither be created nor destroyed. It exists. It flows from one state to another. It flows through all things."

"And the gods?"

"The gods are the source of all wisdom, the source of all life, the directors of that force," Cela answered.

"Priestess," one of the members of the council said, "how are we to show respect to that force? How do we honor the gods if we are not willing to offer the ultimate of what we have? In doing so, we confirm our belief in the constancy of life. We confirm our belief in the gods. What better means than our sacrifices?"

Cela had returned with Dagga five days after she had cut her neck. She went directly to the High Priest. She told him where she had gone and her vow never to participate in the sacrifices again. She did not tell him of the offer of her own life. Immediately, the council was called together. Now she stood before them, trembling, aware of the seriousness of her actions. She knew that there was the very real possibility that she would be exiled from the Wise Ones and her people.

"She has defied the gods. Her actions will result in punishment for all the people," one of the priests of the council interrupted.

The High Priest raised his hand for silence. "The priestess will answer the question put to her," he said. He turned back to Cela. "You refuse to participate in the sacrifices? Explain yourself."

"The People of the Sky taught us many things," Cela began. "They are the source of our knowledge. They instructed us to use what we have learned for the good of our people. This means a lifetime of study, learning, and working from the moment we awaken until we sleep at night, and even then, our sleep is often guided by the gods. It is all done for the good of the people. In this respect, we are no freer than our captives and slaves. Is this not the ultimate sacrifice we have to offer? Our lives of service? Not blood! What need do the gods have for blood? That is easy enough to come by."

Loud murmurs erupted from the council members.

"Would you have us destroy the basis of our beliefs?" Luc shouted. "The priestess has defied the gods. If we allow her to remain, we will all suffer. Tell me, how will the good of the people be served then?" he demanded.

Fear ran through Cela as the angry sounds of the council priests made it apparent that most of the priests agreed with Luc.

"The gods are angry with her. I have seen it!" Luc

shouted.

"No!" Cela retorted. "They are not!"

"How can we believe you, Cousin? You do not even divine as we do. We know the will of the gods, not you."

"They speak to me, too!" Cela said, her anger obliterating her fear of Luc. "They speak to me in the *sky*," she said deliberately, "and I feel no anger from them. They have accepted *my* blood. I will offer no other!"

Cela dramatically pushed the hood of her gown off her head. Her eyes were blazing as she lifted her head and tilted it to the side. The gasps from the priests were explosive. There, extending from the side of her neck to the front of her throat, was a scar five inches long, still bright in its early stages of healing.

It was several minutes before the High Priest could quiet the shouting of the council priests. He walked to where Cela stood. His eyes narrowed as he surveyed her neck. He then turned his gaze upon her. His eyes penetrated through her, and Cela was almost knocked physically backward by the force of the power projected from his eyes.

"You offered yourself as a sacrifice?" he demanded.

"Yes. I will never again offer the blood of another," she answered boldly.

His eyes burned into her. Cela felt her resolve weakening but steeled herself and returned his gaze. Time seemed to stop as they stood there, their eyes locked on each other, separate, invisible forces surrounding each of them, gaining strength. Cela could feel the life force swirling around her, penetrating her skin, seeping into her bones, stirring her blood, empowering her. Then suddenly, the High Priest's eyes widened in surprise? Confusion? *Fear?* He visibly faltered and stepped back abruptly. The spell was then broken, and he turned away from her.

"The Priestess Cela's actions could undermine all of our teachings," he blazed. "Her behavior could confuse the people who need our guidance. Nothing will be spoken of this. The priestess will keep her hood on at all times. She will not participate in the sacrifices."

Several of the members of the council protested. The High Priest turned on them with a vengeance that belied his frail health.

"The will of the gods regarding the Priestess Cela is clear," he said, pointing to Cela's neck. "Who among you dares to defy them?"

She saw the priests shift uncomfortably, their fear and confusion apparent. Even Luc was quiet. When there was no response, the High Priest declared the matter settled. Slowly, the priests began to filter out of the woods. Cela stood until they had all left and then turned to walk out alone. She had reached the edge of the glen when Luc stepped out from behind a tree.

"You may have fooled them, Cousin, but you haven't fooled me." An evil smile appeared on Luc's lips. "No matter. You can escape the sacrifices, but you cannot escape your spring rites. It was decided while you were gone, Cousin. You have been chosen for the fertility ceremony, and I shall initiate you."

✳ ✳ ✳

Derek frowned. He opened the door and stepped out into the garden. He squinted his eyes into the distance. Damn! There it was again: that feeling in the air, like a sudden change in barometric pressure, and yet, the sky was unusually clear. He saw Jennifer at the top of the hill. She seemed to be slumped against a tree. Why? Then he saw her push herself away from the tree. Her first few steps seemed uncoordinated and he thought she might fall, but then she started running. He watched as the late afternoon sun shone on her long, red hair. *Jenny, with your hair of fire.* Then she disappeared over the hill.

CHAPTER 6

"**W**ell, McHugh, I'll say one thing. You sure kept busy while I was away," Nina said.

The two women were sitting at Nina's kitchen table. It was Monday afternoon, and they had just returned from the airport.

Nina laughed. "Now let me get this straight. The professor turned out to be Lord Rannoch, the younger. He rescued you from a storm. Then you spent four days and nights with him at his hunting lodge—just working, right? Another woman showed up and you left, after arguing with him. Next, you met Lord Rannoch, the earl, no less. He invited you to tea. His son arrived, and you realized who he was. He became angry; you became angry. You left again. Have I got this right so far?" Nina asked with humor.

"You make it sound like a plot in a book," Jennifer said with chagrin.

Nina considered Jennifer's statement with a wicked grin. "I'd need to add a romance between you and the earl's son for that. You would have had to sleep with him while at his lodge."

Nina smiled, making a joke. The look on Jennifer's face caused her smile to fade instantly. She looked at Jennifer incredulously. "Jen, did you sleep with him?" she asked with uncertainty. When Jennifer didn't answer, Nina's eyes widened. She sat forward in her chair. "Jen? Oh, no, you did. I don't believe it!"

"Calm down, Nina. Of course I didn't. What kind of a question was that?" Jennifer could read the uncertainty on Nina's face. "Nina!"

"Okay, okay, just checking. I mean, you have been out of circulation for a long time." Nina screwed up her face mischievously. "Actually, you never were in circulation."

Jennifer rolled her eyes in response.

"Besides, there is John, right?" Nina asked.

"I forgot. I need to call John's office," Jennifer said, glancing at her watch. "Someone should be there now. May I use your landline?"

"Of course," Nina said.

Jennifer stood and walked to the phone, dialed the number, and waited.

"Dr. Bracken's office," a female voice answered.

"Hello, Margaret, this is Jennifer Bracken."

"Mrs. Bracken! I'm sorry. I thought your flight wasn't due in until this afternoon. Do you need a car sent for you?" the secretary asked.

"No, Margaret. I'm still in Scotland. I wasn't able to make the flight today. I'm not certain when I'm returning. Just let John know that I called."

Margaret was saying something, but Jennifer was distracted by a knock on the door. She turned to watch as Nina opened the door. Derek! She stepped back, partially concealing herself behind the wall.

"Miss Bouvay?" Derek asked.

"Yes," Nina answered.

"Good afternoon," he said pleasantly. "My name is Derek Rannoch. I would like to speak with Miss McHugh, please."

"Lord Rannoch," Nina acknowledged.

Derek smiled easily. "I'm pretty much known as Derek. My father is the earl, but he prefers to dispense with formalities." He extended his hand. "And you are Miss McHugh's friend, the writer?"

"Yes, my name is Nina," she said as she shook Derek's

hand. "Jen's inside. She's on the phone, but she should be through any minute. Would you like to come in?"

"Thank you," Derek said.

Nina led Derek into the kitchen.

"Margaret, I must go now. Good-bye," Jennifer said hastily and replaced the receiver.

"It appears I am interrupting," Derek said smoothly.

"No, I was just finishing," Jennifer said with reserve.

"My father is of the opinion that I had something to do with your leaving yesterday."

"Your father is a perceptive man," Jennifer responded.

Derek appeared unmoved by Jennifer's barb. He nodded his head. "He insisted that I deliver this to you personally," Derek said as he held out a small envelope. "It's an invitation to tea tomorrow. I'm certain my father would be delighted to meet your friend, Miss Bouvay, as well," Derek said graciously, looking toward Nina.

Jennifer was silent.

"Jen?" Nina asked.

Jennifer glanced at her friend. There was a question on Nina's face. Jennifer had made no move to take the envelope from Derek's outstretched hand. Nina nodded her head in Derek's direction, so Jennifer walked around the table to where Derek was standing. As she reached to take the envelope, Derek's fingers brushed hers. Warmth spread at lightning speed from her fingertips where he had touched her, causing her heart rate to increase, the blood to rush through her body, and every nerve to come alive. Jennifer pulled her hand back quickly. How could her body respond like that? Didn't it know she was angry with him? Was it going to be like that every time he came near her?

"You're wondering if I'm going to be present again," Derek said, reading Jennifer's mind.

"You're mistaken. What you do is of no interest to me," she responded.

"Then shall I tell my father that you accept his invitation?"

Jennifer hesitated again. Derek was still holding the invitation. "What are you afraid of?" he asked quietly, his eyes challenging.

Jennifer inhaled sharply. Derek Rannoch was far too perceptive. If she refused the invitation now, it would only add credibility to his statements.

"Nothing," she said with more force as she took the invitation from his hand. "Tell your father that I appreciate the invitation. I'll be there."

Derek nodded his head, a twinkle in his eye. He turned to Nina. "Miss Bouvay, it has been a pleasure meeting you. Now, if you will excuse me, I must be going."

Nina walked with Derek to the door. As soon as he left, she looked back at Jennifer. "Jen, old friend, you want to tell me what that was all about?" Nina asked.

"What? I don't know what you're talking about," Jennifer replied evasively.

"You were positively rude to him. You're never rude to anyone. And then when he handed you that invitation, you almost jumped out of your skin."

When Jennifer didn't answer, Nina smiled. "You didn't tell me Lord Rannoch was so sexy," Nina said easily.

Jennifer glared at her.

"Don't tell me that in all those days and nights you spent with him you failed to notice," Nina said teasingly. "He's hot, McHugh! Very masculine."

"All I did those days and nights was talk and answer his endless questions."

"Surely you took some time off."

"Only to eat and sleep."

"So tell me about him."

"What is there to tell?" Jennifer asked with irritation.

"Well, at some time, you must have talked about something other than your visions."

"It's not important."

"Of course it is."

"Look, Nina, I don't want to talk about this. Derek

Rannoch is not going to help me. I've wasted four days telling him about the visions, and he's told me nothing."

"Let's get back to that," Nina said, pulling out a chair and sitting down. "He wants you to go with him to these sites, right?"

"Yes," Jennifer said wearily. "He seems to think that I could describe them better if I were actually there."

"How would that help?"

Jennifer sighed. "He said that it's difficult to place the date without that information. Apparently, some of the megaliths have changed over time."

Nina thought about what Jennifer said. "Hmmm. Makes sense to me, Jen. I think you should go with him."

"What!" Jennifer turned on her friend.

"You want to get to the bottom of this, right? Shamus said that Derek Rannoch is a leading authority on prehistoric civilizations. He's a well-respected archaeologist, and he's offered to help. What more could you want?"

"Nina, I can't go with him. What if I have another episode right in front of him?"

Nina shrugged. "Then you tell him the truth. Maybe you should have done that to begin with."

"And have him think I'm crazy like John does? He never would have given me the time of day."

"You don't know that for certain. Just give it some thought, will you?" She grinned at Jennifer. "Besides," she said wickedly, "do you know how many women would jump at the chance to travel with Lord Rannoch to exotic prehistoric sites?" Nina cocked her head. "I wonder if I could have a vision, too," she said playfully. "How do you do it, Jen? Do I need to buy a crystal or stare at a candle or something weird like that?"

"No crystals or candles. You might have to vomit once or twice," Jennifer said sarcastically.

"Oh, yuck," Nina said, sticking her tongue out.

Nina's good humor was infectious. Before Jennifer realized it, she was laughing with her friend.

They spent the rest of the evening relaxing. Shamus came over and joined them for dinner. Jennifer sensed that had she not been there, Shamus would have spent the night with Nina. After he left, Jennifer asked Nina about it.

Nina smiled. "There will be time for that. Right now, you're here."

"My feelings won't be hurt if you want to go to his house some night, or I could go to a hotel."

"Would you stop it?" Nina interrupted.

Just then the phone rang. Nina answered it and then handed the receiver to Jennifer. "It's John."

"Hello, John," Jennifer said.

"Just what are you doing, Jennifer?" John demanded immediately. "I thought you said you would be returning today."

"I'm sorry, John. I couldn't."

"Why not?"

"I've explained that to you."

"Your hallucinations? Are you still trying to turn them into reality?"

Jennifer was silent.

"Jennifer, you listen to me. I've indulged your erratic behavior long enough. This is your last chance. I'll have Margaret book you on the first available flight tomorrow. You can call first thing in the morning to confirm the flight. The jet will be waiting for you in New York. Don't cancel this one or you'll regret it."

Jennifer's jaw tightened. "What are you saying, John?"

"The business day has not yet ended here. I'm going to make a few more calls as soon as I hang up. Just don't try to use your credit cards or bank card. It could be embarrassing for you." John's voice was like ice.

Jennifer blinked. John had never threatened her before, nor had he ever spoken in such a mean-spirited manner. He was distant, yes, even cold, but always polite. She was having a hard time reconciling the man who was speaking to her now with the man she had been married to for the last year and a half. It was a moment before Jennifer replied, and when she did, her voice was calm and controlled. "How could I have been so easily fooled? You really are an ass, John."

Jennifer quietly replaced the receiver. She looked up to see Nina watching her.

"You don't look so good, McHugh," Nina said sympathetically. "What happened?"

Jennifer quickly recounted her conversation with John.

"Would he really do that?" Nina asked when Jennifer finished.

Jennifer glanced at her watch. "He already has," she said.

Nina looked at her friend. "Are you going back?" she asked. "Look, Jen, if it's the problem of money, I can give you some—as much as you need."

Jennifer sighed. "I can't ask you to do that. I don't know what I'm going to do. I don't want to go back. Not now. I'm not sure I ever want to return to John."

"Never return to John, meaning?"

Jennifer didn't answer.

"Divorce?" Nina asked with surprise.

Still, Jennifer didn't answer.

"Listen, Jen, you're not thinking clearly right now. With everything that's been going on, now is not the time to make a decision like that—not when you are preoccupied with these visions that you've been having. John is a bastard for what he did, but maybe he did it because he cares about you, and it's the only way he knows of getting you back."

"What? You're defending him?"

"No. You know how I feel about John, but I just don't want you to rush into anything. Face it, sweetie, the last several years of your life have been a trial. You've been going through the motions of living. And now these visions. One day at a time, okay, McHugh? One day at a time."

* * *

"Camp, Bolton, and Husk Law Firm," the secretary answered.

"This is John Bracken. I would like to speak to Timothy, please."

"One moment, Dr. Bracken. I'll see if Mr. Camp is available."

"John, it's good to hear from you," Timothy Camp said a moment later.

"I need to talk to you," John said.

"Of course. What can I do for you?"

"Not on the phone. I'll come to your office."

"Sounds serious. Is anything wrong, John?"

"Friday afternoon, three o'clock," John said.

"Let me have my secretary check. . . ."

"Three o'clock. I'll see you then."

* * *

"Are you sure you won't come, too?" Jennifer asked.

It was Tuesday afternoon, and Jennifer was changing her clothes. It was a beautiful, warm spring afternoon, and she was expected at Thornhill within the hour.

"I'd love to," Nina answered, "but I think Lord Rannoch included me just to be polite. This is your invitation. You look nice," Nina added.

Jennifer was struggling with her mass of hair, trying to secure it on the top of her head.

"Just wear it down," Nina suggested.

"Really?"

"If I had all that long, red hair, I'd never put it up. It's gorgeous."

Jennifer shrugged her shoulders and removed the pins. "Okay. I guess I'd better be going."

"You know how to find the house?"

"Yes, Nina," Jennifer said with exaggerated patience and smiled. "I was there before, remember?"

Jennifer's impression as she drove up to Thornhill was exactly as it had been a few days earlier when she had come upon it by accident. It was breathtaking. The ancient, gray stones shone in the afternoon sunlight. The massive towers reached up to the sky. The only thing missing was a moat to surround the castle, but this part of Scotland rested on rock. The top soil was fertile, but not very deep. Centuries ago, it would have been impossible to dig a moat through the rock. With a start, Jennifer shook her head. How did she know about the rock? She was certain Lord Harold had not mentioned it when she was here previously.

She stopped the car and stepped out onto the drive. She couldn't help but smile as she looked at the house and its surrounding grounds. It emitted such a feeling of comfort and safety. It was as though the stones radiated a warmth that moved deep inside her, touching every organ, muscle, and bone, all the way to her soul.

The massive door opened immediately, and Harold Rannoch stepped out.

"Miss McHugh, I'm delighted you decided to accept my invitation," he said as he walked toward her. He glanced up at the clear sky. "I believe the sun is shining just for you."

Jennifer smiled. "Thank you for inviting me. Are you always so charming to brash Americans who trespass on your property?"

"Who's to say you weren't invited?"

"Pardon me?"

Harold Rannoch motioned back to the stone castle. "Thornhill. It does have a life of its own. Perhaps you were invited." Lord Harold saw the question upon Jennifer's face. "Come," he said, "let's walk in the garden. I've asked that tea be brought out there."

Jennifer took the arm that Lord Harold offered, and the two of them walked around to the side of the castle. "Thornhill has seen a lot of history," he began as they walked. "The oldest part—of which little remains—was built during the twelfth century when David the First was King of Scotland. He embarked on an ambitious building spree, erecting abbeys and castles, most of which were in the southern and southeastern parts of Scotland. This was one of the northernmost castles established. My ancestor, who became the first Earl of Thornhill, was a mixture of Norman blood and ancient Scottish clan. He had fought with David, and as a reward and a means of securing the land, King David granted him this land. Scotland was embroiled in constant battles back then. The clans were fighting battles over territorial rights, and Scotland was fighting with England over border disputes.

"For the next three hundred years, Thornhill was torn apart by blood divisions. You see, the earls chose wives from the English and Norman nobility, as well as the ancient Scottish clans, all in an effort to build a network of alliances. Unfortunately, as the fighting raged, Thornhill was forced to choose a side, and no matter with whom Thornhill sided, it was raising arms against its own kin.

"Finally, in the late 1200s and early 1300s, a choice had to be made. The Earl of Thornhill allied his house with those fighting for formal independence from England. He lost two sons at the Battle of Bannockburn, but Scotland achieved her independence for another three hundred years, until the time when it would again formally unite with England."

Harold Rannoch continued to talk as they sat in the garden. He told Jennifer of the introduction of the Stuart line into Thornhill following an alliance that the Scots made with the French during the fifteenth century. He recounted the tragedies that Thornhill suffered during the Reformation and again following the alliance of Thornhill with its distant relation, Mary Stuart, Queen of Scots.

He explained how, following the execution of Mary by her cousin, Elizabeth the First, Thornhill continued to experience tragedy as Presbyterian Scots fought the Catholic James the First, who became king of both Scotland and England upon Elizabeth's death.

"Thornhill again lost some of its sons when Cromwell invaded Scotland and defeated the Scots decisively at Dunbar in 1650," he said. "A century later, the Scots made a final fight for independence in the support of Bonnie Prince Charlie in an attempt to restore the Stuart line to power. Shrewdly assessing the overwhelming strength of the English and the Duke of Cumberland, the then Earl of Thornhill quickly arranged a marriage of his son to another English princess, thereby preventing the execution of the earl and his family by the English victors. In return, the earl agreed to support the English and not to support another insurrection. Throughout it all, Thornhill remained a haven and protective fortress for those within its walls, its family a strange mixture of ancient Scottish clan, Norman, French, and English," he concluded.

Harold Rannoch looked up and smiled. For all his gentle charm, Jennifer sensed he was an astute man with a quick mind. She had been enraptured by his story. When he had described the turmoil of the past and the losses that the inhabitants of Thornhill had sustained, she hastily wiped the tears that had appeared in her eyes. She knew he had seen them, but he pretended not to notice, no doubt so as not to embarrass her.

"So what do you think about it now?" he asked, motioning to the structure behind him.

"A lot of pain, a lot of tragedy through the centuries— still, I don't sense that," she said seriously. "There is peace here."

"Precisely," Lord Rannoch said. "The politics of the past eight hundred years have hurled tragedy upon tragedy on Scotland and her people, but inside these walls, Thornhill has kept her family intact." Harold Rannoch smiled suddenly. "Not that they all have been admirable characters, mind you. Some of them were real scoundrels."

"Who were real scoundrels?" a feminine voice asked.

Jennifer looked up to see a woman coming out of the house. Ahead of her, two young boys ran straight toward Harold Rannoch. "Grandfather!" they shouted as they threw themselves into the waiting arms of Lord Harold. Jennifer watched as both boys began talking at once, and Harold Rannoch smiled, indulging each boy.

"Boys," the woman said, "your grandfather has a guest," she admonished in a gentle voice.

Jennifer looked over to the woman who was obviously expecting a third child soon. She smiled at Jennifer and offered her hand. "I'm Ann Warrick," she said kindly. "Please forgive the intrusion. I'm afraid my sons have forgotten their manners."

"They have indeed," Harold Rannoch quipped, still smiling at the boys. "Boys, let me introduce you to my guest."

The boys wiggled on their grandfather's lap, but turned quietly toward Jennifer.

"Miss McHugh, my daughter has already introduced herself. May I present my grandsons, Andrew and Anthony Warrick?" Harold Rannoch gave each boy a subtle push and they stood. Each walked over to Jennifer and bowed slightly; then they offered their hands.

"How do you do, Miss McHugh," the older boy said. "I'm Andrew."

Jennifer shook the boy's hand.

"I'm Anthony," the younger boy said.

"You're supposed to say, 'How do you do' or 'Hello' first," the older brother whispered in the younger brother's ear.

"Ann, Miss McHugh is an American visiting Scotland for the first time. She's staying with her friend who is renting one of the cottages on Thornhill."

"I hope you are enjoying your visit," Ann Warrick replied warmly.

"I am," Jennifer said. "Your father has been telling me something of Thornhill's history."

"Ah, that explains the reference to scoundrels," Ann laughed. "And I think these two are keeping up the family tradition," she said as she looked at her sons.

"Please sit down, dear," Harold Rannoch said to his daughter.

"Perhaps I should take the boys inside. Are Derek and Edward here?" Ann asked.

"Derek should be back soon. Edward is in London. He'll be back tomorrow. The boys will be fine." Harold looked over at his grandsons. "Why don't you two run and play for a few minutes?"

"Just don't wander off too far," Ann admonished.

"Can I ride, Grandfather?"

"Wait until Uncle Derek comes home," Ann said. "Perhaps he can take you."

Andrew started to dart away and then turned back quickly. "A pleasure to meet you, ma'am." He gave a quick bow, and then the two boys darted away, their laughter echoing off of the gray stones of Thornhill.

"I probably should be going now," Jennifer said as she glanced at her watch.

"Oh, please stay," Ann said as she sat down next to them.

"I would like to, but I've already been here later than I had intended."

"I hadn't realized the time," Lord Harold said. "I'm afraid I have talked all afternoon. I hope I haven't kept you from some other appointment."

"I've enjoyed the afternoon," Jennifer said.

"You haven't seen the house yet. You must agree to come back again so that I can show it to you."

"I would like that very much."

"He'll hold you to that, Miss McHugh. There's nothing

he loves more than Thornhill and Scotland," Ann said, smiling.

"My family, Thornhill, and Scotland," Lord Rannoch corrected, "which includes you, my dear, and those wild little Highlanders of yours," he said, referring to Ann's sons.

Harold Rannoch stood. "I will walk you to your car, Miss McHugh. Oh, but before you leave, my son left something for you. If you will excuse me, I will get it."

He returned a moment later with a large envelope. "These are for you. Derek said that you would understand what they are," Lord Harold said as he handed the envelope to Jennifer. She resisted the impulse to open the envelope and, instead, said good-bye to Ann Warrick and allowed Lord Rannoch to escort her to her car. She thanked him for a wonderful afternoon and promised to return again to see the house itself.

As she drove away from Thornhill, she reached over with one hand to open the large envelope. Inside were many pages with Derek's writing. She briefly scanned the first page while trying to keep her eyes on the road. With a start, she realized that the papers were notes that he had made while she was telling him the contents of her "documents." The pages were divided in half, with a line drawn down the middle, the left side containing her descriptions of various rituals and practices, and the right side covered with notes Derek made describing similar practices in other cultures. Jennifer drove a little farther until she could no longer see Thornhill behind her, and then she stopped the car on the side of the road and reached for the papers.

The first entry detailed the initial ceremony Jennifer had related to Derek. Derek's notes were meticulous. He described the direction that the priests and priestesses circled the megaliths and the number of times they moved around the structures. Following his arrow to the right side of the page, Jennifer frowned as she read. Derek described practices conducted by ancient Druids. He penciled in dates in the margin followed by a large question mark. As Jennifer read, she felt her palms grow cold and clammy.

According to Derek's notes, the number three was important in the Druids' religious ceremonies. They also believed in "walking in harmony" with the sun and circled three times in the same direction that Cela's people did. They were known to engage in human sacrifice.

As Derek described the sacrifices conducted by the Druids, a feeling of premonition came over Jennifer. Suddenly, the words "large wicker baskets" leaped out at her. Derek had indicated that the Druids used to burn their victims in baskets.

When Jennifer felt the familiar nausea, she assumed it was because of the clarity of Derek's notes and the obvious parallels between Cela's people and the Druids that Derek described. She swallowed quickly and looked up, trying to focus on the hills before her. She felt her stomach cramp as the bile rose up into her mouth. She dropped the papers in her lap and reached for the steering wheel in front of her. She squeezed her eyes shut as the swirling vertigo and sickness came over her.

✳ ✳ ✳

827 B.C.

Cela watched from behind the rocks, trying to control the tide of feelings rushing within her own body. The woman cried out in pleasure, and a few moments later, the man's body quieted. The two lie naked, entwined together in the afternoon sun. The woman whispered something, but Cela could not hear what she said. The man laughed a full, deep laugh. Cela watched as the man withdrew himself and stretched out next to the woman. He was lying on his side facing the woman, his hand lightly caressing her hip. The woman spoke again and stood up. She grabbed her discarded clothing and dressed while the man watched. The two exchanged words again, and the woman smiled warmly at the man as she left. The man lay there a moment and then, almost reluctantly, reached for his clothes. He had only a rough tunic, sandals made of animal skin, and most importantly, a bronze shield, sword, and knife. He slipped the tunic over his powerful shoulders and stood. He reached down, put on the sandals, and then sat back on the ground, content to rest after his afternoon of lovemaking.

Cela had been standing in one position for a long time, afraid to move, lest the lovers know of her presence. Now, however, it was time to leave. As she turned, a twig underneath her feet snapped. The warrior sprang up immediately, his sword in hand.

"Who's there?" the warrior demanded. "Show yourself!"

Cela crouched down in the bushes, her heart racing. Maybe he wouldn't see her. She heard a rustle and realized he was coming toward her at a run. Cela stood and turned to bolt away just as Dagga bore down on her, his sword raised for attack.

"Priestess!" he exclaimed as he recognized her.

Cela stopped, her eyes drawn to the sword held above her head.

"What are you doing here?" Dagga demanded roughly as he lowered his sword. He looked around. "You are alone?" Seeing no one, he turned back to her. "How long have you been here?"

Dagga had been so surprised to see the Priestess Cela that he had forgotten himself. He realized now how he had questioned her and was also aware that, as a priestess of the Wise Ones, she could order his death simply for his show of disrespect.

Tightening his jaw, he bowed slightly. "Can I be of service, Priestess?"

"No," Cela answered.

She stepped past Dagga and walked through the bushes back to where he and the woman had been lying. Dagga's shield and knife still lay on the ground.

"You were watching?" Dagga asked, the anger in his voice barely restrained as he stopped beside her.

"Yes," Cela answered quietly.

"The act between a man and a woman should be private, not entertainment for another, even a priestess."

"I did not watch you for that reason," she said.

"No? It is said that the Wise Ones are taught sex magic and that they mate before each other."

Cela closed her eyes. "You make it sound so barbaric," she said softly. She opened her eyes to look at Dagga. "We do not mate before each other. The mating is before the gods, and it is only at the spring fertility rites. One priest— usually the High Priest—and one virginal priestess. It is a great honor for the priestess who is chosen for the fertility rites," Cela finished quietly.

Dagga sensed distress in Cela's voice and his anger faded. Again he frowned. "Will you sit, Priestess?" he asked. He noticed that she was trembling slightly, but she moved to a nearby rock and sat down, pushing the hood of her robe back, freeing her hair as she did so.

He stared at Cela. He saw her blush slightly, and then she looked away. He thought he began to understand. "You are to be initiated with the next moon?" he asked gently.

"Yes," she whispered, her face still averted.

Dagga considered the young priestess before him. He knelt down on one knee. "I believe it is natural for a woman, even a priestess of the Wise Ones, to be nervous— perhaps even fearful—of the first time she is with a man."

Still she did not look at him. "It is not the act that I fear, but the man," Cela whispered.

"But Priestess, you have told me that priests are instructed in the means of giving pleasure." He smiled slightly. "Men are not such fearsome creatures, I assure you."

Cela turned to him. He was surprised by the desperation he saw in her eyes. "You don't understand. I have been chosen for the fertility ceremony. I am the one to be initiated before the gods, before the others," she cried.

Dagga pulled back slightly. "So it will not be done privately." He stopped when he saw her eyes filling with tears. "Priestess, you said it is a great honor to be chosen for this," he said gently. "The High Priest has honored you."

"The High Priest will not be initiating me. He is old and frail. Luc will be taking his place. Luc will initiate me before the others."

Suddenly, Dagga understood. He knew of Cela's fear of her cousin and suspected that her fear was justified.

Cela's lips were trembling as she spoke. "Luc wants to hurt me, and he will. He will give no consideration to my virginal state. He will not give my body time to prepare itself for him. He will not ease himself into me. He will cause me as much pain as he can. And I must do nothing. I cannot disgrace myself. I cannot fail in my duty."

"But Priestess," Dagga said softly, "he would not dare to hurt you. The others will be present. You said so."

"They will be chanting, their faces averted from the act. They will only know if I cry out, and I must not do that. That's what he wants. He wants me to defile the ceremony. He wants me to fail. He will do everything he can to make me appear unfit."

The image of Luc on top of Cela filled Dagga's mind. He was a warrior of many battles. Although he had no taste for it himself, he had seen many a woman of the defeated tribe raped by victorious warriors. Rage flowed through him as he looked down upon this priestess whose life had somehow become entwined with his own.

"I will do what I must," Cela said. "I am a priestess of the Wise Ones. I will not fail my people. I will submit to him this one time, as is required, but I will not bear a child resulting from this mating. I will not do that, although it will be expected."

Dagga didn't understand. "A baby from just one sex act? Priestess, a woman does not get with child each time—"

"I am a priestess of the Wise Ones. You need not instruct me in the starting of life within the womb," she said sharply. She stopped and closed her eyes. "I am sorry I spoke to you in anger, Dagga." She opened her eyes and looked at him. "A woman's body cycles as the moon, bleeding commencing every twenty-eight eves. On the fourteenth eve, the gods are waiting with a life ready to begin again. My bleeding started today. I must tell the High Priest, who will schedule the fertility ceremony on the fourteenth eve of my cycle. It is expected that a child will result. That symbolizes the gods' blessing upon our people and the land."

"This is true, Priestess?"

"Yes. It is one of the many mysteries that we understand but do not teach the people."

They were silent as Dagga momentarily forgot about what Cela would soon endure and contemplated this new knowledge. Cela broke the silence.

"You were gentle with that woman," Cela said softly. "You gave her pleasure."

"Is that why you watched?"

"I came upon you by accident. When I saw you, I. . . ." Cela turned away again.

"Did what you see frighten you, Priestess?"

"No, on the contrary. I felt stirrings within myself that I've never felt before. Each time you touched her body—I would that it had been me there instead of her."

Cela suddenly jumped up and ran away, leaving Dagga to contemplate her astonishing words. Her voice had been so soft that Dagga was not certain that he had heard her correctly. It was not possible! Even to touch a priestess was a death sentence, as well he knew. How could she say such things to him?

But he had touched a priestess—this priestess. When she

was a child of ten years, he had carried her away at the order of the Priestess Ega, certain that his own death would follow. He had found himself again touching the priestess when he had carried her away from the ceremonies from which she had fled. She was no longer a child then. She was a young woman, as she was now. He knew her body well, for he had cared for her after she had cut into her neck. He had covered her nakedness with her discarded robe. He had sheltered her from the cool night air with his own body. He had fed her and given her water to drink while maintaining pressure on the delicate skin of her neck. He had held her within his arms while she slept. The thought of her being torn into by the Priest Luc filled him with rage.

* * *

"Jenny! Jenny! Can you hear me?"

Jennifer stirred. Her head was resting against the steering wheel of the car. Automatically, she clutched her midsection with both arms. It had been this way each time: the rushing sound, the nausea and sickness as she was entering and leaving Cela's world. She knew it would pass. If she could just avoid vomiting. She grimaced as she swallowed the bitter bile that arose in her throat.

With a shock, she realized that someone was beside her, helping her out of the car. She looked up into Derek's worried face. She didn't resist as his arm came around her. "I just need some air. I'll be all right," she said.

"You're trembling."

"It's nothing, really."

"Come over here and sit down," Derek said as he led her off the road. Jennifer sat down on the grass and pulled her knees up. She rested her arms and her head on her knees, closing her eyes. She tried to take deep breaths to relax.

Derek squatted down in front of her. With his hand, he reached up and gently pushed Jennifer's hair out of her face.

Even though Cela and her world had faded from Jennifer's consciousness, the emotions that they had evoked remained. Jennifer swallowed as she recalled Cela's arousal when watching Dagga and the woman.

"You're very pale," Derek said softly.

He was so close. Was it Cela's desire for Dagga that Jennifer felt or was it her own desire for Derek? She could feel her heart pounding and her body warming.

For a moment, neither of them moved, and then he frowned. He withdrew his hand and sat down on the grass next to her. "Are you ill?" he asked with concern.

"No. I was just feeling a little dizzy." Jennifer tried to cover her awkwardness. "I guess I'm just tired," she said, forcing a smile.

"You didn't hear me when I approached your car. I'd say that was more than just a little dizzy spell."

"Thank you for the papers," Jennifer said.

"We did have an agreement, as you stated. Have you read them yet?"

"Just the first page. That's what I was doing when I parked on the side of the road."

"I hope they're helpful. As I explained to you, I was unable to authenticate your civilization. All I could do was point out similarities between your culture and others that we know existed. Any relationship between the two is purely speculative. There is nothing to substantiate the existence of your civilization."

"I understand, and I'm sorry about the way I acted when I left the hunting lodge and again at your father's house. I was rude. I'm not usually like that."

"No apology is necessary," Derek said kindly.

"Still, I'm grateful for your help. I'm sorry that I couldn't give you what you wanted."

Derek shrugged. "If you change your mind and decide to allow someone to examine the documents, I would like the opportunity."

Jennifer hesitated. "Professor Rannoch—"

"It's Derek."

"Derek, I don't have any background in this area. I'll understand if you refuse because I still can't show you the documents, but would you consider going over your notes with me? I read the first page. I don't even know who the Druids were."

Derek raised his eyebrows.

"It's important," Jennifer said. "I wouldn't take up your time if it weren't."

Derek stood and offered his hand to Jennifer. Cautiously, she placed her hand in his, and he pulled her to a standing position in front of him. Jennifer swallowed, again conscious of her nearness.

"On one condition," Derek said as he released her hand.

"What condition?"

"Go with me to the sites. Tell me what they looked like according to your documents."

"That's blackmail."

"Maybe in America. In Scotland, it's considered a shrewd bargain. What do you say?"

Jennifer was torn. She was afraid to travel with him, but she had to know about Cela and her people. This last episode was the strongest yet. She knew they were not going to stop, and she desperately wanted to understand what was happening to her.

"For how long?"

Derek shrugged. "We can leave tomorrow. We'll go to the Lake District, then to Stonehenge and Avebury."

Jennifer considered what he said.

"Do you agree?" Derek asked.

"All right," Jennifer finally said.

Derek held out his hand. "An agreement, then," he said as he shook her hand. "Now, you said you haven't eaten today. Why don't you join me for dinner tonight? Come with me now, and we can start discussing my notes."

Derek's offer surprised Jennifer. "Go with you to the lodge?" she asked.

"No, to my home—Thornhill."

"But I thought you lived at the hunting lodge."

"No. I work there occasionally when I don't want to be disturbed."

"I can't just show up at your father's home," she said, hoping to find a polite way to refuse Derek's invitation.

"You're not. I'm inviting you. It's my home, too. My father will be delighted to see you. My sister and her family will also be there. It will give us time to go over my notes and plan our schedule for the next week."

"I think I would be intruding. It sounds like a family evening."

"You'll be my guest. Let's go." Derek motioned to his car, which was parked on the other side of the road.

"But I can't just leave my car here."

"Why not? Jenny, this is my land. This is Thornhill. Shall we?"

Derek took her arm and guided her across the road to his waiting car.

"The papers," she said as he reached for the door of his car. Jennifer ran back across the road, retrieved the papers from the front seat of her car, and then returned to where Derek was waiting with the door open. She slid into the seat as Derek closed the door.

She sat in silence, absently running her hand along the envelope in her lap, as Derek drove back to Thornhill. He parked the car and came around to open the door for Jennifer. As she stepped out, the full force of Thornhill hit her again. She paused, feeling the centuries of human emotion that Thornhill had witnessed. She glanced at Derek, aware that he seemed to be studying her. She felt herself blush under his scrutiny. As they approached the house, he saw another car parked near the entrance.

"It looks like we have another guest," he said as he took Jennifer's arm and walked up to the massive doors. Once inside, a man greeted them in the great hall. "Jeffrey," Derek said casually, "tell Clara that we have another guest. Miss McHugh will be joining us for dinner."

"Of course," the man said. He turned to Jennifer and bowed his head slightly. "Miss McHugh," he said and then addressed Derek. "They're in the garden room."

"Thank you," Derek said and took Jennifer's elbow as he began to walk. He opened a door, and Jennifer immediately recognized the room with windows overlooking the garden beyond. Inside, several people were laughing and talking, and they all looked up as Derek entered. Jennifer hesitated, but Derek placed his arm on her back and gently guided her into the room.

Harold Rannoch came over immediately. "Miss McHugh, I was afraid you would not keep your promise to come back and visit. I don't know how my son found you, but I'm delighted that you are here."

Jennifer smiled gratefully at this kind man who had taken steps to put her at ease.

"Father, Miss McHugh and I are going to be working together this next week."

"Oh?"

"Miss McHugh has recently come into the possession of some documents detailing a prehistoric civilization. We'll be traveling to London tomorrow."

"You must think me terribly self-absorbed," Harold Rannoch said to Jennifer. "I'm afraid all I did was talk about Thornhill this afternoon. You are interested in prehistoric civilizations?"

"I enjoyed our discussions of Thornhill immensely," Jennifer replied.

Ann walked over to where Jennifer stood. "It's nice to see you again, Miss McHugh. I was feeling badly about interrupting you and my father this afternoon. I hope you will be joining us for dinner."

Derek reached out and hugged his sister as another man walked over. Derek released Ann and turned. "Ah, Robert, I see you are still lusting after my sister," he said, nodding to Ann's advanced state of pregnancy.

"Derek!" Ann cried.

"Well, what would you call it? The good vicar here couldn't keep his eyes off you when you first met. Looks like he still can't."

Robert Warrick laughed at his brother-in-law as his arm came around Ann's shoulder.

"Miss McHugh, please forgive my brother," Ann said. "He spends so much time crawling around ancient relics that he forgets how to behave when he returns to civilization." Ann smiled warmly at Derek and then turned again to Jennifer. "Miss McHugh, I would like you to meet my husband, Robert Warrick."

Robert extended his hand to Jennifer. "It's a pleasure to meet you, Miss McHugh." Then he smiled. "And Derek is correct. I'm a minister, and I met Ann when she was a bridesmaid at a wedding ceremony that I was performing. And it's true. I could hardly concentrate on my official duties; I couldn't keep my eyes off her. After the ceremony, I sought her out and pursued her relentlessly until she agreed to marry me."

"Pursued her? Is that what you call it? Father was concerned that there would be an infant baptismal before a marriage."

"Derek, enough!" Ann cried, the laughter dancing in her eyes. She stepped away from her husband. "And you're a minister," she lovingly chided Robert. "You should know better than to encourage such talk." She turned to Jennifer. "Miss McHugh, why don't we sit down and leave them to their bawdy male conversation. And mind you," she said to the men, "watch what you say when the boys return. That means you, too, Father."

The three men laughed as Ann and Jennifer walked over to the sofa and sat down. "I hope they haven't embarrassed you," Ann said. "Please call me 'Ann.' May I call you Jennifer?"

"Of course," Jennifer smiled.

"Tell me about the work you and Derek will be doing," Ann asked as they sat.

Jennifer explained that she was interested in a prehistoric civilization that possibly existed in England and Scotland. "My friend took me to the University of Edinburgh where I met your brother. He has agreed to help me. We spent several days last week going over the details."

"How exciting," Ann said. "You are an archaeologist also?"

"No."

They were interrupted by the sound of the door opening. A woman entered with Andrew and Anthony. She and the boys walked immediately to where the men were standing.

"Uncle Derek!" Andrew said excitedly. "Elizabeth took us riding."

"We were going to wait for you, but you took too long," Anthony said to Derek.

"You certainly did," the woman said, smiling. "Your father tells me that you've been home for two weeks, and you haven't called me." The woman pouted prettily.

"I'm sorry, Elizabeth," Derek said. His arm came easily around her as he kissed her on the cheek. "I hope he also told you that I've been working since I arrived home."

"That's hardly an excuse," Elizabeth said. "I finally had to come over to see you for myself."

"Boys," Ann said from the sofa, "did you thank Elizabeth for taking you riding?"

"Thank you, Elizabeth," they both echoed. "Can we go outside now, Mama?"

Ann smiled. "Yes, but stay near the house."

"Can we take the dogs with us?" Anthony asked eagerly.

"Of course," Harold Rannoch said. "I'll have Brandon get them. He can go along with you."

Lord Harold excused himself and left the room, taking the boys with him. As soon as he was gone, Elizabeth turned back to where Jennifer and Ann sat.

"Elizabeth, I would like you to meet Jennifer McHugh," Ann said. "She's from the United States. She and Derek are working on a prehistoric civilization together."

The woman walked over to where Jennifer and Ann were sitting. Despite the smile on her face, her eyes narrowed. She quickly surveyed Jennifer from head to toe and then extended her hand. "I'm Lady Elizabeth Shearing," she said. "Are you another student of Derek's or a secretary?" The condescension in Elizabeth's voice was barely concealed.

"I'm neither," Jennifer said calmly, eyeing the woman directly. She knew that Elizabeth was expecting Jennifer to explain herself, but she remained silent. Jennifer had met the "Lady Elizabeths" of the world more times than she cared to remember. They made up the bulk of John's social circle.

"Elizabeth, would you care to sit down?" Ann intervened. "I'm afraid the men are being rather roguish at the moment, my husband included."

As Elizabeth sat down, Robert and Derek ambled over to where the women sat. Jennifer was grateful for their presence—less chance of Elizabeth focusing her condescension on Jennifer.

When Lord Harold returned, he turned to Derek. "Have you noticed Issy and Bruce acting peculiarly since you returned home?" he asked.

"If you are referring to their refusal to leave Jennifer's side, then yes, I have," Derek answered.

Lord Harold looked at Jennifer, a quizzical expression on his face. "Yes, indeed," he said, but didn't elaborate as Clara announced that dinner was ready.

When they moved into the dining room, Jennifer found herself seated next to Lord Harold and across from Derek. Elizabeth was on Derek's right side. Derek's family was gracious in their inclusion of Jennifer in the conversation. At one point, however, Derek was again teasing his sister and brother-in-law.

"Marriage is wonderful, Derek. You should consider it yourself," Robert Warrick said.

Before Derek could respond, Elizabeth slipped her arm through his. "That's precisely what I have been telling him," she purred as she looked up at Derek and smiled. Her comment was followed by laughter around the table. Jennifer could see that Elizabeth was in love with Derek, but what of Derek? What about his assistant? She was just puzzling the dilemma when she caught Derek's eyes on her. He seemed to be studying her, and she could feel herself blush under his scrutiny. Then he smiled at her—a gentle smile that she had seen before when they had worked together at the hunting lodge.

When dinner was concluded, Derek announced that he and Jennifer had work to do and that they would be in the library.

"Derek, is that really necessary?" Elizabeth asked.

"Yes, Elizabeth. We leave for London tomorrow."

Derek leaned over and kissed Elizabeth lightly on the cheek. Then he stood and walked around to Robert and Ann. After saying good night to them, he led Jennifer out of the room. They walked down a hall and through double doors into a large room whose ceiling extended a full two stories high, its walls filled with books on all sides. Derek turned on the lights and motioned for Jennifer to sit on a sofa placed before the fireplace. He walked over to a desk and returned with the notes he had made at the hunting lodge.

"One of the puzzling aspects of your civilization is the predominance that megaliths and stone circles have in their ceremonies," Derek began.

"I don't understand," Jennifer replied.

"They used the megalithic monuments in their religious ceremonies. You said that those sites were sacred to them."

"Yes."

"Did they build them?" Derek asked.

Jennifer frowned. Did Cela's people build them?

"No," she replied. "They were built by the Ones Who Came Before."

"What does that mean?" Derek asked.

"The people who lived there before—their ancestors."

Derek sat back. "There are over nine hundred stone rings in the United Kingdom. They're in the shapes of circles, eclipses, ovals, and the like. The earliest ones form parts of chambered mounds that date back to the Neolithic periods, 4000 B.C. to 3000 B.C. Most of them, like Stonehenge and Avebury, were probably erected around 2000 B.C.—the end of the Neolithic age and the beginning of the Bronze Age. Yet, your civilization made molten bronze. That would place them, if they existed," Derek emphasized, "anywhere from 1200 B.C. to 600 B.C. If there are any remains that can be dated with carbon-14. . . ." Derek stopped, seeing the question on Jennifer's face. "Do you know anything about radiometric age-dating?"

"No, nothing, but I would like to. What is it?"

"In simple terms, it is a means of determining the age of an object that contains radiocarbon," he began. Jennifer frowned. "Radiocarbon, known as carbon-14, is a weakly radioactive form of carbon that is formed in the atmosphere. There, it combines with oxygen to form radioactive carbon dioxide—again, with very weak radioactivity—nothing harmful. This radioactive carbon dioxide is taken up by plants during photosynthesis. When the plant, or animal that ate the plant, or piece of grain, or pollen, or anything else that is carbon based, dies, the carbon-14 in it begins to decay. The older the object, the less carbon-14 left in it. We can measure the amount of carbon-14 in an object, compare it to a recently decayed sample, and using the known half-life of carbon-14, calculate the age of the artifact with astounding accuracy." He paused. "But without an artifact, I can't date your civilization any better than the estimation I gave you based on their use of molten bronze."

"There are no artifacts," Jennifer said.

"All right, say these people didn't build the monuments but have the tradition of using them. Many of the monuments have been changed through the years. The microscopic remains of cremated bodies found in Stonehenge, for example, date back to 2800 B.C., plus or minus two hundred fifty years. The stones themselves appear to date from different time periods, suggesting the monument had been changed or added to through the centuries. The earliest stones date from around 2800 B.C. and the more recent ones from around 1100 B.C.

"That's why I want you to go with me to Stonehenge and the other sites you've described. Based on what you've read, you could reconstruct the sites as they were presented in your documents. Then we could cross-reference your description with what we know already. And there's another reason for you to go. You've alluded to the fact that many of these monuments served as astronomical observatories. That, in itself, is not a new hypothesis. However, the problem we encounter is that the stones and patterns don't always line up to confirm their status as observatories. Some of the sites are ruined, or, in some cases, poorly restored. Many of them are below the surface."

"Below the surface?"

"Yes. Changes in the terrain and weather over thousands of years have resulted in soil deposition on top of remains, especially if they weren't tall when constructed or if they have fallen down through the centuries. We have techniques to uncover parts of the structure that are underground: ground penetrating radar, soil resistivity, magnetometry, laser detection, each of which has its usefulness, depending upon the terrain and other mediating structures. You knocked that equipment down at the lake site the second time we met," he added pointedly but with the hint of a smile. "But any attempt to ascertain the original alignments is too often guesswork at best. If you have information as to how the monuments originally looked, it would be invaluable—provided the information can be validated, of course," he added.

Jennifer hesitated to speak. She was *out of her element*, as they say. She had never heard of the archaeological techniques he mentioned. She knew nothing of prehistoric civilizations. "I see patterns, but I don't know where they are all located," Jennifer said softly.

"What?"

Jennifer blinked, alarmed. "Based on what I read in the documents, I can visualize the patterns of the stones, but I don't know where the monuments are located," she said quickly, uncomfortable lying, but accepting it as necessary.

"We'll start with the ones that we've located."

"All right," Jennifer said.

Derek smiled and then explained his plans for the next week. They would take several days driving to the London area. That way, they could stop at some of the prehistoric sites along the way. He was convinced that Avebury was another of the monuments that Jennifer had described, and it was not far from Stonehenge.

It was late by the time they had finished and left Thornhill. Derek insisted on driving Jennifer back to Nina's. He said that he would have someone return Jennifer's car to Nina's cottage tomorrow. As Derek was driving away from Thornhill, he glanced over at Jennifer.

"I apologize for Elizabeth's behavior this evening."

"She's in love with you," Jennifer said simply, surprised at her own feelings of jealousy.

"No, Elizabeth is a family friend. We've been friends since childhood. That's all there is to it."

Neither of them spoke the rest of the way to Nina's cottage. Derek's talk of Stonehenge and the other megalithic structures had stirred up images in Jennifer's mind—images from Cela's world. The images were very strong, pulling at her. When they arrived at Nina's, Derek walked Jennifer to the door.

"You were very quiet in the car," he commented as she reached for the door.

Jennifer turned to face him. She had known him for such a short time, and yet, she wanted him to remain here, standing near her, close enough to touch. She frowned slightly. How was it possible to feel such an attraction to someone? Such a pull? Such a need? It wasn't just a physical attraction, although that was there. Sexual feelings, definitely. But it was more. She liked his company—talking, laughing. She cocked her head in thought. Safe. Secure and safe was how she felt with him.

Derek frowned. "What is it?" he asked.

She could see the genuine concern in his eyes, soft, full of expression, searching her face. "The monuments," she said hesitantly. "They weren't all observatories. Most were built in specific patterns; the patterns identified the people, but, more importantly, the patterns identified places—similar to the writing on a road map. You look on the entire map, read the megalithic pattern, like the name of a town, and follow the course to your destination."

Derek watched Jennifer turn and walk inside the house, leaving him standing there to contemplate her strange words. A map? What was she talking about? He was tempted to knock on the door and ask for an explanation, but something stopped him: it was the look in her eyes as she spoke. In the end, he drove home with his questions unanswered. There would be plenty of time next week to ask for an explanation.

CHAPTER 7

Nina listened as Jennifer spoke on the phone. It was ten forty-five in the morning, and they were both sitting in Nina's kitchen. Jennifer had waited to place her calls after the banks in Scotland were open. The first call she had made had been to American Express. Then she had placed similar calls to MasterCard and Visa. She hung up the phone with a look of determination on her face.

"Well?" Nina said.

"He closed out my checking account. It's empty. I can't get cash advances from my credit cards because he has canceled them also." Jennifer removed a packet from her purse. "I have about two thousand dollars in traveler's checks left."

"That's about fourteen hundred pounds. Professor Rannoch is driving, so you need money for food and lodging. You should have plenty."

"I'm so mad at John right now, but I shouldn't be. It's his money. He can do whatever he wants with it. I know how to support myself," Jennifer said, "but this does put me in a difficult position. I haven't worked since I married John, and I can't just walk into the offices of the London Symphony or hang a sign up saying 'violin lessons.' All I have is John's two thousand dollars, and that may have to last me a while. Maybe going with Derek isn't the wisest thing to do right now," Jennifer said with doubt. "I should save that money."

"Going with him is the right thing to do, Jen. You can't walk away from this now."

"But two thousand dollars isn't going to last very long."

"If you need money, I'll give it to you. I want you to stay with me, McHugh, until this is settled."

Jennifer smiled tenderly at her friend. "We don't know how long that will take. I can't depend on you indefinitely."

"Why not? Listen, Jen, you are far more important to me than any amount of money. Don't you know that? Besides," Nina said with a wink, "I've got plenty of money—more than I will ever need. Now are you all packed?"

"Yes. I still can't believe I'm doing this," Jennifer said with a sigh. "I hardly know him, and we're going to be traveling together."

"Jen, despite the disagreement that you two apparently had, he seems kind. He's also willing to help you."

Jennifer didn't answer.

"There's something else, isn't there? I sensed it the day he came over here."

Jennifer frowned.

"There's something going on between you two."

"There's nothing between us."

Nina knitted her eyebrows together. "You're afraid of him," she said slowly. "Anyone who walked into the kitchen that day could have felt the sexual tension between you two. That's it, isn't it?"

"I don't know," Jennifer whispered as she wrapped her arms about herself. "He just has to come within a few inches of me, and I. . . ." Jennifer looked up. "I never felt this way with John. Never."

A look of understanding appeared on Nina's face. "I guess I'm not surprised. What about Derek?"

Jennifer took a deep breath. "The last night at his hunting lodge, he kissed me. I wanted him to make love to me—more than anything I've ever wanted in my life—a man I'd only known for four days. And it's not just the physical feelings that scare me. It's more than that. When I was at the hunting lodge and telling him about the visions, I felt . . . I felt safe with him."

"Safe?"

"I think he's a part of all this," Jennifer whispered.

Nina whistled under her breath. "I assume that by a part of all this, you mean what has been happening to you since you arrived? These visions?"

"Yes. I can't explain it."

Nina sighed audibly. "How much do you know about him?"

Jennifer shrugged. "Just that he's a professor and the son of the Earl of Thornhill. His father and his sister and her family seem like very nice people. I like them. He has a brother whom I haven't met, and he has a lover, his assistant. I also met a Lady Elizabeth at Thornhill. From what I could see, everyone—especially Lady Elizabeth— expects that Derek and she will marry one day."

"Maybe it isn't such a good idea for you to go," Nina said softly. "I don't want you to get hurt by all this."

Hearing the sound of a car outside of Nina's cottage, Jennifer stood. "I think it's a little late to change my mind now," she said.

* * *

John Bracken walked into the office of his attorney and sat down.

"What's so urgent, John?" Timothy Camp asked, sitting behind the desk in his office. "My secretary said it couldn't wait until Friday."

"It's Jennifer," John said directly.

"Jennifer?"

"She's been acting rather peculiar lately. I think she has it in her head to leave."

"Leave?" Despite his usual rule of maintaining a professional, calm detachment, Timothy Camp leaned forward, alert.

"Yes."

"Leave you? Are you talking about a separation, John, or a divorce?"

"I don't know. We haven't discussed it. She's been in Scotland for most of the past month."

"I see," Timothy Camp replied, his brow furrowed at the ramifications of a possible divorce.

"I want to know what the consequences would be to me if she asks for a divorce."

"I'm sorry, John. I hadn't realized that there was a problem between you and Jennifer."

"The consequences, Timothy," John said tersely.

"That depends on the grounds and what she asks for. Is there anything that would make the court particularly sympathetic to her?" he asked, hoping his worst thoughts wouldn't be confirmed by John.

John looked angrily across the desk at his attorney. "She suspects that I've had an affair. She doesn't know for certain."

"I see." Timothy cleared his throat. "Have you?" When John didn't answer, Timothy sighed loudly. "I need to know if I'm to assist you."

"Call girls. Professionals. Once a week," John said, gritting his teeth.

"And should I assume these prostitutes have particular skills that a court might consider outside the realm of conventional sexual activity?"

John glared at him, giving him the answer he was afraid of. Timothy Camp's law firm represented not just John, but John's father and a vast amount of wealth. John's father would be furious if John's behavior did anything to jeopardize that wealth, and, as unfair as it might be, Timothy would be held partially responsible. Timothy bit back the scathing retort that was in his mind, instead returning to professional objectivity.

"Surely you realize that if the court becomes aware of your sexual activities, Jennifer is likely to garner sympathy— the innocent wife, the deviant husband. You've been down this road before, John. Your ex-wife signed an NDA as part of the divorce settlement. She's not going to talk. Does anyone else know of your particular . . . tastes?"

"For Christ's sake, Timothy!" John exploded. "She heard a few of the board members' wives talking. I don't know the particulars. She asked me if I was having an affair. That's all!"

"All right," Timothy said. He sighed again. "We'll leave it at that for now. What about Jennifer?"

"An affair? Never."

"That could be a problem then."

"When we married, she had no money of her own. The assets we have are mine."

"I'm not certain the court would see it that way. All a good attorney would have to do is show how she supported you in the role of a good wife these past . . . how long?"

"Less than two years."

"Your social and business worlds blend. Jennifer fulfilled a role in that. This isn't California, John, so you don't have to worry about a fifty-fifty split, but her attorney could build a hell of a case if Jennifer is so inclined."

"What about the trust fund?"

Timothy sighed. Here was the issue. For a second, he thought about the possible conflict of interest that could result by representing both John and John's father, but he quickly dismissed it. He knew where his law firm's loyalty lay. "That's another matter. Jennifer can't touch that."

"I know that! What happens to it if we divorce?"

"There's nothing I can do about it. Your father is quite clear on that. Your divorce from your first wife cost the family millions, John. If you divorce again, you forfeit it all, and I can no longer represent you. I will represent your father and oversee the distribution of your portion of the trust: one half to your son and the other half to your sister."

John slammed his fist down on the desk, causing Timothy to jump.

"Is your father aware of the difficulties you and Jennifer are having?" Timothy asked when he had recovered.

"It's none of his damn business!"

Timothy waited a moment before speaking. "Just how severe is the trouble between you and Jennifer?"

John said nothing.

"Look, John, Jennifer seems like a reasonable person. My advice to you would be to see what you can do to change her mind. A reconciliation isn't totally out of the picture, is it? Has she seen an attorney?"

"What? No, we haven't even discussed it. She hasn't mentioned divorce."

"Then I suggest you see what you can do to reconcile with her." He paused. "And you might consider suspending your . . . other activity."

* * *

"The Celts arrived in Great Britain between 550 B.C. and 450 B.C.," Derek said as he and Jennifer drove south, leaving Edinburgh behind them. "We do know that the Druids were a privileged class among the Celts. They were healers, teachers, musicians, judges, and, most importantly, priests. When the Romans invaded England, starting around 300 B.C., Caesar wrote extensively about them. He gives accounts of their worship of the gods as well as their human sacrifices. When the Romans finally conquered England in 43 A.D., one of the first things they did was to outlaw the Druid class."

"And there are some similarities between the Druids and the civilization I described to you?" Jennifer asked.

Jennifer was sorting through the papers on her lap as Derek drove. She had been nervous when he had first picked her up at Nina's cottage, but Derek's relaxed manner soon put her at ease.

"Quite a few, actually," Derek answered. "The early Greek scholars also wrote about the Druids. They give us an even earlier account than Caesar. The method of human sacrifice is probably one of the most obvious. Human sacrifice was practiced by many ancient civilizations, but the Druids are the only ones we know of who put their victims in wicker baskets or cages and then burned them alive. You described a similar practice from your mystery civilization. Perhaps even more provocative is the triple sacrifice practice."

Jennifer looked over at Derek, a question on her face.

"You said they sacrificed to the air, fire, and water. The Druids did the same thing, and," he said with emphasis, "they also divined by the convulsions of their victims who had been impaled or shot with arrows. You referred to that practice several times. They sacrificed to their gods, and they believed in reincarnation."

"Reincarnation," Jennifer said with a frown. Cela's people believed that life continued after death. That was why they had no fear of death. Warriors fought with little regard for their own lives or concern for those they killed. The Wise Ones taught the people this.

"What about the stars?" Jennifer asked.

"The stars? All we know is that they studied the stars extensively. They tracked the movements of the constellations and predicted the eclipses."

"Just like Cela's people," Jennifer muttered to herself. She studied Derek's notes before her. "What is 'deas-iul?' "

"Oh," Derek smiled. "That may be reaching a bit. It is a ceremony still practiced in The Highlands of Scotland today. It means 'sun-wise.' A pregnant woman will walk three times around the chapel for an easy delivery. The people also dance from the right to the center to the left, following the pattern of the sun. They circle three times, beginning in the East. It's in a lot of the ancient Scottish and Irish celebrations.

"When the Romans outlawed the Druids in England," Derek continued, "many of the Druids escaped to the north into Scotland and Ireland. The number three and circling in the direction of the sun permeates the early rituals of the Church as well. Those practices were probably incorporated into early Christian ceremonies around 400 to 500 A.D. because the people had practiced the ritual in their pagan ceremonies prior to Christianity. It made the transition to Christianity easier for the people."

Jennifer leaned back against the seat of the car, closing her eyes. They had been driving for several hours. Derek had proved to be a wealth of information, and Jennifer was having difficulty absorbing it all.

"But you don't believe that the people I read about were Druids," she said with her eyes still closed.

"No. The dates are wrong. The dress, the crude huts, the earth mounds that the people lived on, and the early formation of bronze points to a civilization that lived somewhere around 900 B.C. As far as we can tell, the Druids came several hundred years later."

"The stone circles and other megaliths?"

"We believe the Druids used some of them, but they certainly didn't build them. As I told you, those predate the Druids by several thousand years in some cases. They also predate your civilization. Most of the megalithic circles and mounds were built during the Stone Age."

"The people I read about didn't build them; the Ones Who Came Before did. The People of the Sky told them what patterns to use."

Derek nodded and said nothing. So far, Jennifer had avoided asking a question that had been on her mind since they first began discussing Derek's notes. She took a breath and opened her eyes.

"What about the People of the Sky?"

Derek shrugged his shoulders. "The Druids made no references to them. We know that the Druids did worship flight, though. It was very important to them. They studied the flight of birds and kept ravens and wrens. They were obsessed with the ability to fly. But there are no references to the belief in people who came out of the sky."

As Derek drove, he glanced at Jennifer. "That distresses you. Why?" he asked.

Jennifer was uncomfortable with Derek's ability to read her thoughts. How could she explain something to him that she didn't understand herself? The belief in people who came out of the sky and taught the Wise Ones was the essential foundation of Cela's civilization, and Cela was descended from the People of the Sky.

"There are other ancient civilizations that make references to beings who come from the sky," Derek said.

Jennifer looked at Derek with surprise. He smiled.

"That makes you happy, Miss McHugh?" he teased gently.

Jennifer smiled, self-consciously.

"The references are not as specific as yours are," he cautioned. "The Aztec Indians of Mexico believed in winged gods or people who came down from the sun. They carved their images into stone. In fact, it is a prevalent theme of that civilization. Perhaps even more compelling are the Nasca lines in a desert off the Peruvian Coast. We've had difficulty dating them, but they probably were constructed around a time similar to the construction of Britain's megaliths. Outside of Nasca, there are long, straight lines that intersect. They are located in the middle of the desert, and they form a complex pattern. Some of them have been shown to accurately predict the solstices and other astronomical events. Even more interesting is the shape of a large bird next to the lines. The total bird can only be seen from the sky. It is thought that this ancient civilization also believed in beings of some kind coming from the sky, for carved into a nearby mountain is a warning to the people to keep out of the way of those coming down out of the sky."

Jennifer was very still as a strange feeling came over her. Cela knew those patterns! She may not consciously recognize them yet, but Jennifer was sure they were in Cela's memories, and it would not be long before Cela realized them. Cela was beginning to have images of other lands and other symbols. Recently, she had seen a vast body of water that was alternately pulled and repelled by the forces of the moon. She had envisioned herself moving over the top of that water and coming upon land again—land dotted with stone symbols that reached to the sky, just as the People of the Sky had instructed. These images and memories were Cela's gift, a gift from a godlike young man of the People of the Sky to a young virgin named Mora, Cela's great-grandmother.

"Jennifer? Jenny, are you all right?" Derek asked with concern.

Jennifer shook her head to clear it.

Derek frowned slightly and then reached over with one hand and took the papers from her lap. "I think we've had enough for a while." He shuffled the papers into a pile between them. "We've been at this for almost three hours. You must be getting hungry."

Jennifer smiled slightly. "A little," she said.

"Good. No more discussion of the Druids or your civilization. In another half hour, we'll be entering one of the most beautiful areas in England. It's the land of William Wordsworth and Beatrix Potter. I suggest we stop at a local pub, have lunch, and then take a long walk. A lot of tourists come to the Lake District, but I'm sure we can avoid them," he said with a smile. "I know this area well."

Jennifer felt herself slowly relax as she listened to Derek's voice. They drove past the remains of Hadrian's Wall, and Derek told her of the fortification that stretched over seventy-three miles from sea to sea. It had been built by the Roman Emperor Hadrian to keep the wild tribes of the north out of Roman England. As he described the fierce tribes of the north, Jennifer smiled. "Your ancestors, no doubt," she teased.

"Without a doubt!" he had replied with a smile.

Soon Jennifer found herself overtaken with the beauty of the area. There were mountains here, like in Scotland, but not as fierce looking. These were mostly green, their peaks separated by valleys—valleys of green dotted with lakes, some large and some small, the lakes separated by green grass or thick forests. Derek was following a small, winding road over a gentle foothill. She could see buildings with docks on the water's edge, the blue-brown water sprinkled with boats.

Derek glanced at her. "Too many tourists," he said. "Can't blame them. It's a very nice area."

A half hour later, he drove into a small village and stopped the car before a row of buildings. The cobblestone street—narrow and flanked by an odd mixture of two-story, red brick buildings, their bricks slanted up and down, and smaller, wooden frame buildings, their slats slightly more horizontal than the bricks—was quiet. As Derek opened the door for her, she glanced to the right and then to the left, grateful that another car had not come along, for there wouldn't have been room for two cars on the tiny road, one with a door open.

"Come," he said as he reached for her arm. He guided her into one of the wooden buildings and into a small pub containing only four tables. It was early afternoon, and only a few men remained at the bar. Derek greeted them and then motioned for Jennifer to sit down at the nearest table. She watched as he walked over to the bar and began talking with the man behind the bar, both of them leaning forward with their elbows on the bar, Derek asking questions and the man nodding his head. Then the man laughed at something Derek said and filled two mugs, handing them to Derek.

"I hope you don't mind, but I took the liberty of

ordering lunch for us," Derek said as he sat across from her and handed her one of the mugs. There's not much of a choice in a small place like this. It's a matter of finding out what they have on hand. It will be good, I promise you," he said with a smile. "How's the ale?" he asked as he motioned to Jennifer's glass.

She raised the heavy glass to her lips and took a sip of the strong, dark liquid. Her eyes widened as she swallowed. "It's good," she said politely.

Derek smiled. "It's not like your American beer. Drink it slowly. It may take some getting used to," he added with humor.

She had only drunk half of her glass when the man behind the bar called out to Derek. Derek stood. "Shall we go?" he asked Jennifer.

Jennifer was confused. "I thought we were going to have lunch," she said as she stood up.

"We are," Derek replied. "This time of year, warm, sunny days in England are rare and are to be enjoyed. Would you care to join me for a picnic, Miss McHugh?" he asked with mock formality.

Derek paid the owner of the pub and then they left, each carrying packages wrapped in paper.

"What all did you order?" Jennifer asked as they got into the car. "It looks like there's enough food for days." She started to unwrap one of the packages.

"It's a surprise," Derek said as he reached for the package. "You must wait."

"I'm starving," Jennifer replied.

"Patience, Miss McHugh. Only a few more minutes. It will be worth it."

He drove out of the village, following a narrow road that climbed over the gentle hills. At last, he pulled the car off the road.

"We have to walk a bit," he said as he reached for the packages of food and handed some to Jennifer. As she stepped out of the car, she paused.

"It's beautiful here," she said.

Derek smiled. "Just wait."

They started to walk across a pasture toward a wooded area. The grass was a rich, soft green, the kind that was so often associated with English lawns. As they reached the woods, Derek directed her through the trees. When they emerged a few minutes later, Jennifer stopped abruptly. They were on top of a hill, its grass lush. Below was a small lake with water so clear, it reflected the few white clouds that were in the blue sky above. Occasionally, small yellow wildflowers dotted the green carpet. The entire area was enclosed by the woods that they had just walked through.

Derek smiled when he saw the delight on Jennifer's face. "This way," he said. "We'll find a spot to eat, and then we can walk around the lake later."

They descended the hill about halfway and then stopped. The grass was amazingly soft as Jennifer sat down on the ground. Derek sat next to her and began to unwrap the packages of food. There were thin slices of roast beef, cheese, and a loaf of dark bread, as well as an assortment of delicious-looking tarts accompanied by homemade jams and rum butter. Finally, Derek removed a large carafe of dark ale and two glasses.

For the next hour, they relaxed and talked as they ate the lunch prepared by the small village pub. Derek was right: the food was delicious. At one point, as Derek was telling her of the area and its more famous inhabitants, he asked her if she had read much of William Wordsworth or Samuel Taylor Coleridge, both of whom had made their homes in this area.

Jennifer laughed. "I might have; I don't recall. I should warn you, professor, I was a mediocre student at best. The only subject I was good at was music. My mother was a musician and the music teacher in my school."

"Was?"

"Yes, she died last year."

"I'm sorry, Jenny," Derek replied softly. "And your

father?"

"He doesn't know I exist. He was a visiting artist at Juilliard, where my mom was a student. He and my mom dated a few weeks. She never told him about me."

"Do you have any other family?" he asked kindly.

They had finished eating and both were lying back on the grass, looking up at the sky as they spoke.

"I was an only child," she said. "Mom never married. She didn't even date. She focused her life on me and music. But you have a younger brother, right?" she asked, hoping to direct the conversation away from herself. Thinking about her mother was still difficult, and her father? He was an egomaniac who was married with a family when he dated her mother—something he had neglected to tell her mother.

"Is your brother an archaeologist, too?" Jennifer asked.

"No," Derek laughed. "Edward is a lawyer."

"Tell me about him," Jennifer encouraged.

"Edward works for the government of Scotland. International law and finance are his specialties. He champions the cause of Scotland whenever he can." Derek went on to explain the hardships that the people of Scotland endured during the depression and World War II. "There was a mass exodus of Scots leaving their country because they couldn't find work," he explained. "The economy was in shambles. Scotland was—and still is—in an unusual predicament. We are part of Great Britain and, for the most part, subject to the greater power of England. That has, over the centuries, resulted in economic growth for England at Scotland's expense. Edward believes that Scotland can still remain a part of Great Britain but negotiate more favorable economic agreements. Right now, he's overseeing Scotland's interests in the off-shore drilling in the North Sea and dividing his time between Edinburgh and London. He lives at Thornhill, however.

"When are you returning to the States?" Derek asked, changing the subject.

Jennifer frowned as she looked up at the sky. "I don't know. I had intended to visit Nina only a few weeks when all this started—when I found the documents," she hastily added.

Derek turned toward Jennifer and propped himself up on one elbow. "What's your interest in the documents, Jenny?" he asked softly. Despite his quiet tone, there was intensity in his voice. "Most people would have turned them over to a university or museum. They wouldn't have gotten personally involved."

"I wanted to be certain that they were authentic before I did that."

"But there's no way to determine authenticity unless you allow the documents to be examined."

"I told you I can't do that," Jennifer said, turning to face Derek.

Derek stared at her. "Eventually, you'll have to if you want the truth. It's vital, Jenny. Even if just a portion of what you read is true, do you realize the implications?"

Jennifer was silent.

"You don't have to give them to me. I could give you a list of reputable scholars in Great Britain, Europe, or even the United States, if you prefer, or you could walk right into any major museum in the world. However, if the documents were found on British soil, there might be some legal battles if you turn them over to another country."

When Jennifer didn't respond, Derek stood up and reached his hand down to her. "Come on, it's getting late. Let's go for a walk. We can come back for this," he said, indicating the remains of their lunch.

For the next hour, they walked around the lake. It was secluded, surrounded by hills and distant mountains. Derek explained that this lake had not yet been discovered by tourists, which was why there were no docks, pubs, or boats. They watched as ducks flew down to the lake and then left. Occasionally, they would hear a rustle from the bushes under the trees as some animal scurried away at their intrusion. Jennifer felt relaxed and carefree as they laughed and talked.

"This part of England, the northwest part," Derek said, "was not always so peaceful." He gestured to the calm water, lush, green grass, and plentiful trees that created an idyllic setting. "Beginning with the Roman occupation and all through the Middle Ages, it was a bloody battleground. Celtic tribes battled with the Romans. Medieval kings and rulers fought for control of the area for hundreds of years. Castles and monasteries were built and destroyed over and over." He smiled at her. "It's hard to imagine now."

Jennifer paused and looked out over the peaceful water. "It's so beautiful. I can't imagine why anyone would ever want to leave here, but you have Thornhill," she added. "Nothing compares to that," she said as they resumed walking.

"And there aren't beautiful places in Chicago?" he teased.

"The Midwest is similar to this," she said as she gazed around, "but it's not the same. There's a sense, a feeling here—especially in Scotland." Jennifer looked up at Derek. He was smiling. "You're making fun of me," she accused.

A deep, rich laugh erupted from his throat. "Never, milady," he said as he bowed. "I agree completely."

"Sure you do," Jennifer said with a laugh as they walked on. A few minutes later, Jennifer spoke. "Do you have what you want out of life, Derek? You have a wonderful family, a successful career. Is there anything else that you want?"

"Hmmm," Derek said as they walked. "Fate has been kind to me. My work is my passion, and, as you said, my family is wonderful. And we agree," he said with a wink, "I live in the most beautiful place on earth. I don't think there's much more that I could ask for." They walked on in silence a few minutes, then he turned to her. "What about you?"

Jennifer looked up at him. "If I tell you the truth, you won't think me foolish?"

"I asked you, didn't I?"

Jennifer looked ahead. "I want a sense of belonging somewhere. I don't know if I can explain it."

Derek seemed to consider what she had said. "I think I know what you mean," he said and then he smiled. "And are a husband and children in your plans, too?"

"Having a happy marriage and children are very important to me, but that requires the mutual desire of two people, doesn't it?"

"Interesting reply," Derek commented.

"And what of you? Is Lady Elizabeth to be the next Lady Rannoch, or is Miss Bensen in line for that title?" Jennifer asked, trying to keep the tone of her voice casual.

Derek laughed. "No, Elizabeth is just a family friend, and Linda is not interested in getting tied down to just one man. She never stays in any place for more than a year at best. My guess is I'll find her resignation on my desk when I return to the university."

"But aren't you supposed to produce an heir or something like that?"

Again, Derek laughed. "Thornhill and its title will pass to me upon my father's death. Should I die without a son, it would then pass to Edward. Should he neither marry nor produce an heir by the time of his death, then it would go to Ann's oldest son."

They returned to the site of their picnic and gathered their things.

"This was lovely," Jennifer commented as they prepared to return to the car. "I don't know when I've spent a nicer afternoon. I mean that. Thank you."

"I'm glad you enjoyed it," Derek said as he smiled. "Since you agreed to come with me, the least I can do is make it a pleasant trip for you. And you have surprised me, Miss McHugh. You have turned out not to be the person I thought you were when we first met, or the second time, either."

"Oh," Jennifer said, "the vomiting." She knew she

should feel mortified. She had vomited on him—twice! But instead, she felt comfortable with this man. She felt happy. And *safe.*

"Yes, well, that, in itself, is difficult to top," Derek said, "but you also damaged some very expensive equipment and destroyed my measurements."

"What about you?" Jennifer countered. "You frightened me. You chased me down the hill and grabbed me."

"I did, didn't I?" Derek said, a twinkle in his eye, as they began to walk again. "But then I rescued you from the rain and gave you shelter at the hunting lodge."

Derek's good nature was infectious, and Jennifer couldn't help but laugh. "Do you know this area well?" she asked, changing the subject.

"Yes. I've done a lot of work here. Cumbria has one of the greatest concentrations of prehistoric megaliths, stone circles, henges, and mounds in England."

Jennifer stopped suddenly. "Are there any near here?"

"Of course. The entire Lake District is not more than thirteen by nine kilometers in area. Cumbria occupies just a part of the Lake District. Would you like to see some of them?"

Did she? A feeling of fear passed over Jennifer. What if she experienced one of the episodes in front of Derek? Did she really want to risk that happening?

"We could actually stay here tonight and drive to Stonehenge tomorrow, if you would like," Derek continued. "There's a manor house not far from here where I've stayed. They maintain a few rooms for guests. I'm certain they can accommodate us."

Jennifer was desperately trying to decide what to do. Would seeing these sites be any different from looking at Stonehenge tomorrow? She knew the risk she was taking when she had agreed to come with Derek.

Despite the fact that they were walking and Jennifer had kept her face averted, Derek glanced at Jennifer several times, as though he knew that she was troubled by something. "Why don't we drive over to the manor and secure rooms for the night?" he said. "Then we can visit some of the megaliths before dark. You said there were others in the documents you read. Who knows? Maybe one of these will be among them."

Jennifer did not have to ponder Derek's statement for long. She had no clear picture in her mind; rather, it was a feeling she had. She was certain that Cela knew the megaliths they were about to visit.

* * *

"Margaret," John said as his secretary entered his office, "I want a flight to London. I can leave any time after two o'clock today. And check on connecting flights to Aberdeen, Scotland."

"Of course, Dr. Bracken, and shall I cancel your appointments scheduled for tomorrow?"

"Better cancel them for the rest of the week," John said with irritation. "I'll let you know my plans once I meet with Jennifer."

* * *

Derek pulled the car off the road. As he turned off the engine, he squinted up at the sky. "It's too bad it's clouding over. The stones at Castlerigg make some interesting patterns when the sun hits them. But even without the sun, the view is fantastic," he said as he smiled.

Jennifer took a deep breath and stepped out of the car. She could hear her heart pounding in her chest. She hastily wiped her palms, clammy from her nervousness, on her pants as Derek came around the car and stopped before her. He knitted his eyebrows together and cocked his head as he looked at her as though he sensed her discomfort. Then he smiled and gently took her hand in his.

"It's this way," he indicated as they began to walk. "A bit of a climb, but well worth it," he said.

It felt good—her hand in his as they walked together. There were areas where the path narrowed and he would step in front of her, still holding her hand. Several times, he put his arm around her waist to help her climb over boulders. All the while, he talked, his voice soothing.

"Probably one of the earliest studies conducted on this area was in the mid-seventies," he said as they walked. "A researcher named Glover photographed the midsummer sun setting over the stones. The tallest stone casts a shadow—a black line that extends across the hills for more than a mile. Archaeologists have tried to link the shadows to the equinoxes and seasons, although not successfully."

The first sight that greeted Jennifer when they reached their destination was the view of the mountains in the distance. From where she was standing, she could see across several valleys. It was magnificent. Then her eyes were pulled to the stones standing alone in the grass before her. Derek had begun to speak again and stepped ahead of her. He was pointing to the stones as he spoke, his back to her. As Jennifer's eyes riveted from stone to stone, she frowned. Some were missing! That was when she felt her stomach cramp and the feeling of nausea assail her. She clutched her midsection. *Not now,* Jennifer whispered silently. *Not here. Please. Later. I'll be ready later. Please!*

To her astonishment, the violent contraction diminished, leaving only the faint taste of bile in her mouth. She looked at the stones. She had seen them! It had occurred in only a fraction of a second, but she had seen them as they looked in Cela's time.

Derek turned just as Jennifer took a step forward. He

frowned. "Jenny? Are you all right?" he asked with concern.

She looked up at him and swallowed quickly. "I felt dizzy for a second." She looked back across the expanse of the hills. "Heights sometimes bother me," she said. They didn't, of course, but it was all she could think of to say. She smiled. "I'm fine now."

Jennifer walked over to where Derek was standing. Hesitantly, she reached out and touched the nearest stone. It was short, scarcely reaching her waist. As her hand rested upon the top of it, she could feel its force. She knew this place; Cela knew this place.

"This stone has been moved," she said contemplatively.

Surprise registered on Derek's face. "What do you mean?" he asked intently.

"It's been moved. It's out of alignment." She glanced across the ring. "And there are stones missing: there and over there," she said as she pointed. She frowned as she surveyed the circle before her. "These do not predict the equinoxes. There are others for that. These indicate directions. They're high up on this hill so there is no obstruction. No matter the season or time of day, the shadows created by the sun as it moves across the sky indicate direction. At a distance, the pattern created by a few stones, while useful, could be missed. The pattern of a shadow, amid the stone formations and cast for a long distance, however, would not be missed."

Jennifer was so absorbed in seeing the stones from Cela's perspective that she was unprepared for Derek's sudden grip on her arm. She was startled as Derek turned her toward him. His eyes seemed to pierce through her. "Directions for whom, Jenny?"

She began to tremble. Cela knew. Jennifer swallowed. She knew also, although she didn't know if she believed it herself.

"Jenny?"

"Let go of my arm."

Derek released her. "No one could see the shadows you

speak of unless they were right here among the stones. You said it yourself—the circle is on top of this mountain. It could not be seen below, nor could it be seen across the valleys," he said as he indicated the mountains in the distance. "A traveler would be unable to see the stones or the shadows, even if the stones did, at one time, indicate directions. How could it have been of any practical use situated up here?" he asked.

"I'm going back to the car," Jennifer said as she turned.

"Wait!"

"No," Jennifer said, shaking. "You wanted me to tell you if Stonehenge was different. Well, I just told you this is not as it once was. That's what you wanted, wasn't it?"

Jennifer turned and started running back down the hill. She knew she had done it again: she had overreacted and had spoken in anger to cover the emotional upheaval she was feeling. Each time this happened, she lashed out at Derek, as though it were his fault. She could hear Derek curse loudly behind her, and then he caught up with her.

"Slow down," he said as he reached for her arm, "you're going to fall." He was beside her and took her hand firmly in his. He didn't speak as they descended together, but she could feel the tension in his body.

When they reached the car, he opened the door for her. After walking around the car and sliding in behind the steering wheel, he swore again.

"Castlerigg was not one of the sites you previously described to me," he said as he started the engine. "How do you know about this site, Jenny?" When Jennifer didn't answer, Derek turned toward her. "You didn't tell me everything, did you?" he questioned. Jennifer stiffened. "There are more documents, aren't there? You've read more."

Inwardly, Jennifer breathed a sigh of relief. He was angry because he thought she had withheld some information from him. He assumed she had lied to him.

"Were you going to tell me about them?" Derek asked.

"It's not what you think. There's not a lot more to tell," Jennifer said. "I didn't even realize I knew that place until I saw it. I told you before that I read about several places, but I don't know where they're located. I just remember what they looked like during Cela's . . . a long time ago," she finished lamely.

"Really? I'd say you did more than just tell me about stones back there. You just described something that no other archaeologist knows. And you still refuse to show me the documents? Damn it!"

Jennifer didn't answer. She could feel Derek's anger; she didn't need to see how tightly he gripped the steering wheel, the tension in his neck, the pulsing on his temple. Neither of them spoke on the drive to the manor house.

When they arrived, Jennifer went straight to her room. Derek stopped briefly to tell Mrs. Levens, the owner, that he and Jennifer would eat dinner in their separate rooms tonight. He declined tea and went to his room. He closed the door behind him and began to pace. Jennifer was lying to him—of that he was certain. But why? What was she hiding? Why hadn't she told him of the other documents? And damn it all! Why wouldn't she show them to him? She had come to him and asked for his help. He had aided her as best he could with the information she had given him. She had been eager to learn all that he could tell her. He had also sensed that there was something about her documents that was deeply unsettling to her. Had she come upon them illegally? Why else would she refuse to show them to him?

Jennifer was an enigma. Her smile was honest, not contrived for its effect on others. She had a stubborn streak in her; Derek had witnessed that. She possessed a gentle strength, too, the kind you could depend on. He suspected that she had a passionate nature, also. Still, something was wrong. She was very troubled, and for some reason that he could not explain, he felt the need to help her, to protect her. But protect her from what? Instinct told him it had to do with the mysterious documents or the manner in which she had obtained them.

Derek stopped pacing and sat down on the bed. His father liked Jennifer. It seemed to Derek that his father had not spent that much time with her to have formed such a staunch opinion, but he had. His father had said that Jenny was special, "a very perceptive young woman," and that she had "good blood running through her." Derek had laughed at his father, although he had to admit that his father was usually a good judge of character. Derek frowned. He liked her, too, and he liked being with her.

Dinner was served early that evening. He sat down before a small table in his room where his dinner had been placed. While he ate, he reached for some papers on his bed. For the past hour, he had been making some sketches. He was trying to envision the Castlerigg Stone Circle as Jennifer had described it. Then he estimated the positions of the shadows that the sun would make as it made its way across the sky. Derek was not an astronomer; his study of prehistoric sites, however, had necessitated a basic understanding of the science. He frowned as he studied the angles he had drawn on the papers. He needed satellite images of the stones.

He wanted to talk to Jenny, but not just about Castlerigg. He also wanted to know if she was all right. Something kept nagging at the back of his mind, but he couldn't quite bring it into focus. He wasn't worried, though. This often happened to him when he was working on a new archaeological project, sifting through seemingly meaningless pieces of information. Eventually, the missing pieces would become clear to him; they always did.

Jennifer stared at the food before her. She had no appetite. Derek was angry; she knew that. What was she to do? It was not going to be possible for her to continue to

Stonehenge with him. His questions about her documents were becoming too insistent. She would have to arrange transportation back to Scotland.

She walked to the window. The sky had been a mix of clouds and sun today, but now, the sun could be seen on the horizon, setting in silver and pink colors. Below the window stretched the formal gardens of Cowden Hall, still visible in the fading light of the day.

The house had been built in the eighteenth century by a noble family. The descendants of the family still owned the hall, but the inheritance taxes of England had forced the elderly woman who owned it to open up several of the rooms for guests. Mrs. Levens was a warm, gentle woman who made her guests feel like they were all special. They didn't mind spending the exorbitant rates she charged, for she treated them like royalty.

Cowden Hall was famous for its garden. As Jennifer looked down upon it, she could see the pattern of the maze that the neatly trimmed hedge made. There were stone paths that weaved among the brightly colored flowers. Benches were placed under the trees throughout the garden. Everything was neat and orderly. As Jennifer was staring at the patterns of the garden below her, the garden was suddenly replaced by other patterns, all created by the positions of huge stones. She shook her head, and the garden reappeared.

"All right," she whispered softly. "I'm ready now."

She reached for a sweater laying on the top of her unpacked suitcase. She left her room, closing the door quietly behind her. Her footsteps were light as she descended the massive oak staircase and made her way out the back door of the manor house into the gardens. She hesitated only a second when she felt the first wave of nausea hit her. Swallowing, she walked quickly around one of the paths, following it to an opening where yellow-and-red flowers shone in the sunset. She barely made it to the bench when she swayed from the dizziness. The next contraction of her stomach was violent as the garden faded from her consciousness.

✳ ✳ ✳

827 B.C.

"Cela, where are you going?" the older priestess asked.

Cela turned to Lodi. She had spent the afternoon in Lodi's hut, receiving her final instructions before her initiation at the fertility ceremony the following night.

"Forgive me, Lodi, but I must be alone," Cela said.

"You are still nervous, Child?" the Priestess Lodi asked.

"I will do what is expected of me."

"Expected? Child, this is a great honor."

"I know that, but it is one that I would gladly give to another."

"I don't understand."

"I fear my cousin, Luc."

"He is but a man. I trained him myself in the arts of pleasure. You understand the ways of men. What is there to fear?"

"Forgive me, Lodi, but I see more than you do." Cela turned to leave.

"Do not go far. The winter has left the wolves hungry. Many of them have not retreated to the north yet. It is not safe."

"I will take a guard with me," Cela said.

Cela walked out of Lodi's hut and followed a path to the edge of the huts of the Wise Ones. Several guards sat around, talking among themselves. Cela stopped before them and they all immediately stood, awaiting her command.

"Warrior," she said, sighting Dagga standing among them. "Accompany me."

Cela turned and began to walk, knowing that Dagga would fall in behind her. She followed a path leading away from the compound of huts. She walked in silence, her hood obscuring most of her face. She walked from the highest hill of the Wise Ones' lodgings down and up the three ramparts until she reached the lowest ground level. She exited through the tall, wooden fence and its gate and started walking across the field, its grasses high.

Dagga immediately positioned himself to her side and slightly ahead of her. His eyes scanned the surroundings as they walked on in silence until the settlement was no longer visible behind them. They reached an area of rolling hills and lakes and began to climb upward. Dagga turned to see if Cela required assistance carrying the large hide that she had brought with her. She avoided his gaze and continued to climb.

When they reached the top, Cela found a place where the grass was soft and short. The area was heavily forested, but the site she selected was in a clearing, and she could see for great distances. The ground, however, was damp, and she was grateful for the hide she had brought with her. The large hide would keep her dry and warm should the evening temperatures become colder. Cela sat down on the hide, positioning herself so that she was facing west. From this vantage, she could watch the sun go down behind the hills. Her view of the sky would not be obstructed.

Dagga did not sit immediately but walked around, ever on alert. After assuring himself that there were no immediate threats and that an enemy, be it human or animal, could be easily detected in its approach, he returned to where Cela sat.

"May I sit, Priestess?" he asked. Dagga would never have asked the other priestesses or priests for permission to sit. He would have stood until they spoke to him.

"Of course," Cela said gently. Then she returned her

gaze to the west, watching as the sun moved toward the distant hilltop.

Dagga had been carrying his bronze shield and sword. A dagger was secured at his waist. He wore laced boots made of animal skins and a leather garment that wrapped around his waist, overlapping in the front and ending above his knees. This gave him great freedom in movement, necessary for a warrior. He also wore a vest made of animal skins, which he removed before sitting down.

As Cela sat, staring at the horizon, Dagga periodically scanned the area for potential danger. As the hours went by, he began to relax. He shifted his position frequently and occasionally stood to restore the blood flow to his lower limbs. He glanced at Cela, who seemed immobilized. She did not even appear to be aware of his existence. He had seen others of the Wise Ones behave similarly. He did not understand all of their ways, but he had been told that the Wise Ones were able to speak to the gods at such times, and that great wisdom was often given to them at these moments.

Dagga watched now as the sun set and the distant sky glowed a brilliant orange. Cela's face seemed transfixed as she stared at the sky. Dagga did not know how long Cela would remain, but he knew that with the night air, the dampness would increase. They would need a fire.

It took Dagga a while to find dry twigs and logs that would burn without smoke. He didn't want to attract any human enemy with a noticeable fire. He managed to keep Cela in his sight while he gathered the wood and assembled it near her. Even when he struck the flint stones together to provide the spark he needed, Cela did not alter her position or her gaze.

The sun had fully set an hour before Dagga saw movement. He watched as Cela lowered her head to her chest. He thought he detected a slight trembling of her shoulders underneath her robe. He waited.

"Dagga," she finally said. Her voice was soft and he

moved closer.

"Priestess?"

"Please sit," she said, keeping her face down. She indicated a place next to her on the soft hide.

She was sitting with her feet tucked beneath her. Dagga cautiously moved next to her, kneeling beside her.

"I have something to ask of you," she began, her face hidden beneath the hood of her robe. "Please understand that this is not a command. What I ask of you is yours to accept or refuse. If you refuse, we will speak no more of it. It will be as though the words were never spoken. Do you understand?"

"These are strange words coming from a priestess, but yes, I understand."

Dagga waited in silence for Cela to continue.

"Tomorrow, I am to be presented at the fertility rites. This is my duty, and I will do so, but if it is possible, I would like to go to that ceremony not as a virgin."

Dagga stared at Cela. What was she saying?

"I do not want my first time with a man to be with Luc. I will endure him, as I must, but help me," she whispered softly, her voice strained. "I do not want him to be the one to remove my virginity. And I will not bear his child," she said with force.

Dagga was shocked. Surely he misunderstood Cela's words. "Priestess, what is it that you are asking of me?"

Cela smiled briefly as her lip trembled. "I have been instructed in the act, but I do not know what precedes it. What do men and women say to each other? What did the woman with the dark hair say to you the day I saw you both together? What did you say to her? I am not like her. Perhaps you do not even find me," Cela searched for the word, "desirable."

"I do not believe the words I am hearing," Dagga exclaimed, jumping up.

"I'm sorry," Cela said suddenly. "I understand that men are attracted to different traits in a woman. You do not find me pleasing. As I said, we will speak no more of this. We will return immediately." Cela's voice choked as she spoke, and Dagga knew that she was crying. She started to rise, but he reached out to her, positioning himself in front of her. He knelt before her, his hand resting on her shoulder. Gently, he pressed her back down into her sitting position. She lowered her head so he could not see her face.

"Priestess," he said softly, "what you ask is not possible."

"I understand. You need not say more."

Dagga placed his fingertips under Cela's chin and gently raised her head. She looked at him, her eyes moist from tears running down her face. He slowly pushed the hood of her robe off her head.

"What you ask is not possible because you are not an ordinary woman. Were you so . . . ." He smiled. "You have hair of fire, Priestess," he said as his hand moved down her long, red curls, the light of the nearby flames reflecting off Cela's hair. "It sets a man's blood on fire." His hand moved to her face. "Your face would haunt a man's dreams, for rarely is skin so fair seen or lips so. . . ." Dagga stopped himself as he felt his own manhood stir. "Were you a common woman, Priestess, men would fight to the death for the prize of what you have just offered."

"And you, Dagga?" Cela whispered.

"I would have been the victor, Priestess, and would have taken you for my own."

She hesitantly placed her hand on his chest. "Then, please, do this for me now."

"How can you ask such a thing? You must be a virgin at the ceremony. The priest, Luc, is no fool. What will happen when he discovers that you have already been with a man?"

"He will not know."

Dagga shook his head. "Priestess," he said patiently, as though instructing a child, "he will know. There is evidence. A man can tell."

"No. He will not suspect because what I dare do is

unthinkable to him and to all the others. And," she paused, "there are ways known to some of the priestesses that are not known to men, even the priests. The expected evidence of my virginity will be there."

Dagga frowned.

"Luc will hurt me; I know that," Cela said. "But the pain will pass." She paused, her voice soft. "I would not wish to leave this life with my only experience with a man having been Luc. That is what I see lying ahead of me." She looked up at Dagga. "I want to feel what I felt when I watched you with that woman. I wanted to be her then. I want to be her now. Just for tonight, I do not want to be that to which I was born. I do not want to be a priestess of the Wise Ones. I want simply to lie in your arms."

Dagga studied the young face before him. "I fear for your life, Priestess," he said with emotion.

Cela smiled. "Dagga," she said, "you have not learned well while with us. This life, as we know it, ends when it is to end. There is nothing to fear in that. The life force continues. Do you fear the setting sun? Of course not, for it will rise again the next day. So does life continue. The sun sets and rises when it is intended to. Each cycle of our lives begins and ends at the appointed time. There should be no fear, nor should there be sorrow. The only sorrow would be if the sun rose and failed to shine." Cela paused and grew serious. "There is one more thing you should know. I lied to the Priestess Lodi. I told her my body started its lunar rhythm a day later than it actually did. Tonight is the time when a child will be made."

Dagga was incredulous. "If I lie with you tonight, it will result in a child? My child?"

"Yes. Everyone will assume the child is the result of the fertility ceremony. There will be great rejoicing. It will be seen as a symbol of the gods' favor upon our people for the coming year."

Dagga detected the sadness in Cela's voice. He understood. "I will never be a father to this child."

"No," Cela said.

"The priest, Luc?"

Cela shrugged. "He will be High Priest soon. He will have no time for a babe."

"The child will be raised as a priest among the Wise Ones?" Dagga asked.

"A priest or a priestess," Cela said.

"This is possible? The child will have the gifts of the Wise Ones?"

"Ah," Cela sighed, a far-off look on her face. "The child will have more than that. The child will have the gift of the skies."

"You speak in riddles, Priestess. I am a warrior. I do not understand this."

Cela smiled. "I am only just beginning to understand it myself. It was there, within me, but there was no one among the Wise Ones who understood it. There was no one to teach me how to use the gift."

Cela waited. The silence was so prolonged that she was reluctant to look at Dagga. She was afraid that he would refuse her. Suddenly, she felt his nearness, the touch of his fingertips upon her face.

"It is forbidden to touch a priestess of the Wise Ones," he whispered, his voice strained with passion. When his lips gently sought hers, Cela was shocked at the desire that spread throughout her. How often had she found herself looking at this man's body, secretly desiring it for herself? But Cela recognized something else guiding her at this moment, for this was the man who had—contrary to all the customs and laws of her people—rescued her, kept her safe, held her in his arms, and cared for her when the demands placed upon her had been more than she could bear. She shuddered slightly.

Dagga pulled his face back from hers. "You're trembling. Do not fear. I will go slowly. I will be gentle."

"I know," Cela said. "I do not tremble for fear of you." Her breathing had become deeper and her pulse quickened. "I tremble for want of you."

"Cela! Child, where have you been?" Lodi demanded when Cela walked into her hut the next morning. "You have been gone all night. We were worried. We sent warriors to look for you."

"Yes, Lodi, I know. I encountered them on my return."

"Your mother was very frightened."

"I will go see her to tell her that I am safe. First, though, I must speak to you."

"When you said you were going out, I thought you would return with the nightfall."

"I have returned now," Cela said calmly.

"It is daybreak!"

"I am aware of that, Lodi."

"This is an important day for you—for all of us."

"That is why I have come to you. I must speak to you about the ceremony tonight."

"Child, I don't understand your reluctance," Lodi said. "You have been given a great honor." Lodi paused. "What troubles you?"

Cela drew herself up, squaring her shoulders, her gaze direct. "Do you know who I am?" she asked.

"What?" Lodi frowned, her confusion obvious.

"Do you know who I am?" Cela asked again.

"Of course I know—"

"I am the great-granddaughter of *Mora*," Cela emphasized.

It was a moment before Lodi responded. Cela saw her eyes widen suddenly in understanding. "Yes," Lodi said again, this time her meaning clear, "I know who you are."

"Then you must help me."

"What is it that you ask of me?" Lodi inquired.

"It is possible for a woman, who is not a virgin, to lie

with a man and appear to be a virgin, is it not?"

Lodi's eyes clouded over. "That is not something that we teach."

"Yet, it is knowledge that you possess, for you learned it from Mora, and she learned it from a young man who was of the People of the Sky—the young man who started her first child within her."

"Why do you ask me this?" Lodi asked in a hollow voice, her face pale in the firelight of her hut.

"Luc holds a great hatred for me. I do not know why. We are cousins. I have sensed this hatred since I was a child. He chose me for this ceremony because he knows he can hurt me then, and he will."

"Child, Luc has been instructed. I, myself —"

"He will disregard all that you have taught him. But that is not why I'm here. I will submit, as is expected, and I will endure whatever he does. I know the importance of this ceremony. But," Cela said as she advanced upon Lodi, "he will not be the first. I will not come to him a virgin. I will not bear his child."

"What are you saying?" Lodi whispered.

"This past night, a child was begun. Now teach me what I must do to appear a virgin at the fertility rites tonight."

Lodi's eyes widened in shock. She did not speak for a moment. When she did, her mouth was dry and the words came out raspy. "How is that possible?"

Cela smiled for the first time. "The usual way, Lodi. Need I explain the act between a man and a woman to you?"

"What priest?" Lodi demanded.

"Not a priest. An ordinary man. A man of honor and bravery. One who touched me with kindness and gentleness, one who took me to heights of passion that might surprise even you."

Lodi gasped. "You wish to deceive Luc and the others?" she asked incredulously.

"The only deception would have been the ceremony

itself," Cela snapped. "The ceremony is supposed to symbolize the continuity of life, the gift of the gods. Luc would have defiled the ceremony, as he still will. But it will not affect the people now, for I shall go through the ceremony and a child will be born—a child who is truly a gift from the gods, for she will carry the blood of the People of the Sky."

Lodi did not speak. She turned and nervously paced the confines of her small, round hut, rubbing her hands together as she paced, glancing at Cela and then back at the floor of her hut, her brow furrowed in concentration. Cela finally spoke.

"It has been a long time since the People of the Sky came to us, Lodi. The High Priest is the only one left who was alive when they were last here among us. When he leaves this life, there will be none of us who have ever seen them. We will teach of the stories we have heard, never having seen them ourselves."

Lodi turned, fear in her eyes. "You do not believe they will return?"

"I do not know. I do not have the gift of seeing in the future as others do."

"They must! We need them! There is so much that we do not understand," Lodi cried.

Should Cela confide in this woman? Did she dare tell her what was slowly forming in her mind? Perhaps it would help to convince her of the importance of what Cela was requesting. "There is another way," Cela said at last.

"What are you talking about?"

"What if we could go to them?" Cela said.

A look of confusion crossed Lodi's face. "The Wise Ones go to the People of the Sky? Child, you aren't making any sense. We cannot move through the sky as they do. We cannot. . . ."

A look of shock appeared on Lodi's face, her eyes wide, the color draining from her face. She blinked and hesitantly walked to where Cela stood. "Child?" She hesitantly placed her hands on each side of Cela's face.

"Soon, Lodi, soon. I can feel it. My whole life, I have seen the stones of other places. I have always seen them from the skies. In my dreams, I move through the skies. In my waking hours, the stars and the sun call to me. Sometimes I feel so helpless because I can sense the sky pulling at me, and yet I can't move. It's here, Lodi, inside of me," Cela said, taking the older woman's hand and placing it on her chest. "And it's getting stronger and stronger. It won't be long now, I'm certain."

Lodi stepped back, a look of wonder on her face. It was a moment before she recovered, then she reached her hand out and led Cela over to hides that were placed on the floor of her hut. She motioned for Cela to lie down and then walked over to the wall where she kept the tools of her trade. She returned a few minutes later, carrying something small in her hands.

"Luc will expect some resistance when he enters you," Lodi began. "That is easy enough to accomplish simply by shifting the position of your body and altering the angle of entry. I will show you in a moment. More importantly, he will expect to see virginal blood." Lodi smiled. "That is what this is for," she said, opening her hand. Lodi talked for several more minutes, instructing Cela in the art of deception. When she finished, she paused and then spoke again. "Now, let me show you how to change the angle. May I?" she asked Cela.

Cela eagerly nodded her head. Lodi gently pulled Cela's robe up to her waist and spread her knees. Her fingers were gentle and knowledgeable as she touched Cela's womanhood.

"Your lover was very skilled," she commented in objective appreciation. "Usually there is some tenderness and tearing beyond the virginal tissue. I see none of that. Now, lying in this position, this will likely be the angle of Luc's manhood when he prepares to enter you," Lodi began.

Cela emerged from Lodi's hut some time later. After assuring her mother, Ega, that she was safe, she joined the other priests and priestesses in their daily training. At one point in the midafternoon, Cela's path crossed Luc's. Her first instinct was to shrink from his malevolent glare, but then she stopped and looked him directly in the eyes. She no longer feared Luc or what he would do tonight, for his touch would mean nothing to her. She smiled softly to herself as she remembered Dagga's caress and a night that had exceeded anything she could have imagined possible. All the pain that Luc could inflict would not hold any power over her now, for it could come nowhere near the power of Dagga's touch and the pleasure that it brought. Therein lies the simple truth.

✳ ✳ ✳

Derek walked across the hall to Jennifer's room. He knocked on the door and waited. When there was no answer, he knocked again.

"Jennifer?" he called as he opened the door and looked inside. He saw her untouched dinner on a table and her suitcase laying on the bed. He turned and went back into the hall and down the steps.

"Looking for Miss McHugh?" Mrs. Levens asked. "I think I saw her go out into the garden a few minutes ago."

"Thank you," Derek said.

The sun had set, but the sky was still fairly light. Derek entered the garden and looked about. He didn't see her at first, so he started walking on the nearest path. He rounded a hedge and there she was, sitting on a bench under a tree.

"Jenny!" he called.

There was something peculiar about the way she sat there, staring out into the garden. He called her name again.

This time, she visibly jumped and turned her head in his direction. She was not that far from him, and Derek could see the look of confusion on her face. It was as though she didn't recognize him at first.

"Jenny? I want to talk to you," Derek called as he started walking toward her.

Suddenly, Jennifer jumped up and turned. She began to run in the direction opposite Derek, her steps clumsy at first. The move had so surprised Derek that it was a second before he reacted. It didn't take him long to catch up with her. Reaching her, he put his arms on her shoulders and spun her around. He frowned when he saw her face.

"Jenny, are you all right?"

He could feel her trembling beneath his hands, her breath ragged, her face pale, her eyes avoiding him. She averted her face, but not before he saw the first tear roll down her cheek and something else.

"What's on your sweater and your lips? Did you just vomit again? Jenny, are you ill?" he asked with concern.

"No," Jennifer managed to choke out as she hastily wiped her arm across her lips and clutched her abdomen. "I'm fine. It's always like this afterward," she mumbled.

"What is? What are you talking about?"

She pulled back. "Let me go," she said quietly.

"You're crying," Derek said. "Come inside with me," he said, moving his arm around her shoulders.

"No."

"Look," he sighed in frustration, "I don't care about the documents. I don't care where you found them or how you got them." He paused as he turned her face toward his. "I care about you, Jenny. You." He heard her gasp and her eyes widened. "Let's go inside," he said softly.

Jennifer slowly pulled away from Derek. He didn't fight her but waited for her to speak. "I don't think that would be a good idea right now," she said. "It would be too easy to get confused."

"We'll just talk, that's all," he said reassuringly as he

placed her hand in his and started walking toward the manor house.

Derek entered Jennifer's room with her and closed the door behind him. He helped her remove her fowled sweater, and then she immediately put some distance between them.

"You didn't eat anything," he said, glancing at the tray of food still sitting on the table.

"I didn't have much of an appetite."

Derek nodded and sat down in a chair next to the bed. He watched as Jennifer started to pace. Finally, she spoke.

"I don't think I should go with you to Stonehenge tomorrow," she said.

"Why not?"

She turned to him. "I think that should be obvious after today."

Derek smiled. "You surprised me today at Castlerigg. I won't be surprised tomorrow."

"You're not going to be satisfied until you have the documents in hand, and that will never happen."

"Never is a long time, Jenny."

"Time? I don't know what time is anymore," she said, tears threatening again as she wrapped her arms about herself.

Derek frowned. What was she talking about?

Jennifer walked over to the bed and removed the packet of notes that Derek had given her. "May I keep these?" she asked.

"Of course. I made them for you."

She unzipped her suitcase. "I can't stay here tonight. I must return to Scotland."

"Don't you think you at least owe me an explanation?" Derek asked in a steady voice.

Jennifer reached for the papers again to place them in the suitcase. As she did so, she knocked several of them to the floor. Derek immediately rose from his chair and reached down to help her pick them up.

"What's this?" she asked as she lifted one of the papers.

Derek leaned over to see what she was looking at. In the margin of the paper that she was holding were some markings, not letters, but something that, to the trained eye, resembled ancient cuneiform with its wedges placed together to form an alphabet.

"Oh, I was just speculating," Derek said. "It's nothing. At one point, I had hoped that there might be a connection between the language of your civilization and some other, but you said that you didn't know what language the people spoke. Your documents didn't make reference to it, and you said the documents were written in English. You also said that your civilization didn't record their knowledge in writing but passed it down by verse and memorization."

Jennifer's eyes were transfixed on the paper as she traced her finger over the marks that Derek had made in the margin. "Why did you stop?" she whispered, her fingers continuing to move unconsciously on the paper.

"Stop what?" Derek asked, his senses fully alert.

"The letters," she said, a hollow ring in her voice as she continued to look at the paper.

He turned quickly, looking around the room. There was a small writing desk across the room. He darted over to it and opened several drawers until he found what he was looking for. Jennifer was still staring at the markings when he returned to her. He held out a paper and pen.

"Write them, Jenny," he said, his voice commanding.

"What?!" she asked with surprise, making eye contact with him for the first time since picking up the paper.

"Write them," Derek again instructed.

"I can't. I don't know how." She frowned.

Derek sensed her agitation. It was palpable. He took her arm and led her to the desk.

"I don't want to do this," she said, her voice shaking, her arms stiff, resisting his attempt to have her sit.

He heard the fear in her voice. What was she afraid of? More importantly, how did she recognize the Ogham letters? Very few historians or archaeologists were experienced enough to translate that prehistoric form of writing.

"Derek, please," she whispered.

She was pleading with him, and his first instinct was to take her in his arms to comfort her, to protect her. Instead, he pulled the chair out and nodded for her to sit. When she did, he placed the pen in her hand. He saw tears forming in her eyes, but he didn't relent.

"Just do it, Jenny," he commanded.

Jennifer squeezed her eyes shut, then opened them and looked at the blank paper Derek had given her. He watched as she wiped a tear away, her hands trembling. She looked up at him, her eyes, her expression that of someone lost. His heart clenched, but he simply nodded to the blank paper.

She began making a series of marks, haltingly at first, her hand trembling, but then her strokes became more fluid. He watched in amazement as her hand flew across the paper with speed and accuracy. When she finished, she placed the pen down on the desk next to the paper—a paper that was now covered with thirty distinct markings.

Derek picked up the paper. "What is this, Jenny?" he asked, his voice steady, devoid of emotion.

"Their alphabet," she said, fear laced in her voice.

Derek examined each mark. "Thirty characters instead of thirty-six," he said, "and they're not as developed as the later Etruscan letters. Still, there are sixteen radicals, and the remaining letters are extensions or mutations of the sixteen." He looked at Jennifer. "Who used this, Jenny?"

Jennifer swallowed. "The Wise Ones," she finally answered. "They didn't commit any of their secrets—their rituals, the combinations of herbs used in healing, or the method of reading the stars—to writing. The writing was used to send simple messages to each other."

"Do you know what this is?" Derek demanded, his eyes penetrating into hers. "It's the Druidic alphabet, Jenny!

There are some changes, but the basics are there, enough that there is no doubt as to what each letter is. It's called Ogham Writing. The only major difference is that your alphabet is missing six letters. Your alphabet is made up of thirty letters. The Druidic alphabet, as we know it to be, contained thirty-six letters."

He grabbed her shoulders, pulling her to a standing position, and turned her to face him. "You're missing the six Roman letters, Jenny—the ones added to the Druidic alphabet by the Romans," he said to emphasize his point. He still held her shoulders, his hands gripping her. "Jenny, at the time your civilization wrote this, Caesar wouldn't have invaded England for at least another half century. Your civilization would not have known the six Roman letters!"

CHAPTER 8

"John, this is such a pleasant surprise," Lady Pershing said. She was sitting across from John in the dining room at Lord and Lady Pershing's London home.

"I apologize for calling you on such short notice," John Bracken replied. "I wasn't certain I could get a connecting flight."

"We're delighted you called," Lord Pershing said. "You really must take time off from your busy schedule more often and visit us."

"That's what Jennifer says," John said smoothly.

"Where did you say she is?" Lady Pershing asked.

"She's been spending the month visiting a girlfriend. Her friend is an author currently living in Scotland. Jennifer has been helping her with some research."

"How interesting," Lady Pershing said politely.

"Will you be staying long?" Lord Pershing asked.

"A few days—just enough time to see something of Scotland—and then Jennifer will be returning home with me."

"You both must stop here before you return home," Lady Pershing said.

"What time did you say your flight leaves for Edinburgh?" Lord Pershing asked.

"Nine o'clock."

"We'll have you there in plenty of time. Let's enjoy our dinner," Lord Pershing said.

Alison Blasdell

* * *

"You came to me asking for my help!" Derek said. "You're the one who wanted to verify the existence of this civilization you had uncovered. Jenny, you can have the proof you want. All I need is one artifact that has the Ogham writing on it and that can be carbon dated."

"I told you I can't give you anything!" Jennifer retorted.

They had been arguing the past hour. Derek was angry, but how could she tell him that she hadn't realized she knew the alphabet of Cela's people? Cela knew it, of course. An uneasy feeling was growing inside Jennifer, for she was discovering that she knew specifics of Cela's world without actually having experienced them in one of the visions. The stones at Castlerigg's Stone Circle were proof. Jennifer had not seen those yet, but Cela had seen them at some time, and consequently, Jennifer knew them also. How could that be?

"I must have been crazy to have gotten involved in this in the first place," Derek exploded. "No archaeologist in his right mind would have even begun without something in hand. Just what do you expect me to do, Jenny? You give me little bits of information and then snatch them away from me. And there's another thing—you could not have just read about the Druidic alphabet. No one picks that up easily. Who are you, Jenny, and what kind of game are you playing?" Derek demanded. "You must have spent time studying and practicing these letters to have written them so easily. You haven't been telling me the truth, have you?"

When Jennifer didn't answer, Derek spun around and walked to the door. "I don't like being played for a fool, Jenny," he said angrily. "I'll see that the bill is taken care of and leave the car for you. I'll find some other transportation. I'm leaving in the morning. Here, you might as well take these. I won't need them," he said bitterly as he threw some papers onto the bed and left, slamming the door behind him.

Jennifer sat there a few moments, unable to move. What had she expected? She was angry, too. She told him from the beginning that she couldn't give him the documents. So why did she feel so dismal, so alone now? She should be glad he was leaving; she could return to Nina's. But Nina knew the truth, even if Jennifer hadn't wanted to admit it. The truth was that Jennifer had never felt more alive than when she was with Derek Rannoch. Even when he was angry, as he had been the past hour, she felt comfortable, natural with him. The force of his emotions, no matter what they were, seemed to penetrate her, as though they were a part of her.

So what now? Was it time to return to reality, go back to Nina's, pack her things, and return to Chicago and try to put her life back together? Could she do that? Could she forget about Cela and her world? Could she forget about Derek Rannoch?

Jennifer brushed a tear away and stood up. Her movements were mechanical as she removed her clothes and selected a nightgown. When at last she turned out the light in her room and lie down in the bed, she was crying freely. Even if Cela's world were to forever remain a mystery, she didn't want to return to Chicago. That life meant nothing to her now. This is where she wanted to be; this is where she belonged. Somehow, she knew that intuitively. Could she start her life over here? There was Nina, but she couldn't build her life around Nina, for who knew how long Nina would remain in Scotland.

"You're dreaming, Jenny," she whispered to herself, the tears cascading down her face, dampening her pillow. "This is all just a fantasy—Cela, Derek Rannoch—it's all fantasy." When she finally fell asleep, it was with the intent of making plans to return to Chicago as soon as possible.

Derek stirred in his sleep. He had not gone to bed but had removed his shirt and sat down in a chair, his feet propped up on the ottoman. He hadn't even been aware that he had drifted off to sleep.

When he returned to his room after arguing with Jennifer, he paced the room and finally sat down. "Why?" he kept asking himself. "Why won't she show me her documents? What's she hiding?" He was certain that she was concealing something. He also had sensed her fear. Why was she frightened?

He was pondering this when his thoughts were interrupted, and he suddenly sat up in the chair. He felt something. There it was again, that peculiar feeling, like the air was charged with an electromagnetic field. He had once been caught in an electrical storm in the deserts of Egypt. It was similar to that. Something you couldn't see, but all the electrons in your body were suddenly scrambling in response to an external force. He cocked his head. He could have sworn he heard a woman cry out. Jenny?

Jennifer reached for the light beside her bed. She couldn't sleep, so what was the use of trying? Her eyes scanned the room. There, on the writing table, were the papers that Derek had thrown onto the bed when he left. He hadn't even told her what they were when he threw them.

Jennifer pushed the comforter back and stepped barefoot onto the floor. She walked over to the table and picked up the papers. She recognized the sketches immediately: Stonehenge! He had drawn it as it presently stands. She didn't have to look at it long to see that something was wrong. To the east of the outer circle, Derek had drawn a single stone marker some eighty yards away. There were supposed to be two stone markers standing next to each other. Where was the second one? What had happened to it? It was important for accuracy. In midwinter, the full moon rises over the space between the *two* heel stones. It was a valuable sign of an impending solar eclipse. The moon would not align properly over one stone.

On the morning of the summer solstice, the sun rises between the two heel stones, creating a shadow that divides the altar stone in half. The preceding eve of the summer solstice was very important: that was the eve of the fertility rites of the Wise Ones— Cela's fertility rites. Jennifer's hand began to tremble as she touched the place where the absent stone should have been drawn. She had not even completed her thought when she experienced the most violent attack yet. Her stomach knotted and contracted. She clutched herself in pain as the room began to spin and the bile rose to her throat. Then the vortex was pulling her down into its depths.

✻ ✻ ✻

827 B.C.

"Are you ready?" Lodi whispered.

Cela was standing outside of the circle. Only the Wise Ones were present. Neither the common people nor the warriors were allowed to witness the fertility rites. Guards had been posted beyond the earthen circle that surrounded the giant stones. She watched the priests and priestesses, their hoods drawn over their heads, walking solemnly around the stones as they chanted. Three fires burned in the center of the circle enclosing the altar stone. Sweet-smelling rushes had been placed on the ground in front of the altar where the ritual mating would take place. Luc, standing before the altar, was wearing only a leather cloth that hung down from his waist. His body, covered with the symbols of fertility painted in red, glistened in the torchlight.

Cela listened as they chanted. They were calling upon the People of the Sky now, entreating them to return. Cela bowed her head and tried to calm the pounding of her heart. One of the priests was beating on a dried animal skin that had been stretched between two poles. The rhythm that it created drove the priests and priestesses as they chanted. Suddenly, there was silence, and the Wise Ones all turned to the inner circle where Luc stood.

"They're ready for you, Child," Lodi whispered.

Cela swallowed and lifted her head slightly. She would not let him see her fear. She was a priestess of the Wise Ones. She was a daughter of the People of the Sky. As Cela slowly walked forward, the circle parted to admit her. As it did, two priests came forward to where Luc stood. Ceremoniously, they untied the leather apron he was wearing and removed it. Cela hesitated when she saw Luc standing there, his manhood, half the symbol of life, ready and waiting for her. He was watching her, malevolently assessing her reaction, hoping to see her fear.

Two priestesses followed behind Cela to assist her. It comforted Cela to know that Lodi was one of them. If she just didn't have to look at Luc, it would be much easier. She gazed at the ground before her as the circle of priests and priestesses closed behind her. A few more steps and she would be there. When at last Luc's feet came into view, Cela stopped. Still, she did not look up. She felt Lodi and the other priestess step up behind her. Together, they lowered the hood of Cela's robe. In her hair, the sacred mistletoe had been entwined. Despite the warmth of the three fires that surrounded her, Cela felt a chill as the priestesses removed her robe. There was a deep vibration as one of the priests struck the skin drum, and the priests and priestesses turned away from the two naked people standing before the stone altar. As the priest beat out a rhythm on the drum, the Wise Ones began to circle, chanting. They had their hoods up and kept their faces forward as they circled.

Suddenly, Luc laughed, the malevolence of the laugh shaking Cela's soul. In the next moment, she could have sworn that she heard another male voice call to her. It was all that she needed. She raised her eyes and met Luc's squarely. She knew Luc expected to see her terror, but instead, she met his gaze with a challenge of her own. He reached out and took her shoulders in his hands, his fingers digging in painfully. When she didn't respond, he squeezed her arms harder, his fingers sinking into her delicate flesh. She involuntarily winced but then gritted her teeth. Keeping her eyes locked on his, she raised her chin defiantly. Then she deliberately taunted him by turning her face from him so that he could see the scar that stretched from the side of her neck to the front of her throat—forever a reminder that *she* had the protection of the gods.

When his fist struck her face, her head reeled back from the sheer force of it. Cela was shocked by Luc's reaction, for never had she dreamed that he would be so openly violent during the fertility rites. His behavior was a defilement of the ceremony. No priest would dare do such a thing!

She glanced around quickly. The priests and priestesses were chanting feverishly now, and none of them heard or saw Luc strike Cela. She cringed as she felt him grab her arms again. He picked her up as though she were as light as a bird. In the next instant, she felt the air go out of her lungs as he slammed her down upon the cold stone altar, and pain spread across her back. She twisted her head, confused. Luc was supposed to place her on the soft reeds arranged on the ground in front of the altar. She felt his hands upon her thighs as they dug into her, spreading her legs apart. Cela gritted her teeth and squeezed her eyes shut.

Luc slammed into Cela with a vicious force, ripping tissue that Dagga had so skillfully prepared before entering her. The pain shocked her, and her eyes flew open involuntarily. At that moment, the sky opened up to her. The stars reached out to her in solace, and at last, Cela, daughter of the skies, understood.

She saw fear spread across Luc's face. His body faltered. In terror, he grabbed her shoulders as she breathed in deeply and moved toward the sky. He was still on top of her, and they were floating several feet above the stone altar. He lost his balance.

"No!" he screamed in rage. "No!"

He managed to raise his fist and bring it crashing down into her face. Her reaction to the pain was immediate, and Cela's body returned to the stone, slamming down upon it. He struck her two more times and then grabbed her head with both hands and pounded it down on the stone. She was not aware of Luc finishing and removing himself from her.

Luc's scream caused Lodi to look up from where she was standing. She and the Priestess Cupa did not circle with the other priests and priestesses, but kept their hooded faces cast downward during the fertility rites. They, along with two priests standing beside them, were to clothe Cela and Luc when the act was completed. The four now stood there, the horror on their faces barely concealed by their hoods. They had not been close enough to see what had prompted Luc's violent attack. They had only seen him beat Cela with his fists and then complete the rite. The four stood there, paralyzed. This—the most sacred of all their ceremonies, a celebration of the gift of life from the gods, an invocation for the blessings of the gods—had been nothing more than the brutal rape of a priestess of the Wise Ones.

Lodi was the first to move. She ran forward, covering Cela's body with the white cloth that was to have been her ceremonial robe.

"Child?" Lodi's voice faltered as she reached out to Cela.

Cela groaned as she rolled to her side, her body trembling from the assault. "Is it finished, Lodi?" Cela asked, her voice barely audible.

"Yes, Child."

"Please, help me, Lodi. I can't see. I want to leave," Cela said.

Already, Cela's eyes were swollen shut, purple welts covering her eyelids. Blood oozed out from the multiple lacerations on her face caused by Luc's knuckles tearing into her skin.

"Of course, Child," Lodi said as she reached to help Cela sit up.

"But they are to receive the sacrifices now," Cupa whispered to Lodi. "The ceremony must be completed. The Priest Luc and Priestess Cela must drink the blood of the first sacrifice. Look," she said as she pointed, "they are bringing the first prisoner forward to be sacrificed."

"No, Cupa," Lodi said forcefully. "The Priestess Cela does not attend the sacrifices, even this one. The High Priest himself has so ordered it," Lodi countered as she finished dressing Cela.

"Give me your arm, Lodi. I must walk out as a priestess of the Wise Ones," Cela said weakly.

"We'll hold you," Lodi said as she took Cela's arm and Cupa rushed to Cela's other side.

Together, the two priestesses pulled Cela's hood down, covering her bruised and bleeding face. Already, the back of Cela's white robe was stained red with blood oozing from the cuts on her back and head.

Lodi and Cupa were struggling to support Cela as they walked. The three women managed to exit the outer stone circle when Cela stumbled.

"Lodi, my head hurts," Cela cried softly. "I can't walk," she said as she collapsed onto the ground, the two priestesses unable to support her.

Just as the two priestesses reached down to Cela, a shadow fell over them. Lodi looked up in alarm to see a warrior of the guard. The look on his face caused her, a priestess of the Wise Ones, to instinctively cower. She knew she should order him away—after all, *she* was the priestess, *she* had the authority—but the powerful eyes that met hers carried death. This was a warrior who wielded death without fear, and right now, she and Cupa were within his sphere of furor.

Lodi grabbed Cupa's arm and pulled her out of the warrior's way as he boldly reached down to Cela. Lodi watched as his powerful arms, ever so gently, turned Cela onto her back. He tenderly picked her up, cradling her in his arms, his own eyes revealing his pain. In that instant, she knew who he was; there could be no other. Astonishingly, Cela had taken this warrior as her lover. It was his child that she carried within her.

Lodi scrambled to her feet. "Warrior," she said respectfully, "please follow us. The Priestess Cupa is a healer," she said, pointing at Cupa.

Lodi turned to Cupa, who, like she, recognized a purveyor of death and was standing, paralyzed, eyes wide. Lodi took Cupa's arm and pulled her forward, leading the way back to Cupa's hut. When they reached the round hut, Lodi motioned for the warrior to enter, carrying Cela in his arms. "Place the Priestess Cela here," she said, motioning to the soft hides on the floor.

"Lodi, what do we do?" Cupa glanced at the warrior who was gently lowering Cela to the ground. "He touched her," she whispered to Lodi.

"He has been her protector since she was but a child. The laws do not apply to these two," Lodi answered.

"But—"

"I will explain later, but now, you must use your skill to heal Cela."

"Of course," Cupa said.

Lodi turned to the warrior, now kneeling beside Cela. "Warrior, what is your name?" she asked.

"Dagga," was his singular reply.

"Dagga, we must care for the priestess now." She hesitantly reached out and touched his massive arm. She saw the fierceness come into his eyes again and made a quick decision. "You may stay, but you must keep out of sight. Please, come stand back here," she said, indicating the dark walls of the hut.

Dagga took one last look at Cela and then did as Lodi bid. Lodi followed him to the recesses of the hut. "You must remain silent," she whispered to Dagga. "None can know you are here." She didn't wait for a reply but retreated from the shadows back to the center of the hut.

"We must remove the robe so that I can see the extent of her injuries," Cupa said. Both priestesses carefully lifted Cela's head. She cried out and opened her eyes.

"Did I perform the ceremony befitting a priestess of the Wise Ones?" Cela asked, struggling to speak.

"Yes, Child, none other could have done as well."

Lodi's smile turned to a frown when she saw Cela grimace in pain. Cupa's experienced hands were gently moving over Cela's face and then to her arms and shoulders where deep-purple marks had appeared.

"The bones of her face and arms are intact," Cupa said. "Help me turn her onto her side."

Lodi gently assisted as Cupa dabbed the blood off Cela's back. The rough stone altar had sliced into Cela's skin, and already, the soft hides onto which Cela was placed were stained with blood. Cela cried out as Cupa parted the sticky, matted area on the back of her head.

"I don't think the skull is broken, but I can't be certain. Let's roll her onto her back again," Cupa said.

Once Cela was positioned, Lodi gently probed the bruised and torn flesh of the young priestess's womanhood. When she finished, Cupa stood up and moved to the side of her hut. Lodi could hear Cupa as she sorted through the paraphernalia of her trade. She returned a moment later, her arms laden, and knelt beside Cela.

"Cela," she said as she gently touched the young priestess, "I want you to drink this. You will sleep, and while you do, Lodi and I will care for you."

She held the beaker-shaped vessel against Cela's lips until Cela had swallowed all of its contents.

"All will be well, Child," Lodi said. "We will stay with you."

The sedative Cupa had administered began to take effect, and Cela's body grew lax.

"Lodi, get some water and we'll clean the wounds first," Cupa said.

It was a slow process. They started with Cela's back. The cleansing caused the wounds to bleed again, but Cupa seemed unconcerned. Lodi watched as Cupa plucked some leaves off a plant. She knew that the People of the Sky had brought the plant to her people long ago. They instructed the Wise Ones on how to cultivate the plant and protect it in the cold winters. The healers of their people grew this, along with many other medicinal plants that the People of the Sky had brought to them.

This plant had hairy stems with purple flowers, but it was the power in the leaves that Cupa sought now. As Cupa crushed the leaves in her specially shaped pottery, Lodi could smell the minty scent the leaves emitted. She looked down at Cela's face. When applied to Cela's wounds, the scent would help Cela to relax, although there were other plants that could do that as well. Cupa chose this plant because when the oil in the leaves was applied to a wound, the edges of the wound would tighten, shrinking the size of the wound and stopping the bleeding.

Lodi was assisting Cupa to push the leafy powder onto Cela's wounds when there was a commotion outside of Cupa's hut. The two priests who had assisted Luc in the fertility rites entered the hut.

"How is the Priestess Cela?" one of them asked, his voice a mixture of concern and anxiety.

The other priest stepped forward and knelt beside Cela's sleeping form. His eyes went to her bruised and bloody face.

Cupa gently rolled Cela onto her side. She pulled the

garment back, revealing the bloody lacerations on Cela's back and head.

"He did not prepare her, either. He entered before she was ready. There is a lot of tearing," Lodi said.

Both priests looked at the two priestesses.

"She is young; she will recover," Cupa offered in answer to their unspoken question.

"Will there be a child?" one of the priests asked with doubt in his voice.

"Yes, there is a child," Lodi answered.

The priest looked at her with a question on his face. Lodi said no more.

"The Priestess Cela reads the sky like no other," the priest who was kneeling beside Cela said. "She tells me of lands that are not in my memories or in any of our teachings."

"The High Priest Luc fears her gift and her lineage," the other priest said.

Lodi and Cupa looked up quickly.

"The High Priest Sham left this life tonight," he said in explanation. "Luc is now the High Priest. Tomorrow, we will offer the body of Sham, and Luc will be initiated as the new High Priest."

The priest's ominous tone of voice said what his words did not.

"Look at this child!" Cupa said, directing their eyes to Cela. "This was done by Luc! What will happen to us? Have the gods turned against us?" she cried in desperation.

"The Priestess Cela must be protected," Lodi said, for Lodi alone fully understood just how much of a threat Cela would be to Luc and his quest for power. She also knew the importance of Cela's gift and the legacy of the child that she carried.

"The High Priest Luc would not be so bold as to harm her now," one of the priests said.

As the Wise Ones in the hut contemplated a situation that was totally new and frightening to them, Lodi glanced to the corner of the hut. Even in the dark, she saw the hand of the warrior gripping his sword with a force so great, the muscles in his powerful arm bulged out.

✽ ✽ ✽

"Jenny? Jenny!" Derek cried as he crossed the bedroom to where she was slumped on the floor against the wall. He knelt down beside her and brushed her hair out of her face.

"You're crying! What happened? Are you hurt?" he asked as he put his arm around her.

"Derek, what are you doing here?"

"I heard you cry out."

Jennifer closed her eyes and rested her head against Derek's chest. "No," she mumbled. "I didn't cry out. That's what he wanted, but I didn't."

"What?"

"No, not me—*she* didn't cry out," Jennifer whispered as she fought to clear the images of Cela's ordeal from her mind and the sickening feeling from her stomach.

"Jenny?"

"Derek, let go of me!" Jennifer cried as she turned and vomited.

In one swift movement, Derek had Jennifer in his arms and carried her out of her room and across the hall to his own. He entered his room, pausing only a moment to kick the door shut behind him. He carried her over to the bed, threw back the spread, and carefully laid her down. Jennifer squeezed her eyes shut and waited for the feeling to pass; it always did. It was just that this episode had been the worst. Jennifer was still reeling from the violence that Cela had experienced.

"You're ill, Jenny," Derek said with concern.

"No, I'm not sick. I had a bad dream, that's all," she said

weakly.

"I think I should call Dr. MacNeal."

"No. Please, don't do that. I'll be all right in a minute," Jennifer said as she waited for her world to right itself again. "It's always like this. It will pass."

Derek sat down beside her and took her hand in his. He watched with concern until, at last, her body quieted, the trembling and vertigo gone.

"Are you all right now?" Derek asked.

"Yes, I'm fine. It's gone, like it never happened."

Derek frowned. "It must have been some nightmare. Do you have these often?"

"No," Jennifer said, "not often." She glanced at his bare chest and felt her face flush. "I'm so sorry," she said, feeling mortified at seeing the remnants of her stomach contents on his chest.

"Don't worry about it," Derek said reassuringly. "I'm getting used to it. Stay there."

Derek walked to the bathroom. Jennifer watched as he washed her vomit off his chest. He returned with a damp cloth and a glass of water.

"I'm so embarrassed," she said as she wiped her lips and chin with the cloth and then drank the water Derek offered.

"Don't be embarrassed. I'm probably partly responsible by insisting that you work so hard lately."

Jennifer pushed herself up in the bed. Self-consciously, she glanced down at herself and blushed. She was wearing a short silk chemise cut low in the front with thin straps that crossed in the back. She pulled the sheet up, covering her chest, and drew her knees up.

She thought she saw a smile threaten on his face before he stood up and retrieved his shirt that lay on the back of the chair. As he was putting it on, Jennifer spoke.

"I'm sorry, Derek. I woke you."

"I hadn't gone to bed yet," he said as he pulled a chair next to the bed and sat down. "I think I should call a doctor."

"No, please don't. I . . . I have a problem sometimes, but it's nothing serious. As you can see, I'm fine—except for being dreadfully embarrassed. I'm sorry I disturbed you."

"You didn't disturb me. I was awake and feeling guilty. I owe you an apology for the way I acted." He paused. "You can be a very stubborn woman, Jenny McHugh."

"I know your work means a lot to you. I would help you if I could."

They talked for the next half hour, carefully avoiding the subject of the documents.

"I can tell you what you want to know about Stonehenge," Jennifer said at one point. "I looked at your sketches. I can replace the missing stones to restore the original pattern. I can also draw the carvings and paintings that were on the sarsen uprights."

Derek's jaw dropped open in surprise. "You know about those? We've only recently had equipment sophisticated enough to discern the carvings, and we have but a few laser-generated, partial images at that. Three thousand years of exposure to the elements has ground them away."

Derek shook his head as though to clear his thoughts. "Jenny, if you have documents detailing. . . ." He abruptly stopped talking and studied Jennifer's face until she turned away, uncomfortable under his scrutiny.

"In the morning," he said, surprising her. "I don't want to push you again. If you want to tell me about it in the morning, we will discuss it, but for now, you need to sleep. You can stay here."

She looked at him, a question on her face.

"Go ahead and sleep in the bed," Derek said. "I've slept in chairs before and in worse conditions than this when I've been in the field."

"I . . . I can't stay here."

"Why not?"

"This is your bed."

"But I'm not in it. I'll sleep here, on the alert, should your nightmare return," he said lightly.

"I don't need you to watch over me."

"I know you don't, but it's in my blood. I come from a long line of chivalrous nobility, pledged to protect fair maidens."

"My own white knight?"

"Better than that, milady. An earl of the nobility outranks a knight," he said with humor.

Jennifer couldn't help but smile as she shook her head.

"Tell me," Derek continued, "have the men in your life always felt this need to come to your aid? I suspect that you have the ability to coax the protective nature out of us."

Jennifer was quiet a moment. "There haven't been that many men in my life," she finally answered.

Derek raised his eyebrows. "I find that hard to believe."

"There's only been one, and that seems like a lifetime ago."

"Did you love him?"

"It was a mistake. I didn't know what love was then."

"And there hasn't been anyone since?"

"No."

The silence grew between them, and then Derek broke the spell.

"Have no fear, milady," he said lightly. "I shall protect you from all manner of evil."

He stood up from the chair and turned off the lamp beside the bed. As he returned to his chair, Jennifer watched him in the darkness. The drapes at the window remained open, and the room was illuminated by a shaft of silver light coming from the full moon in the sky.

"Sleep, Jenny," he said softly as he leaned back in his chair.

Jennifer awoke suddenly. She was breathing deeply. The room was still cast in darkness, with the exception of the light filtering in from the moon. She had been dreaming. Images of Cela and Dagga filled her mind. This had been a dream—nothing more—but from one perspective, it had been more disturbing than the visions. This left her with a feeling of emptiness and longing that was far worse than the sickness of the visions. She sat up in the bed.

"Jenny?"

Jennifer turned in the darkness to Derek. The silence between them seemed to stretch on until Derek stood. Jennifer's heart was beating wildly when he sat on the edge of the bed, facing her. He seemed to be studying her face with an intensity that took her breath away. When at last he lowered his lips to hers, Jennifer trembled slightly. It wasn't just the touch of his lips that was having such a powerful effect on her, it was his scent, the warmth radiating from his body, the feel of his fingers on her neck, his physical presence so close to her. She felt his hands move up to her hair, and he grasped it in his fingers. When he pulled back from her, she held her breath. He tilted her head back slightly, and then she felt his lips upon her neck. She was surprised at the reaction of her body to his touch. The desire that flowed through her was a new and powerful sensation.

He released her hair, and she felt his fingertips brush against the top of her shoulder, pushing the thin strap of her gown down over her arm. His lips immediately traced the path of his fingers. When he reached up with the other hand to loosen the other strap of her gown, the soft silk slid effortlessly down, revealing the tops of her breasts.

Once again Derek paused, his eyes searching hers. She could feel the force of his passion, still restrained. At that moment, despite the longing of her body, she almost pulled away, for she realized something else: Derek was touching more than just her body. His intimacy went beyond the physical, and with a sudden clarity of thought, Jennifer realized that what was about to take place could forever change who she was.

He caressed her slowly, his hand moving on the top of her silk chemise. Any reservation Jennifer had disappeared the instant he pushed the soft silk down, freeing her breasts to his kisses. Jennifer inhaled sharply, surprised at the sensations that flooded through her. All conscious thoughts faded, and there was only Derek's touch and the demand that she felt in her own body. Wherever his fingers or lips touched her, he left a searing heat. When he once again pulled away from her, she wanted to cry out. She had never felt such passion before, and she never wanted it to end.

Derek gently pushed her back on the bed. His eyes bore into hers as he removed his shirt. Once again, he leaned down over her, his lips finding hers as his hands caressed her breasts, his fingertips lightly teasing the nipples. He was lying on her, and she was aware of his passion straining through the fabric of his pants. Derek shifted his weight slightly, and she felt his hand move down over her hips, pushing the silk chemise down. Jennifer lost herself in the sensations she was experiencing, the tide of pleasure that was building inside of her. She was hot and cold and tingling all at once. The incredible sensations she was feeling beneath his lips and fingertips seemed to be pulling and centering themselves in one place on her body. When Derek's hand moved down over her abdomen, Jennifer was shocked at how her legs seemed to part with a will of their own.

He leaned over her, kissing her as his hand brushed against her inner thighs. Jennifer twisted, the desire she was experiencing almost more than she could bear. The feeling was both a sweet pleasure and a wild demand that made her want to scream for release. When at last she felt his fingers gently touching her, a moan escaped her lips. His fingers moved expertly across her slick folds, intimately probing, touching, stimulating, sensing her response to each movement he made, until at last he centered in on what, for Jennifer, was unbearable. When her release came, it was in an explosion of indescribable pleasure that made her cry out. She clung to Derek, her entire body trembling. He pulled away from Jennifer and stopped immediately when he saw the tears in her eyes.

"Jenny?" he whispered with concern.

She buried her face in his neck, unable to look at him.

"What is it?" he asked softly.

"That's the first time I. . . ." Her voice was muffled as she spoke, her lips upon his neck, her face hidden.

He moved his head back to look at her. Jennifer glanced down, avoiding his eyes, unaccustomed to the intimacy she was experiencing.

"That never happened to me before," she said shyly.

Derek's eyes widened in surprise. He grasped her to him forcefully, enfolding her in his arms. He kissed her face, her hair, and held her tightly.

"Your previous lover must have been very inept or one selfish bastard," he spat out, cradling her in his arms.

A few minutes passed and neither of them spoke. Jennifer rested in Derek's arms, relishing the feeling. Then he kissed her forehead and pulled away from her slightly. There was a twinkle in his eyes as he looked at her. She felt her face flush under his gaze.

"You're blushing," Derek said. "Who would have thought it possible?" he teased.

"Are you making fun of me?"

Derek laughed a deep, throaty laugh, but before Jennifer could respond, he kissed her. The kiss was leisurely at first, but then, as his own passion mounted, it became more insistent. She was surprised at the immediate response in her own body, the contented feeling of just a few minutes ago replaced with a new hunger.

Once again, Derek's fingers caressed and teased, driving Jennifer wild with desire. When she thought she could bear it no longer, she felt his hand move to her inner thigh and then to her most sensitive area. Instinctively, she thrust toward him, anxious for that sweet release. He accommodated her, gently touching, stroking. She was riding on a tide, rushing toward a climax, when suddenly, Derek withdrew his hand. He had been kissing her neck, and she cried out in frustration.

"Not yet," he whispered hoarsely as his lips continued to move upon her neck and chest.

She was vaguely aware of him removing his remaining clothing, and then he was pressed against her, his weight above her. The feel of his body against her only made her more aware of her desperate need for him. He did not enter her immediately, but stroked her and kissed her until Jennifer felt on fire. When at last he moved into her, a cry escaped Jennifer's lips. He had so aroused her that each movement that he now made drove her wild until she once again felt her body rhythmically contract in waves of pleasure. This time, the release coming from his movements inside of her was far more intense than it had been when he had deftly stroked her with his fingertips. She clung to him, taking him into herself, moving with him, blending into him, until at last she felt him thrust deeply once more and shudder as he buried his head in her hair.

"Ah, Jenny," he moaned, "my Jenny."

She could hear his ragged breathing in her ear and feel the thunderous beating of his heart against her naked breasts. She held him as his breathing slowly quieted and gently stroked the muscles of his back. She couldn't recall ever having experienced such contentment in her life—or such tender intimacy as she felt at this moment. She closed her eyes and prayed that, for a few more minutes, time could stand still for her and she could be bound to Derek forever.

When at last he moved to lie beside her, she couldn't hide her disappointment with the separation. Derek laughed softly.

"The night is still young, milady," he said with a heavy brogue, "but I need a few minutes to recover."

He kissed her tenderly and then slipped his arm beneath her head, pulling her against him. Powerful emotions swirled around in Jennifer's head, in her heart: joy, contentment, intimacy, peace, safety.

"There's so much I would like to say to you now."

Derek touched her lips. "There is no need. Your eyes say it all," he said gently.

They settled into an intimacy that only lovers know as they talked, teased, and made love during the night. The first rays of sunlight were beginning to filter through the window when Jennifer at last fell asleep in Derek's arms.

Jennifer was dreaming when a noise, drifting in from the window, caused her to stir. Derek wasn't in the room. She glanced at her watch and jumped out of bed, laughing as she picked up her discarded nightgown and slipped it on. She stuck her head out into the hallway and then quickly crossed to her own room. She dressed hurriedly, pausing only long enough to carefully apply her makeup and brush her hair. When she descended the oak staircase to look for Derek, there was a bounce in her step that hadn't been there previously. What would he say when he saw her? Would the recollection of the night cause her to blush when she saw him? She reached the bottom of the stairs, her heart racing in anticipation, her skin flush with excitement.

Cowden Hall had a large room at the bottom of the stairs with several well-placed sofas, chairs, and tables where its guests could linger. There was also a library that had been converted to a dining room where guests could dine on small, linen-covered tables, the walls of the room still lined with books. Jennifer was preparing to go into that room when she heard someone call her name. Just then, Derek also looked up from where he was sitting and smiled at her.

"Jennifer? Jennifer Bracken! What a surprise!" a woman said.

Jennifer whirled around to see Lord and Lady Pershing enter from the door that led to the garden. She froze in horror as the couple approached.

"Jenny?" Derek said as he came up behind her.

"Jennifer, how nice to see you," Lady Pershing said. "Is John here?" she asked as she looked around.

"Where is that husband of yours?" Lord Pershing asked. "He didn't mention that you two would be here. I thought he was flying to Edinburgh."

"John isn't here," Jennifer said mechanically, rooted where she stood.

"I don't understand. After dinner last night, we drove him to the airport. He had a late flight to Edinburgh," Lady Pershing replied.

"John . . . John is here?" Jennifer asked incredulously.

"Yes. Oh, don't tell us that we spoiled his surprise. You didn't know he was coming?"

"I . . . I—"

"Jennifer, perhaps introductions are in order," Derek said stiffly as he stepped up beside her.

Jennifer felt like she had just been kicked in the stomach. It was difficult to breathe or speak. Her heart ached so much that she couldn't face him; she couldn't look at Derek. A chill ran through her. She listened to her own voice, as though it were coming from a distance.

"Lord and Lady Pershing, this is Derek Rannoch. He is a professor of archaeology at the British Museum and at the University of Edinburgh."

"How do you do," Lord Pershing said as he extended his hand to Derek. "Dr. Bracken, Jennifer's husband, said that she was doing some research for her author friend. How is it going?"

"I think Mrs. Bracken has gotten what she came for," Derek replied.

"Wonderful! And do you know Dr. Bracken, too, professor?" Lord Pershing asked.

"No," Derek replied. "I've not had the pleasure."

"My dear, John must not have known that you would be here. He should have arrived at Miss Bouvay's last night," Lady Pershing said.

Jennifer stood there, mute and frozen.

"Perhaps you should call Miss Bouvay to see if your husband has arrived," Derek said politely. "I think we're finished with our work. You will, of course, want to return to Scotland as soon as possible."

Jennifer was vaguely aware of the Pershings exchanging more pleasantries and then of saying good-bye to them. She felt Derek's hand upon her elbow.

"Derek," she began weakly.

"Not here," he said through clenched teeth.

He guided her, not too gently, back up the steps and down the long hall. He went directly to her room. Only when they were inside the room and the door was closed did he release his tight grip on her elbow. Jennifer turned around and, through her tears, saw not only anger but loathing in his eyes.

"Tears, Mrs. Bracken?" he spat out. "It is *Mrs.* Bracken, is it not? You're married!"

Jennifer lowered her head.

Derek swore explosively. "What? No explanation?" he ground out. "Surely you've thought of this possibility, too. You thought of everything else!"

"Derek," Jennifer stuttered. "It's not what it seems."

"Of course it isn't!" Derek shook his head. "You're very good, Jennifer," he said cruelly, "very good, indeed. Let me see if I have this correct. You're the poor, neglected wife of a, by the looks of your clothes, fairly wealthy doctor. But you're bored. So you come to Europe to visit a friend and to find some excitement. And, if I can believe anything that you've said, which is highly doubtful, your husband is not that good in bed, either, so you're also looking to get—"

"Don't say it!" Jennifer interjected, tears in her eyes.

"You're a hell of an actress, Mrs. Bracken. Last night was probably one of your best performances. Tell me, does he know about this? Does he even suspect what you do?"

"Damn you!" Jennifer shouted.

Derek suddenly advanced threateningly toward her. He grabbed the front of her shirt, pulling her roughly against him. "How dare you involve my family in your sordid scheme," he accused. "You ingratiated yourself with my father. You came to my home. You met my sister and her family," he shouted. "Did that add extra excitement, dining with an earl and his family?" Derek was within inches of Jennifer's face. She wanted to pull away from the furor and loathing she saw in his eyes, but his grip was too tight. "By God, if I ever see you on Thornhill again, you'll wish you had never set foot in Scotland!"

He released her, and she almost fell backward from the force of it. Derek turned and walked to the door. He opened it and then stopped. With his back to her, he spoke one last time.

"Tell me one thing; I think you owe me that much. Were there ever any documents?"

Jennifer stared at his back, wanting to cry out to him, but not knowing what to say.

"No," she said softly.

Derek paused, only a moment, and then stepped through the door, slamming it as he left. Jennifer crumbled to the floor, the pain and desolation more than she could bear.

"Damn you, Jenny! Damn you to hell!" Derek swore as he crossed the border into Scotland. He had tried to tell himself that it didn't matter. So what? She got the best of him. He should forget it. After all, hadn't he entered into his share of casual relationships, too? Yes, but never dishonestly, never like she had. And to think that he thought she was different, that there was something very special about her. There was something special all right: she was a first-class liar.

Derek swore again. There never were any documents. She had lied about that, too. She had played him for a fool and he went along, against his better judgment and all his scientific training. How could he have been so gullible? So stupid! *Because she got to you, Derek, she really got to you.* He

237

couldn't help but recall images of Jennifer: her face as she smiled, her hair, the feel of her body against his. Then there was her eagerness to learn, her curiosity, her vulnerability— or so he thought! By the time he reached Thornhill in midafternoon, his fury had only intensified.

Harold Rannoch heard the massive front doors of Thornhill slam. He'd been in the library, going over the ledgers of the estate. Upon entering the hall, he saw Derek as he started up the stairs, suitcase in hand. Lord Harold immediately recognized the angry strides of his son.

"Derek! I hadn't expected you back so soon," his father said.

"My plans changed, Father," Derek replied, his rage barely concealed.

"And Miss McHugh? Has she returned also?"

"Miss McHugh," Derek ground out, "is not my concern. She can rot in hell for all I care. Now if you'll excuse me, I'm going to unpack," he said, pausing only long enough to wait for his father's nod of dismissal.

"Derek, will you join me for tea when you are finished?" Harold Rannoch asked, curious about what had provoked his son's anger.

Derek paused on the steps but did not turn around. "Of course, Father. Give me a few minutes."

Derek continued up the stairs and disappeared.

"I couldn't help but overhear, Father. Who is Miss McHugh?" Edward Rannoch, Derek's brother, asked as he entered the large hall.

"A young woman with whom I was very impressed," Lord Harold replied, a frown on his face.

"It appears she had an effect on Derek, too," Edward replied.

"So it would seem."

"I've never seen my brother that upset over a woman," Edward commented. "This should be interesting," he added as they walked together down the hall.

＊ ＊ ＊

"Jen! I thought you would never get here. John has been calling every hour," Nina exclaimed when, at last, Jennifer arrived at her cottage.

Jennifer placed her suitcase on the floor and removed her sweater.

"You look awful," Nina said, surveying her friend's face.

Jennifer ignored Nina's comment. "When is John expected?" she asked, her voice flat.

"I told him you would call when you arrived," Nina said, suspicion in her voice. "Jen? What is it?"

"I'd like to bathe and change my clothes first. It won't take me that long to pack."

"Pack? What are you talking about? Tell me what happened."

"I can be ready to leave in an hour. Will you call John and tell him that?" Jennifer turned and started walking toward the bathroom, dismissing Nina.

"No! I won't call and tell him that or anything else—not until I know what's going on. You haven't said a word to me."

"I would think that would be obvious," Jennifer said. "John has shown up unexpectedly; I'm returning with him. Now if you won't make the call, I will."

Jennifer walked past Nina into the kitchen. She reached for the phone when Nina grabbed it away from her. "Don't get snarky with me, McHugh," Nina said. "I know you. Something is wrong, and it has nothing to do with John being here."

"Give me the phone, Nina."

Nina stared at her friend, still holding the phone.

"Damn it, Nina, give me the phone!" Jennifer shouted.

Nina set the phone down on the table, carefully watching as Jennifer, her hands trembling, picked up the receiver.

"What's the number?" Jennifer asked quietly.

Nina walked to the kitchen cabinet and returned with a piece of paper. She laid it down on the table. As Jennifer picked it up, Nina placed her hand on Jennifer.

"Jen," she said softly, "don't go. Don't run away."

"There's no reason to stay," Jennifer said quietly, her voice faltering for the first time.

"Wait, will you? Don't call John yet. It's only three o'clock. There's plenty of time."

"Not if we can get an evening flight out of here."

"An evening flight to where? There won't be any trans-Atlantic flights leaving this late. Why don't I call him and tell him you've been delayed? I'll tell him you'll be arriving early tomorrow morning."

Jennifer looked at Nina. "I know you're trying to help, Nina, and I appreciate it, but this is best, really it is."

Nina watched with resignation as Jennifer dialed the number. She listened as Jennifer spoke with John, her voice a monotone. Then Jennifer quietly replaced the receiver and turned to Nina.

"He's coming over as soon as he can check out. He's going to see if he can get an evening flight to London. We'll leave London in the morning."

"Why are you doing this? What about your visions? Are you giving up on those?"

Jennifer shrugged, heaviness in her movements. "I don't know that I'm any closer to the truth now than I was when this first started. I can't just wait around for them to happen. What would be the purpose in that?"

"You're going to walk away from it?" Nina asked incredulously.

"I can't live my life for something that might be an illusion."

"You don't believe that for a second, and neither do I."

"Maybe not, but I've got to get on with my life," Jennifer retorted.

"A life back in Chicago?"

"Yes."

"With John?"

Jennifer didn't answer.

"You don't love John."

Jennifer turned and started walking toward the bedroom.

Nina ran after her, caught her arm, and turned Jennifer around to face her. "Tell me that you love John. Go ahead, say it."

Jennifer clenched her teeth. "No, I don't love John. Is that what you want to hear? I don't. And I never will. I'll always be grateful to him for how he cared for my mother and me, but you were right all along. I see John for what he really is."

"Then why are you leaving with him?"

"I can't stay here," Jennifer said.

"Why, Jen, why can't you stay here? There's nothing for you back in Chicago."

"There's nothing for me here, either."

"I can't believe you're giving in like this and are actually going back with him."

Jennifer stared at her friend and then turned. Nina followed her into the bedroom.

"Forget about the bath," Jennifer said angrily as she placed one of her suitcases on the bed. "I'll just pack and be ready when John arrives."

"You haven't even said his name," Nina said softly.

If Nina had any doubt about what was wrong, it was removed when she saw Jennifer's response. Her hands stopped in the middle of her packing. She seemed frozen. When she spoke, Nina had to step closer to hear her.

"That's because I'm not as strong as you are, Nina. I'm not as strong as Cela, either."

Nina walked around to Jennifer and gently turned her so that they were facing each other. "You're not leaving because John has come for you, and you're not leaving because you've given up on the visions. You're leaving because of Derek Rannoch. What happened, Jen?"

Slowly, Jennifer sat down on the side of the bed. It was difficult for her to speak at first, but gradually the events of the past few days came out, including the night spent with Derek and the arrival of Lord and Lady Pershing. Nina held Jennifer in her arms until at last she stopped crying.

"Oh, Jen, I'm so sorry," Nina murmured. "Don't go. Stay with me."

"I can't. I can't stay here. This is Thornhill, Nina. This is Derek. Scotland is Derek. Don't you see?"

"Don't run away."

"He was so angry, Nina. He hates me. He threatened to throw me off Thornhill."

"You love him, don't you," Nina said softly.

"I lied to him. I could have told him any number of times that I was married, and I didn't. I lied to his family as well. Nina, if you could have seen the loathing in his eyes."

Jennifer stood up abruptly. "I've got to hurry or I won't be ready when John gets here."

"You're in love with Derek Rannoch. You slept with him. How can you go back to John now?"

For the first time, Jennifer laughed, although it was a bitter laugh. "I couldn't bear to have John touch me now, but that won't be a problem. John stopped making love to me shortly after we returned from our honeymoon. Five times in eighteen months of marriage—that's how many times we've had sex. Four times on our two-week honeymoon and one time after we returned home. We've had separate bedrooms for over a year." Jennifer turned to Nina. "When I get back to Chicago, I'm filing for divorce."

Nina sighed. "John will not make this easy for you. You know that."

"John doesn't love me."

"You said it yourself. He doesn't like to lose," Nina said.

Both women looked up as they heard a car stop in front

of the cottage. A moment later, there was a knock on the door.

"I wish you wouldn't do this," Nina said fervently.

"Will you let him in while I finish packing?" Jennifer asked.

Reluctantly, Nina left Jennifer sorting her clothes and walked to the door. She opened it to find John standing there, his gaze cold.

"Nina," he said.

"Come in, John. Jennifer's almost ready."

John stepped inside. It was an awkward moment as they both stood there, unable to think of anything to say. The moment was broken when Jennifer walked into the room, a suitcase in each hand.

"I left the sweaters, pants, and boots that I bought. I don't think I'll need them," Jennifer said.

"Jennifer," John said as he stepped before her. He put one hand on Jennifer's shoulder and leaned over to kiss her on the cheek.

Nina watched as Jennifer flinched as though she had been struck and immediately moved away from John.

"What time is our flight?" Jennifer asked, trying to sound casual.

"Six o'clock. We're flying to London tonight and then to Paris in the morning. I thought we could spend a few days there before returning."

Nina saw Jennifer stiffen.

John reached for Jennifer's bags. "We'd better hurry," he said. "Good-bye, Nina."

John walked to the door and then paused, turning to wait for Jennifer. Jennifer reached for some papers rolled up and tied with string.

"Will you see that these are returned?" Jennifer asked as she handed them to Nina.

Nina glanced at the roll, a question on her face.

"They're for Derek?" Nina asked softly.

Jennifer nodded her head.

"You can come back anytime, Jen," Nina whispered as she hugged Jennifer to her.

Jennifer resisted the impulse to look back at Nina as John drove the car away. Instead, she closed her eyes and leaned her head back so that she would not have to look at Scotland. Even with the light rain that had started, she knew the power of the fierce Grampian Mountains, their tops now obscured by gray clouds. She could envision the misty meadows, their green carpet interrupted by massive boulders, some resting alone, others congregated in groups of differing sizes; the purple heather, so colorful and peaceful; the thistle, beautiful but unforgiving if one was foolish enough to breach it without sturdy shoes, socks, and pants made of wool or waxed cotton; and the woods, where a girl having an image of a civilization that existed three thousand years ago could become lost and found by a pair of Irish wolfhounds and their master.

Jennifer's mind drifted to a vacation she and her mother had taken when Jennifer was twelve years old. Her mother carefully saved money during the year so that she and Jennifer could take a vacation each summer. They would pick a different state or National Park that was within reasonable driving distance. Teaching music in a public school provided a decent salary, but it didn't leave a lot for "extras," as her mother called vacations, going to movies, or eating out in restaurants. Their one extravagance was season tickets to the Chicago Symphony Orchestra—that and Jennifer's violin.

Her mind came back to the vacation. Her mother drove to Colorado and all the way up to Pike's Peak. The vista was beautiful, spectacular even. Jennifer mentally counted all the places she and her mother had gone: Mount Rushmore, the Grand Canyon, the East Coast, the West Coast, the Gulf States. So many beautiful places. And what of John? He had taken her to Paris, Rome, Venice, Madrid, but none of those places had seeped into her very bones, stirred her blood, or claimed her as its own like this land did. Was it because of the visions she had of Cela and this place during prehistoric times? Or was it the man who had become the heart of Scotland, the man who gave her love, the man she had deceived.

Her eyes were still closed, but she squeezed her eyelids together, hoping to stop the tears that had begun. She became aware of John speaking to her. He said something about Paris. His voice jolted her from her thoughts of Derek and Cela. She opened her eyes but kept her face averted from John. She was seated next to her husband —a man she neither knew nor loved.

"John," Jennifer began. "I don't want to go to Paris. Can we just fly back to Chicago tomorrow?"

"I thought it would give us some time together. We haven't had much of that."

Jennifer sighed. "There's something I want to tell you."

"It can wait," John said, interrupting. "I know that you've been unhappy lately. Maybe that's why you had those spells. I guess I've expected a lot of you, and with my schedule, I have not spent much time with you. I plan on changing that, and to begin, I planned a few days in Paris for just the two of us."

"Why are you doing this, John?"

"Jennifer, you're my wife, and I'm sorry that the demands placed on me have come between us. I'll see that it doesn't happen again," he answered. He smiled at her and then focused his attention on the road ahead.

Jennifer sat there, astounded at John's words. She shook her head. John was going to a lot of effort, saying words that, up until a short while ago, she'd been longing to hear. Had he spoken them sooner, however, would she have realized what she did now? He was saying all the right things, but there was no emotion behind his words, no love, no passion. It was a business relationship. As his words echoed in her mind, she felt no stirring within the depths of her being. Nothing. She almost felt sorry for him.

Two days later, Nina stopped her car in front of the massive, gray stone structure. She smiled. Jennifer had described it perfectly. Thornhill was impressive. No wonder Jennifer had been so affected by it.

Nina reached for the rolled-up papers on the seat next to her and got out of the car. She was contemplating what she would say when she knocked on the ancient oak door.

"Hello," Nina said as a man opened the door. "My name is Nina Bouvay. I have some papers for Lord Rannoch, Professor Derek Rannoch, that is."

"Won't you come in? I'll see if he's available. Miss Bouvay is it?" the man asked.

"Yes," Nina answered. "Thank you."

The man led Nina to a small room pleasantly furnished with overstuffed, comfortable chairs, plants, and books. She hadn't waited long when the door opened and Derek Rannoch entered.

"Miss Bouvay," he said politely, but with some restraint.

For a moment, Nina couldn't think of what to say. She fumbled with the papers in her hands.

"Jen asked me to return these to you," she said as she held them out.

Derek stepped forward and took them. Nina saw his eyes narrow as he recognized the rolled-up papers.

"Thank you," he said, his face controlled. "It was kind of you to bring them over, although it was not necessary," he added.

Nina nodded, unable to think of anything else to say.

"I'll walk you to your car," Derek said.

As he reached for the door, Nina spoke. "You're wrong about Jennifer," she said.

Derek's hand froze on the doorknob.

"She never meant to deceive you," Nina said.

"There really is nothing to discuss," Derek said, a

hardness coming to his voice.

"Please, you don't understand."

"Thank you for bringing the papers over," Derek said as he opened the door and stepped into the foyer. He stood aside for Nina to go before him. She took a step and then stopped.

"Jennifer didn't tell me everything, but she said enough that I could figure out the rest for myself. She didn't deliberately set out to deceive you. It just happened."

"I do not wish to discuss this with you, Miss Bouvay. Mrs. Bracken is of no concern to me."

"And what about Jennifer McHugh?" Nina asked.

"I believe they are one and the same, a fact that she omitted."

"But not intentionally."

"Not intentionally?" Derek laughed sarcastically.

"I call her 'McHugh,' " Nina began. "I always have, especially since she married John Bracken. The man is a real ass. I don't know what she told you about him, but—"

"She said nothing. I'm not interested in Mrs. Bracken or her husband. Now if you will excuse me," Derek said.

"Jen did not come to Scotland looking for excitement with you or any other man. Believe me, a man was the furthest thing from her mind. As a matter of fact, she did everything she could to put distance between you two. She didn't want to go with you, if you will recall."

Derek said nothing, but started walking toward the large front door. Nina caught up with him.

"She didn't plan on getting involved with anyone." Nina could see that her words were having no effect on Derek. "Did you bother to ask her if she was married?" she blurted out.

Derek stopped and turned cold eyes on Nina.

"Jennifer McHugh is the most honest person I know," Nina said quickly. "You spent several days with her on two different occasions. You should know that."

"Honest? Like she was about the documents?"

Nina hesitated. "She told you about that?"

"That there never were any documents? Yes, but only after I demanded to know. Until then, she led me to believe that she was in possession of documents that described an ancient civilization."

Nina hesitated. She chose her next words carefully. "What else did she tell you about her information?"

"What was there to say? She lied about that, too." Derek opened the front door and then turned to Nina. "I'm certain that under other circumstances, your loyalty to your friend would be admirable. I have no interest in it, Miss Bouvay. Thank you for returning the papers."

Derek held the door open for Nina. As she walked through, she paused and turned.

"Professor Rannoch, you're an intelligent and educated man. Your reputation as a noted archaeologist is well known. You, of all people, should know that things are often not as they appear on the surface and rarely are as simple as most people think. You're wrong about Jennifer—very wrong."

Nina turned and walked out the door.

"Who was that?" Edward Rannoch asked as he walked into the foyer.

Derek turned to his brother.

"Nina Bouvay," Derek answered, a scowl on his face.

"Nina Bouvay," Edward said, repeating the name as he knitted his eyebrows together. "Ah, Miss McHugh's friend. What did she want?" he inquired of his brother.

"She was returning some sketches that I gave to Jenny. Here, burn these!" Derek said as he thrust the roll of papers into Edward's hands and stalked away. He didn't see Edward smile as he looked down at the rolled-up papers in his hand.

CHAPTER 9

Jennifer followed John up the staircase in their house, each step a labor. She and John had returned from Paris a few hours ago. It was odd. When they had driven into the driveway, she was struck by the fact that she felt nothing as she surveyed the house where she had lived for the past year and a half. Yet, the first time she had seen Thornhill, she had been overcome with emotion, and that was before she had even known it was Derek's ancestral home. She'd felt such a feeling of peace, protection, and welcome when she had first come upon its massive, gray stone walls. She also had a sense of belonging, a sense of home. How could that be? Now, of course, she could not separate thoughts of Thornhill from thoughts of Derek. They would be forever intertwined.

She hastily wiped her eyes of the tears that threatened. She welcomed the feeling of numbness that had settled over her in Paris, for not to feel was far better than the pain she felt when she thought of Derek—a pain that was threatening to break through again.

John entered his bedroom with their luggage, followed by the housekeeper, Irene Lynch.

"It's nice to have you back, Mrs. Bracken," Mrs. Lynch said. "Shall I unpack for you?"

"Later, Irene," John said.

"Very well," Irene said and excused herself.

Jennifer stood at the doorway of John's bedroom.

"I missed you, Jennifer. This room was very lonely without you," he said.

"John," Jennifer ventured, "I haven't slept in this bedroom for over a year. I can't stay in this room now."

For a brief moment, Jennifer saw John's face harden, and then his expression changed. He came over to her and took her hand in his.

"Jennifer, I've tried to be patient. We've been apart a long time, and I'm the first one to admit that I wasn't a very attentive husband before you left. All of that is going to change. I understood when you wanted separate rooms in Paris, and I went along with that. But we're home now. We've got to get on with our lives . . . our marriage. I want things to be like they were when we were on our honeymoon, and they can be."

Jennifer withdrew her hand from his. How could she tell him that she couldn't stand his touch? He'd made an effort while they were in Paris. He'd been attentive, charming, and solicitous. She had almost forgotten that he could be that way, the way he'd been when they first met. Jennifer had been vulnerable then and easily fooled; she was not so naive now.

"Why, John? Why do you want this marriage to work? We're not right for each other, and you know it," she said softly.

John stiffened. "Jennifer, you're tired, and you've had a difficult past few months. Let yourself get reestablished here before you start thinking rash thoughts. We are right for each other.

"I've thought about it while you were away. I need you, Jennifer. You have a way of grounding me. You're sweet, kind, and innocent. That's rare in a woman nowadays. I want to take care of you. I want to make you happy." He paused, a pained expression on his face. "If it's about sex, I told you before we married that I had some difficulties—"

"John," Jennifer interrupted, "I don't want to hurt you, and I'm aware of how hard you've been trying, but it's not going to work. We're wrong for each other. I'll always be grateful to you. You came along at a time in my life when I needed some stability and support. You gave that to me. But you don't love me, John. You don't. We can't just suddenly manufacture feelings of affection or passion."

John's eyes narrowed briefly, and she saw him tense. Then he took a deep breath.

"Jennifer, I've tried to give you everything. I took care of your mother. I gave you this house, clothes, a car. And I'm sorry . . . I'm sorry I objected to your pursuing a career as a violinist. That was wrong of me. You're very gifted. If you still want to do that, I'll support you." He paused, judging her reaction. "And I apologize for closing your accounts and canceling your credit cards while you were in Scotland," he added. "They'll all be activated again first thing in the morning."

"John, it's not a matter of money; it never has been. I don't care about the house, clothes, or car. Those things are important to you, not to me."

John sighed. "Jennifer, I've tried to be a good husband to you. All I ask is that you not make a hasty decision. Give it some time. That's not asking too much, is it?"

"We don't belong together. A divorce would be the best thing for both of us. I'm not angry." Jennifer smiled sadly. "I don't want anything from you, John—not money, not this house, not even the car. I'm prepared to leave with what I came in with."

"Two weeks. Give me that. Don't you think you owe me that much?"

Jennifer closed her eyes. She almost felt sorry for John.

"Stay, Jennifer," she heard John say softly. "Stay here. Stay with me tonight. Let me make love to you."

Jennifer opened her eyes and stepped back quickly, out of his reach.

"All right, if that's rushing things too much, sleep in your room," John conceded, "but give me two weeks. Please, Jennifer. I'll make no demands of you, and then, if at the end of two weeks you still want a divorce, I'll not object. Just don't make a rash decision right now."

Jennifer thought about what John said. Would a few days matter? Did she owe him that? "All right, John," she finally said, "I won't change my mind, but I'll stay two weeks."

"Thank you. We can be civil, can't we? Friends at least?" John asked as he picked up Jennifer's luggage and carried it to her room.

At the end of the first week home, Jennifer was ensconced with her violin in the library. John had been true to his word: he placed her violin, the file cabinets with all her music, and her music stand in the library where she could play undisturbed. At first, she was hesitant. She hadn't played the violin since her mother died a year ago. Her fingers, neck, arms, shoulders, back, even her heart and lungs—no longer conditioned to meet the demands of hours of playing—rebelled with aches and pains of their own and left her sweating and breathless. But soon, the patterns of nerve impulse and muscle response, deeply engrained in childhood, resurfaced, and she once again found solace in the sweet sounds produced by string and bow.

She had just finished playing Sibelius's Concerto in D Minor when she heard a knock on the library door. John hesitantly stepped into the room.

"I didn't want to interrupt you," he said. "I waited until you finished. That was amazing, by the way," he added.

"Thank you," she said and placed her violin and bow on the table. They both had been overly polite this past week, like strangers who were afraid to offend.

"When your mother first told me you were gifted and a prodigy, I assumed it was maternal pride speaking, and then I heard you play for her. You are truly a gifted violinist. You should be playing on the world's great concert stages, not closed up in a library. I'm sorry I did nothing to encourage you to seek a professional career."

"John, we've discussed this before. There's no need to apologize. I never wanted the world stage. I still don't." She shrugged her shoulders. "I like the library."

John gestured magnanimously around the library. "Then it's all yours. Now, it will soon be time for dinner, and I have a surprise for you."

Jennifer frowned slightly and stood. "What is it?"

"Come with me," John said. When she hesitated, he walked to where she was standing. "Please."

John led her up the stairs and paused in front of her bedroom. He opened the door and stepped aside for her to enter. When she didn't move, he held his hands up in front of him. "I won't touch you, I promise," he said. "Please."

Jennifer walked into the room to find a dress laying on the bed. She walked over to the bed and picked it up—a beautiful, black silk cocktail dress.

"Here," John said, holding out a slim box.

"John, what are you doing?" Jennifer asked.

"Just open it."

Reluctantly, Jennifer took the Cartier box in her hand. She opened it to find a stunning diamond and ruby bracelet inside.

"John," she said as she began to shake her head. "Don't do this. I can't accept this."

"Why not? I want you to wear it with the dress tonight."

"Tonight?"

John smiled as he withdrew two tickets from his pocket.

"We have tickets to the symphony, and then I made reservations at your favorite restaurant. And," he said looking over at the dresser in the bedroom, "those are for you also."

Jennifer turned to see a bouquet of red roses.

"John, please don't do this. The symphony, the gifts— they don't change anything. I'm still leaving."

"I know, Jennifer. I asked you to stay for two weeks, and you are. I want you to have the bracelet, and you love the symphony. This is my way of saying thank you for the first week. We don't have to leave for another hour," he said as he looked at his watch. "Why don't you relax in a hot bath, put on the dress and bracelet, and we'll have a nice evening: the symphony, dinner, and that's all. I promise. I know this doesn't change things."

An hour later, Jennifer stood before the mirror in her room. She had pulled her hair up on top of her head and wore the diamond and ruby earrings that John had given her on their honeymoon. They matched the bracelet perfectly. She looked at her image in the mirror. The black dress was beautiful. It had a closely fitted bodice and waist and then fell straight down her hips, the short skirt ending above her knees. Jennifer stared at the seductive image in the mirror and wished with all her heart that she was wearing the dress for Derek.

She turned away abruptly, stopping the painful thoughts before they went any further. She had managed to keep busy the past week and deliberately shut him out of her mind. The nights were different. She couldn't control her dreams. She couldn't constrain the memories her body had of him, and she would wake up, her face tear-streaked and longing for him.

John was waiting in the foyer as she descended the staircase. "You look beautiful, Jennifer," he said when she stopped before him. "This evening is for you. I want you to relax and enjoy yourself."

He was a perfect gentleman the entire evening, but even hearing Vivaldi's Four Seasons and Mozart's Violin Concerto No. 3, followed by several glasses of wine at dinner, couldn't penetrate the lonely despair she felt inside.

"Thank you for going with me this evening," John said kindly when they returned home and he walked her to her bedroom door.

"It was very thoughtful of you to plan it all," Jennifer said.

"It was the least I could do. Good night, Jennifer," he

said and turned and walked down the hall to his room.

"Good night," she called and then entered her room and closed the door.

Jennifer had been asleep for several hours. Derek permeated her dreams—his smile, his voice, his touch. When she felt his warm breath upon her neck, she moaned softly and turned to feel his lips on hers. The weight of his hand upon her breast caused her to stir.

"Jennifer, it's okay. It's me," a male voice whispered.

It took a second for Jennifer to come fully awake. When she did, she realized John's hand was on her breast.

"John! Get off me!"

"You looked beautiful tonight, Jennifer." His voice was husky and smelled of bourbon.

"Stop that!"

"I know it's been a long time. Just relax."

His hand moved to her side, and he grabbed the delicate fabric of her gown and pushed it up over her hips. He was wearing a robe, and as he moved over her, the robe parted and she felt his nakedness against her.

"What are you doing? Let go of me!" she said as she instinctively resisted him.

"Don't fight me on this, Jennifer. I'm your husband."

"Stop it, John!" she said, gritting her teeth. She planted her hands on John's shoulders and tried to push him off of her, but he grabbed her hands and pinned them down beside her head. She felt his knees between her legs, spreading them.

"No!" Jennifer shouted as she twisted beneath him. She was able to wrench one hand from his grasp, but he quickly grabbed it again.

"Stop fighting!" he growled.

She brought her knee up and hit him in the side. He cried out and tightened his grip on her wrists. He forced all his weight down on her, finally spreading her legs. In the process, her nightgown had moved down again, effectively blocking his entry.

"You wanted a baby," he spat out. "Well, that's what you'll get tonight."

"No!" Jennifer shouted.

"Stop struggling!" he said.

For a split second, Jennifer quieted. John freed one of her hands so that he could move her nightgown aside. In that second, Jennifer doubled her fist up and, using as much of her body weight as was possible, smashed her fist into John's nose. There was a faint crunching sound as her fist connected with his nasal bone and cartilage, followed by a guttural scream. John lurched to the side.

Jennifer scrambled off the bed and ran to the light switch by the door. She turned the light on and whirled around to see John sitting on the bed, cradling his face, blood dripping from his hands.

"Jesus Christ, Jennifer! I think you broke my nose!" John shouted.

"You're damn lucky I didn't break more than that!" she shouted back.

"Get me some tissue!"

"Get them yourself!"

Her initial fear was rapidly being replaced with fury. John got off the bed and gathered his robe about him with one hand. With the other, he held his nose and walked into her bathroom.

"Fuck!" he swore.

She heard the water run, and then he emerged a minute later. He was holding tissue to his nose.

"It's broken!" he said, glaring at her. "What the hell did you think you were doing?" he said angrily.

"Me? You tried to rape me!"

John laughed sarcastically. "You're my wife, Jennifer. I would hardly call that rape. As usual, you're overreacting again."

"Overreacting! Get out of here!"

"You wanted a baby. Well, you could have had one!"

"Are you crazy? I would never consider having a child with you—not now, not ever."

"Are you sure, Jennifer? This might be your last chance," John said tauntingly. "This is the fourteenth day in your cycle. You could have the child you've always wanted."

Jennifer stared at him in horror. She couldn't believe what she was hearing. "How do you know that?" she demanded.

"I'm a doctor. You started your period while we were in Paris. It wasn't hard to calculate," he spat out.

"You bastard! You take one more step near me, and I swear to God I will break more than your nose. Get out!"

John walked to the door. "Perhaps in the morning, when you've calmed down, we can discuss this."

As John left the room, he closed the door behind him. Jennifer stared at the door and then turned around. John's blood was already staining the white sheets of her bed. She walked slowly to a chair and sat down, the adrenalin of a few minutes ago still rushing through her body. At last, her tears began to fall, brought on by feelings of loneliness, grief, and rage.

* * *

"Elizabeth! What are you doing here?" Derek asked as she entered his bedroom and closed the door behind her.

"I saw you return from taking your nephews riding. I thought you would probably come up here to change your clothes before joining your family. I snuck away when no one was watching," she said with a grin.

"So I see," Derek said with surprise.

"I thought you might need some help," Elizabeth said. She walked over to Derek and put her arms around his

257

neck. "I still remember the first time," she said seductively.

Derek laughed. "In your father's stables. We were . . . what . . . sixteen? I was clumsy and awkward. I didn't know what I was doing. And you were afraid someone would find us."

"Hmmm," Elizabeth purred. "You weren't that bad. We understand each other, Derek. We come from similar backgrounds. We're two of a kind."

"Where's this leading, Elizabeth?" Derek asked as he gently disengaged himself from her.

"Here," she said as she reached for him again and kissed him.

"Elizabeth," Derek said gently, "I don't think—"

"Shhh," she whispered. "I'm not making any demands. We've been friends a long time. I see no reason why we can't enjoy each other."

"I'm flattered, but we're not the same people we were at sixteen," Derek said kindly as he backed away from her grasp. "I'll walk downstairs with you."

✻ ✻ ✻

"The wording of the trust is specific," Timothy Camp said. "If you get a divorce—no matter what the reason—you forfeit your shares of the trust fund."

"You're my attorney. I expect you to see that doesn't happen," John Bracken said angrily.

"Did Jennifer actually ask for a divorce?"

"I got up this morning, and she was gone. My housekeeper said she took a cab to the airport."

"Maybe she just needed some time to herself. I thought you two were getting along."

"That stupid old man!" John swore.

"Your father? Not really, John. Many a family fortune

has been destroyed by the time the attorneys and courts finish hammering out the terms of a divorce. Your father is bound and determined that will not happen to his fortune. And I don't have to remind you how much your previous divorce cost."

"Then don't remind me," John ground out angrily.

Timothy sighed. "Have you even discussed this with your father?"

"My father and I are not exactly on good terms."

"Listen John, if this is just a rift between you and Jennifer, maybe you should tell her about the conditions of your trust fund. She may not be quite as eager for a divorce then."

"That would be a little difficult right now. She's on a fucking plane to Scotland."

* * *

"He did what!" Nina exclaimed. She had picked Jennifer up at the airport in Aberdeen and they were driving back to Cormara.

"He held me down. I fought him as best I could. When he wouldn't stop, I punched him in the nose," Jennifer said.

"Oh, Jen."

"You know what the worst part is? He had carefully orchestrated the entire evening," Jennifer continued, "from calculating the exact day of my cycle, to buying a dress and a diamond and ruby bracelet, getting symphony tickets, and even making dinner reservations."

Nina sighed audibly. "So what now?"

"I met with an attorney just before I left. His name is Steven Cole. My mother had taught his children in school, and I gave private violin lessons to his daughter. He was very kind. He let me come over to his house Sunday afternoon before I caught my flight. He'll start the divorce proceedings immediately." Jennifer paused. "I was hoping I could stay with you for a while."

"You can stay as long as you like."

"I want to pay you."

"Absolutely not!"

"You're renting the cottage and buying food. I can help with the expenses," Jennifer said.

"No, you can't."

"Nina, I don't know how long I'll stay in Scotland. I don't want to take advantage of our friendship."

"You're insulting our friendship right now," Nina said reproachfully. "Listen McHugh, if I showed up on your doorstep in Chicago, would you expect me to pay you for letting me stay with you? Would you limit how long I could stay?"

"Of course not."

"I think I've made my point," Nina said in a superior tone.

Jennifer glanced at her as Nina burst out laughing.

"It's good to have you back, McHugh. I've missed having my best friend in my life. I don't know where you went, but you disappeared after you married John. That fiery little redhead with the braids was gone, and in her place was a quiet, dutiful, sad woman. Finally, I have my friend, Jenny McHugh, back." Nina giggled. "So how hard did you hit him?" she asked with a wink.

Jennifer winced. "I broke his nose."

Nina burst out laughing, slapping her hand on the steering wheel as she drove. When it looked like she wasn't going to stop laughing, Jennifer interrupted.

"It's not funny, Nina," she chided her friend.

"Oh, yes it is, McHugh," Nina said, tears of laughter running down her face.

"What do you plan to do while you're here?" Nina asked

when they arrived at the cottage.

"I haven't thought about it. I just had to get out of Chicago."

"I have a suggestion."

Jennifer looked at her, a question on her face.

"You still want to get to the bottom of these visions, and you were making progress with the help of Derek Rannoch."

"No," Jennifer interrupted.

"Wait. Let me finish," Nina said. "I don't think you can count on any help from Derek, but you still have the notes he made for you. Why not do some research of your own? He's given you a starting point."

Jennifer was silent a moment, the idea taking hold. Could she do that? Did she know enough that she could investigate the possibilities of Cela's civilization existing? Certainly she could start by learning all she could about the Druids. Derek had drawn many parallels between Cela's civilization and the Druids, who came several hundred years later. She could also read more about the ancient stone monuments and megaliths that were now a part of her memories.

"How would I start? Internet?" Jennifer asked.

"Always start with the Internet. It can provide you with a rudimentary knowledge base. But then you're going to need reference books for a more thorough understanding of the subject matter.

"As a tourist, you can use the public libraries in Scotland, but you can't check books out. I think what you will need is more likely available in the university library in Edinburgh. You may not want to drive back and forth every day, though.

"There's a little pub in Cormara that is owned by a man and woman who happen to have a daughter who works at the university library. She's helped me in the past. When there are references that I want to keep for a while, I leave a list with her parents and she checks them out for me. I pick them up at the pub and usually leave a couple of pounds for her for her trouble. When I'm through with the books, I just return them to the pub. You can search the university's holdings online. Then make a list and let Claire know which ones you want first."

"Claire?"

"Claire MacFarland. She's the one who works at the library. Charlie MacFarland, her father, owns the pub. He's Scottish and his wife is English. Tomorrow we can drive into town and I'll introduce you. Then you can get started."

By the end of the week, Jennifer had established a pattern. She awoke early and, while Nina still slept, went for a walk in the nearby foothills. When she returned, she ate breakfast with Nina, then she searched the Internet, finding articles to read and compiling a list of books she wanted.

Nina took her to the pub and introduced her to Mr. MacFarland. He was a friendly man who had kindly agreed to pass the list on to his daughter. He suggested that Jennifer return the next Monday for the books she had requested.

On Sunday morning, Jennifer arose early. The sky was threatening rain again, and she wanted to walk before it rained. She slipped on a raincoat and headed toward the foothills. She walked for some time, contemplating how she would approach her research tomorrow. The sky was overcast and the wind was cool as it blew through her hair. When she felt the first wave of nausea, she was surprised, for she had been thinking about what time she would go to Charlie MacFarland's pub tomorrow. In just seconds, she was unconscious and lying on the ground.

* * *

827 B.C.

"Lodi, I am fine," Cela protested. "I have remained in this hut for three days."

"We thought it best that you avoid Luc's initiation as High Priest," Lodi responded.

"I am grateful for that, but Luc is now the High Priest, and I must resume my duties and my studies."

They were interrupted when a priest entered Lodi's hut.

"The High Priest requests the Priestess Cela's presence," the priest said.

Lodi frowned and looked to Cela. Neither woman spoke.

"He is waiting," the priest said.

"The Priestess Cela has not been feeling well," Lodi answered.

"It is all right, Lodi. I will go to Luc," Cela said.

"Shall I come with you?" Lodi asked.

Cela smiled. "That will not be necessary."

When she arrived at Luc's hut, the priest stepped aside for her to enter alone. Cela found Luc talking with several members of the High Council. They each nodded at her in greeting and then left, leaving Cela alone with Luc.

Cela stood quietly, waiting for Luc to speak. She trembled slightly in his presence, unable to completely forget the night of her initiation.

"Priestess," Luc said in an authoritative voice, "you will move your personal items to my hut."

"What?" Cela gasped.

"You will reside here with me."

It was a moment before Cela could find the words to protest Luc's latest means of intimidating her.

"I cannot do that, Cousin," she said, bowing her head slightly as a sign of respect. "I have neglected my duties and studies. I must return to them."

"You may study with the Wise Ones during the day, but at night, you will attend me." There was a lascivious expression on his face that he did not try to hide.

Cela swallowed, trying to quell the fear building inside of

her. "I cannot do that," she said.

"Can't?" Luc challenged, anger blazing in his eyes.

"It would not be wise," Cela responded, gaining courage as she rapidly formulated her response. "I now carry a child," she said, touching her abdomen. "To repeat the sex act with you would endanger the life of the child."

An evil laugh erupted from Luc. "You must take me for a fool, Cousin! There is no danger to the child now, and I will finish with you long before your belly is swollen with the child."

Anger surged through Cela, giving her courage. She stepped forward, her eyes narrowing. She stopped within inches of her enemy. "And I tell you," she said, her voice deadly, "that lying with you one time will kill the child within me."

Luc drew back, shock on his face. "You speak falsely!" he replied. "You would not cause the death of your own child."

Cela sensed the doubt in his voice. It was all she needed. "Are you certain, Cousin? If this child were not to be born, it would be the worst possible omen for you as High Priest. The people would look upon it as a curse from the gods—a curse on the one chosen as the new High Priest."

In a fury, Luc raised his fist to strike her.

Cela did not flinch. "Go ahead, Cousin," she said calmly. "Hit me and kill the child now."

Luc shrieked a horrible, animal-like sound. Dagga, who was standing nearby, entered, his sword drawn. Luc's fist was still clenched in a fit of rage and poised above Cela's head. He looked up and saw Dagga with his unsheathed sword raised, ready to attack.

Cela was certain Luc assumed Dagga had entered to protect him, the new High Priest. She also knew that Dagga would likely kill Luc if he touched her. Time seemed suspended as the two elite Wise Ones, cousins, glared at each other.

Finally, Luc lowered his fist. "Escort the priestess back

to her hut!" he commanded.

Dagga bowed and stood aside for Cela to pass. He silently followed her away from Luc's hut. It was not until they were well away from the lodgings of the Wise Ones that Cela paused and turned to him.

"How is it, Dagga, that you are always near when I am in danger or in need of help?"

"I believe, Priestess, that your gods have willed it so."

She considered what he said. "Perhaps you are right," she said and smiled. "You can replace your sword; there is no longer the need for it."

Cela waited until Dagga had done as she asked.

"I am not returning to my hut," she began. "I need to be alone. I need to be far from here. You will accompany me?"

Dagga bowed. "As you wish, Priestess."

Cela walked for several hours, Dagga beside her. At one point, Dagga spoke.

"Priestess, you are all right? You have recovered?"

Cela paused. She understood what Dagga was referring to. She knew he had carried her back to Cupa's hut after the fertility rites.

"Yes," she said softly. She placed her hand on his arm. "Dagga, you must never raise your sword against the High Priest, no matter what happens to me. It will mean your death."

"I am a warrior. I expect my death."

"I know that, but there is more to consider here than just your death," she said, trying to patiently explain the implications of such an act. "To have a warrior strike a Wise One—it can't be. It must never happen. It would cause chaos, and the people cannot survive in chaos. They need order and leadership. They need the Wise Ones. Such an act would surely lead to the destruction of our people."

"And what of your life, Priestess?"

They began walking again. "My mother came to Cupa's

265

hut to be with me after the fertility rites," Cela said. "When I looked at her face, I knew something was wrong. At first, I thought she was just concerned about my injuries, but then I realized it was something more than that. My mother has the gift of seeing into the future." Cela paused. "Although she said nothing, I know she saw my death. I do not believe that this life will be a long one for me."

"Priestess!" Dagga said, grabbing her shoulder and turning her to face him. "Leave this place. There are Wise Ones in other lands. Go to them!"

Cela placed her hand on Dagga's where it rested on her shoulder.

"I cannot do that, Dagga," she said gently, touched by his concern. "But there is something that I must learn before I leave this life. It is important. That is where we are going today."

Cela removed her hand and started walking again. Dagga fell in beside her. At midday, they came to a small grove of trees. On the other side of the trees was a meadow. Cela stopped at the trees.

"Dagga, I must be alone now. I want you to guard the entrance to this grove. See that no one approaches. I will be in the meadow beyond. You must not watch me. You must face away from the meadow."

Dagga frowned.

"No matter what happens," Cela said.

"Priestess . . ." Dagga began, firmness in his voice.

Cela smiled. "Do not fear for me, Dagga. Today is not the day that this life ends for me. We will return to our huts by nightfall."

It was clear that Dagga did not like Cela being beyond his watchful eye, but he accepted her order and planted his feet before the grove, his eyes watching for any intrusion from man or beast.

Cela walked through the trees and emerged on the other side into a meadow. She knelt down in the knee-length grass, the sun directly above her. She remained there, kneeling in the meadow, for a long time. It was important that she clear her mind of thoughts of Luc, Dagga, her mother, or her people. She must not think about the child she carried or about the future.

Slowly, she began to relax. She could feel the warmth of the sun upon the top of her head and the mattress of grass beneath her. Her breathing slowed. Finally, she raised her face to the sky.

"Teach me," she whispered. "I am Cela, your daughter. Teach me," she repeated.

As she continued to focus on the blueness of the sky, she could hear the birds chirping in the distant trees. The soft breeze of the wind caressed her face. She concentrated on the sounds around her. Soon, she found herself hearing the minute rustle of a single blade of grass and the sound of the wind as it lifted the birds into the sky.

As Cela listened to each sound, the sounds began to come together, so that soon she realized that she was no longer hearing the single flight of a bird as it moved or a bee as it swarmed, but rather, she began to hear the life force as it flowed through each being. The force itself had a sound that permeated all living things. She heard it as it danced about her, through each flower, each blade of grass, each bird, and each insect. It was everywhere. She was surrounded by it. Then she felt it. It soared through her body, connecting her to all living things. She was deafened by its sound as it swirled through her muscles, bones, and heart. She felt its force gathering inside her, blinding her, and then it seemed to explode, bursting within her in shimmering lights. Suddenly, she understood. The force was there, waiting to be directed.

Cela focused on the expanse of the sky. It was effortless, as natural as breathing. Her body lifted up, unfolding as it did. She ascended slowly, at first, as the sky came closer. She glanced down and watched as she left the grass below her. She looked up and, taking a deep breath, let her body expand in weightlessness and soar upward. She skimmed over the tops of the trees, the wind lifting her up. Below her lay the earth with its grass, trees, flowers, and rocks. She could see great distances as she moved through the sky. She raised her head, arched her neck slightly, and flew more vertically toward the clouds. She felt no fear, but suddenly, caution overcame her. She did not fully understand this new power that was carrying her into the expanse of the sky. Despite the exhilaration, she slowed her movement. Glancing back, the trees were small and she could no longer see the grass and flowers. For a second, she hesitated.

"Go no farther," an inner voice cautioned.

Cela turned and came rushing back. There it was: her meadow. Beyond, she could see the small figure of a man—Dagga—as he stood guard. She relaxed and slowed her speed as she moved through the sky, the earth coming closer. Finally, she let her feet touch the grass.

* * *

Jennifer rolled onto her side, her breathing labored. She swallowed quickly. Perspiration formed on her forehead and on the palms of her hands. Her head was spinning in a sickening vertigo. Her stomach cramped, and she lifted herself up on her elbows, vomiting onto the grass. She squeezed her eyes shut and waited for the vortex to release her.

When at last she felt her racing heart slow down and her balance return, she sat up. She took some deep breaths and looked around. That didn't make any sense. Cela flew. *We flew!*

She stared at the rocky foothills, a patchwork of green grass peppered with gray boulders jutting up everywhere. It was rough terrain. How did she get here? She ran her hand across her forehead and stood. The ground was hard underneath the coarse grass that grew on soil only a few inches thick. Fortunately, she hadn't hit her head when she lost consciousness. Physically, she felt fine, other than the bad taste in her mouth.

She started the climb downward, careful of her footing. She stumbled a few times and was forced to reach for the large rocks for support. By the time she arrived at Nina's cottage, her hair and clothing were wet from the rain that had begun to fall.

An hour later, Jennifer was seated on the brightly flowered sofa in Nina's cottage. She had bathed and changed into dry clothing. Nina handed her a drink.

"Sip it slowly," Nina warned. "The Scots know how to make whiskey," she said as she sat down next to Jennifer.

Jennifer took a sip of the liquid, feeling its burn as she swallowed. She welcomed the distraction it brought.

"You're upset about this last vision," Nina stated. "Why? What happened?"

"Maybe John was right after all," Jennifer muttered as she took another sip of the famous malt whiskey of Scotland.

"What are you talking about?"

Jennifer took a deep breath. "The visions. Maybe they're hallucinations after all."

Nina screwed up her face. "Why would you say that?"

"I honestly believed that I was seeing a past civilization—something that was real at one time. I had no explanation as to why I was able to see this, but I believed in it. That was why I went to Derek in the first place, but now—"

"Now what?"

"I don't know if what I see is, or was, reality."

"I'm sorry, McHugh, I don't understand anything you're saying," Nina answered.

Jennifer shook her head and leaned back in the sofa.

"Do you remember me telling you about the People of the Sky that Cela and the Wise Ones believed in?"

"Yes. You said they believed that people came out of the sky and taught them everything they know."

"Yes, and the People of the Sky were humans, like them, but sent by the gods."

"So?"

"In my visions, I've never seen these people. I thought it was a legend that Cela and her people believed. Cela was descended from one of them." Jennifer paused. "These people were supposed to be able to fly; that's why they called them the 'People of the Sky.' The Wise Ones have been waiting for them to return. The last time their history says that the People of the Sky visited was in the time of Cela's great-grandmother, Mora," Jennifer added.

"So what happened? Did they return?"

"No, but Cela flew, or at least I think she did," Jennifer said with doubt.

"What do you mean, 'Cela flew'?"

"Cela used to have dreams and images of things, seeing them from the air. Well, this time, she flew. She finally discovered the secret of the People of the Sky. She flew!"

"You mean like a bird?"

Jennifer smiled weakly. "Not exactly. She didn't have to move her arms."

"Are you sure this wasn't just a dream that she had, or maybe an out-of-body experience?"

"I don't know. It was so real, Nina. I saw her move through the sky. I *felt* it. I was her, or at least I was a part of her, inside of her. *I* flew through the sky, Nina. It was just as real as the rest of the visions have been." Jennifer paused. "But that's not possible, is it?"

Nina frowned.

"Do you see what I mean?" Jennifer asked. "Am I just making up this fantasy in my head? Hallucinating, as John said?"

"Forget about John."

"There's another problem," Jennifer said. "All my life, I've dreamed that I could fly. Ever since I was a little girl. When I was asleep, I would dream that I could fly. This was just like my dreams, only so much better. I can't even describe it to you. So is this just a figment of my imagination like the dreams? Am I creating all of this in my mind?"

Nina looked at Jennifer shrewdly. "I had forgotten about that. When we were kids, you told me that you flew in your dreams."

"But people can't fly now, and they never did. So is this all just my fantasy?"

Nina shrugged. "I don't know. Maybe Cela was dreaming also, or maybe she was in some sort of self-hypnosis. That's possible, isn't it?"

"I suppose so," Jennifer said with doubt, "but that's not like Cela. It seemed so real," she repeated. "You can't imagine what it was like to move through the sky like that," Jennifer whispered. A tear began to form. "In all my dreams, I never imagined it could be like that. It's as though by defying gravity and the physical laws, the body sets the soul free at the same time. The spirit and the body are truly joined with the life forces, and you soar through the sky."

The room was silent, and then Nina broke the spell.

"All right. That's a little weird. Next thing you know, you'll be hearing the phone ring before it does or bending spoons," Nina said with humor.

Jennifer couldn't help but grin sheepishly as she wiped her eyes.

"But seriously, Jen, I don't know if Cela flew. I don't really understand any of this, but I trust you. Something incredible is happening. I would suggest that you continue with your plan. Find out all you can about that time period and just see what comes next."

Jennifer took Nina's advice and the next day drove to

Cormara and stopped at the MacFarland's pub.

"Ah, Miss McHugh," Charlie MacFarland said when she entered.

"Good afternoon, Mr. MacFarland," Jennifer replied with a smile.

"Claire got these books for you," he said as he placed three books on the bar. "She said she will have more for you next week."

"Thank you," Jennifer said, taking the books in her arms. She looked around the pub. "Is it too late for lunch?"

"Not at all. Let me find a nice table for you," Charlie MacFarland said as he walked around the bar. His establishment was small, with a bar dominating the room and eight small tables placed about the room. He pointed to a chalkboard on the wall, indicating that those were the dishes available for lunch. With his assistance, Jennifer selected from the menu and settled in for a pleasant lunch.

People entered the pub, calling a greeting to Charlie MacFarland as Jennifer ate and read from one of the books. When she had finished her meal, she pushed the plates aside and continued reading. At one point, Charlie removed the dishes and Jennifer looked up with embarrassment.

"I'm sorry," she said, glancing at her watch. "I hadn't realized the time. You probably want to close."

"Not at all. The bar stays open all day. There's no need to hurry," Charlie MacFarland said kindly.

That was the beginning of a pattern. For the next two weeks, Jennifer arrived at Charlie's pub at noon. She ordered lunch and then worked at the table the rest of the afternoon, leaving around four o'clock. She developed an easy relationship with Charlie. The people of Cormara who frequented Charlie's pub came to know her by name and would call a greeting to her as they entered the pub. They became accustomed to seeing her reading at the table and typing on her laptop computer. Jennifer finished the first books, and Claire brought more for her.

Charlie always saved a table for Jennifer, and when

business would slow, he'd frequently sit at her table and talk for a few minutes. Jennifer never minded the interruptions, and Charlie always brought a glass of dark ale for her to drink. Sometimes the other customers would join them for a few minutes before returning to their homes or businesses. She enjoyed the relaxed friendliness of Charlie's customers.

One day, when she was especially engrossed in her reading, a shadow passed over her table as a man stopped next to the table. Jennifer smiled and looked up, expecting to see Charlie with two mugs of ale. She froze when she saw the familiar face staring down at her.

"Mrs. Bracken," Derek said, his eyes piercing, his anger barely concealed. "I thought you had returned to Chicago."

A myriad of feelings rushed into her body, seeing him standing so near after all this time. How long had it been since she had seen him? Six weeks? She felt her heart leap, her body come alive. A night didn't pass that she didn't dream about him and awaken, longing for him. And every day since returning to Scotland, she had to force herself not to think about him, knowing that she could never put him out of her heart. She took her time answering.

"I did, and then I returned to Scotland several weeks ago. There were some things I needed to do," she said lamely, unable to stop the warmth that was spreading throughout her.

"So I see," Derek said, his voice hard. He reached down and picked up one of the books. "*The Druids,*" he said, reading the title. He placed the book on the table and reached for another one. "*The Mystery of the Standing Stones,*" he read. He returned the book to the table. "So that's how you did it." His eyes narrowed.

"Pardon me?" Jennifer said.

"Your Bronze Age civilization," he answered. Derek stepped closer to the table and picked up her notebook. He glanced through several pages and then to her laptop computer. "Very thorough, and these must be the mysterious 'documents.' No wonder you wouldn't show them to me." He returned the notebook to the table.

Jennifer began to understand. She started to protest when Derek interrupted her again.

"You don't have to do all this work to get a lover, Jenny, unless, of course, you are particularly attracted to the academic type."

His cruel words caused tears to spring to her eyes. For a moment, she couldn't breathe, the ache in her heart so great. Then she sprang to her feet and hastily dashed the tears from her eyes.

"I never read anything before I came to your office that day. I'm doing this now only because you will no longer help me." Her hurt transitioned into anger, and she advanced on him in a fury, causing him to take a step backward. "You think you know everything, don't you?" she spat out. "The great Professor Rannoch. Oh, excuse me, *Lord* Rannoch. Here!" she said, turning and grasping the large book with the pictures of the standing stones. She thrust it roughly against his chest. "Take it. It's wrong anyway. It's useless! They're all wrong! You're wrong! It's right before your eyes, but you're too damned sanctimonious to see it. All you can see is my mistake. You can go to hell!"

Jennifer whirled around and grabbed her purse and laptop. She ignored the surprised looks from Charlie and his customers as she ran out of the pub, leaving Derek holding the book and staring after her.

CHAPTER 10

"Jeffrey!" Derek roared to the longtime employee of Thornhill. "Where's Edward?"

Derek had just returned from Charlie MacFarland's pub. He called to both his father and his brother and found no one home. He found Jeffrey in the kitchen.

"Lord Edward flew to London this morning. He isn't expected back until Friday."

Derek swore. "Where's my father?"

"I believe he's in the sheep barn. Is there something I can do, Lord Derek?"

"No," Derek muttered as he walked out of the kitchen. He withdrew his cell phone and punched the numbers with unnecessary force.

"Edward, do you remember the roll of papers that Nina Bouvay brought over six or seven weeks ago?" he asked when he heard his brother answer his phone.

"Good afternoon to you, also," Edward said in response to Derek's abrupt speech. "I'm in a meeting. May I call you back?"

"No. This will only take a minute. Nina Bouvay. She's a friend of Jennifer McHugh. You came into the hall just as she was leaving. I gave the papers to you."

"The ones you asked me to burn?"

Derek swore. "You destroyed them?" he demanded.

Edward laughed. "Relax, brother. No, I did not destroy them. I suspected they must be fairly important to have

275

caused you such anger—either that, or the owner was important. They're Miss McHugh's, correct?"

"Where did you put them?" Derek asked, ignoring his brother's teasing.

"They're in the library, in the bottom drawer of the map table."

"Thanks, Edward," Derek said.

"Sure. You'll explain all of this to me when I get home this weekend?"

"I'm not certain I can," Derek said.

Derek found the papers in the library where Edward had placed them. Sitting down, he turned on the light and unrolled them. His brow knitted together as he looked at the first sketch. It was the one of Stonehenge that he had drawn. Jennifer had changed it. She had added some stones and moved others. He noticed immediately that she had added a second Heel Stone to the east. She also had written an explanation for the second stone. Derek read in rapt attention as she described the effect the pair of stones would have when the midsummer sun and the midwinter full moon rose over them. He studied the pattern created by the stones she had added and those that she had moved slightly. She had removed the two Station Stones and the Slaughter Stone completely. Interesting. And she placed stones in the North and South Barrows that, to date, had not been suggested by archaeological examination.

He leaned back in his chair. Jennifer's Stonehenge was much more symmetrical and complete. Furthermore, she had drawn an avenue leading from Stonehenge westward to the River Avon.

A second paper had a small scale drawing of Stonehenge and the surrounding plains. He recognized Durrington Walls to the south, but she had drawn other henges and mounds that, to his knowledge, didn't exist. As Stonehenge had been modified over thousands of years, he wondered what year her sketches were meant to represent. There had been several other smaller pieces of paper inside the roll. Derek had hastily pushed them aside in order to study the sketch of Stonehenge. Now he shifted his attention to the other papers. They were all quickly drawn on Cowden Hall stationery. Jennifer had obviously used the paper in the writing desk in her room to draw these before she left. He spread them out on the desk, swearing under his breath as he let his eyes scan over each one. "What kind of a game is this, Jenny?"

There were six sketches of megalithic formations. Some had shadows caused by the sunlight; others did not. He recognized three of them immediately, one of which was in Wales and one in Ireland. When had Jenny gone to Wales and Ireland? She never mentioned traveling to either country. The other three were different. He looked at them, one at a time. He imagined them missing some of their stones. That was it! He knew these three formations, too. Jenny had just added stones again.

Derek spread all six sketches on the desktop. There was something more here. He just couldn't determine what it was. He swore again. Something was nagging him at the back of his mind, and it was more than just the fact that she had added or moved stones and drew new shadows on some of them. What was it?

He picked up each sketch individually. For the next hour, he stared at them, still unable to uncover what he was looking for. It was there; he knew it. This was not the first time that an archaeological puzzle had presented itself to him. He would discover it, even if it took all day and night.

There was a knock on the library door and Clara, the maid, entered.

"Lord Derek, would you like tea now?" she asked.

Derek looked up and rubbed his eyes.

"Yes, Clara, thank you. I'll take it in here."

Derek stood and walked to the window. He looked out across the expanse of Thornhill as Clara placed the teapot

and plate of scones on a nearby table. When she left, Derek
filled a cup and wandered back to the desk. He was about to
take a sip of the tea when he glanced down on the table
where the six drawings were spread out.

"Damn!" he suddenly shouted, his eyes riveted to the
sketches. "That's it!"

Derek set his cup down roughly, spilling its contents on
the desk. He hastily grabbed the sketches and a leather
portfolio. Shoving the papers inside of it, he took large
strides out of the library. As he passed Jeffrey, he shouted,
"I'm going to the old shearer's cottage, the one that Nina
Bouvay is leasing."

Without further explanation, he rushed out the door and
to his car.

Derek's anger hadn't abated by the time he reached the
cottage. He had tried to put Jennifer out of his mind after
the morning at Cowden Hall. That's when he discovered the
depth of her deception. She had lied about possessing
documents detailing a Bronze Age civilization, and she had
not told him she was married. Would she have ever told
him? It was by accident that they had encountered Jennifer's
friends at Cowden Hall. Obviously, he was just a fling for
her, an exciting affair, and the archaeological deception was
a triumph.

Derek swore as he turned off the engine and stepped out
of his car. Finding her at MacFarland's Pub only confirmed
his conclusions. She had gained her knowledge about the
Bronze Age and prehistoric megaliths from modern-day
publications. And yet, there was something about her
sketches that kept nagging at his subconscious. He knew
there was a flaw in his logic, and he aimed to discover it
now.

He knocked on the door and didn't have to wait long for
Jennifer to open it. For a brief moment, he faltered at seeing
her reddened eyes but steeled himself. "I want to talk to

you," he stated without a greeting as he entered the cottage.

"Well, I don't want to talk to you," Jennifer said as she left him standing inside the door and walked into the kitchen.

"I want the truth for once," Derek said, following her into the kitchen.

Jennifer whirled around. "Are you sure you would know it, *Lord* Derek?" she sarcastically challenged.

"Dispense with the *Lord*," Derek said.

"Why? It suits you," Jennifer fired back.

"Like *Mrs.* Bracken suits you?"

The color drained from Jennifer's face and she looked away. "The fact that I'm married is nobody's business but my own. And it never would have been yours if . . . if. . . ." She kept her face averted, but Derek heard her voice catch.

He had forgotten how easily Jennifer could stir deep feelings within him. Even now, as angry as he was, he wanted to take her in his arms, to erase the existence of this husband of hers forever. He had been fooling himself for six weeks now, saying that she didn't matter, that she was no different from the other women with whom he'd had a relationship at some point in his life. But she was different from the others, and it did matter. He couldn't explain why—he didn't understand it himself—but Jenny mattered.

"You must leave," she said quietly, staring at the space in the floor between them.

"Not until I get some answers," he stated.

"You've already gotten your answers," she said as she raised her eyes to meet his.

"Not all of them," he said as he withdrew the sketches from his portfolio. He laid each of her drawings out on the table. When he had all six laying there, he stepped back.

"Something was bothering me about your drawings," he said, "and I couldn't determine what it was. I know you added stones to some of the formations and sketched shadow patterns, but it was more than that. It wasn't until I had moved away from the desk and then returned, just like this," he said, grabbing her elbow and turning her to face the table, "that I realized what it was that was bothering me.

"They're all aerial views of the monuments, as though you flew over them and took photos from an airplane. Not one of them is a view from the ground. None of the formations—the shadows that you drew—could be completely seen from the ground. This one, Long Meg and Her Daughters, is in Cumbria," he said as he pointed to one of the sketches. "Because of the height of the one stone, it's always photographed from the ground to show the difference in heights of the stones. I didn't even recognize the formation at first, and I've seen it hundreds of times, but always from the ground."

Derek paused a moment. "Why, Jenny, why did you draw them like this? Why did you draw them as they would appear from above?" He looked at her. When she didn't answer, he grew more insistent. "What are you trying to do? Is this another one of your games?"

Derek knew he was pressing her unkindly, but he had to know. Had everything between them been a lie?

Jennifer tilted her chin up with a look of determination. "You know all the answers, remember?" she said.

Her lip was trembling, and Derek felt his heart soften. Why? Why couldn't she be truthful with him for once? He looked down at the pictures, pointing to one of them and then another. "You indicated the direction of each sketch in the corner. You placed an *N*, indicating the north."

He ran his hand through his hair in frustration. "You once told me that, although some of the monuments had astronomical significance, their main function was to be part of a map. I questioned you about that at the time. I couldn't understand how a traveler on foot would be able to see all the megaliths. You didn't mean that they were for a traveler on foot, did you? Who were they for, Jenny?"

Derek reached down and picked up one of her sketches. "Who would see these as you have drawn them, Jenny? Who?" Derek asked insistently.

He was standing inches from her and saw something in her eyes. Pain? Sadness? "The People of the Sky," she finally answered, her voice barely above a whisper.

"The gods that your civilization believed in?"

"They weren't gods. They were people who. . . ." Jennifer faltered a moment. "They were people who had the ability to fly. They were the messengers of the gods. They came from some other place. They taught the Wise Ones everything they knew."

"And these?" Derek asked, indicating Jennifer's sketches.

"The pattern made by the stones and henges was specific. Each stone formation indicated a place and the tribe of people who had created it, like the name of a town on a map. It was a symbol that could be read from the sky. The People of the Sky would look for the symbol as they flew."

Derek stared at her, astounded by her revelation. "Like a landing strip, Jenny?"

"No," she said softly. "They didn't use spaceships or aircraft. They could defy gravity and just move through the air with their bodies."

It took a moment for Derek to contemplate the enormity of her words. He looked back at the sketches. "Are there more?" he asked.

"Yes, many. In lands with dense jungles, it was necessary to build larger monuments—stone pyramids that could be seen among the trees from the sky," she finished quietly.

He picked up one of her sketches again and held it out to her.

"How do you know this, Jenny?"

Derek saw Jennifer's lip tremble, and she looked away.

"Tell me," he said softly as he reached out to her, his fingertips lightly touching her chin, turning her to face him.

"I can't," Jennifer replied.

"Please," he said.

"I'm sorry. I can't."

Derek sighed, feeling defeated. He handed her the sketch

he was holding.

"I'm sorry, too, Jenny." The silence hung in the air, and then Derek spoke one more time. "Good-bye."

Jennifer bit her lip and nodded her head.

"Good-bye," she whispered.

Derek turned and left the room.

* * *

"Jen," Nina called from the kitchen. "A phone call for you."

Jennifer frowned as she walked into the kitchen. "For me?"

"Yes. Steven Cole, your attorney."

Jennifer glanced at her watch. "It must be the middle of the night in Chicago."

Nina handed the phone to Jennifer and waited.

"Steven?" Jennifer answered.

"Good morning, Jennifer. I hope I didn't call too early," he said.

"No, not at all."

"Good. I thought I would let you know how things are going. Your husband has refused to speak with me. I have spoken with his attorney, Timothy Camp. According to Camp, John does not want this divorce and is going to fight it all the way."

"Fight it? What do you mean?"

"He won't make it easy."

"But he can't stop it, right?"

"No, he can't stop it, but he can delay it. I've been doing some background work. His previous wife signed an NDA as part of her divorce settlement, but there's something there—something that John doesn't want us to know."

"Like what?"

"I don't know yet. Do I have your permission to hire a private investigator?"

"What?"

"It's standard procedure in cases such as this."

After a few more words, Jennifer reluctantly agreed and hung up the phone.

"Well?" Nina asked impatiently. "What did he say?"

"John doesn't want the divorce and is going to try to delay it," Jennifer answered.

"That doesn't surprise me. John's an ass," Nina said and then smiled when she heard a car stop in front of the cottage. "Shamus is here. Look, Jen, John may delay the divorce, but he can't prevent it. Forget about John. Let your attorney handle it, and you stay here with me.

"Come in, Shamus," Nina called when she heard Shamus knock at the door. She turned back to Jennifer. "We want you to go with us today," Nina said.

Jennifer frowned. A week had passed since Derek had brought the sketches to her and confronted her in Nina's kitchen. Jennifer had tried to resume her study of the Bronze Age and Druid civilizations, but she only ended up crying. Derek, Scotland, England, the Bronze Age, Cela— they all swirled around in her mind, intertwined, and at the heart of them all was Derek, the man she had lied to and who wanted nothing to do with her.

"I wouldn't be very good company, Nina," Jennifer replied.

"That's exactly why you should come with us. You need to do something fun. Jen, you're in Scotland, and these are the Highland Games. You know you want to go," Nina coaxed.

"Yes," Jennifer agreed, "I want to go, but what if he's there?"

"What if who's there?" Shamus asked.

Both women turned as Shamus entered the cottage.

"Shamus, you look so handsome," Jennifer exclaimed as she admired his Highland dress.

Shamus bowed slightly and smiled. "Thank you, Jennifer."

"I agree," Nina said as she kissed him on the cheek. "A man in full Highland regalia is a sight to behold. Tell Jen about it," she said as she motioned to his clothing.

Shamus turned back to Jennifer.

"Yes, please do," Jennifer encouraged.

Shamus smiled again. "Of course. The pattern of the fabric, the plaid, is actually called a tartan," he explained. "Originally, the tartan was the clan fabric that was draped over the shoulder. Each clan would spin their own wool and then dye it, getting their colors from the plants that grew where they lived. They each created distinct patterns. The word 'tartan' has come to mean the plaid fabric in the kilt as well."

"But why not pants?" Jennifer asked.

"The tartan, or kilt, was once a very functional garment. It allowed the clansman freedom of movement and was very practical in the damp moors. Pants would have been continuously wet and difficult to dry. Bare legs could dry quickly. Of course, they used a lot more fabric than we use today. Originally, it wrapped around the top of the torso, too. That provided added warmth and could actually be used as a sleeping bag at night." Shamus smiled and looked down at his own kilt. "My family comes from the Macneill of Colonsay clan."

Jennifer looked at the rich fabric, a mixture of green, blue, black, and white. Shamus was wearing a tweed jacket and sweater as well. He had gray tweed socks that reached just below his knees.

"A properly dressed clansman always has his knife tucked here, just in case," Nina added.

Jennifer noted the knife sticking out of Shamus's right sock. Shamus laughed.

"It's called a sgian dubh," he said. "And you ladies will appreciate this as well," he said as he lifted a pouch made of animal skin that hung from his waist. "It's a sporran.

Originally, it was to hold one's valuables, including a daily ration of oatmeal. There are no pockets in the kilt," he added in explanation.

"And what is that on your hat?" Jennifer asked, referring to a pin on the soft cap Shamus was wearing.

"The hat is a Highland bonnet, and this is the badge identifying my clan," he said as he removed the hat so Jennifer could look at it more closely.

She held the hat in her hand and lightly traced the badge with her fingers. "It must be wonderful to feel such a sense of history, of belonging," she said wistfully.

"I believe you are one of us, Lass," Shamus said in a heavily accented brogue. "Your name is McHugh, is it not?" Shamus smiled.

"See, you must come with us," Nina said to Jennifer and then she turned to Shamus. "She's worried about seeing Derek Rannoch," she explained.

"Nina!" Jennifer exclaimed.

"Jen, he knows all about you and Derek."

Jennifer didn't know what to say. She was embarrassed, but then Shamus put his arm around her and winked.

"I think you'll enjoy the games, Jennifer, and don't worry," he said. "I've got one of my grandmother's famous feelings: it's going to be a good day."

The short drive into Cormara was pleasant as Shamus told both women of the events of the day. Despite his vivid descriptions, Jennifer was unprepared for the sights and sounds that greeted her once they arrived. The entire town was involved in the celebration. A large, grassy area on the edge of town had been set aside for the games. The road was blocked, and areas were roped off for the dances and music. Men were walking in their colorful tartan plaids. Jennifer could hear music from every direction. The excitement of the people was contagious.

"It's wonderful, Shamus!" Jennifer said excitedly.

The games had already started, and they stopped to watch those in progress. Shamus explained that the games had their origins in the fairs organized by the tribes or clans long ago.

"The games were tests of strength. The clansmen demonstrating the greatest strength were selected to serve in the clan's army," Shamus said as they paused to watch a race being run up the steep hillside, then winding around again and returning to the flat area sectioned off.

A great roar erupted from the crowd as the victor crossed the finish line. Jennifer, Shamus, and Nina watched as the weary man, breathing hard, stepped up to receive his award. Jennifer stiffened when she saw Lord Harold Rannoch step forward to congratulate the runner.

"It's tradition," Shamus said gently. "Lord Harold is the ranking nobleman of the games."

As Jennifer watched, she saw Lord Harold's daughter, Ann, step forward. She was flanked by two men: Derek and, Jennifer imagined by the resemblance, his younger brother, Edward. Jennifer couldn't take her eyes off Derek. He looked magnificent. His kilt was predominantly red plaid, and he, too, was wearing a dark tweed jacket and hat. She felt a rush of feelings flood her body with warmth. Just then, Derek stepped away from Ann, and Jennifer saw another woman take his arm. Even at this distance, she recognized Lady Elizabeth Sheering. She must have said something amusing, for Derek looked down at her and laughed.

"Jen?" Nina said, interrupting Jennifer's thoughts.

Jennifer turned to see concern on both Shamus and Nina's faces. They glanced at Derek and back at her.

"I heard some bagpipes over that way," Jennifer said quickly as she pointed in a direction away from Derek. "I think I'll just wander over there and listen to the music for a while. You two don't mind, do you?"

Nina nodded with understanding. "No, go ahead. We'll be here by the games."

Derek had just finished congratulating the winner of the race when he turned to say something to his sister. As he did, a flash of sunlight caught his sight, burnishing like fire. He inhaled sharply, recognizing that blazing, red hair at a distance. "Shit," he swore under his breath.

"Derek? Are you all right?" his sister, Ann, asked.

"Yes, of course," he answered.

Ann glanced in the distance to see what had provoked her brother. Then she turned back to Derek and placed her arm through his. "You're a good man, Derek," she said.

"Not so good, Ann. I lost my temper and said some harsh things."

"Oh? To a woman?" When Derek didn't answer, she squeezed his arm gently. "A gentleman would apologize."

Jennifer was grateful to Nina for her sensitivity and to Shamus for his kindness. Perhaps returning to Scotland was not such a good idea after all. One thing was certain: if she was going to stay for a while, she must learn to separate Derek from Scotland. She could not allow herself to be reminded of him by everything she saw and heard.

As she walked, she stopped to watch some children dancing. Two swords had been placed on the ground at right angles to each other in the form of a cross. The children were dancing above them, their feet nimble as they touched the ground without disturbing the swords, their arms alternately held up in the air. Each child wore the traditional kilt, knee-length socks, and a white shirt. Their steps were lively and quick, and Jennifer could not help but feel her mood lighten as she watched them dance.

When the children finished, there was a roar of approval from the people watching. Jennifer joined in, smiling. The swords were retrieved, and Jennifer heard the first distinct sounds of bagpipes as a parade of pipers in full dress appeared. There must have been at least two hundred of them, walking three abreast. They all had black coats trimmed in silver with tall, black hats topped off with plumes. She could see the different patterns and colors of the kilts, each clan being represented by about a dozen pipers. They wore a piece of the tartan cloth draped across their chests and up to their shoulders. The sound of their combined bagpipes captivated Jennifer as she watched, mesmerized, taking the sound deep within her where it resonated.

"They say only a true Scotsman can appreciate the sound of a bagpipe," a male voice said close to her. "To others, the sound is worse than death."

Jennifer recognized the deep timber of Derek's voice. Every nerve fiber within her leapt, recalling the one night spent in his arms. She had discovered passion that night but was not fooled by it. Her feelings for Derek ran much deeper. She loved him.

"Every instrument has its own soul," she said without turning around. He was just inches from her, but she kept her face forward. She wasn't certain if it was the power of the music or Derek's proximity, but her eyes moistened with emotion. "If a musician recognizes that uniqueness and honors the soul of the instrument, well then," she shuddered, "the sound returned is of such perfection that the music penetrates the bones, stirs the blood, and touches the human soul."

The seconds hung in the air, and then she felt his hand on her shoulder. She turned to see him looking down at her as though studying her. His gaze was so penetrating that she felt overtaken by its power.

"Who are you, Jenny?" His voice was soft, but his eyes reflected intensity, and what, confusion?

He blinked and shook his head as though to clear it of his thoughts. Then he smiled at her, his countenance casual. She hastily wiped the tears from her eyes and smiled tentatively.

"You like music," he said.

Jennifer shrugged her shoulders. "It was the only thing I understood. I was a poor student, graduating from high school with a mediocre *C* average. Math, science, social studies, literature, history—I was not very good at any of it. I only attended one year of college." She paused. "My mother was a classically trained musician. I understood and loved music from the moment I was born." Again, she felt her face blush from embarrassment.

"Do you play an instrument, Jenny?" he asked.

She hesitated. *A prodigy. They said I was the most gifted prodigy they had ever seen play the violin. Destined to be one of the greatest violinists in the world.*

"I used to," was all she said and looked back at the bagpipes. "Not the bagpipe," she added.

Derek laughed. "Did you know that the bagpipe didn't even originate here? It's believed to have originated in the Near East and to have been introduced to Scotland by the conquering Romans. Some changes were made, and it became a military instrument of The Highlands, similar to the bugle used to signal troops in your country."

He smiled again. "It's said that the dreaded sound of the Highland piper alone sent terror through the English ranks. Following the defeat of the Scots by the English at Culloden in 1746, the bagpipe and the kilt were actually outlawed for a time. Some probably wish they still were," he added with humor.

Jennifer smiled. She'd been so tense around Derek since she returned. She had forgotten how easy it was to talk with him, how comfortable he made her feel, how safe. She looked back at the pipers who had come to a stop, forming three lines. "You're so fortunate to be a part of all this," she said softly.

"Here," he said as he removed his hat.

To Jennifer's surprise, he placed it on her head. As he adjusted it, he pushed her long hair back.

"Now you're a part of it, too," he said, smiling.

"I can't wear this. Shamus said that the hat, or bonnet as he called it, was important to the complete dress. Your clan symbol is on it. You can't let someone else wear it."

Derek burst out laughing, a deep, rich laughter. "My father is the Earl of Thornhill, the ranking nobleman of Scotland and patron of these games. I can give my hat to whomever I please, although you should know that today you are an honorary member of the Stuart Clan of the Marquis of Bute. The Marquis of Bute was descended from one of King Robert the Second's illegitimate sons, mind you." Derek's eyes were twinkling.

"Conceived in the hunting lodge, no doubt," she replied.

"Ah, you remembered," he said, laughing again. "Will you walk with me, Jenny?"

She nodded her head and strolled beside him as he explained the specifics of some of the dances they saw and games being conducted.

"The games were originally a clan event designed to test the strength, stamina, and skill of the clansmen. Any man of fighting age was expected to compete. They used the materials available."

"Like wooden poles?" Jennifer asked as they stopped to watch the competition.

"Yes. Those poles are actually tree trunks called *cabers*. Throwing them requires a great deal of strength, as does throwing hammers. Foot races up steep hills tested endurance."

"And that?" she asked as they began walking again.

"Round stones were taken from streams and placed on the ground. The men used a stick to hit the stones to a target. It required accuracy."

"The beginning of golf?" she asked, excited by her conclusion.

Derek nodded his head and smiled.

"And did the men dance?" she asked as they approached men dancing around swords placed on the ground.

"Yes, the warriors were expected to compete in the

Highland dance as well. Stamina and agility were required for the dance. Of course, fighting skills such as wrestling, archery, and swordsmanship were also included in the games.

"The chief of the clan chose his warriors based on the games. But it wasn't all serious competition. It evolved into a clan gathering celebrating with music, food, and socializing."

They were watching the dancing when Derek's father appeared.

"Derek, there you are," Lord Harold said. "Miss McHugh! How nice to see you again. I thought you had returned to America."

Harold Rannoch extended his hand to Jennifer.

"I had, but I returned a few weeks ago," Jennifer said.

"I'm delighted that you have," Lord Harold responded. "Are you enjoying the games?"

"Very much," Jennifer replied.

Just then, Robert and Ann Warrick approached with their sons. Lady Elizabeth Sheering was with them.

"You remember my daughter, Ann, and her family," Harold Rannoch said, "and Elizabeth Sheering."

"Of course," Jennifer said.

Robert Warrick offered his hand. "It's a pleasure, Miss McHugh."

"Jennifer," Ann said warmly, "I'm glad you've returned. Father was positively disappointed that he never got to give you a full tour of Thornhill when you were here before. You must indulge him this time," Ann teased.

Everyone laughed and then Harold Rannoch spoke again.

"And this is my youngest son, Edward. Edward, this is Miss Jennifer McHugh," Lord Harold said.

Derek's brother stepped forward. "Miss McHugh, at last we meet. I've been quite curious. It appears you have cast a spell over my entire family, and now I can see why," he said kindly.

Again everyone laughed, and then Lady Elizabeth spoke.

"Derek, we thought you'd gotten lost," she said as she placed her arm through his possessively. "They're about to confer the awards and are waiting for your family."

"I'm sorry, Father," Derek said. "I lost track of the time."

"I understand," his father replied, smiling at Jennifer.

"Miss McHugh," Edward said, "would you care to join us for the ceremony?"

Everyone turned to look at her.

"We'd love for you to," Ann added.

Jennifer's heart was pounding. She looked at Derek but couldn't read his thoughts. He appeared to be measuring her, waiting to see what she would do. Lady Elizabeth's eyes narrowed.

"Thank you," Jennifer said, "but I must return to my friends."

Lord Harold nodded his head in understanding. "Perhaps you will accept my invitation to tea at Thornhill?"

Jennifer hesitated. She glanced at Derek, but his face was impassive.

"Say yes, Miss McHugh, but if he's planning on giving you the full tour of Thornhill, you'd better allow several hours," Edward Rannoch said conspiratorially.

"Yes, I would love to," Jennifer said. "Thank you."

"Good." Lord Harold nodded his head. "And now," he said, turning to his family, "we had better return to our duty."

Derek smiled secretly to Jennifer and leaned close. "Ah," he whispered in a brogue, "the heavy weight of duty."

She stood there, paralyzed, emotions racing through her. He turned to leave with his family when Lady Elizabeth grabbed his arm.

"Derek, you need your bonnet!" Lady Elizabeth interjected.

Derek's family looked back at Jennifer. It was an awkward moment, for Elizabeth's meaning was clear: she did not like Jennifer wearing Derek's hat.

"Oh," Jennifer said as she reached for the hat to return it to Derek.

"I think it looks good on Miss McHugh," Derek's brother said.

"So do I," Derek said. "I can do without my bonnet, Elizabeth. Come, we've delayed the award ceremonies long enough."

"Good-bye, Jennifer," Ann called as the family turned to leave.

Jennifer began to retrace her steps back to where she had left Nina and Shamus. Her heart was pounding, and her thoughts were in turmoil. She glanced over her shoulder and saw Derek and his family in the distance. Was this what it was like for those countless mistresses whom Derek had jokingly told her about? Did they give their hearts to the previous Lord Rannochs through the centuries, never to be a part of the family? Derek and Lady Elizabeth were destined to be married.

But why had Derek just been so nice to her? He'd been so angry when he discovered she was married and that she had lied to him about possessing documents. Then when he had found her at MacFadden's Pub, he had been furious. Obviously, Derek had not told his family about their night together at Cowden Hall or that she was married.

Jennifer reached up and touched the hat on her head. She could almost feel his hands as he placed it there and brushed her hair back, causing her heart to race just thinking about him. She swore softly under her breath. She could abide his anger easier than his kindness, for his anger she could fight. She could not fight the longing that his kindness brought.

"Jen! Where have you been?" Nina asked.

Jennifer looked up to see Nina and Shamus approach.

"We've been looking everywhere for you," Nina said as she scrutinized Jennifer. "Your face is flushed. Are you feeling all right?"

"What?" Jennifer replied, touching her cheeks. "I'm fine."

"You didn't have another vision, did you?" Nina asked with concern.

"No, Nina, I'm okay. I'm thirsty, though."

"Shall we sample some of the local food and drink?" Shamus offered easily.

They purchased food and found a place to sit on the grass and eat while watching the events. At one point, Nina looked casually up at Jennifer.

"Nice hat," Nina said. "Where did you get that?"

Jennifer shrugged her shoulders. "I was watching some children dancing, and it fell off one of the kids. He didn't seem to notice, so I just picked it up."

"What!" Nina said in horror. "Jen, you can't just take someone's hat."

Jennifer burst out laughing.

"Relax, Nina. Jennifer is teasing you," Shamus said with a twinkle in his eye. "If I'm not mistaken, that is the Stuart Clan badge, the Earl of Thornhill's family, I believe."

"Jen, how did you get that?" Nina demanded. When Jennifer didn't answer, Nina persisted. "Did you talk to him? Did Derek Rannoch give you that?"

"It doesn't mean anything, Nina. He was just being kind."

"What do you mean? Tell me what happened," Nina said.

"Shamus, explain this next game to me," Jennifer said calmly, deliberately ignoring Nina.

Jennifer and Shamus started laughing, and when Jennifer refused to answer Nina's questions, Nina finally stopped asking.

They spent the next two hours watching the various games and listening to the music. Jennifer was intrigued by the Gaelic language that she heard in several of the songs. Shamus didn't speak Gaelic but said that his grandparents had. He was able to comprehend some of the lyrics.

As late afternoon approached, Jennifer watched as large piles of logs were placed at various locations. She asked Shamus about them.

"This is midsummer's night. Fires will be lit after dark, and people will continue to sing and dance."

Jennifer stilled as ancient images materialized in her memory.

"What's wrong, Jen?" Nina asked. "You just turned white as a ghost."

Jennifer shook her head. "Nina, I don't want to stay for that."

"What is it?" Nina asked. "Shamus?" she said, looking to him for support.

Shamus stepped forward. "Jennifer, are you feeling all right?" he asked.

"Yes. I'm sorry, I didn't mean to alarm you." Jennifer smiled weakly. "It's just that the images of the fires at night are too strong. The eve before midsummer's day was an important festival for Cela's people. Their fires would light up the hills. They conducted human sacrifices around the fires. I can still see it." Jennifer wrapped her arms about herself in an effort to steel herself against the grisly memories.

"We don't have to stay," Nina said, putting her hand on Jennifer's shoulders.

"Thanks," Jennifer said with relief. "I don't want to push my luck. I'm afraid of what those bonfires would trigger."

"Are you feeling all right now?" Shamus asked.

"Yes, but I do think I'll go get something cold to drink," Jennifer said.

"I'll come with you," Nina volunteered.

"That's not necessary," Jennifer countered. "Stay here with Shamus. I'll be right back. Would you two like something?"

"Shamus?" Nina asked.

"No, thank you," he answered.

"Me, neither," Nina said.

"Okay. I won't be long," Jennifer said.

Jennifer left Shamus and Nina sitting in the grassy area on the edge of town where the games were being played. She started walking back toward the streets of the town where food and drink were sold. A parade of pipers crossed her path, and she stopped to listen. She was enjoying the unique sound of the instruments when she felt the first cramping of her stomach. She gasped in surprise and in pain. Not here! It couldn't happen here among all these people!

She turned and started walking rapidly away from the food vendors. As the nausea increased, she felt her heart begin to pound. She searched desperately for an escape and started to run, feeling powerless as the vortex began to swirl around her. She reached the area where cars were parked but couldn't find Shamus's vehicle. Her head was spinning, and she could taste the vile secretions in her mouth.

In the distance, she saw the remains of a small medieval church. If she could just reach it, she could be hidden from the crowds of people walking to and from their cars. Her face was drenched in sweat as she repeatedly swallowed, trying to delay the sickness that she knew was coming. The roaring noise in her head was disorienting by the time she reached the remains of the walls. She stopped, the vertigo overtaking her. She bent over, clutching herself, as her vision faded, and she sank down into unconsciousness, her body pressing into the rough gorse.

Derek was standing among his family, discussing the last game.

"I told you he would win!" Elizabeth Sheering boasted. "You owe me ten pounds, Derek Rannoch."

"Remind me never to go to Monte Carlo with you," Derek said as he withdrew some notes.

"Monte Carlo sounds wonderful. Let's go!" Elizabeth said.

Edward laughed and made some comment that made Elizabeth burst into laughter, followed by Harold Rannoch and the others.

Derek was enjoying the joke when suddenly he stopped laughing. He frowned. There it was again—that strange feeling. He looked at Elizabeth, his father, and brother, but they continued talking. He shook his head; perhaps it was nothing. He was about to join the conversation, when Ann laid her hand on his arm.

"What was that?" she asked, a puzzled look on her face.

"What?" Derek asked.

"I don't know. I felt. . . ." Ann stopped and shrugged her shoulders.

"You felt that?" Derek asked with surprise.

"Something," Ann said. "The air. . . ." She looked around. "I don't know. It was very strange. Maybe I imagined it. It's gone now."

Derek clenched his fists. "I still feel it, Ann. It's not gone, it's just moved, and by God, this is not the first time I've felt it, either," Derek said in a deadly whisper.

"Derek?" Ann said with alarm.

Suddenly, he bolted across the grass, away from the games. He wasn't certain where he was going, but he knew that wherever it was, he was getting closer. The air seemed thick and charged. He reached the meadow where the cars were parked and paused a moment. It was near; he could sense it. He suddenly felt desperation deep within himself. He broke into a run, past the cars and into the field. It was there, he knew it, just beyond the chapel ruins. A cold sweat broke out on his forehead as, with trepidation, he rounded the corner. His heart leapt into his throat when he saw her. The sun reflected off her hair, casting a blinding, fire-like light that was surrounded by a shimmering vortex of charged air. He saw her stumble and then bend over, clutching her midsection.

"Jeneeeeeee!" Derek screamed as watched her pitch forward and then slowly sink to the ground.

* * *

827 B.C.

"The others will notice that you're gone," Lodi said.

"Tell them that I wasn't feeling well and that you thought it best that I be alone for a while so that I can rest, or tell them the truth: that I have at last discovered the gift of the skies but am still waiting for the gods to guide me in its use. For that, I must be alone," Cela said.

"How long will you be away?" Lodi asked.

"Three days, maybe less."

"Must you travel at night? Why not wait until the morning?"

"Everyone will be attending the festival tonight. My absence will not surprise anyone since I avoid the sacrifices. We will travel tonight and find a place to sleep. In the morning, I will go into the sky," Cela said.

"Isn't there danger?" Lodi asked with concern.

"Only in that I have never gone far before. I've always kept our lands in sight," Cela said.

"You should not do this alone."

"Who among the Wise Ones is there?" Cela countered.

There was no one.

"You're taking the guard Dagga with you?" Lodi asked.

"There is none that I trust more," Cela answered.

"He knows?" Lodi asked with surprise.

"No. He guards the entrance to the grove and waits. Lodi, do you know where to meet us with the supplies?"

"Yes, child, I'll be there."

It was sunset when Lodi pushed through the thick bushes. Dagga and Cela stepped forward.

"I brought the warm skins as you asked and enough food for three days," Lodi said.

Dagga raised his eyebrows when he heard Lodi mention three days, but he said nothing. He stepped forward and took the bundle from her hands. After Lodi left, he turned to Cela.

"Priestess, it is not my position to question you, but for your own safety, I must ask where are we going?"

They began walking.

"We're going back to the grove of trees and will stay there for the night," Cela answered as they began walking. "We'll leave when the sun comes up," Cela said.

"And then?" Dagga asked.

Cela had been thinking about how to explain this to Dagga. Six times now they had gone to the grove of trees, and Dagga guarded the entrance. Each time, Cela was away for a longer period. Dagga had expressed concern the last time when she came out of the grove just before sunset.

"I will explain later," Cela said. "For now, I just want to leave without being seen."

They had been walking for less than an hour when Dagga suddenly stopped, his hand up. Cela had heard nothing. She looked at Dagga, a question on her face. He indicated for her to be quiet and crouch down behind the nearest bushes. He joined her there, his sword drawn. A moment later, a young man and woman burst through the bushes, laughing. They tumbled to the ground and removed their clothes. Dagga started to move when Cela motioned for him to remain. Cela and Dagga could see the couple clearly through the bushes. Cela waited a moment longer and then indicated that they would leave in the opposite direction.

Dagga and Cela emerged from the bushes and resumed their walking. Cela, silent, her brows knit together, her steps labored, brooded as they made their way across the plains.

"Priestess," Dagga said after an hour of silence, "is the journey too much for you?" He absently glanced at her swollen belly, now in her sixth month of pregnancy.

"No, Dagga, I am fine," she replied and then stopped.

She could see the concern on his face, the fierce face of a warrior. She knew his strength, his power. She also knew his gentle touch. She smiled slightly. "Truly, I am fine."

When at last they reached the grove of trees, it was dark. Dagga built a small fire, and they ate in silence. He sat across from her, his head bent down as was expected when in the presence of a priestess of the Wise Ones. Cela was deep in thought and was surprised when she heard him speak.

"Priestess, something troubles you."

Cela looked up into his fierce face. "I am frightened," she said simply. "Things are not as they once were, and I am concerned for the people." She paused. "Dagga, you are a warrior. What are the warriors saying? What are the people saying?"

Dagga boldly stood and walked around the fire. He sat down next to her. "The people do not say anything; they never do. The warriors. . . ." He shrugged his shoulders. "The new High Priest has made war upon many—even some tribes that have been our allies. That is not wise. He takes men who have been in the fields all their lives and puts a sword in their hands. They are farmers, not warriors. You know the ways of your people. Warriors begin training as boys to be fit for battle as men. A man with little training with the sword should not be sent into battle.

"The High Priest's insistence upon battle has resulted in many deaths among our warriors and people, but he doesn't see that. When he looks at a man, he sees only a vessel to serve him, be it hunter, farmer, or warrior. He does not see a man."

Cela understood what Dagga was saying. Since becoming the High Priest, Luc had launched a campaign of destruction. There seemed to be no end to his quest for power. He had forsaken the intellectual focus of the High Council and embarked upon a path of war against the neighboring tribes. He even convinced the High Council to attack Ere, the land across the water that Cela had warned the old High Priest about. Few of their warriors returned from that disastrous assault. Still, Luc pressed on, and the number of sacrifices grew following each battle.

Cela knew that there were those among the Wise Ones who disagreed with Luc's actions. Luc's power was formidable, however, and none had opposed him yet. It was most important that the people not become confused or sense any division among the Wise Ones.

"We need help," Cela said softly. "We need the People of the Sky to return to us."

A short time later, Dagga made a bed on the ground for Cela. He indicated that he would stand guard and that she should sleep. Cela tried but was unable to relax, for she felt as though she was carrying the weight of her people on her shoulders. Tomorrow, she would go far from this land of her people. She did not know where she was going. She only knew that she had to find the People of the Sky—and she had to go alone. She could wait no longer. Luc's power continued to grow, creating division among the Wise Ones and weakening the people. But there was another reason why she could not delay her journey any longer. Soon, the child within her would be born. She dare not leave it for fear of what Luc might do.

Suddenly, she was awakened by Dagga's voice. "Priestess? It is the child?"

Cela sat up. "What?"

"You cried out in your sleep," he said.

He was kneeling next to her, and she could see the concern on his face. "No, Dagga, the child is fine. Here," she said, reaching for his hand, "see for yourself."

Cela placed Dagga's hand upon her abdomen. Even in the moonlight, she saw his eyes widen in surprise.

"This does not hurt?" he asked.

Cela smiled. "No. You have never felt a child move while still within its mother?"

"No," Dagga said. "I do not have a mate."

"Why not?" Cela asked.

"I do not choose to have one," Dagga said simply.

"Yet you can still lie with a woman when it pleases you?" Cela asked.

"Yes," he said.

"It is not so for me," Cela said. "Among the Wise Ones, we also may choose our mates. However, it is different for me. A few days after my initiation, Luc sent for me. Do you remember that day when you came into his lodge?" Dagga nodded his head and Cela continued. "It was his intent to mate with me. I refused. I told him that the child within me would die if I were to lie with him. He was very angry, of course, but believed what I said. I cannot let him doubt me, so I have not been with a man since the fertility rites."

"But Priestess, women still lie with their mates while the child grows within."

"I know," Cela said, smiling slightly. "I did not tell Luc the truth. He was not certain but could not take the risk that I might end the child's life, so he left me alone." She hesitated. "And there are none among the Wise Ones whom I desire."

"Priestess, why do you not leave this place?"

"I am a priestess of the Wise Ones. It is my duty to remain."

"I do not understand the ways of the Wise Ones, but I understand the ways of men, Priestess. The High Priest is not wise among men. He wishes only to increase his power through fear. He looks for enemies where they do not exist. Many have been killed."

"That is another reason why I cannot leave my people."

Cela was suddenly aware that Dagga's hand was still upon her. She looked down at her abdomen, and Dagga hastily removed his hand.

"Please," Cela said softly, "it is good to be touched again."

Dagga gently replaced his hand. There was such comfort

and strength in his touch. Cela lay back down upon the skins.

"Priestess," Dagga said, his voice strained. "I think I had better go watch from there," he said, indicating the area where he had been guarding.

She placed her hand upon his, halting him.

Dagga had thought often about the Priestess Cela. She was a priestess of the Wise Ones, and as such, beyond his understanding, beyond the boundaries of his life. And yet, he had known her as a man knows a woman. His life had been inexplicably intertwined with hers.

When he had seen what Luc had done to her, he wanted to kill the High Priest. And yet, the ways of the Wise Ones were none of his concern. Why should this child-woman evoke such feelings in him? Had she cast her spell upon him when she was but a child and he had carried her away from the ceremony? Or was it the time when he had seen her lay the blade across her own neck. And what of his feelings now? Had any man ever felt as he did now, feeling the child stir within her? Would that she were only a common woman. Then he would be content to spend the rest of his days and nights at her side, and he would allow no man to come between them. He would die for her now, and not just because he was a warrior, a member of the elite guard, and expected to do so, but because he. . . ."

"Dagga," Cela whispered, interrupting his thoughts.

Her breathing had quickened, and a flush appeared on her face. He was aware of her unmistaken desire. He moved his hand to Cela's breasts, gently cupping them. Her body had changed since he had first taken her that day six months ago. Her small breasts were now full, her body voluptuous. When he lowered his lips to hers, Cela's arms came up around his neck.

Cela awoke the next morning to the sound of birds in the trees above her. She smiled. The glow of the night spent in Dagga's arms was still upon her. She turned on her side and saw him standing not far from her. His back was to her as his eyes scanned the area.

"Why could you not have made him one of the Wise Ones?" she whispered to the forces around her. "Why could he not be a child of the People of the Sky, too? He understands the needs of our people better than many of the priests do."

"Priestess?" Dagga said as he turned and saw her studying him.

He was standing there, his chest bare, the hide drape that he wore hanging from his waist, reaching the middle of his thighs. His sword was at his waist. His body was powerful and muscular, and yet his touch had been gentle, sensitive. Cela turned her face from his gaze. The sun would be up soon. She must leave. She would need the light of the sun to guide her on her journey. If only she did not have to make it alone.

Dagga walked over and knelt beside her, holding a cup containing cool, clear water. As Cela took it from his hands, she was again moved by her feelings for this man whom the gods had sent to her—this man who had started the life of the child growing within her. She lowered her eyes and drank from the cup. Dagga then offered food and sat down beside her as she ate. When she had finished, she drew a deep breath. It was time to leave. She would have to explain to Dagga.

"Dagga," she began. "I must go now."

"Go? Where will you go, Priestess?"

"The same place that I have gone the other times. I will need you to remain here, as before, and wait for me This time, however, I may be gone several days."

Dagga frowned. "Priestess, where have you gone before? Have you not remained in the glen, beyond the trees?"

"No."

Fierceness came upon Dagga's face. "To have left without an escort was foolish! How far did you go?" he demanded.

Did Cela dare tell him the truth? Only Lodi, Cupa, and her mother knew of her quest to find the People of the Sky. None of the priests knew. Did she dare share this powerful secret with one who was not born to the Wise Ones?

"Dagga," Cela began. "I hold a powerful gift within me that I have kept hidden from the Wise Ones. My mother and the two priestesses, Lodi and Cupa, who cared for me after my fertility rites, are aware of what I have discovered. None of the others know. The High Priest does not know. First, I must tell you the story of a young priestess called Mora."

Cela told him the story of her great-grandmother, Mora, and of Mora's secret mating with a man of the People of the Sky. Then she told Dagga of how Mora had unveiled the secret shortly after Cela had fled her first sacrificial ceremony.

"For so long, I wondered what my special gift would be. All of the Wise Ones have something: the ability to heal, to see things that are not yet, the understanding of animals and plants, computations. I could read the stars, but all priests and priestesses can do that. Then I started seeing lands where I had never been—lands that none among the Wise Ones had ever seen. I saw them all from the sky. The stars, sun, and clouds would call to me. I didn't understand . . . not until the night of the fertility rites.

"Dagga, I am a daughter of both the Wise Ones and the People of the Sky, and now I understand. Come with me, and I will show you," Cela said as she placed her hand in Dagga's.

They stood and walked together out from under the trees to the glen beyond. Cela did not release Dagga's hand until they were in the middle of the glen. Then slowly, she took several steps backward, stopping when a distance of twenty feet separated them. Her eyes held his for a moment.

Then she took a deep breath and her body lifted up. Still she stared at him, and then she was gone, soaring into the sky.

Dagga was unaware that he had dropped to one knee when Cela's body left the earth. He had to arch his neck to see her, and he could see that her eyes were still on him, watching him, and then she turned, and he saw her move off as a bird might. First, she went high into the sky over the glen, and then he watched her turn and come back, soaring above him. He had to twist around to follow her flight as she went over the trees, disappearing from his sight. He stood quickly, scanning the sky above him, and then she was there again, above the trees, coming toward him. Dagga jumped back, still clutching the handle of his sword as she lightly touched back on the ground.

She took a step toward him, and Dagga withdrew his sword. He raised it in the air above her, its deadly blade gleaming in the sun.

"Dagga!" she cried as her hands instinctively covered her bulging abdomen.

He saw the fear in her eyes, and then she did the unthinkable: she sank slowly to her knees in front of him, her head bowed.

"My life is in your hands, as it has been countless times before," she said.

It was a moment before he could move. His legs were trembling—something that they had never done in all his battles, even when he had stared death in the face. Cautiously, he took a step forward, his sword still poised. He transferred the sword to his right hand and then hesitantly reached out with his left. He touched her hair, red and shining in the sun. He reached down to her chin and slowly raised her face to his. She looked the same; she felt the same under his touch. Her eyes were gentle and trusting, the eyes of a child he had cared for so long ago.

He deliberately lowered his sword to her shoulder. He placed both of his hands on the handle and brought the blade up against her neck. With one slight movement, he could kill her. Still, she did not remove her eyes from him.

"Priestess," he said, "you offer your life too easily to your gods. You should not tempt them so often." The blade lay against the scar upon Cela's neck, poised and ready to kill.

The hint of a smile appeared through Cela's moist eyes. "I am not a fool; I am a priestess of the Wise Ones. I have been trained in the arts of sacrifice. Are you the one who will deliver me to the gods? If so, then I have chosen well, for I did not choose a priest who thirsts for blood to appease the gods, nor a man who kills for fear of that which he does not understand."

Dagga swore. "A curse upon your gods for thrusting a crying child-priestess into my arms long ago!"

This time Cela did smile. "But, my warrior lover, they also thrust a woman into your arms."

"I am not certain it is compensation enough, for the woman is strange and beyond my understanding," Dagga said.

He slowly removed his sword and returned it to its scabbard. Then he reached out and took her hands, helping her to stand.

* * *

"Jenny! Jenny!" Derek cried as he cradled Jennifer in his arms.

Jennifer moaned and then rolled onto her side. She could feel Derek's arms around her, holding her.

"Derek, let go of me. I'm going to be sick!"

She turned away and crawled a few feet from him as her

stomach contracted and emptied its contents onto the ground. When the vomiting stopped, she sat back on her heels, her hands resting on her thighs, waiting for the vortex to release her. She closed her eyes and took slow, deep breaths. Then she felt Derek's hand on her back—so comforting, so safe, but she couldn't hold on to that feeling. She was going to have to face him.

"I'm all right," she said weakly. "Just give me a minute."

"Jenny, you're ill!" Derek said with concern.

"No . . . no I'm not. It's always like this afterward. I'll be fine in just a minute."

Already Jennifer could feel her stomach calming and her heart slowing. A moment later, she was feeling as though nothing had happened. If it weren't for the bitter taste that remained in her mouth, there would be nothing left of the sickness of a minute ago.

She reached up and wiped her lips off with her hand. If only Derek weren't here! She needed a drink to rinse her mouth, and she must look a fright. Then another thought occurred to her. How long had he been there? What had he seen?

"What are you doing here?" she asked hesitantly, keeping her back to him.

When he didn't answer, Jennifer turned. He was looking at her in a peculiar way.

"What did you mean when you said, 'It's always like this'?" he asked.

"What?"

"You said, 'It's always like this afterward.' What is?" Derek repeated.

"I don't know what you're talking about," Jennifer said, panic rising within her.

Derek's eyes narrowed. "I think you do. What happened just now, Jenny?"

"Nothing. I just felt sick to my stomach. I probably drank too much of your famous malt liquor," she said, trying to make light of the situation.

"Like the night in your room at Cowden Hall? The night you said you had a nightmare and were sick afterward?"

"What are you talking about? That was different."

"Are you sure?"

"Why are you making such a big deal out of this?" Jennifer asked. "I drank too much, like some ridiculous teenager. I felt sick to my stomach and came out here. I hardly wanted to vomit in the middle of the crowd."

Jennifer stood up quickly, and Derek was instantly beside her.

"You're lying to me," he said.

"Of course I am. That's all you think I can do, isn't it?" Jennifer said sarcastically. "Fine. I'm going back. Nina and Shamus are probably looking for me."

Derek reached out and grabbed her arm, preventing her from leaving.

"What happened just now, Jenny?"

She didn't answer. She needed to get away from his perceptive scrutiny. She tried to pull away from him, but he held her firmly.

"This has happened before, hasn't it?" he demanded. "And it has nothing to do with drinking, and it has nothing to do with nightmares."

His eyes narrowed. "When I found you lying on the ground in the rain outside of the hunting lodge." His grip tightened. "And when I came upon you in your car on Thornhill. Christ! The restoration room at the museum! How many times has this happened?" he demanded.

Jennifer's lip quivered. "Ten times, maybe more," she said softly, lowering her face.

"What is it, Jenny? What's wrong?"

Derek was standing close to her, his hands gripping her shoulders. Jennifer was fighting the tears that were forming.

"Let me go," she whispered as the first tear cascaded down her face. "Please."

"No. The truth, Jenny! What just happened to you?"

Jennifer shook her head slowly back and forth as she

squeezed her eyes shut. "Just let me go, Derek. Please."

"I can't."

With a last ounce of resistance, Jennifer tried to twist away. "Leave me alone!"

Derek only tightened his grip. "Tell me the truth for once! I'm not letting you go—not until you tell me what just happened to you."

"What just happened?" Jennifer shouted, the tears falling freely now. "I'll tell you what just happened. The same thing that has happened each time before. I get this terrible pain in my stomach, a roaring sound in my ears, and so dizzy I can hardly stand, and then, the next thing I know, I'm seeing life through the eyes of a girl who lived over two thousand years ago.

"I'm actually there. It's as though I'm inside of her. I know and *feel* everything she does. I'm in her world, her time. I'm living in a world that ended thousands of years ago. And when I'm there, it's just as real to me as this is right now. And then," Jennifer said, laughing hysterically, "suddenly, I'm back here, my head spinning, and so sick to my stomach that I often vomit. Then it's gone, as though it never happened, except that I remember everything.

"Her thoughts are in my head, along with her feelings. I remember what the people wore; what their huts looked like; how they conducted their ceremonies; what they believed; how they made their weapons; cured their sick; how they *wrote*," she said pointedly. "I remember how they tracked the movement of the stars and built stone monuments to people who came down out of the sky."

Jennifer could see the shock on Derek's face.

"Let me go!" she screamed, pulling out of his grasp.

She started to run. She had gotten only a few feet when she felt his arms come around her. He spun her around and crushed her to him. Jennifer didn't resist, but buried her head in his chest and cried as Derek held her in his arms, gently stroking her hair.

CHAPTER 11

"**I** think it's time we talked, don't you?" Derek asked.

Jennifer had ceased crying. In some ways, it had been such a relief to finally tell him what had been happening. Now, however, she was afraid to look at him. She was standing very still, her head resting on his chest, his arms still around her. She shrugged her shoulders.

"There's not much more to say," she said quietly.

"I think there is, but not here," Derek said as he gently separated himself from her. He reached down and picked up his hat that Jennifer had been wearing. "Come with me; we'll go where we won't be disturbed."

Jennifer allowed herself to be led back to the cars.

"Where are we going?" she asked, still avoiding Derek's face. "Nina and Shamus will be looking for me."

"I'll take care of it," Derek said.

He led her to his Land Rover and opened the door for her. Hesitantly, Jennifer got into the vehicle.

"Are you going to be all right?" he asked.

Jennifer nodded her head, trying to assure him without looking at him.

"I'll be right back," he said.

Derek turned and walked quickly toward the games. Jennifer leaned her head back on the seat and closed her eyes. She would have preferred that Derek never find out, especially now. What must he think? What could she tell him? She felt so confused. She'd been so certain that somehow she was seeing something that had happened in the past, and she really believed that—up until the last two episodes. That was when Cela had flown. Jennifer had almost decided that Nina was right. Cela had been in some kind of hypnotic state and had thought she had flown, or perhaps it had been an out-of-body experience.

Jennifer covered her face with her hands. What now? What she just saw could not have been an out-of-body experience because Dagga had seen it, too, and it had frightened him. It had frightened him so much that he had almost killed Cela. He saw her fly, and he didn't understand it. That was not self-hypnosis on Cela's part. Cela was not fantasizing to escape something that she did not want to see. Cela had flown! It was real, and like everything else with Cela, Jennifer had experienced it, too.

Her thoughts were interrupted by the opening of the car door. Jennifer glanced quickly at Derek and then focused her attention forward as he slid into the vehicle.

"Did you find Nina?" she asked.

"Yes," Derek said as he started the engine and backed the Land Rover out of the parking space.

"What did you tell her?"

"That you were coming with me," he said simply as he eased the vehicle out onto the road.

Jennifer felt uncomfortable in his presence. What must he think of her? "Derek," she began, "I don't think there is anything more that I can tell—"

"Not here," he interrupted. "Wait. There'll be plenty of time."

Jennifer glanced furtively in Derek's direction. He seemed to be concentrating on the road ahead of him. She wanted to break the silence but didn't know what to say.

"You must think I'm out of my mind," she ventured. When Derek didn't answer, she persisted. "Well? Say something! I can't just ride along, wondering if you're thinking that I'm crazy."

"Why didn't you tell me the truth in the first place?"

Derek asked, his eyes still focused on the road.

"Would you have believed me?"

"You didn't really give me a chance one way or the other, did you?"

"And you haven't answered my question," Jennifer replied.

Derek was silent. She watched him as he drove, displaying no emotion, his focus on the road ahead of them. At least he wasn't angry. Jennifer abandoned trying to get Derek to tell her what he was thinking. She leaned her head back and closed her eyes. When she felt the car turn once more and slow down, she opened her eyes.

"Here?" she said with surprise.

"There won't be any interruptions," Derek said as he turned off the motor and stepped out of the Land Rover. He walked around to Jennifer's door and opened it.

Jennifer hesitantly stepped out and stopped, letting her eyes rest on the massive gray stones of Thornhill. Despite the anxiety she felt about talking to Derek, the stones still worked their magic on her, soothing her. She felt reassured as she and Derek walked together up the steps to the large oak door. The door opened and Jeffrey appeared.

"Lord Derek," he said, stepping aside. "Miss McHugh." He bowed slightly to Jennifer as she walked into the entry hall.

"Would you like anything to drink?" Derek asked Jennifer.

"No," Jennifer said.

Derek turned back to Jeffrey. "We don't wish to be disturbed for any reason, Jeffrey. We'll be in my rooms."

Jeffrey nodded slightly, his face a mask lacking expression.

"This way," Derek said to Jennifer. He led her through the hall to the massive stairs, wide enough for four people to walk beside each other without touching the stone wall that anchored the stairway or the ornate, carved banister. They ascended the staircase to the second floor, and then

Derek turned to the right. He led her down a hall and opened the door, standing aside for her to enter.

Jennifer stepped inside the room and paused. It was a sitting room, furnished with a sofa, several chairs, and tables placed in front of a large, gray stone fireplace.

"Make yourself comfortable," he said as he walked past her into a connecting room. Jennifer watched as he turned on a light in the next room. She could see a desk positioned in the middle of the room and rows of books lining the walls. She turned and, in the opposite direction, could see a bed in the next room, its massive four posts supporting a tartan plaid, identical to the one that she had slept in at the hunting lodge when she had first come to Scotland. She turned around as Derek returned. He carried a notebook, pen, and laptop computer.

"Where would you like to sit?" he asked.

Jennifer shyly selected a chair in front of the fireplace. Derek positioned himself in a chair across from her, placing his notebook on a table next to the chair. He sat back and looked directly at Jennifer, causing her to look away.

"Do you want to tell me what's been happening to you?" he asked.

Jennifer took a deep breath. "This isn't easy. I don't know where to begin."

Derek shrugged. "At the beginning. How long has this been happening?"

"The first time was at the British Museum in London."

"It never happened in The States?"

"No."

"Nothing like this has ever happened to you before, not even as a child?" Derek asked.

"No, nothing."

"Why did you come to Britain?" Derek asked pointedly.

"Not for the reason you thought," Jennifer said defensively. She jumped up and started pacing, then stopped before a window. She looked out through the centuries-old, heavy leaded glass onto the expanse of

Thornhill's land and took a deep breath. "It's true that I'm married," she began with agitation. "I have been for almost two years. And no!" she said as she spun around to face Derek, "I did not come here looking to have an affair with you or any other man," she blazed as she held Derek's eyes. Then she turned back to the window.

Jennifer was silent, hoping Derek would say something. She wanted to look at him but she was afraid, so when he didn't speak, she took another deep breath to calm herself. "I met John when I was nineteen years old," she began softly. "I was young, inexperienced, and emotionally exhausted. My mother was dying; I was trying to take care of her and work to support us."

For the next several minutes, Jennifer recounted the circumstances of her marriage to John. "The day before the luncheon at the British Museum," she continued, "I found out that John, my husband, was having an affair. Apparently, it was going on before we married, and he continued after we married." Jennifer shrugged her shoulders. "That explained his disinterest in me."

She continued to look out the window as she spoke, avoiding eye contact with Derek. The only time he interrupted was when she hesitantly told him how John had stopped making love to her when they returned from their honeymoon and how he had insisted that they have separate bedrooms from that point on. "We had sex four times during our two-week honeymoon. I thought I must have done something wrong," Jennifer said. "I'd never been with a man before my wedding night, and there never had been anyone else until . . . until you." That was when she heard Derek swear softly in disgust. Still, she didn't turn around until she had finished, and then she returned to her chair across from him.

"So now you know it all," she said as she sat down. "The first time I had an episode was in the basement of the British Museum where you found me. I had just confronted John about his affair, or what I've since learned to be multiple affairs with . . . with call girls," she said with some embarrassment. "I flew to Scotland the next day. I convinced myself that whatever the episode had been, it was the result of too much alcohol and hitting my head when I fell."

"Did you tell anyone about it?" Derek asked.

"No," Jennifer said, shaking her head. "Not that time. But a few days later, it happened again when I was out walking by myself in the hills around Nina's cottage."

Derek was studying Jennifer as she sat before him. "And the day you knocked down my equipment?" he asked.

"That was the third time. I wasn't aware I had fallen onto your equipment. I don't remember any of that. I only remember what happened back in Cela's time."

"Go on," Derek said.

"I was really scared after that. I told Nina what had happened, and she insisted that I talk to Shamus. He did some blood test and an MRI of my head." Jennifer paused, her throat tight. "All the test results were normal; there was nothing physically wrong with me. I returned to Chicago, and John had all the tests repeated. Again, everything was normal. That's when John suggested I see a psychiatrist."

Derek raised his eyebrows but said nothing.

"But then, something occurred to me. It was strange. After those first few times . . . ." Jennifer stopped. "I still don't know what to call those experiences. Anyway, I realized that I knew things that I had never known before. I knew about plants and herbs that were used for healing. I knew how to make bronze. I knew the names of the constellations. How could I be making up delusions with such accuracy? That's when I decided to come back to Scotland. I had to know if there was any truth to what I had been seeing. Nina scheduled the appointment with you at the university. I had no idea that you were the same person who found me at the British Museum and whose equipment I had damaged in the mountains."

"Why did you tell me you had documents?"

"Actually, you gave me that idea. I just wanted to talk to someone about what I had seen. I couldn't tell you the truth, for fear of what you would think. It is pretty crazy. If it hadn't happened to me, I wouldn't believe it myself. You asked me if I was in the possession of some documents," Jennifer continued. "I said yes. I didn't know what else to say."

"So when we were at the hunting lodge, each document that you described was actually one of the times when you lost consciousness and saw this other time period," Derek said.

"Yes. That's why I couldn't tell you how many there were. I didn't know if they were going to continue."

"That explains something else that was bothering me," Derek mused.

"What?"

"Your description of the civilization was never objective. It was very personal."

They talked some more and then Derek interrupted.

"So you had never read anything about prehistoric monuments, the Bronze Age, or the Druids before?" he asked.

"Not that I'm aware of. I started reading when I returned this last time. That's what I was doing at Charlie MacFarland's pub the day that you came in. Derek, I really believed that what I was seeing actually happened thousands of years ago. I did, that is, until recently. Now I don't know what to believe."

"What happened recently?" Derek asked.

Jennifer jumped out of the chair and began to pace nervously. Derek didn't press her but waited quietly. Finally, she stopped before the window, her back to him.

"Cela flew," she said softly.

Jennifer told Derek of Cela's grandmother and of the People of the Sky. Then she recounted the events of the last two visions she had.

"She really flew through the sky and Dagga saw her.

But," she said, turning around to face Derek squarely, "that's not possible, is it? John says that these are all delusions, fantasies that I'm creating in my mind. Maybe I am." Jennifer paused a moment. "You see, ever since I was a child, I have dreamed in my sleep that I can fly. They were my favorite dreams, so exhilarating and so real." Jennifer frowned. "But these visions are different. They're not just about flying."

Derek frowned and reached for his notebook. He opened it to a blank page and started writing. Then he turned back to the other pages.

Jennifer returned to her chair. "Those are the notes you made at the hunting lodge?"

"Yes," Derek said. "Do you mind if I ask you some more questions?"

"No," Jennifer said.

For the next several hours, Derek queried Jennifer about the episodes she had already discussed with him, as well as the ones she had experienced since she last saw him. She was surprised to find that he was interested in not only the objective details about Cela and her people, but also the personal aspects of Cela's life.

When Jennifer finally finished, she sat back in her chair. Derek was quiet, scanning the volumes that he had written. She had been extremely detailed in her recollections, with the exception of a few times. He looked up.

"What happened the night before the fertility rites? You said that Cela met with the warrior, Dagga." Derek glanced back at his notes and then looked up expectantly.

"It's not important," Jennifer said. She felt herself blush and looked away.

A look of understanding came into Derek's eyes. He closed his notebook and leaned back in his chair.

"Did they make love?" Derek asked directly.

Jennifer hesitated before answering. "Yes," she finally said. "It's Dagga's child that she carries, although the Wise Ones think it is Luc's."

"I see. And the fertility ceremony? Tell me about that," Derek said as he opened his notebook again.

Jennifer began recounting the events of the ceremony. She stopped when she came to the part where Cela was brought forward. How could she recount the rape to him? It was too painful.

Derek, however, sensed her discomfort. "Ritual fertility ceremonies have been a part of most ancient civilizations at one time or another," he offered. "Again, my interest lies in finding similarities between the practices of this civilization that you have been seeing and the documented practices of other civilizations."

Jennifer swallowed and looked down. "I can't talk about that," she said quietly. When Derek didn't respond, she looked up to see him watching her quizzically.

"Jenny," he finally said, "when you go back into this world, do you observe everything from a distant point, as a third party might, or are you actually living at that time, too?"

Jennifer frowned. "I see things through Cela. I see what she sees; I feel what she feels."

"As though you are the young woman, Cela?" Derek asked.

Jennifer shook her head. "I don't know. I don't have any control over what she says or does. It's her world, but it's like I'm inside of her, a part of her. I feel her thoughts, emotions, and anything physical that happens to her."

Derek's brows knitted together. "What language does Cela speak?" he asked.

Jennifer paused. "I don't know."

Derek cocked his head, a peculiar expression on his face.

"What?" she asked.

"You didn't know you could write using Ogham lettering, either—not until you saw it on my notes. If I gave you a piece of paper and asked you to write down everything you did today using Cela's pre-Druidic Ogham, you could do it, couldn't you," he stated.

"Yes," she said with some surprise, "I could." She looked back at Derek. "It doesn't make any sense, does it?"

Derek smiled and closed his notebook. "One of the first things I learned in archaeology was to stop trying to place occurrences into preconceived notions of how they should be. To do so imposes a severe limitation on the probability of discovery."

Jennifer smiled for the first time. "Thank you, Professor Rannoch."

"My pleasure," he said, bowing slightly. "Now, you must be hungry. It's late, and neither of us has had dinner. My family has probably already eaten, but I'm sure we can find something."

He stood up, waiting for Jennifer. She glanced at her watch and saw that it was eight o'clock in the evening.

"I should probably go back to Nina's."

"How important is this to you?" Derek asked, his voice serious.

"What do you mean?"

"Well, we don't have any artifacts or anything else that we can use to substantiate the existence of your civilization. There is nothing here that can be revealed to the scientific community—nothing that can be published or discussed. However, if you're serious about this, there is a lot that can still be done."

"Like what?"

"Look for more similarities among civilizations. I suspect that there is a lot more in your head than you have told me."

Jennifer stiffened. "I have told you everything!"

Derek smiled slightly. "You misunderstand me. I mean that there is a lot more in your memory that still needs to be brought out—little details that you glossed over or thought were unimportant—things that you know and you're not even aware that you know, like the night you saw the Druidic alphabet." Derek looked at her forehead. "How many more prehistoric monuments are in there?"

Jennifer smiled slightly. "A lot. I just don't know where they are."

"If you can draw them, I can find them," Derek said.

"You're still willing to help?" Jennifer asked.

"Are you willing to put in the time and work that will be necessary?"

"Yes. Yes!" Jennifer cried and threw her arms around Derek's neck impulsively.

Derek gently separated himself from her. "Jenny," he said, "this will be a working relationship, nothing more. I don't want to give you any false impressions about our relationship."

Jennifer stepped back, mortified. She turned away. "I'm sorry."

Derek sighed. "You're married, Jenny. You not only lied to me about that, you lied to my family as well. There are some things that are inviolate; marriage and family are two of them. Had I known you were married, I never would have slept with you."

Jennifer detected the hardness that had come into Derek's voice.

"It doesn't matter now," Derek said, "as long as we understand one another."

Jennifer was both embarrassed and hurt. What had she expected? "We understand each other," she said, "and now I think I would like to go back to Nina's."

"Very well. We'll start first thing in the morning," Derek said as they walked down the hall to the stairs. "It would probably be a good idea if you moved in here for a while. We'll be working at odd hours in the day and night."

Jennifer paused slightly. Didn't he know how difficult it was for her to be this close to him? Didn't he know how much she wanted him to take her in his arms again? Could she stay in his house knowing that his only interest in her was academic?

"Well," a feminine voice said as Derek and Jennifer descended the steps, "I didn't realize you had a guest."

Elizabeth Sheering stood at the bottom of the steps.

"Elizabeth, I didn't know you were here. I'm sorry. Have I kept you waiting?" Derek asked as he reached the lower floor.

Elizabeth's eyes narrowed. Derek laughed.

"Elizabeth, I must drive Miss McHugh back to the shearer's cottage, and then I'll come back to eat. I'm starved."

"Really?" Elizabeth asked him. "And why do you have such an appetite?"

"Pull your claws back in, Elizabeth. Jennifer and I will be working together. I'll be back in a few minutes," Derek said.

Jennifer sat beside Derek in silence as they drove back to Nina's cottage. She felt emotionally drained. She was also hurting. Derek and Lady Elizabeth obviously had a relationship. They probably had for some time. So what was the night at Cowden Hall? Had that meant anything to Derek?

At last, Derek pulled his Land Rover up in front of Nina's cottage. He turned off the engine and paused before getting out of the vehicle. "You're very quiet," he said to Jennifer.

"There's a lot to think about," Jennifer said. She looked directly at Derek. "You believe me, don't you?"

"Yes," Derek answered.

"Why?" Jennifer asked.

Derek shrugged his shoulders. "I have my reasons. Call it instinct."

Jennifer frowned as she considered his answer.

"What do you think is happening to me?" she asked.

"That I can't say. This is out of my field of expertise. I suppose you could get different opinions from people who delve into this sort of thing. Those who believe in reincarnation would say that you were Cela in another life. Another theory would be that you are biologically descended from Cela and subconsciously have her memories as well as other genetic traits. Then it's also possible that you are not connected in any way to Cela, but that you've stumbled on a link between the present and the past. After all, what is time except another dimension?"

"It frightens me," Jennifer said.

"I know it does," Derek said kindly.

"Which of those explanations do *you* think is true?" Jennifer asked.

"I don't know. Are you Cela? Are you descended from Cela? Did Cela select you? I don't know what's happening to you any more than you do." Derek paused. "I will tell you something, though."

"What's that?"

"I don't think you should fear what's happening to you. I don't think you should be afraid of the visions, and I don't think you should fight them. If you are Cela reincarnated, you have nothing to fear from yourself or from recalling a previous life. If you are descended from Cela, again, you have nothing to fear from these memories, which are a part of both of you. If you have nothing to do with her, but her spirit has somehow selected you . . . well . . . from what you have told me about her, there's no reason to think that she would wish you harm.

"I doubt if your fear or your resistance will stop the visions from happening," Derek continued. "On the other hand, acceptance may make it easier and give you the answers you're looking for."

Jennifer considered what Derek said. "I'm surprised to hear you talk that way. You're a scientist and, from what I can see, fanatical about objective scientific verification."

Derek smiled. "Perhaps that's why I can believe as I do. Through every age of man, there have been events that were unexplainable—things that could not be explained by empirical reasoning. There are more mysteries associated with the universe than there are scientific facts."

"I'll have to think about that," Jennifer said, smiling

slightly. "Thank you," she said suddenly. "Thank you for believing that what's happening to me is real and not just my imagination."

"I know it's real," Derek said simply. "Now, we have a lot of work to do tomorrow. I'll pick you up in the morning," Derek said.

He walked around to Jennifer's door and then walked with her up to Nina's cottage.

"Good night, Jenny," he said and then turned and left.

When Derek arrived back at Thornhill, he found that his sister and brother-in-law had already left to return to their home in Cormara. Harold Rannoch had retired for the evening. Derek stopped in the kitchen and found some food to take up to his rooms. He opened the door to his sitting room to find Elizabeth waiting for him.

"Elizabeth, I didn't really expect you to wait," Derek said as he walked into the room. "Did you have dinner with the family?"

"No, I waited for you. I told you I would," Elizabeth said in a sultry voice. "I'll even stay the night if you would like."

Elizabeth walked over to Derek and took the food out of his hands. She set it on a nearby table and then turned. Placing her hands on his chest, she seductively slid her hands up until they were around his neck, then she kissed him deeply.

Derek didn't respond, but instead, he gently pulled back from her. Elizabeth looked up, curving her lips down in a pouting expression, and reached for the buttons on Derek's shirt.

"Elizabeth," Derek said kindly, "what are you doing?"

"Don't you know?" Elizabeth answered playfully.

Derek stepped away from her. "Elizabeth, I don't mean to be insensitive, but you don't want to do this. This is not us; it hasn't been since we were teenagers. I care about you, but not in this way," he said clearly.

"It's Jennifer McHugh, isn't it?" Elizabeth demanded, her eyes narrowing.

"I don't want to discuss this with you."

"Why not? Do you think I'm blind? What was it that Edward said? Miss McHugh has cast a spell over all of you? Just what is it about her? Your father's eyes positively light up when she's around. Ann acts like Miss McHugh is her best friend. Even Edward, who just met her today, couldn't keep his eyes off of her."

"You're imagining all this," Derek said as he turned away from her.

"I'm not imagining anything at all. Just what is Jennifer McHugh to you?"

Derek turned around. "Elizabeth, you and I have been friends a long time, but that does not give you the right to probe into my personal life."

Elizabeth's eyes widened. "You're in love with her," she accused.

"You don't know what you're talking about."

"The hell I don't," Elizabeth exclaimed. "I have watched you have one lover after another ever since we were teenagers. I know you, Derek. And this Jennifer McHugh is different; she means something to you. You're in love with her. What I can't imagine is why? What can you possibly see in her?" Elizabeth demanded.

"That's enough, Elizabeth," Derek said coldly.

"How do you think this makes me feel?" Elizabeth shrieked. "I've been in love with you since I was sixteen years old. But have you noticed? No. I'm just Elizabeth, family friend, someone who's always been around. I hated it each time you slept with another woman, but I also realized that you weren't serious about any of them. I always thought that when you were finally ready to settle down, we would get married, just as our families expected us to do. But all that has changed now, hasn't it? Jennifer McHugh is the one you've chosen to marry."

Derek sighed. "Elizabeth, I'm sorry. I didn't know you felt this way. I never meant to mislead you. Had I known how you felt, I would have told you that marriage was not in my plans."

"Not until now," Elizabeth snarled. "Not until she came along."

Derek straightened. "There's nothing between Jennifer and me other than work."

"Don't tell me that. I know you too well, Derek. I can see it in your eyes when she's around. You're different with her. Everyone can feel the electricity between you two."

"You're mistaken."

"Are you sleeping with her?" Elizabeth demanded.

Derek fought to control his anger. "Elizabeth, jealousy is not becoming; neither is playing the part of a shrew. I suggest that you leave before either of us says anything we may regret. As you said, we have been friends a long time."

"Don't patronize me! I have a right to know what your plans are. You owe me that, Derek."

"I don't have any plans with Miss McHugh," Derek exploded. "She's married!"

The silence in the room was oppressive as it hung in the air. Elizabeth's jaw dropped. Derek turned away and walked over to a table.

"Is that the truth? She's married?" Elizabeth asked, her voice calmer now but filled with uncertainty.

"Yes," Derek said quietly without turning to face her.

Elizabeth didn't respond immediately, but when she did, Derek was surprised by her words. "We're quite a pair, you and I," she began softly. "I'm sorry, Derek. I regret what I said a few minutes ago, and I'm sorry about you and Jennifer. I am. I know what it's like to love someone whom you can never have. I guess I've known it all along. I knew that you would never love me and that, eventually, someone would come along and you would look at her the way I dreamed that you would look at me. Well, my worst fear has come true. You've met someone. I'm sorry for you; I'm sorry she's married."

Elizabeth turned and walked to the door.

"Wait," Derek said as he crossed the room to where she was standing. "Elizabeth, I never meant to mislead you. You're right, of course. Our families. . . ." He ran his hand through his hair in frustration. "I was wrong. I did nothing to dispel their expectations for us. And you . . . I just assumed that you felt as I did. I didn't realize that you still had feelings for me. I was insensitive and callous. I'm sorry." He paused, then continued. "I care about you, Elizabeth. I always will, just not—"

Elizabeth put her fingers to Derek's lips, silencing him. "I know, Derek. Now give me a kiss on the cheek and let's say good night."

Derek kissed her and then smiled at his childhood friend. "Good night, Lady Elizabeth."

Derek awoke early the next morning. He knew that his friend, Nathaniel Sheffield, arrived early at his offices at Oxford University. Nathaniel Sheffield was a professor of anthropology and history, and the two had collaborated often in the past. Derek placed the call to Oxford and was rewarded by hearing Nathaniel answer the phone himself.

"Nathaniel! This is Derek Rannoch," Derek said into the receiver.

"Derek, my boy. Good to hear from you. I thought you had gone to Scotland for the summer."

"I did. I'm calling from Thornhill."

"How is your father?"

"He's fine, thank you."

"Glad to hear it. Give him my regards," Nathaniel said.

"I certainly will," Derek replied. "Nathaniel, I would appreciate your help with some research. It's out of my field of expertise, and I would like to know where to start."

"Anything. If I can help, you know I will," Nathaniel replied. "What's this about?"

"I need to know if there has ever been any reputable documentation of human beings flying—defying gravity and flying under their own volition."

"Are you sure you want to do this?" Nina asked Jennifer as Jennifer closed her suitcase.

"I thought you would agree that this is the best approach," Jennifer replied.

"Oh, I do. I think it's great that Derek will help you, and I'm glad that he knows the truth. I just don't think it's such a good idea to stay at Thornhill. Jen, I don't want you to get hurt. You're in love with him."

"That doesn't matter. He's certainly not in love with me. He made that clear. He'll never forgive me for lying to him and his family about being married. He said it himself: we have a working relationship; that's all. Besides, he has Lady Elizabeth."

Both women looked up as they heard the sound of a car approach.

"That will be Derek," Jennifer said as she picked up her suitcase. "You have the number at Thornhill if you need me. If Steven Cole calls, ask him when I can call him back and let me know."

"Your attorney? You bet I'll call you," Nina said. "The sooner you divorce John, the better."

When Derek and Jennifer arrived at Thornhill, Harold Rannoch greeted them at the door.

"Miss McHugh, Derek told me that you two will be working together. I'm delighted that you're here. Perhaps you could find time in your busy schedule for a visit with me. I know my son, Miss McHugh. He can become totally absorbed in his work, foregoing sleep and meals. Don't allow him to do that to you."

Jennifer laughed. Derek introduced her to Clara, the

maid, who showed Jennifer to her rooms. They were on the second floor but in a different wing than Derek's. The rooms consisted of a small sitting room, decorated in bright, chintz-upholstered chairs, a bedroom, and a modernized bath. Clara offered to unpack Jennifer's things for her and then escorted her back downstairs. She explained that Lord Derek was waiting in the library.

Jennifer entered the library to find Derek and his father talking. Lord Harold turned and smiled at her.

"Remember what I told you. Do not let my son overwork you," he said to Jennifer and turned to Derek. "I'll leave you two to your work."

After Lord Harold left, Derek explained his plans to Jennifer. Having reviewed the notes he had made at the hunting lodge, he wanted to start at the beginning again with Jennifer, recounting each vision. "I suspect that your account may be slightly different now," Derek began. "Unconsciously, there were probably some things you omitted the first time, especially since you wanted me to think that you had acquired the information from reading some documents."

They spent the remainder of the day in the library. That evening, Derek walked her to her room. He stayed out in the hall as he said good night to her. The next morning when she arose, she found one of the large Irish wolfhounds lying outside her door. Jennifer jumped back in surprise as the huge beast stood up, wagging its tail. Cautiously, Jennifer made her way, the dog beside her, down to the dining room to find Derek waiting.

Derek immediately saw the uncomfortable look in Jennifer's eyes and laughed. "I forgot that you're not accustomed to dogs," he said as Jennifer sat down at the table. "Do you remember Issy?" Derek asked, pointing to the dog that was lying on the floor a respectable five feet away from where Jennifer sat. "You two met at the hunting lodge. She remembers you. She seems to think that you are her responsibility," Derek said. "Last night when I returned from a walk, she went straight to your room and posted herself outside your door. I took her out with me again this morning, but I see she found her way back to your room."

When Derek saw the doubt in Jennifer's eyes, he reached over and gently touched her hand where it rested on the table. "You have nothing to fear from her or any other man or beast. She'll protect you with her life, if necessary, Jenny."

For the next three days, Derek and Jennifer worked continuously. They had breakfast together—usually while Derek related his analysis of the information they had discussed the day before—and then they retired to the library. They worked until lunch was served. Harold Rannoch usually joined them for lunch, where Jennifer had a reprieve from Derek's constant questioning and analysis. Then they would resume their work in the library. Some days, Derek would have tea brought in late in the afternoon. Other days, he would decline the tea in favor of continuing to work, relentless in his quest for the details of Jennifer's visions.

During the evening, Jennifer, Derek, and Lord Harold dined together, where Lord Harold would enthrall Jennifer with more stories of Thornhill and its history through the centuries. All too soon, though, Derek would indicate it was time to return to the library where they would work late into the night.

On the morning of the fourth day, a package arrived for Derek. He and Jennifer were sitting with Lord Harold and Ann, who had just arrived. They were all having breakfast together when Jeffrey brought the package into the dining room. Derek looked at the return label.

"It's from Nathaniel Sheffield at Oxford, a friend of mine," Derek said as he opened the package. He quickly scanned the pages. "This is better than I expected," he said excitedly. "I need some time to read this, and then we can discuss it."

"Does this mean that you are actually giving Jennifer some time off?" Ann asked. She turned to Jennifer. "Father says that Derek has had you working in the library from sunup to sundown."

"Jennifer, if you would like, I could take you on a tour of Thornhill," Lord Harold offered.

"I would love it," Jennifer replied enthusiastically.

"Derek?" Lord Harold asked.

"That would be fine, Father," Derek replied and then turned to Jennifer. "I'll meet you in the library at ten o'clock."

"I think I'll join you two," Ann said. "The walk will do me good. This baby is not due for another month, but it feels like it will be any day now."

Lord Harold helped his daughter rise, and then the three of them started exploring Thornhill. Jennifer walked beside Ann and Lord Harold, his daughter's hand tucked in his arm, as they ascended the great staircase. When they reached the first landing, he motioned to the right.

"The family's rooms are down this wing, renovated in the early eighteenth century into three-room suites, then in the early twentieth century with electricity and plumbing, and again in 2005 when we modernized the baths in each suite of rooms. We did the same for guest accommodations down this wing," he said as he pointed to the left, where Jennifer was currently staying. "But what I think you will find most interesting is this way," he said as he started down the family wing but then turned abruptly into a narrow hallway, pausing only to flip a switch that illuminated the long hallway with iron wall sconces, the only source of light, creating a tunnel-like atmosphere, complete with curving ceiling overhead. The walls were the same gray stone, the floors a matching gray slate that was ubiquitous throughout the castle. They emerged fifty feet later into a rectangular foyer.

"My dear," he said, turning to Jennifer, "this is what remains of the original castle built in the twelfth century, under the reign of David I, by the first Earl of Thornhill. Only a few walls from the original keep remain, but those walls and buttresses have been incorporated into the renovations in the family wing that we just left.

"The original keep was a square structure some four stories high. We're entering on what would be called the second floor in America, the first floor in Scotland. Below us is the ground floor, the remains of which have also been assimilated into our modern kitchen area. But the entry to the original keep was built on the next floor up to make it more difficult for an enemy, intent on attacking the castle, to breech. This door is the original castle door, made of wood, sixteen inches thick, and reinforced with iron grating. It swung open using a chain and cogwheel system. Now, of course, because of its weight, it's kept open permanently."

Jennifer closed her eyes briefly, the power of this part of Thornhill reaching out to her. She could feel her heart pounding in her chest, the blood rushing through her body. It was with reverence that she crossed the threshold of the door, her senses fully alert, reveling in the smell of stone and wood, her fingertips lingering on the massive wood of the door, every nerve in her body responding to the stones of Thornhill.

"You can see the original wall here," he said as he walked over to the wall. "It was ten feet thick. When the structure was renovated in the eighteenth century, these walls and their buttresses were integrated into the walls of the current family suites, the kitchen, and smaller family rooms on our ground floor."

Lord Harold turned to his daughter. "My dear, I want to show Jennifer the original living quarters of the lord and his family, but you shouldn't climb the steps."

"Nonsense, Father. Derek, Edward, and I have been running up and down these steps since I was a small child.

This one might as well start now," she said, placing her hand over her enlarged abdomen, "but at a walk, not a run." She smiled at her father and stepped ahead of him. "Careful, Jennifer," she said as she started up the steps, glancing backward briefly and grabbing the wooden railing. "These are the original steps of stone. They're in remarkably good condition, but, as you can see, uneven and worn in some places. My grandfather had the wooden railing installed along with the lights."

Lord Harold gallantly nodded to Jennifer to follow Ann. Jennifer reached for the wooden railing, grateful it was there, for the steps were indeed uneven and narrow, an upward winding tunnel, the walls on each side a mere three feet apart.

"Shall we stop on this floor, Ann?" Lord Harold asked, climbing behind Jennifer.

"No, Father, I can make it to the top. We'll stop on our way down to show Jennifer the great hall. I want her to see it from the upper floor balcony first." Lord Harold started to object, when Ann continued. "Besides, if I go into labor, it won't be the first time a baby has been born up here," she said as she emerged from the walled steps into a hallway.

"Ann!" her father scolded as he entered the hallway behind Jennifer.

"I'm teasing, Father," she said, smiling and patting him on the arm. "I'm fine."

Lord Harold hung his head down, shaking it back and forth, but when he looked up, he was smiling. "You're every bit as bad as your brothers," he said to Ann, and then he turned to Jennifer. "Shall we continue?"

Jennifer laughed. She was warmed by the humor and love she saw in Derek's father and sister. "Yes, please," she said.

"In the late thirteenth to early fourteenth centuries, this part of the original keep was reconstructed. Directly below us is the great hall, two stories high, which you can see from several small balconies on this floor. The living quarters of the lord and his family were on this floor. We have kept the original furniture and tapestries, articles of daily living," he said as he absently waved his hand around, "and maintained this part of the house," he paused, "out of respect and appreciation."

He turned to Jennifer and paused, his gaze direct, a question on his face. He seemed puzzled. "When we first met, my dear, I was struck by your impression of Thornhill. Most people, when seeing it for the first time, see a medieval castle, dark and foreboding, imagining a dungeon, knights in armor, battling. But you told me it was solid, faithful, comforting, and protective of its inhabitants. Even when I told you of the countless battles and tragedies of Thornhill, you said it was peaceful, caring." He smiled. "You were correct. Thornhill is first and foremost a home for its family. It has been since its beginning."

Jennifer thought he was waiting for a response, but she had none. His words, while interesting, were unimportant. Her focus was elsewhere: something she couldn't see was pulling at her consciousness, entreating her, inviting her, *welcoming* her.

"Come along," he said, resuming his narration. "There's an entrance to the upper deck of the chapel at the end of the hallway," he said as he pointed. "Back then, all castles or keeps had their own chapels within their walls." Then he turned to a large oak door. "And these were the apartments of Lady Gwenivere, wife of the fifth Earl of Thornhill. It is said. . . ."

"Jenny!" Jennifer whispered. She suddenly felt dizzy and placed her hand against the closed door to the rooms of Lady Gwenivere for support. The rushing sound began in her ears and her stomach contracted. The vortex was mounting around her. She could feel it. But oddly, it was not overtaking her. Something was stopping it; something was intervening. It swirled around her but was unable to swallow her. She inhaled sharply and she was there: Lady Gwenivere! She was a part of Lady Gwenivere —just as she had been a part of Cela—but something held her, keeping her anchored here in the present.

"Your son, milady," the chambermaid said as she placed the newborn baby in her arms.

Gwenivere took the baby, wrapped in soft wool, its face pink, eyes closed in peaceful slumber. She touched its cheek, soft as a rose petal, and tears came to her eyes. "Surely the greatest gift God has ever bestowed on mankind is a child, created from love," she whispered. Her reverie was short-lived, however, as the door to her room was flung open and his lordship entered, his stride angry, his face contemptuous, his eyes cold.

"I understand you have delivered a son, milady, robust and well," he sneered. "We are indeed fortunate, considering you carried the baby for a mere seven months."

"Her name was Gwenivere," Lord Harold repeated.

Jennifer did not turn around, but kept her hand where it rested on the wood of the massive oak door, her eyes fixed beyond the great door—seeing, feeling. She was, at the same time, aware of Lord Harold staring at her.

"Her name was Gwenivere, but he called her 'Jenny,' " Jennifer said. "She gave birth to her son in this room, and even then, she was not aware that her masked lover and husband were one and the same."

Jennifer had spoken in a soft, ethereal voice. She stared at the door, transfixed. She could see it all. She was there. She could feel the baby in her arms, her heart swelling with love. And the year was 1736 A.D.

"Jennifer?" Ann said as she placed her hand on Jennifer's back. "Jennifer? How did you know that?" Ann asked.

Ann's touch broke the spell and Jennifer jumped. She turned to see Lord Harold and Ann staring at her, shock on their faces. Unconsciously, she wrapped her arms around her midsection to quell the vortex that was, although receding, still present. She looked up as she heard a familiar voice.

"There you are," Derek called in greeting as he entered

the hallway of the old castle.

"That's only a family story passed down through the generations," Ann said to Jennifer. "There's no written record of Lady Gwenivere ever having a masked lover. No one knows how the tale even started."

"How did you know that, Miss McHugh?" Lord Harold asked.

"Know what?" Derek asked when he reached them.

Ann quickly repeated what had transpired. Derek looked from his father and sister to Jennifer. Lord Harold and Ann were still staring, waiting for an answer. Jennifer looked at Derek, silently pleading with him.

He shrugged his shoulders. "I've told Jennifer stories of Thornhill's colorful past," he said with a good-natured wink. "Now," he said, turning to his father, "I hate to break up your morning, Father, but Jennifer and I must get back to work."

"Of course," Lord Harold said, recovering. "I lost track of the time," he said in apology.

They all returned to the main floor, and Jennifer thanked Lord Harold and Ann for the tour. She then went with Derek into the library. No sooner had Derek closed the door than he turned and stared at her.

"I never mentioned Lady Gwenivere to you," he said.

"You must have," Jennifer said nervously.

"No, I didn't. How did you know that?"

"I . . ." Jennifer looked about the room, as though seeking an answer to Derek's questions.

"Jenny?"

"I don't know!"

Derek stared at her a minute and then took her hand in his.

"Let's get out of here for a while," he said.

Jennifer didn't resist, taking comfort in his hand clasping hers as he led her out of the library. He paused before the door to grab two sweaters and then led Jennifer outside, still holding her hand. He didn't release it until he reached his

Land Rover.

They drove in silence for ten minutes. At last, Derek pulled the Land Rover off the side of the road. They were in the Grampian foothills. In the distance, the stark, gray rock mountains reached into the gray sky. He walked around to open the door for Jennifer and then again took her hand. The area was rocky, necessitating maneuvering around boulders and climbing up paths of rough grass and thistle, trampled down by sheep, until he found a soft patch of grass. He handed Jennifer one of the sweaters to put on and pulled one over his own head. Then he nodded for her to sit and eased himself down next to her.

They were very close, their arms touching, as Derek looked up to the sky, searching among the expanse of gray. Then he turned to Jennifer. "What happened back there?" he asked.

Jennifer sighed. "I don't know," she began. "I was walking with your father and sister, and we stopped before a door. Your father said that they were the apartments of Lady Gwenivere, the wife of some earl in the past." Jennifer shook her head to clear it. "Suddenly, I knew who she was. She loved him desperately."

"Who?"

"Her lover. He was wearing a mask when he first abducted her. He called her 'Jenny,' and he was the father of her baby. She didn't know that he was also her husband. Derek, I can tell you exactly what those rooms on the other side of that door looked like during her time. For a few seconds, I was a part of her, seeing what she saw, feeling what she felt as she held her newborn baby in her arms."

"How do you know this?"

"I don't know. I just know it. It just came into my head," Jennifer said lamely.

"You didn't lose consciousness or get sick?"

"I felt dizzy when I touched the door and I thought I was going to get sick, but something stopped it. Something held on to me."

"Something?"

"It was like . . . it was like it was holding on to me, keeping me anchored in the present, keeping me safe even while I was back in time, back with Jenny."

Derek was silent for so long that Jennifer was tempted to look at him, but she kept her gaze forward.

"Anything else?" he finally asked.

"I felt something . . . something when we entered the old keep, and then, standing there by her rooms—it felt very natural . . . familiar." Jennifer leaned forward, her elbows on her knees, and covered her face with her hands.

"Jenny, I've got to ask you again, has anything like this ever happened to you before?" Derek asked.

"No," Jennifer said with exasperation. "Believe it or not, before I came to London and had the first vision, I was a very normal, even boring, person." She was still leaning forward, her face covered.

"Here," Derek said, "you need to relax. Lean back against my arm."

He put his arm behind her and with his other hand, gently pushed her back against him. She found his close proximity comforting and settled into his arm.

"So what do you think?" Jennifer asked.

"I think you should relax and not worry about it."

Jennifer twisted around to look at him. "Not worry!"

"You're a remarkable woman, Jenny McHugh," Derek said. "The past seems to reach out to you, or at least, England and Scotland's past. It appears that Thornhill's does as well. I suspect that this is just the beginning."

"Don't say that!" Jennifer said, sitting forward.

Derek laughed and pulled her back against his arm. "There's no use fighting it, you know. It's a part of you."

"I couldn't fight anything today," Jennifer said. "I'm getting a headache, and my throat hurts from talking nonstop the last three days and nights."

Again Derek laughed. "Then relax and close your eyes, and I will do the talking. I've come across some amazing information that I think will interest you. It appears that your Cela is not the only human being to have flown."

"What!" Jennifer said, again sitting forward.

"Last Monday morning, I called a friend of mine. He's an archaeologist with a special interest in astrophysics. I told him I was interested in historic documentation of people who could fly. That's what I received in the package this morning.

"It appears that throughout history, there have been a number of authenticated, although inexplicable, cases of men and women who could sail into the air, just as your Cela appears to have done. Certainly, the art from almost every civilization—some dating back six thousand years—often depicts human beings moving through the air, but art does not necessarily represent reality. What are really interesting are the accounts of people flying.

"The most reputable is probably the case of Joseph of Cupertino. He was a monk during the seventeenth century. Apparently, he was a very unremarkable man except for one thing: on numerous occasions, he flew. This has been well documented by many influential and respected witnesses of the time. The Catholic Church even canonized him. There are separate reports of Friar Joseph sailing through the air attested to by a pope, two kings, and the Duke of Brunswick, all independently. The descriptions even specify where he flew, how high, and the like.

"There is another account of a young girl in Calais, France who lived during the sixteenth century. Again, there are records of independent narratives by people who were considered reliable, respected persons. These records are also specific in describing the location and just where the girl flew.

"Nathaniel, my friend, included no less than fourteen accounts from Europe and five from Great Britain. That's a total of nineteen accounts that involved verification by multiple, independent witnesses in which the deeds were recorded. There are reports from the Middle East and Asia as well.

"He said there were many more, but they were not as reliably substantiated by people who were respected at the time, so he didn't include them. He can get those if we need them," Derek concluded.

Jennifer looked at Derek incredulously. "What does all this mean?" she asked.

"It means that there are written records—witnessed by people who were considered reliable at the time—of people flying," Derek said.

It was a moment before Jennifer could speak again. Finally, she looked directly at Derek. "I've never heard of this before. Do you believe it?" she asked.

Derek shrugged. "As I said, it's always been a theme in human civilization. Is it possible? Did these people actually fly? I don't know." Derek was silent a moment. "Nathaniel's research revealed one more note of interest." Jennifer detected the change in Derek's voice, portending importance. "With the exception of Friar Joseph, all of these people were subsequently either murdered or disappeared."

"What?"

"It looks like, in most cases, the people of their villages killed them, or the authorities of the times sentenced them to death. Nathanial included the documentation of their deaths as well. As I said, a few just disappeared."

"How can that be?"

"Mass hysteria, similar to the witch hunts of two centuries ago in your own country," Derek said. "The accounts in the Middle East are different, though. Those descriptions were all of people who were members of the Shining Ones, and they were revered by the people."

"The Shining Ones?" Jennifer asked.

"When you first told me of your civilization and its Wise Ones who received their knowledge from the People of the Sky, it didn't strike me as a totally new theme. I didn't say anything about it because, at that time, I was under the impression you had artifacts that could document the existence of a Bronze Age civilization.

"Jenny, you must realize that even with a conservative estimate, the age of the universe, as we know it, is at least ten billion years old. Homo sapiens appeared simultaneously with the last of the Neanderthals around thirty-two thousand years ago. That's thirty thousand years of civilization before the birth of Christ. These early humans created the paintings in the caves of Lascaux. Then we lost track of Homo sapiens until they turned up twenty thousand years later—in 12,000 B.C.—in Jericho, the Indus Valley, Sumer, Crete, and Egypt.

"What happened to them during those twenty thousand years? What happened between 32,000 and 12,000 B.C.? Scholars have been trying to solve that mystery for the past hundred years. There is no evidence of man's development during that twenty-thousand-year period. How, then, did early Homo sapiens, living primitively in a cave in 32,000 B.C., suddenly show up in the Indus Valley in 12,000 B.C. with the knowledge of cutting building blocks with which to construct entire cities, harvesting and storing grain, working metals, navigating, and the ability to craft seaworthy vessels in which they made long ocean voyages?"

"Derek, slow down," Jennifer said as she sat forward. She turned to him. "I know nothing about Neanderthals, caves, Jericho, all these B.C. dates. I never studied any of this, and if I did, I don't remember it. I had one year of college, and I was a marginal student, at best." She shrugged her shoulders. "I'm not as smart as you," she finished, once again feeling embarrassed.

Derek raised an eyebrow as he smirked. "This, from a woman who understands the fine points of metallurgy, can identify every constellation in the Northern and Southern skies and plot their movements through the seasons, has knowledge of prehistoric herbal medicine, can write in an ancient script, and—"

"That's Cela's knowledge, not mine," Jennifer

interrupted.

"No, Jenny, it is yours. You may have acquired your knowledge in an unconventional manner, but your brain comprehends complexities and subtleties and can process and recall a vast amount of information." He paused and smiled at her. "It's true. I would know. After all, I'm a world-famous scholar," he said, laughing at himself. He pulled her back against him.

"Civilizations evolve slowly, gradually, Jenny," he continued when he had settled her against him. "As I said, there should be evidence of this development, and yet, there is this gap in human evolution. For twenty thousand years, mankind appears to have done nothing, and then suddenly, the human race appears with these incredible advances. How could such a colossal leap have been made?

"One notable researcher, O'Brien, states that there was a small band of luminous individuals who appeared out of nowhere. They had a profound effect on our ancestors. They imparted to them the knowledge on which they built their civilizations. O'Brien uses the accounts from the early civilizations of Sumer, Lebanon, the Mesopotamian basin, and the valley of the Tigris and Euphrates Rivers to support the existence of these people. The Sumerians, Babylonians, and ancient Hebrews all tell of these luminous people whom they called the Shining Ones. It is said that they came from the sky, not unlike your People of the Sky, Jenny."

Jennifer was trembling as she listened to Derek. Her mouth was dry as she spoke. "Why didn't you tell me of these people before—these Shining Ones?"

"I assumed your documents were simply supporting a previously espoused theme. Jenny, up until a few days ago, I didn't know the source of your information." The air was thick as Derek spoke his next words. "What I find most profound about your People of the Sky and Cela is that *you* knew nothing of this theory."

"I didn't!" Jennifer said defensively.

"I know," Derek said gently, "and the similarities

between your People of the Sky and O'Brien's Shining Ones are astounding. The writings from the ancient Hebrews and the Babylonians date from 1200 B.C. to 100 B.C. They describe these Shining Ones who came from the sky and imparted great knowledge to our ancient ancestors. This was in the Middle East. Your People of the Sky appeared during that same time period, roughly 900 B.C., in Great Britain."

For a long time, they both sat in silence. Finally, Jennifer spoke.

"I'm frightened, Derek," Jennifer said. "With all these visions . . . and today Lady Gwenivere . . . I don't know what's happening to me."

Derek pulled her close to him, and she leaned back against him, seeking the protection of his arms.

"I don't know what's happening either—reincarnation, a memory passed down genetically to a descendent, or perhaps you've stumbled onto one of our inherent potentials, one that was long ago forgotten by most of our ancestors," Derek said. "But I do believe this: you have nothing to fear. What's happening to you is not bad. Some would even say it is a precious gift."

They sat in silence for a while, Jennifer drawing comfort from Derek's strength. Finally, Jennifer turned to him.

"Do you believe in God?"

"A good Presbyterian Scotsman like me?" Derek said with humor.

"I'm being serious," she said.

Derek thought a moment before he answered. "I've traveled all over the world, Jenny, digging through ruins, trying to separate fact from fiction, and every civilization has had its religion. Human beings seem to have a need to create for themselves a Higher Being. Me? Yes, I believe in God, although I think, as human beings, we have misunderstood and tried to make God in our image. I don't believe we have anything to fear in God. I do not see God as a vengeful force. God is the essence of everything good:

creation, life, love."

Derek was quiet a moment as Jennifer thought about what he said.

"Do you believe that you can talk to God and that He will hear you?" Jennifer asked.

"I certainly hope so, or on more than one occasion in my life, I've been shouting to deaf ears."

Jennifer turned to Derek. "You? Really?"

"What do you mean me, really? What do you think I am?" Derek challenged playfully.

"You were the one who said you were a rogue," Jennifer retorted.

"When did I say that?"

"That night at the hunting lodge when. . . ." Jennifer stopped suddenly, feeling her face coloring.

"Ah, yes, I remember," Derek said.

His face was inches from hers. All the nerves in her body responded. The feelings of comfort and peace of the last hour in his arms were replaced with feelings of passion and desire. She wanted him to kiss her, but he didn't. Instead, he shifted away from her, his eyes pained.

"Jenny," he said softly, "I *am* a rogue, but there are some things in life that are sacred to me—marriage and family are foremost on the list. I don't sleep with another man's wife. I believe in fidelity," he paused, "and honesty," he said pointedly.

Jennifer swallowed, his rebuke crushing her.

"I understand why you didn't tell me the truth about the source of your information, but to lead me to believe you were single, to lie about that, and let me fall. . . ." He stopped.

"I'm sorry," Jennifer whispered, her throat constricting with emotion.

Derek took a deep breath. "I know you are," he said quietly, "but it changes things between us." When he next spoke, his voice was impersonal, professional. "Ann and my father are waiting for us. They'll have lunch ready."

They drove back to Thornhill in silence, Derek immersed in his own feelings. Back there, sitting among the boulders in the foothills, his arm around her as they talked, it was all he could do to restrain himself. He had wanted to take her in his arms, her husband be damned. But then what? He didn't want Jenny simply for a lover. No, he wanted to spend his life with her. There. He admitted it. He was in love with her, and damned if he hadn't been since the moment he had found her lying on the floor at the museum. Was that even possible? To fall in love with someone you didn't know? All right, maybe not love, but he certainly had been unexplainably drawn to her.

He frowned, recalling that day when he had found her at the museum. He had felt something—something that caused him to leave the work he was doing at the time and enter the restoration room where she was lying on the floor, her head bleeding, the newly-acquired spear tip on the floor next to her. The *Bronze Age* spear tip!

Derek shook his head to clear it of the contradictions, mysteries, and revelations swirling around inside of him. They had reached Thornhill. He parked the vehicle and walked around to open the car door for Jennifer. "You go inside," he said. "I'll gather Nathaniel's notes."

Jennifer stepped out of the car and hesitated. He could see her uncertainty. To put her at ease, he placed his hand on her shoulder. "I'll be along shortly, Jenny," he said reassuringly.

She appeared to relax. "Okay," she said and turned toward the house.

Some of Nathaniel's papers had fallen to the floor of the car. Derek reached inside and was gathering the loose papers when he felt the change in the air. Instantly, he whirled around to see Jennifer. She was about twenty feet from the house when he saw her clutch herself and stumble. He heard her cry out and started running. He caught her as she collapsed and eased her down to the ground.

"Jenny!" Derek said, his lips against her ears. "It's all right. You're safe. Nothing is going to hurt you. I'm here, Jenny."

"Derek," Jennifer mumbled as she blinked her eyes and looked up at him. Then her eyes closed, and she was limp in his arms.

She didn't see Lord Harold and Ann rushing out the door to where she lay in Derek's arms, nor did she hear Issy, the great Irish wolfhound, howling as she came bounding out ahead of them to reach Jennifer first.

CHAPTER 12

826 B.C.

"Lodi, someone must stop him!" Cela cried as she felt the contractions of her womb.

"Do not worry about the High Priest now. You must think about your child who is about to be born," Lodi said.

Cela was squatting in Cupa's hut, supported by Cupa on one side and her mother, Ega, on the other.

"I failed," Cela said when the pain passed. "I could not find the People of the Sky."

"You did all that you could, Child," Lodi said.

"No, I need more time," Cela said. "I found the symbols of many different people, but I was alone in the sky. I flew south across waters and came upon a vast land, a land so large. The symbols were there, the great stones were there, but the sky was empty."

"Shhh, my child," Ega said.

"Someone must stop him. No more children must be sacrificed," Cela cried as once again the birth pains gripped her. The sweat was glistening on Cela's naked body, her long hair damp and clinging to her face and breasts, her muscles straining to deliver the infant within.

"Now!" Lodi said. "Your child comes now, Cela."

An hour later, Cela lay resting in Cupa's hut, her infant, swathed in a soft sheepskin pellet, asleep in her arms. Ega, Lodi, and Cupa had removed the soiled grasses that had been placed beneath Cela during the birthing process, and helped her bathe and dress in a clean robe. Now the priestesses sat around Cela and the sleeping baby.

"The High Priest must be told. He will know by now that the child has been born," Cupa said.

Cela closed her eyes and then opened them. "I must go to him then," she said with resignation, her finger gently stroking the baby's face.

"No, Cela. There's nothing that you can do. You cannot stop the ceremony," Ega said.

"But I must try. I cannot allow him to order the sacrifice of ten children in celebration of the birth of this one," Cela said, looking down at her child. "How can I? How can any of you?" Cela demanded.

The priestesses were silent, their eyes cast down, and then Lodi spoke.

"We do not condone the sacrifice of children," she said. "Never in our history has that been a practice of the Wise Ones."

"We were shocked when the High Priest first started sacrificing the captured children following battles. But what can we do? I have implored the gods to give us some direction, but they no longer hear us," Cupa said.

"I fear for us as a people," Ega said. "Something terrible is going to happen. I have seen it, but the vision is still clouded. I see our robes stained with blood."

"Then I must go," Cela said as she struggled to stand, still holding the infant.

"No, please," Ega suddenly said. "I fear for you!"

Cela stopped and looked at her mother. Her mother's eyes were a sea of pain. At last Cela understood as she looked down at the face of her own newborn child. Cela looked back at her mother.

"Mother," she said quietly, "is it my robe that you see stained with blood? Have you seen my death?"

Ega did not need to answer, for Cela could see the answer in her eyes. Cela inhaled sharply and then swallowed. She looked down at her own newborn daughter, sleeping peacefully.

"Is it soon?" Cela asked, her voice strained with emotion with the realization that her time with her infant was going to be cruelly cut short.

"I do not know, my daughter," Ega whispered, her own voice raw with pain.

Cela took a slow, deep breath. "There may not be much time. I must try to stop Luc," she said as she stood.

"No! Please! Do not go to him," Ega begged.

"You cannot stop the sacrifices," Cupa said. "Stay here. I will tell the High Priest that you are weak and that you and the child must rest in my hut tonight."

"She's right, Child," Lodi said. "Stay away from the High Priest."

The three priestesses were trying to block Cela's exit, but she pushed through them, cradling her child against her breast.

"No," Cela said. "I must try."

As she walked to the entrance of the hut, a shadow fell across the opening and Dagga stepped inside. His form completely blocked the entrance. Cela gasped in surprise. Dagga gently placed his hands on Cela's shoulders.

"Listen to them, Priestess. They offer good council," he said.

"I must try to stop him," Cela said to Dagga. "I cannot allow him to order the sacrifice of more children."

Dagga sighed and moved one of his hands to Cela's face. He gently cupped her cheek in his hand.

"Priestess," Dagga said, "the High Priest doubts himself as a man. This causes him to be jealous of any who threaten his power. His anger has no limits. Now is not the time to challenge him. If you care nothing for yourself, then think of your child. Would you have your cousin's anger extend to this one?" Dagga asked as he looked down at the baby.

Cela lowered her gaze to her sleeping child. A tear escaped down her cheek. It was a moment before she spoke. "No," she finally whispered. "I will remain here."

Dagga looked at the sleeping infant in Cela's arms. "Priestess, is it permitted to see the child?" he asked hesitantly.

Cela looked up into Dagga's eyes. With one hand, she brushed the tears away. A smile slowly formed on her face.

"Yes, Dagga," she said gently, "it is permitted."

Cela pulled the sheep's pellet from the infant's face and head, causing it to stir. She held the baby out, placing it in Dagga's waiting arms. She couldn't help but laugh, seeing the surprised look on Dagga's face as he held the child awkwardly against his chest.

"It is so small! The baby has no weight," Dagga exclaimed. "It is well?" he asked with concern.

Again, Cela smiled. "Yes," she said. "She is well. She is very strong."

"She?" Dagga asked.

"Yes," Cela answered. "Have you never held a baby before?" Cela asked, still amused by Dagga's awkwardness.

"No. I do not have a mate," Dagga answered.

A moment of intimate silence passed between them. Then Cela reached out and touched Dagga's arm. He looked up at her.

"She has your hair of fire, Priestess," he said softly.

Cela looked into Dagga's eyes. "I pray that she will have her father's kindness, wisdom, and strength."

It was all that Cela could say, and Dagga knew that. Cela was taking a great risk in saying that much. Although Lodi, Cupa, and Ega were loyal to Cela and would protect her as best they could, they were bound as priestesses of the Wise Ones. Cela could never speak openly of the night that the baby's life really was started. Lodi knew the truth, of course, for she had instructed Cela in the art of simulating virginity. And Cupa had cared for Cela following the fertility ceremony when Luc had so brutally raped Cela. No doubt she also had learned the truth. But Cela had never told her mother, Ega. She hadn't wanted to burden her.

"Cela?" Ega whispered.

Cela turned to her mother. Although Ega was shocked at seeing a warrior and a priestess touch and speak so intimately, Ega was also very wise. She looked at Dagga, and her eyes widened in recognition.

"I must return to my duties," Dagga said roughly. With reluctance, he placed the baby back in Cela's arms. "You will remain here throughout the night?" he asked.

"Yes," Cela said.

Dagga raised his eyebrows, as if questioning her. Cela smiled.

"Yes, I will remain here," she said again. "Too many times the gods have sent you to me, Dagga. I dare not doubt their message tonight."

Dagga looked at Cela, her long, red hair flowing down her back, the baby nestled in her arms. There was no mistaking the warmth in his eyes. Then he bowed his head, as was expected of a guard, and walked out of the hut.

* * *

Jennifer moaned and clutched her stomach.

"Derek! What's happened?" Harold Rannoch asked with deep concern. He was kneeling beside Derek.

"What's happened to Jennifer?" Ann asked with alarm as she knelt beside them.

Derek didn't know how long Jennifer had been unconscious. It couldn't have been more than a minute or two. He could feel her begin to stir, although her eyes were still firmly closed.

"Father, would you take Ann and stand back there?" Derek asked, indicating a place several feet away from him. He didn't know if Jennifer would vomit again, but he remembered her distress because he'd been present when she regained consciousness at the Highland Games. Obviously, his family would need some explanation now, but he didn't want Jennifer to become anxious at seeing them. "Please," he repeated. "She'll be all right."

Harold Rannoch looked from his son to his daughter, doubt on his face.

"Father, will you help me up?" Ann asked, offering her hand to her father.

Harold Rannoch assisted Ann into a standing position and then allowed her to lead him several feet away from where Derek sat, holding Jennifer in his arms. Issy, however, was not about to be dismissed so easily. When Derek motioned for her to leave, she promptly lay down on the gravel drive, resting her face on her massive paws, only inches away from Jennifer.

Once again, Jennifer moaned. She curled up, clutching her midsection, and rolled onto her side. Derek could feel her trembling and saw her swallow several times and reach for her mouth.

"Easy, Jenny," he said soothingly. "You're safe. You're coming back. Don't rush it, Jenny. Let it bring you back slowly."

Through the roaring in Jennifer's ears, she heard Derek's voice from a distance. His words penetrated her consciousness.

"Relax, Jenny. Wait. You're safe. Trust it. It's not trying to hurt you. Let it bring you back," Derek repeated softly.

Jennifer felt herself relax, and amazingly, the violent cramping ceased. Her world was still black, but she felt like she was floating, safely floating. Gradually, she was aware of a light becoming brighter. Soon, she could feel its warmth on her eyelids, and she opened her eyes. Derek was there, his face above her. She stared at him a moment, feeling at peace, feeling safe. She was aware that her head was in his lap, and he was holding her hand. At that moment, she wished that time could stand still. Just then, Derek smiled.

"You're not going to vomit on me again, are you?" he asked teasingly.

"No." She paused, assessing her physical feelings. "I almost did, but no, I don't think I'm going to be sick this time," Jennifer said, her voice weak. She could feel the nausea receding, and the vortex had left. She felt like her body was still quivering, but safe in Derek's arms. Just then, something clouded her peripheral vision as Issy's tongue reached out and licked Jennifer's face.

"Issy, get back, girl," Derek said. "I guess you're going to have to get used to her," Derek said to Jennifer. "When a dog selects a master, there's not much anyone else can do. She's appointed herself your guardian."

"I'll try to get used to her," Jennifer said as she turned her head to avoid the dog's tongue. "Can you tell her to stop that?"

Derek spoke to the dog again, and this time, Issy took a step backward and sat down, still staying close to Jennifer.

"Can you stand up now?" Derek asked.

"Yes," Jennifer said. She didn't want to stand—she wanted to remain here, feeling his arms around her, holding her, her head in his lap. But, reluctantly, she reached her hand out to him.

Derek helped Jennifer stand, and then he raised his hand to brush a leaf out of her hair. That was when Jennifer turned and saw Lord Harold and Ann standing about ten feet away. She froze, her breath catching in her throat.

Derek reached for her hand and took it in his. "It's all right," he said softly, squeezing her hand. "They were concerned about you."

"Jennifer?" Ann said. She walked over to where they stood and gently placed her hand on Jennifer's shoulder. "Jennifer, are you all right?" Ann asked.

Jennifer couldn't look at her. A myriad of feelings were rushing through her: fear, confusion, but primarily embarrassment.

"Why don't we all go inside?" Derek said smoothly, still holding Jennifer's hand.

Ann stepped back, concern in her eyes. Derek turned and, keeping Jennifer's hand in his, started walking toward the house. Harold Rannoch waited for his daughter and then took her arm, following behind Jennifer and Derek. Issy, now apparently assured that Jennifer was safe, bounded ahead of them all.

"Derek!" Jennifer whispered.

He released her hand and put his arm around her waist, pulling her close to him as they walked. "I think we should tell them the truth. We've got to say something," he said as they walked.

"No! Please!" Jennifer pleaded in a whisper. "What will they think of me?"

Derek glanced at Jennifer as they mounted the steps leading toward the door. He released her only long enough to open the door, and then he put his arm around her. "They might surprise you," he said encouragingly, his lips close to her ear.

Jennifer didn't enter but waited beside Derek as Ann and Lord Harold walked inside the house. She kept her face down and avoided looking at them. As Derek turned and indicated that he and Jennifer were to follow, she stopped. As much as she wanted and *needed* his arm around her, she pulled away from him.

"Derek, I can't discuss this with your family," she said. When Derek started to object, Jennifer continued. "Tell them whatever you want. Tell them the truth, if you must, but I can't sit there while you do."

"Jenny, my father and sister—"

"No," Jennifer said as she turned, clearly becoming agitated. "I'm going for a walk."

"Jenny," he said, reaching for her hand and closing his fingers around it.

"Please, I would prefer it this way." Why couldn't she quell the shaking she felt inside? She was trying, but she couldn't handle the visions, which, despite the joy she felt with the birth of Cela's child, were becoming unsettling. Like Dagga, she was worried about Cela. And now there was Derek's family. What must they think of her? How could they possibly understand?

Derek hesitated. "Then I'll come with you," he said.

"No," Jennifer said, shaking her head. "Derek, your father and sister need some kind of an explanation. You go talk with them. I won't go far; I'll stay near the house."

"Are you certain, Jenny? Are you feeling all right?"

She could see the concern in his eyes and was warmed by it. "Yes, I'm fine," Jennifer replied. "If it will make you feel better, I'll take Issy with me," she said as she looked down at the dog that had stopped at the door and was standing next to her.

"I don't know," Derek said with doubt.

"This is not the first time this has happened, Derek," she reminded him. "I know what I'm doing. Please, let me wait outside by myself. I can't face them now. It's too much."

"All right," Derek finally said, squeezing her hand and releasing it. "But take Issy with you. I'll join you later."

Jennifer nodded and turned to walk down the steps. She glanced back once to see Derek standing at the door, watching her. Then she set out walking across the grass of Thornhill, the great dog beside her.

"That's an incredible story," Harold Rannoch said when Derek concluded. "And I sense, by what you didn't say, that you believe Jennifer—that she is actually seeing a past civilization."

"I don't have a scientific explanation for it, but yes, I do believe her," Derek said.

"I believe her, too, Father," Ann said. "I sensed something that day at the Highland Games. It didn't last for long, but I know I felt something."

"I did, too," Derek said, "and that wasn't the first time. I realized later that on at least three other occasions, I was near when Jennifer had one of her visions. I felt it then, too. And her information about that time period is too astounding. There's no other explanation."

Lord Harold shook his head. "Phenomenal. Absolutely phenomenal."

"And the story about Lady Gwenivere?" Ann asked.

Derek shrugged his shoulders. "She said that suddenly she saw it. She saw the room and Lady Gwenivere. More importantly, she felt what Lady Gwenivere was feeling, like she was inside of her or a part of her. That's how she feels with Cela, the young woman of the Bronze Age society."

"And nothing like this ever happened to her before?" Harold Rannoch asked.

"Nothing—not until she came to England and Scotland, and she says that it didn't happen when she returned to America."

"What do you plan to do?" Lord Rannoch asked.

"Jennifer has agreed that we will continue working together. An unbelievable fountain of information is in her head. I would like to search for evidence—all of it circumstantial at this point—that this society that she is seeing actually existed."

"Do these spells hurt her?" Ann asked, the concern evident in her voice.

"They make her sick, or at least they did until this last one. She usually gets sick to her stomach when the episode begins and then loses consciousness. When she comes out of them, she is dizzy, disoriented, and often vomits. Then, after a few minutes, she says the feeling passes and she's fine."

"How awful," Ann said.

"I have a theory about that," Derek said. "The experiences frighten her, as one would expect. I think her fear and resistance are the root of the sickness that accompanies the episodes."

"This is absolutely amazing," Harold Rannoch repeated

again. "Son, have you ever encountered anything like this before?"

"No, Father, I haven't."

"Well, no wonder Jennifer is frightened. Is that why she didn't want you to tell us about it?" Ann asked.

"Jenny is concerned that you will think she is either lying or crazy. Few people know. As I told you, when she came for my help, she didn't tell me the truth. She never intended for me to know about the visions. Her friend, Nina Bouvay, and Shamus MacNeal know the truth," Derek said.

"I see," Harold Rannoch said. "Well, I guess we'll just proceed as we have been. Miss McHugh is an amazing young woman. I must say, I liked her the first day I met her, and there was something else. It was strange. The way she was staring at Thornhill and then the behavior of the hounds. . . ." He paused, drawing his brows together as though puzzled.

"What, Father?" Derek asked.

"Let me think about this," he said. "You should be with Jennifer now."

"All right," Derek said as he stood. "Thank you for understanding," he said to both his father and sister.

"Of course," Ann said. "Please reassure Jennifer on our behalf."

Derek nodded his head in agreement and then walked to the door. However, when he reached it, he stopped. He took a deep breath. "There is one thing more that you should know," he said, without turning to face them. "Jenny's name is not McHugh. It's Jennifer McHugh Bracken. She's married."

"What?" Ann asked as she stood up.

"She has a husband in America. Originally, she came to Scotland to visit Nina Bouvay for a few weeks. As soon as all this is ended, she'll return to him. I just thought you should know," he said in explanation. "Now, if you will excuse me, I'll go find Jenny."

It was a moment before Ann or Harold Rannoch spoke. Ann moved to the window. She saw Derek walking away from the house. In the distance, she could see Issy and Jennifer sitting on one of the small hills that surrounded Thornhill. Harold stepped over to stand by his daughter. They both watched as Derek reached Jennifer. He sat on the grass beside her and took her hand in his.

"He loves her," Ann said softly to her father.

"Yes," Harold replied.

"We have no records of the Druids sacrificing children," Derek said.

Derek and Jennifer were sitting in the library at Thornhill. It was late in the evening. Jennifer had been grateful to Ann and Lord Harold, for both had been kind and reassuring when she and Derek returned to the house earlier in the day.

"Certainly there are descriptions written by the ancient Greeks and Romans describing the methods employed by the Druids when sacrificing adults, but never children," Derek continued.

"That's what Luc has started doing. Cela's people had never sacrificed children before," Jennifer said. "They didn't really involve themselves in war that often, and when they did, young children of the enemy tribes were adopted, not sacrificed."

"How are they sacrificed?" Derek asked.

"What?"

"How do they do it? What method do they use?"

"Derek, please. . . ."

"You don't have to talk about it if you don't want to," he offered, "but the more detailed the information, the better."

Jennifer was silent a moment and then spoke.

"The young children and babies are put in a large wicker basket and carried to the edge of a mountain gorge,"

Jennifer said, a hollow ring to her voice. "Then they're removed from the basket and thrown over the edge."

Derek frowned. "That's not a typical Druidic practice, either. Up until this point, all the techniques of sacrifice used by Cela and her people were used, to the best of our knowledge, by the Druids, too."

"It's been an unusually wet summer for them," Jennifer said, "and with all the wars, they haven't been able to grow any food. The wars have forced the animals north. There's a terrible food shortage, and Cela's people are suffering severe losses from the fighting. Luc's explanation is that the gods are displeased with them because they haven't been sacrificing enough."

"And the other priests and priestesses?" Derek asked.

"Most are disturbed by Luc's leadership but are hesitant to speak openly about it. Things have changed, Derek. Since Luc has become the High Priest, the focus has become war and sacrifice. It wasn't like that before. The Wise Ones spent their time learning, creating, studying."

They talked some more, reviewing Jennifer's latest vision, and then Derek asked questions about the previous episodes. At one point, Derek retrieved his notes.

"What about the People of the Sky? What exactly did Cela see when she went searching for them?"

Jennifer thought about Derek's question.

"She saw monuments that had been erected by people other than her own. She could read the symbols made by the monuments. The few times she encountered people, she hid from them and watched. She couldn't understand the languages they spoke."

Derek raised his eyebrows. "Where did she go?" he asked.

Jennifer frowned. "I'm not certain. I know what she saw and how she found her direction. She used the stars and the position of the sun."

"She flew, or traveled, at night?"

"Most of the time at night, sometimes during the day."

A secretive smile came to Derek's face. He stood up and offered his hand to Jennifer.

"Come with me," he said.

"Where are we going?" she asked.

"Just come with me," he said, a smile at the corners of his lips.

Jennifer frowned but stood, taking Derek's hand. They walked out of the library and through the hall to the front door. Derek grabbed two coats. Jennifer turned around as he helped her put one of them on. After he slipped his on, he opened the door for her.

"Where are we going?" Jennifer asked again.

"For a walk," he answered.

"For a walk?" Jennifer glanced at her watch. "It's almost one o'clock in the morning."

"We won't be long," Derek said, taking her hand.

"But—"

"Shhh," Derek said, smiling.

They walked in silence as Derek led her away from Thornhill. He didn't stop until he reached the top of one of the hills surrounding the great house. He then turned to Jennifer. He was standing very close, and in the moonlight, Jennifer could see his eyes clearly. When he reached up to her chin, she felt her heart race. His hand lingered there a moment, and then he gently tipped her chin up and her head back.

"Tell me what you see," Derek said.

Jennifer jerked her head down and looked at Derek. "What are you talking about?" she asked, confused.

"Tell me what you see," he repeated patiently. "Up there." He nodded to the sky.

There were a few clouds in the night sky, but for the most part, it was clear, a myriad of stars shining in the blackness. Jennifer began to speak slowly, hesitantly, and then suddenly, the information rolled effortlessly off her tongue. She named and described one constellation and star after another. Many of the names she used were unfamiliar, as she was calling each by the names used by the Wise Ones almost three thousand years ago. She paused for a moment and then continued to discuss the rotation that would be anticipated with each season. When she finished, the night air was silent as she continued to gaze at the sky. Then Derek spoke.

"And when Cela left, searching for the People of the Sky, which direction did she go?" Derek asked.

As Jennifer stared into the vastness of the sky, a feeling of comfort came over her. It was as though the sky and the stars were her friends. It was as if she, not Cela, had traveled through the sky, guided by their light.

"She went north first," Jennifer began, "but there were no symbols, no monuments. Then she went west, across a small body of water, and arrived at the island of Ere. There were many stone monuments and earth burrows there, but she didn't find the People of the Sky.

"Another time, she went east and crossed another body of water. This land was dotted with monuments, although Cela couldn't read them all. Many of the patterns were unfamiliar to her. She continued north until the monuments stopped."

"Where was she, Jenny?"

"You mean what was the name of the country? I don't know."

"Can you identify its shape? Would you recognize it on a map?"

Jennifer looked at Derek. "Yes," she said simply, "I see its outline from the sky."

"Good. Did she go anywhere else?"

"Yes. She also went south, across a narrow body of water. There were many symbols there, too. All along the Western Coast and all the way to—"

"To where, Jenny?"

"There were some islands with monuments very similar to Stonehenge," Jennifer said, confusion in her voice.

"What's wrong?"

"I don't know where these places are or where they were. I see them as though watching a home movie shot out the window of an airplane, but I have no idea what country they were in."

Derek could tell Jennifer was becoming frustrated. He put his hand on her shoulder.

"That's all right. It doesn't matter. Can you draw the stone monuments?"

"Yes."

Derek smiled. "Let's go then," he said, taking her hand.

Derek had assembled maps on one side of the desk. For the past two hours, he had tried to decipher where Cela had flown based on Jennifer's description and the maps before him. Then he asked her to draw all the monuments she could remember Cela seeing.

As he watched her, a strange feeling came over him as, one by one, Jennifer drew the positions of the stones. Some of them he didn't recognize, but most of them he did, and incredibly, they were located in the countries where he had surmised Cela must have gone. Derek quickly determined the island of Ere, located to the west, to be Ireland. Although Jennifer had never been there, she accurately drew numerous earth mounds and stone formations known to be in Ireland.

Next, she moved south and sketched megalithic formations that had been on some small islands. Derek instantly recognized the Neolithic remains located on the Channel Islands. When she continued south to "a large land mass," Derek froze as he saw her sketch megalithic remains known to be in France, Spain, and Portugal.

After a while, Jennifer paused, rubbing her eyes. "There's still more," she said as Derek studied one of the sketches she had just made. "Just let me rest a minute, and I can draw some more," she said as she crossed her arms on the table and laid her head down on her arms.

Derek moved the sketches to another table and was examining them, making notations on pieces of paper. "Jenny?" he said as he studied one of the sketches. He paused, looking across the room to where she sat. "Jenny?" he said again. He walked to where Jennifer's head was resting on her arms. He placed his hand on her arm. "Jenny, are you awake?"

"Hmmm," Jennifer mumbled.

Derek smiled. "I guess you've done enough for the night. Come on, Jenny, I'll take you upstairs."

Jennifer stirred. "No, I can draw more. I just need to rest a minute."

"You need to sleep," Derek said, glancing at his watch. "It's three o'clock in the morning. Come," he said as he took her arm.

Jennifer lifted her head up and stood.

"Really, Derek, I'll be fine in a few minutes." Derek was holding her arm as they started walking toward the door. "Here," Jennifer said, "just let me lie down on this sofa for a few minutes. Then I can draw the rest of them."

Jennifer reached the leather sofa and collapsed on it. She was instantly asleep. Derek laughed softly to himself as he reached for a tartan blanket that had been thrown over the back of the sofa. He covered Jennifer with the blanket and then brushed her hair out of her face, letting his hand linger for a brief moment, feeling the thick, silky curls between his fingers. A tide of emotion welled up in him, and he abruptly stepped back. He extinguished the lights and carried all of Jennifer's sketches to a large chair. He turned on a solitary lamp and sat down to once again examine the structures as she had sketched them.

"Derek!" Harold Rannoch said with surprise as he entered the library.

Derek sat up from where he had fallen asleep several hours ago. The sketches still lay on his lap. He glanced at his watch and then looked over to where Jennifer still slept. He motioned to his father. Lord Harold raised his eyebrows when he saw Jennifer asleep on the sofa.

"How late did you two work?" Lord Harold whispered to his son.

Derek rubbed his eyes. "I must have fallen asleep sometime after five," he said. "I want to show you something," he said to his father, "but let's go somewhere else so Jenny can sleep."

Derek stood and gathered Jennifer's sketches. He and his father left the library and crossed into the small family dining room. Clara immediately appeared to see what they would like for breakfast. After she left, Derek spread Jennifer's sketches out on the table.

"Look at these, Father," Derek said enthusiastically. "These were all in her head. She saw all of these prehistoric monuments during her visions. Most of them I recognize, although they have been changed in subtle ways—stones destroyed or carried off by people through the years. There are some that I have never seen, which makes me question what happened to them. It's an unbelievable opportunity," Derek said, looking up at his father. "Talking to Jenny is like talking to someone who actually lived during the Bronze Age." Derek shook his head. "You wouldn't believe what she said the purpose of Stonehenge and other megalithic structures was."

"Jennifer is a very unique woman," Lord Harold said, watching his son carefully. "It makes one wonder about the role fate plays in our lives: Jennifer arriving here and having these visions of the past, you two meeting and your having an interest and expertise in the same time period that she 'sees,' and then there's Jennifer's curious relation to Thornhill. Is there such a thing as coincidence?"

"You're in a very philosophical mood," Derek accused lightly.

Lord Harold smiled and then became serious. "I can understand your professional interest in Jennifer. I believe, however, your interest goes deeper than that. Am I correct?"

It was a moment before Derek responded. "Jenny is special," he finally answered.

"That's all?" Lord Harold asked his son.

"She has a husband," Derek said.

Just then Clara entered, carrying a tray of food. Derek and his father ceased talking, as Derek moved his papers and Clara served them breakfast. After Clara left, Lord Harold spoke.

"Derek—"

"I don't wish to discuss this, Father."

"I don't mean to pry," Lord Harold said. "I'm concerned for you both."

"I know," Derek said. "Now," he said, changing the subject, "how are plans going for your birthday party?"

"Oh," Lord Harold scoffed, "you'll have to ask Ann. I told her I didn't want a party."

"You have a lot of friends, both here and in London. They all want to help you celebrate your sixtieth birthday."

Just then, Jeffrey entered the dining room. "Excuse me, sir," he said as he approached Lord Harold, "but there is a telephone call for Miss McHugh."

"Oh?" Derek said. "Who is it?"

"Nina Bouvay, sir. She said it was important."

Derek stood. "Miss McHugh is in the library. She'll take the call in there," he said to Jeffrey. "Excuse me, Father. I'll tell Jenny there's a call for her."

Derek walked to the library and entered, finding Jennifer still asleep on the sofa. His expression softened as he looked down on her, red hair spread out on the sofa, glistening, inviting his touch, her face peaceful, her complexion creamy with the slightest touch of a freckle here and there from the time they had spent outdoors, her lips curved up in the corner, content in her deep-dream state. He liked having her here in his home; he liked being close to her. He shook his head to stop his thoughts from where he knew they were going.

"Jenny. Wake up, Jenny," he said as he gently touched her shoulder.

Jennifer stirred. She opened her eyes slightly and then closed them again.

"I can't draw anymore tonight, Derek. My eyes feel like sandpaper." She moved against the back of the sofa, making room for him. "Sit down, and you can ask me questions about the ones I've already drawn."

Derek hesitated only a moment and then sat down on the edge of the sofa next to her, not consciously realizing how natural such a casually intimate gesture was for him.

"Jenny," he said, laughing to himself, "it's morning."

He waited a moment for his words to register. Slowly, Jennifer opened her eyes again. She squinted them against the morning light.

"Morning?" she asked.

"Yes. It's seven thirty in the morning, and you have a telephone call."

Jennifer frowned as she tried to wake up.

"It's your friend Nina. She said it was important," Derek said. "The phone is over on the desk. Would you like me to leave?"

Jennifer hesitated. "No, that's not necessary."

Derek stood, allowing her to push the blanket off and stand. She walked to the desk and picked up the receiver.

"Hello?" Jennifer said.

Derek watched as Jennifer frowned and then reached for a pen laying on the desk. "Okay, go ahead," she said. When she finished writing the numbers down, she said good-bye to Nina and hung up the phone. She stared at the numbers a moment and then turned to Derek.

"I need to place a call to Chicago," she said, "and my cell phone is useless here. Is there any chance you could drive me to Nina's?"

"To call Chicago? You may use the phone here. I'll close the door so you can have some privacy."

Jennifer watched as Derek left the room, closing the door behind him. She hesitated only a second and then dialed the number Nina had given her.

"Jennifer," Steven Cole, her attorney, said upon answering the phone. "I'm glad you called."

"I hope I didn't wake you. It must be what, around midnight in Chicago? Nina seemed to think it was important," Jennifer said.

"It is. I thought you should know that I met with your husband's attorney today. By law, both parties must make a complete financial disclosure. Do you know how much your husband is worth?"

"No," Jennifer said, "and I don't care. I told you I didn't want anything from him."

Jennifer could hear Steven rustling papers and then he spoke again.

"Your husband's interest in the corporation, his cash and investments, and the house and two cars are currently valued at about ninety million dollars. He also has a salary of two and a half million a year."

"Steven, I told you—"

"Wait, there's more. Do you know anything about a trust fund set up by John's father?"

"A trust fund? No."

"This is pretty amazing, Jennifer. You might want to sit down for this one. Apparently, John's father made a lot of money in the oil business, or rather, John's grandfather did. John's father controls all that money. He set up a trust fund for his two children, John and Hillary. Upon his death, the money is to be divided evenly between the two of them, but there is a catch. First of all, they can't touch the principal until they reach the ripe old age of sixty-five. That's nine more years for John. Up until that time, they can use the income from the funds anyway they want. At the age of sixty-five, each beneficiary will receive his or her portion of the principal, which, by the way, amounts to one hundred million each.

"There's one more provision, and this is the one that should really interest you. The old man apparently doesn't believe in divorce. I gather he wasn't too pleased about John's first divorce, so some time after that divorce, he added another stipulation to the trust. As the trust currently reads, should any of the beneficiaries—meaning John or his sister—become divorced before the age of sixty-five, they forfeit forever any right to the principal and the interest it generates. It goes back to the trust fund. Your husband will lose a fortune on the day that your divorce becomes final. Even if I do go along with you and we ask for nothing in the settlement, John's still going to lose a bundle."

The line was silent.

"Jennifer? Are you still there?"

"I'm here, Steven."

"Sorry to spring this on you so suddenly. I was fairly certain you didn't know anything about it."

"No, I didn't."

"Your husband's attorney indicated today that John still does not want this divorce and is going to do everything he can to prevent it. He'll probably offer incentives to stay in the marriage—at least until he reaches age sixty-five. He's going to talk to you."

"John's attorney?"

"No, John. I got the impression that your husband would be meeting with you soon."

"I don't want to talk to him."

"I understand. Shall I request a restraining order?"

Jennifer was silent a moment. "No, that's not necessary."

"John can't prevent the divorce, Jennifer. We have additional leverage that I think may hasten the divorce."

"I don't know what you mean."

Jennifer could hear Steven take a deep breath. "Jennifer, are you aware that your husband patronizes expensive prostitutes who cater to wealthy men with particular sexual interests? It's run as an exclusive club of sorts."

Jennifer felt a chill pass through her.

"I gather by your silence that you know nothing of this. It took some digging. Apparently, his first wife used this as grounds for divorce, but she also signed a non-disclosure agreement as part of the settlement. We can use this as leverage to speed up the divorce proceedings."

Jennifer was numb. She told Steven she didn't want to know any of the details of John's club. She didn't want any of John's money. She just wanted it to be over, as quickly as possible.

Jennifer left the library after speaking with Steven and walked to the small dining room. She would have to give Derek and his family a reason for leaving. Hopefully, it would only be a day or two—long enough to confront John and end this forever.

Derek and his father were still seated at the table and rose when she entered the room.

"Ah, Jennifer," Lord Harold said. "I'm glad you could join us for breakfast."

"Actually, I must apologize to you. I need to return to my friend Nina's for a few days."

"Oh? No bad news, I trust," Lord Harold said.

"No. There are just some things that I must take care of. It should take only a day or two."

"Then you will be certain to be here for my birthday, and bring your friend, Miss Bouvay. I shall see that an invitation is sent to her immediately."

Jennifer hesitated. "I'm not certain that I will be able to come."

"My dear, I shall be very disappointed if you are not here, and Ann is counting on your being here," Lord Harold said.

Jennifer glanced at Derek and then turned back to Lord Harold.

"I will try to come," she said.

"Splendid!" Lord Harold said, smiling. "Now, shall I

send Clara to help you pack?"

"No, that's not necessary, but I do need to leave right away."

"I'll drive you," Derek said, stepping away from the table. "Father, if you will excuse me?" he said as he walked to where Jennifer was standing.

Derek accompanied Jennifer to her room and waited while she tossed clothing into her suitcase. "How long do you think you will be away?" he asked her.

"This should take only a few days," Jennifer responded, not looking at him.

"And then?"

"If you still want to continue working," she said hesitantly, "I could return."

They drove in silence to Nina's cottage. Nina greeted them at the door as Derek carried Jennifer's luggage.

"Miss Bouvay, it's a pleasure to see you again," Derek said as he placed Jennifer's suitcase down inside the door. "My father asked that I deliver this to you," he said, holding out an embossed envelope with the crest of the Earl of Thornhill adorning it. "He would be pleased if you and Miss McHugh would join him this Saturday. My sister has planned a party to celebrate his birthday." Derek then turned to Jennifer. "I will see you Saturday," he said, nodding his head slightly.

After seeing Derek to the door, Jennifer and Nina returned to the living room as Nina opened the invitation. She read it quickly and then looked up at Jennifer.

"I read about this in the paper. Derek's father is also retiring. He'll still retain his seat in the House of Lords, of course, but he'll no longer be active in London politics. Apparently, he wielded quite a bit of power in London. This birthday party is supposed to be a big event, with many of London's MPs attending."

"MPs?" Jennifer asked.

"Members of Parliament," Nina answered. She looked at Jennifer. "Derek said he would see you then. What are you doing here? You surprised me when you drove up just now. Is something wrong?"

"Yes."

"Derek again?"

"No, not Derek. I called Steven Cole this morning."

For the next few minutes, Jennifer related the substance of her conversation with her attorney. When she finished, Nina jumped up.

"That bastard! I would not have thought it possible to detest John Bracken more than I already do. You think he's coming here?"

"I don't know, but I thought I'd better be here. I certainly wouldn't want him going to Thornhill."

The next day, just as Jennifer feared, John arrived in the afternoon. Nina answered the door and motioned for John to step inside.

"Jen, the asshole is here," she called to Jennifer. Then she turned back to John. "Watch your step, Bracken," Nina said, her warning clear.

John stepped past Nina and walked to where Jennifer was standing. "Jennifer," he said with restraint.

"Hello, John," she replied.

"I have some work to do in the garden," Nina said. "I'll be out there if you need me, Jen."

When Nina left, John turned to Jennifer.

"I would think you would have had the decency to discuss this divorce with me before sending an attorney to my door," John said tersely. "You left without a word."

"John, I've tried to talk to you about our relationship for the last six months, and each time I did, you told me I was being childish or naive."

"And just what do you think your running away was?"

"I'd say it was justified after what you tried to do to me."

371

John clenched his jaw. Jennifer saw the anger in his eyes; then his face became a mask.

"If we are going to reach an agreement on this matter, then we need to discuss this like adults. That's why I came to Scotland. I booked a room at a hotel in Braemar. Why don't you get your things together, and we can go there now?"

"John, I'm not going anywhere with you, especially to a hotel."

"Do you propose that we stay here in Nina's living room for the next few days while we get this thing settled? There's a lot at stake here, Jennifer."

"Yes, money. I never knew about your father's trust fund. I'm sorry you may lose that, but I still want a divorce." Jennifer saw the muscles in John's face tighten. She knew he was trying to contain his anger. "I don't want a penny from you," she added. "No money. Just a divorce."

"We still must discuss this. I've been a good husband to you, Jennifer. I've taken care of you and your mother. I've given you anything you asked for. I think you owe me the courtesy of discussing the divorce. I understand if you don't want to stay at the hotel with me. I'll stay there and you can stay here. Will you at least agree to dinner tonight?"

"What! Do you think I'm a fool? I remember the last time you took me to dinner."

Again, John clenched his jaw quickly, and then he relaxed.

"A public dinner, and then I will bring you back here," he said. "You can have Nina wait up for you, if that will make you feel better."

"I don't want to have dinner with you, John. I don't ever want to see you again."

"Unfortunately, it's necessary if you want my cooperation in these proceedings."

Jennifer didn't answer.

"Good Lord, Jennifer, I'm not some kind of monster. I'm not going to touch you. What happened the last time was a mistake. I was desperate. I didn't want to lose you. I thought, perhaps a child. . . . I have apologized for that. Now can we just discuss this like two adults? The sooner we can come to an agreement, the sooner we can both get on with our lives."

Jennifer thought for a moment. She loathed the idea of dining with John, but if that would hasten the divorce, she would do it. "All right. I'll go to dinner with you, and then you can bring me back here. Nothing more. Is that understood?"

That evening, John drove to a restaurant in Braemar. They both had been silent as he drove, but once their drinks were served, John initiated the conversation.

"What exactly do you want from me, Jennifer?"

His direct question unsettled her, although she had to admit, she didn't read any malice in his manner or voice.

"I want a divorce, John. That's all."

John smiled slightly. "Your attorney seems to think you need a financial settlement as well."

"John, I don't want your—"

"And I am in agreement with him," he said.

Jennifer stared at John.

"You do think I'm a monster, don't you?" John sighed. "I guess I have been in many ways. I like having things my own way, but you know that more than anyone. You didn't turn out to be the pliable young woman I thought you were, a miscalculation on my part." John smiled. "You've given me a lot this past year and a half, Jennifer—more than you'll ever realize," he said gently.

Jennifer looked at John. It was difficult to remain angry when he was talking like this, yet she knew him, and she cautioned herself against being fooled by his charm.

"You never told me about your father's trust fund," she said, watching him carefully.

John shrugged. "You never were interested in the

money. That was one of the things that set you apart from the others."

"You'll lose the trust when we divorce," she stated directly.

"I'm not going to pretend that doesn't make me mad as hell, Jennifer. It does. Somehow, however, even all that money doesn't matter when compared to the real loss at stake here." John paused. "I know I can't change your mind, but I wish I could. I don't want to lose you, Jennifer."

"Our life together is over, John."

John was silent a moment. "I know that," he finally said. "I'm leaving the day after tomorrow. I have an afternoon flight on Sunday. Can we spend tomorrow together?"

"What would be the point?"

"It's just one day, Jennifer. I don't expect you to stay at the hotel with me. We'll stay in public places. You can show me some of Scotland. The Pershires are here with me. I stopped in London first, and they were flying up here anyway. They have invited us to join them tomorrow."

"I don't want to see them, John."

"We don't have to spend the entire day with them, Jennifer. They've asked about you. They'd like to see you. They know nothing about our personal situation. You don't have to worry about that," John said.

"How did you explain the fact that we are not staying together?" Jennifer asked.

"I didn't. They don't know that."

Jennifer shook her head. "John, I don't—"

"Don't make a decision now, Jennifer. Think about it. We don't have to spend the day with them. Besides, we will have things to settle ourselves."

"Like what you were actually doing the nights you said you were working late?"

John's jaw tensed but he remained silent.

"My attorney told me about the . . . um . . . prostitutes."

She was so angry at him for his betrayal and deception, but she was also hurt and ashamed that he preferred prostitutes rather than her. Feelings of inadequacy and rage swirled around in her head. "Well, aren't you going to say anything?" she demanded when he still remained silent.

"I never meant to hurt you, Jennifer. You're my wife. I love you. If you recall, I told you, before we were married, that because of age and a previous surgery, I had some difficulties. We discussed it again on our honeymoon. I thought we had come to an understanding."

"An understanding! What . . . that you would continue to see prostitutes while we were married?"

"Jennifer," John began, this time his voice laced with steel, "I have always treated you with honor, respect, and kindness. This . . . this other matter is beneath you, and I won't insult your dignity or mine by discussing it. It has nothing to do with us. If that's the reason you want a divorce, then I will cease seeing them. You have my word."

$$* * *$$

"What time did John say he was picking you up?" Nina asked.

It was late Saturday morning. Nina, Jennifer, and Shamus were sitting in the living room of Nina's cottage.

"Eleven o'clock," Jennifer said as she glanced at her watch. "We're going to have lunch together."

Nina shook her head in disgust. "I don't know why you agreed to see him today."

"If that's what I need to do to hasten the divorce, I will."

Nina turned to Shamus. "Can we wait until John gets here before we leave for the earl's party? I don't want to leave Jen here alone with that ass."

"Nina, I'll be fine," Jennifer interjected.

"Of course we can wait," Shamus said kindly.

"You're still planning to come to Thornhill this

afternoon?" Nina asked.

"How can I?" Jennifer countered.

"After lunch, tell John you have plans with us. Have him bring you back here, and you can use my car to drive to Thornhill." Nina hesitated. "I think you should come. Lord Harold and his family want you to come."

Before Jennifer could answer, they heard a car approach. A moment later, John knocked on the door. Jennifer opened the door and stood aside for John to enter.

"John, you remember Shamus MacNeal," Jennifer said as John entered.

Shamus stepped forward, offering his hand. John briefly took in Shamus's appearance. He was wearing his traditional kilt and suit jacket.

"Of course. You're the local physician, as I recall," John said politely as they shook hands. "Nina," John said, nodding his head in her direction.

"We've been invited to lunch by a friend," Nina said. "Jennifer is to join us later this afternoon. You won't mind dropping her off here after your lunch, will you, John?" Nina asked directly.

For a second, John's eyes clouded and then he responded politely. "Of course not. Now, we should be going. The Pershires are waiting in the car."

"The Pershires?" Jennifer said with surprise.

"I'm sorry, Jennifer. I know you didn't want to see them, but they insisted. We've been invited to accompany them to a birthday party. A member of parliament is retiring. Apparently, George Pershire has worked with the man in London, and that's why George and Claudette are here in Scotland."

Jennifer felt herself blanch, and she reached for a nearby table.

"Who are the Pershires?" Nina asked quickly, trying to give Jennifer some time to recover.

"George and Claudette Pershire, Lord and Lady Pershire, are friends of mine. They live in London," John answered and then returned his attention to Jennifer.

"Come now, Jennifer. It won't be that bad. We'll have lunch with them, meet a few of the local royalty, and then we can leave. I promise."

"I can't go," Jennifer said.

"Why not?" John asked.

"Jennifer," Nina interjected, her voice enthusiastic, "John's friends are probably going to the same party we are." Nina turned to John. "What's the name of the man whose birthday it is?"

John shrugged his shoulders. "I don't remember."

"Is the party for Harold Rannoch, Earl of Thornhill?"

"Why, yes, I believe it is," John answered, unable to conceal his surprise.

"This is perfect, Jen!" Nina bubbled. "Now you won't miss the earl's birthday party. He would have been so disappointed if you hadn't come. We'll see you there."

Jennifer stared at Nina, aghast. What was Nina doing? This was a catastrophe!

"Now let's go or we'll be late," Nina said, gently pushing John and Jennifer out the door. She quickly said good-bye to Jennifer and walked with Shamus to his car.

Jennifer allowed John to lightly take her arm as he walked with her to the car.

"Jennifer, it's so nice to see you again. And what a coincidence that we're all in Scotland together," Lady Pershire gushed as Jennifer and John slid into the back seat of the car. "We're delighted you and John can join us today."

"It appears that Jennifer and her friend Nina Bouvay have already met Lord Rannoch. They were also invited today," John said.

"Really?" Lady Pershire said. "I myself haven't had the pleasure of meeting the earl. George has worked with him in London, of course."

"On a few occasions," George Pershire added. "Harold Rannoch is very well respected in London, even if he is an ardent Scotsman," he said, laughing. "Very well connected, too. As I recall, he's descended from kings of both Scotland and England. I suspect a member of the Royal Family will be paying their respects today as well."

Jennifer was distracted as they drove, not listening to the conversation in the car. In her mind, she was conjuring a myriad of scenarios likely to occur when they arrived at Thornhill—none of them good. What would Derek think? What about his family? She was watching the green grass, gray boulders, and low stone walls pass in a blur as they drove, until she was jolted back into the conversation.

"Jennifer, are you still working on research for your friend, the author?" George Pershire inquired.

"Yes," Jennifer answered.

"And that handsome professor. Is he still assisting you?" Lady Pershire asked with a smile. "You're a very trusting man, John," she teased. "Not many husbands would let their wives travel around the country with a man like that."

"Claudette," Lord Pershire admonished.

"Well, would you let me?" she asked her husband.

"This must be it," George Pershire said as he drove up toward Thornhill.

"Oh!" Lady Pershire said as Thornhill came into view. "I heard it was exquisite. Magnificent, isn't it George!"

"It makes my family estate seem rather paltry, doesn't it, dear?" Lord Pershire said as he stopped the car.

The doors of the Pershires' car were opened by valets wearing the tartan of the Earl of Thornhill.

"Your invitation, sir?" the valet said as he held the door for Lord Pershire.

The valet quickly scanned the invitation and then nodded his head. "Welcome to Thornhill, Lord Pershire. The earl and his family are receiving guests in the garden. Please, make yourselves comfortable. If I might, sir, I'll park your car for you."

John and Jennifer stepped out of the car to join Lord and Lady Pershire while the car was whisked away by one of the valets. Tables, covered with white linen cloths and runners of the Earl of Thornhill's tartan, and chairs had been set up on the expansive lawn. Men and women walked among the tables, the dresses and hats of the women creating a sea of color, bright and floral, undulating back and forth. Many of the men wore their ancestral kilts and formal jackets. Others, the English, Jennifer surmised, wore suits or formal day wear.

Jennifer could feel her heart pounding. She swallowed, her eyes darting about for an escape. Perhaps she could say that she wasn't feeling well, and then John would take her back to Nina's. If she was going to say something, she'd better say it now because the Pershires were walking toward the garden. She turned to John, but before she could say anything, he grasped her arm and leaned into her.

"You didn't mention a professor, and I wasn't aware that you were traveling with this man." His voice was cold as he spoke. "Who is he, Jennifer?"

"John, not now," she said as she tried to separate herself from him. "He's a professor of archaeology. He was helping me trace the civilization that I saw when I had those visions."

"Was that all you were doing with him?" John asked maliciously as he gripped Jennifer's arm painfully.

Jennifer jerked her head to the side to face John, her eyes strangely gliding over the walls of Thornhill not twenty feet behind where they stood. Thornhill, its stones strong, protective, comforting. Jennifer gritted her teeth, her eyes locking on John. "Let go of me, John, or I swear I'll—"

"Keep your voice down," John hissed. "We'll discuss this later!"

John loosened his grip. Jennifer glanced sideways at him and could see the fury radiating from his face. At that very moment, she would have given anything to get away from John and Thornhill. She would even welcome one of the visions. At least then, John would stop walking and would carry her back to the car, for he wouldn't want anyone to see her in that state.

She took a deep breath to calm herself. She could see Lord Harold and his family receiving their guests. Derek was standing next to his father. They were about twenty feet away, greeting each guest who arrived.

"John," Jennifer said, "I'm feeling sick. I must go back to the car."

John stopped and turned to look at Jennifer. "You're very pale and you're trembling." His jaw twitched. "Why, Jennifer? You were fine a few minutes ago. Does it have something to do with our conversation about this professor of yours?"

"John? Jennifer? Are you coming?" Lady Pershire asked as she paused, holding her husband's arm.

"Of course," John said.

"I'm not feeling well," Jennifer said loud enough so Lady Pershire could hear.

"Oh? I'm sorry to hear that," Claudette Pershire said. "Is there something we can do?"

"Why don't we ask Lord Harold if there is some place that you might lie down to rest?" George Pershire said.

"George," Harold Rannoch said in greeting.

Claudette and George turned back to their host and his family and closed the distance between them.

Lord Harold extended his hand in greeting. "I'm delighted you could come. It's about time you Londoners ventured into Scotland. And is this your wife?" he asked.

"Yes," George Pershire said, taking Claudette's arm. Lord Pershire quickly introduced his wife. "Please excuse us," George Pershire continued. "We have some American friends with us, but the young woman is not feeling well. I wonder if we might impose on you. Perhaps there is some place she might lie down and rest?"

"But of course," Lord Harold replied, looking expectantly toward the people who had been behind the Pershires. "My daughter can take her inside."

George Pershire turned in time to see Jennifer free her

arm from John's and turn back toward the drive. "Jennifer!" George Pershire called.

"Jennifer, dear," Lady Pershire softly called. "John, bring her back here. She can rest in the house."

"I would suggest that you not call any more attention to yourself," John hissed as he caught Jennifer and placed her arm through his.

There was no escaping the situation, so Jennifer allowed herself to be escorted back to where Claudette Pershire was waiting.

"Lord Harold has graciously offered you a place to rest in his house," Claudette said as the three of them approached Harold Rannoch and his family.

"Jennifer!" Ann Warrick stepped away from her husband and family. "You came!"

John automatically stepped to the side as Ann slipped her arms around Jennifer to embrace her. Jennifer could no longer avoid them all, and she looked up at Ann. Ann, dear Ann, blinked when she saw the distress in Jennifer's eyes.

"We were afraid you wouldn't make it today," Ann said smoothly, taking charge of the situation. "You left in such a hurry Thursday. Are you not feeling well? I'll tell you what, standing in a receiving line is rather tiring on me," she said, looking down at her enlarged abdomen. "Perhaps we should both go inside and rest awhile. Why don't you say hello to my father and introduce me to your friends, and then we can go inside."

"Ah, Jenny," Lord Harold said as he came forward. He surprised Jennifer by calling her by the name that Derek used. Then he further surprised her by taking her hands in his and kissing her on her cheek. Once again, Jennifer was grateful to these kind people.

"Perhaps introductions are not required," George Pershire said as he stepped forward. "Jennifer, I didn't know that you knew Lord Harold and his family. You didn't say a word."

Jennifer was searching for an appropriate reply when she

felt a reassuring touch from Ann.

"Jennifer has been staying with us at Thornhill while she was doing some work with my son," Harold Rannoch said. "George, I don't believe you have met the rest of my family," he continued. "This is my daughter, Ann, and her husband, Robert Warrick. This is my younger son, Edward, and my older son, Derek."

"I beg your pardon," George Pershire said as he shook Derek's hand. "I didn't know who you were when we met previously. Jennifer only introduced you as a professor."

"Derek, when did you meet Lord and Lady Pershire?" Harold Rannoch asked.

"When Jenny and I went to Cumbria to study the megalithic ruins," Derek said smoothly.

"Jennifer, it's nice to see you again," Edward Rannoch said as he kissed Jennifer lightly on the cheek. He then surprised Jennifer by turning to John. "Edward Rannoch," he said, extending his hand.

John awkwardly shook Edward's hand. "I'm John Bracken, Jennifer's husband," John said clearly.

"It's a pleasure to meet you," Edward said.

Ann's arm was still linked through Jennifer's. What must this kind family think of her? She wanted to pull away from Ann and run back to the car, but then Derek stepped forward and extended his hand to John.

"Derek Rannoch," he said as he shook John's hand. Then he turned to Jennifer.

"Jenny?"

"My wife isn't feeling well," John interjected.

"I was about to take Jennifer inside," Ann said.

Jennifer still had not yet looked at Derek; however, the closeness of his presence had been overwhelming. Jennifer turned to Ann. "Thank you, Ann, but I think I would feel better if I just walked a little."

"Of course," Ann said as she gave Jennifer a gentle squeeze before releasing her arm and stepping back.

"Thornhill is at your disposal, Jenny. I believe you know

your way around," Harold Rannoch said with a twinkle in his eye.

Other people had moved up in the line and were waiting to greet the Rannochs. John reached for Jennifer's arm, but she artfully stepped out of his grasp and started moving toward the garden where guests were seated. It was awkward, but thankfully, Jennifer spotted Nina and Shamus seated at a table. She walked toward it, not caring if the Pershires or John followed her. However, as she reached the table, she could tell by Nina's expression that John was following.

Jennifer quickly introduced Nina and Shamus to the Pershires as they all sat down. For the next twenty minutes, Jennifer was silent. She was vaguely aware of Claudette asking Nina about the novels she wrote. Had Claudette read some of them?

"Yes, Jen and I have known each other since childhood, and she finally agreed to help me with the research for my next book," Nina said.

"Oh, yes, with Professor Rannoch?" Claudette asked.

"Yes, Lord Derek has been quite helpful," Nina said smoothly. "I can't possibly do all the field work myself, and it is essential that my historical references be accurate."

Servers, dressed in the tartan kilts of the Earl of Thornhill, passed among the guests, carrying silver trays with glasses of champagne and, of course, the famous malt whiskey of the region. Jennifer reached for a glass of whiskey, noting John's look of surprise and disapproval. The champagne and whiskey were followed with lunch, during which Jennifer accepted another glass of whiskey.

Jennifer heard Nina giggle next to her. "Go for it," she whispered in Jennifer's ear.

An ensemble of bagpipers began to play. The pipers were standing on the steps leading up to Thornhill, far enough away not to compete with the guests' conversations, but close enough to provide a unique background of sound.

"Was there ever a more God-awful sound than that of a

bagpipe?" John quipped.

George Pershire laughed. "It's inescapable around here, old boy," Pershire said, teasing John. "You'll just have to suffer through it like the rest of us."

"No offense, Dr. MacNeal," John said in deference to Shamus, "but perhaps, as the only Scotsman among us, you could explain what you Scottish people see in that instrument."

Shamus smiled in an easygoing manner. "Ah, but I'm not the only Scotsman at the table. Your wife's Scottish blood runs very deep, I believe," Shamus said in a heavy Scottish brogue.

"Really, Jennifer?" John said, his voice frosty. "Don't tell me you like the sound of bagpipes?"

Jennifer lifted her head slightly. "Yes, John, I do. Very much."

"Oh, come now, Jennifer. You're a world-class, professional violinist. You can't possibly compare bagpipes to the likes of the violin."

"I don't compare them at all, John. Each instrument has its own unique soul. The sound of the bagpipe can also stir emotions within a person. That's the purpose of music after all, isn't it?" Jennifer responded, her eyes challenging.

John clenched his jaw. "One would have to be deaf to appreciate that sound."

"Perhaps it's not meant for everyone," Jennifer said evenly.

Just then, the pipers stopped playing and the sound of the bagpipes was replaced by the gentle strains of a harp. Jennifer turned back to John.

"There are actually three national instruments of Scotland: the bagpipe, the fiddle, and the harp. Perhaps you'll enjoy this more," Jennifer said.

"You're becoming quite the authority on Scotland, I see," John said, his anger barely concealed.

"Well, I'm for walking around a bit," George Pershire said suddenly, no doubt to cover the awkward situation.

"What do you say? Shall we all stroll about? Come, there are some people I would like you to meet," he said to John and Jennifer and then turned to Shamus and Nina. "Dr. MacNeal and Miss Bouvay, won't you join us?"

Shamus glanced at Nina before answering. "Perhaps later," he replied.

Jennifer was disappointed that Nina and Shamus were remaining at the table, but perhaps it was for the best. Nina's dislike of John was becoming too obvious.

For the next half hour, the Pershires introduced John and Jennifer to their friends and George's political acquaintances. At one point, Jennifer turned suddenly and looked over her shoulder. Derek was there, staring at her. For the first time that day, their eyes met. Jennifer shuddered slightly from the sheer force of emotion Derek projected. John noticed her reaction and turned to see what she was looking at. When he saw Derek staring at Jennifer, he put his arm around her waist and pulled her roughly to his side.

"Just what is your relationship with that man, Jennifer?" John demanded in a whisper. When Jennifer didn't answer, he bent closer to her. "You slept with him, didn't you?" he hissed.

As discreetly as possible, Derek had kept his eyes on Jennifer ever since she had arrived. After all the hours they had spent together, he could read her body language well. She had avoided looking at him, but he saw the distress in her eyes when she was in the receiving line. He also knew she almost cried when Ann hugged her. Now, as he watched her husband put his arm around her and pull her to his side, Jennifer flinched. Then he whispered something to her. Even at this distance, her husband's anger was apparent. Then suddenly, Jenny pulled away from him and looked him squarely in the face. Her eyes were blazing. He couldn't hear what she said to her husband, but it was enough to cause him to step back from her.

"She's filed for a divorce, you know," a feminine voice said close to Derek.

Derek turned to see Nina.

"She never told you, did she?" Nina said. "Just after she returned from the trip she took with you to Cumbria to examine megaliths, she went home with John and told him she wanted a divorce. John's an ass, you know, but he can be very persuasive. And there's no way he wants to lose Jennifer. He laid a big guilt trip on her—all that stuff about how he took care of her dying mother. Jennifer finally agreed to stay with him for two weeks only, on the agreement that he would give her a divorce."

Nina laughed sarcastically. "All the time, he was planning, though," she continued. "You see, Jennifer has always wanted children, but John said no, there would be no children. John thought he had found a way to keep Jennifer with him: if she were to become pregnant, he could convince her to forget about the divorce."

Derek turned sharply, his eyes narrowing as he looked at Nina.

"Never mind the fact that they hadn't slept together in over a year and have separate bedrooms," Nina said. "One night, after taking her to dinner and the symphony, he sneaked into her room in the middle of the night, held her down, and tried to rape her," Nina concluded.

The response in Derek was explosive. He took an angry stride forward, but Nina reached out and caught his arm.

"Jen's okay," Nina said, restraining Derek. "She can take care of herself." Suddenly, Nina smiled. "Did I ever tell you how Jen and I met?"

Derek frowned and started to pull away. "If you will excuse me," he said tersely.

"Relax," Nina said, still holding Derek's arm. "My family moved to a Chicago suburb toward the end of my first year in school," Nina began. "I didn't know anyone, and I was a plump little girl and the object of a lot of teasing.

"Well, there was this one boy named Bobby Mathews, who was the class bully. One day, I was playing during recess, and he came up to me and started calling me all kinds of names. He grabbed hold of my hair and started pulling it. He wouldn't let go, and I started crying. All of a sudden, this little spit of a girl marched up to Bobby and planted her feet next to him, her hands on her hips. I remember she had the most beautiful, long, red hair with curls all over her head. She was fully a head shorter than Bobby."

Nina smiled. "She told him to let go of me. Well, Bobby was not about to let some little girl tell him what to do. He said something dumb, like 'make me!' The next thing I knew, those clear-blue eyes of hers turned as dark as midnight. She doubled up her fist and smashed it into Bobby Mathew's nose." Nina laughed. "I've never seen anything like it. She broke his nose! Needless to say, Bobby Mathews never bothered me again.

"Bobby had underestimated her. John Bracken made the same mistake." Nina glanced over at John and then looked back at Derek. "I don't know about you, but I think John's nose looks a little crooked, don't you?"

Derek jerked his gaze back to where Jennifer and John were standing.

Nina laughed. "She broke John's nose, too. Yes, sir, Little Jenny McHugh still has a powerful right hook." Nina winked at Derek, released his arm, and walked away. She took a few steps when she turned back. "Falling in love is something new for Jennifer, and she's hopelessly in love with you. You broke her heart once; don't do it again."

"I understand," Derek said. "Thank you."

Nina nodded her head and then walked back to the garden. Derek looked across the lawn to where Jennifer was standing. Her back was to him. A divorce! She had asked him for a divorce just after they had spent the night together in Cowden Hall—even after all the horrible things he had said to her that next morning. And all this time, when he had been angry, thinking she had deceived him, she had not returned to her husband at all. He'd been wrong. He should have trusted his instinct about Jenny instead of letting his pride and hurt dictate his actions.

Derek's heart was racing. He was aware of his brother and father approaching, but kept his focus on Jenny. He saw her husband place his arm around Jenny's waist, and there was no mistaking her reaction as she resisted.

"She's his wife, Derek, not yours," Edward said quietly.

"The hell she is," Derek ground out.

Derek pushed Edward aside and took a step toward the crowd.

"Derek!" Harold Rannoch admonished sternly.

Derek paused only a moment to look at his father, and then he turned and angrily strode through the crowd toward Jennifer. He ignored the people around him, who paused in surprise when he failed to acknowledge their greetings. He came up behind Jennifer and John and clamped a strong hand on John's shoulder, twisting him around. John's eyes widened as he felt the force of Derek's rage, and he took a halting step backward, releasing Jennifer.

Derek turned to Jennifer and held his hand out to her. "Jenny," he said simply, his soul searching her eyes.

Jennifer gasped. He was there, his eyes burning into her. She felt that odd mixture of safety and peace, which she always felt in his presence, as well as intense desire and passion. She thought she heard John say something, but she didn't care. She placed her hand in Derek's. His fingers closed around hers, and then he turned, holding her hand tightly as he strode quickly through the crowd, the people staring openly at them.

Jennifer had to take several steps to keep up with his long stride. He left the garden behind and continued until they could no longer hear the guests of Thornhill. They reached the gentle hills that surround Thornhill and began to climb. Jennifer clung to his hand for support. When they arrived at the top, he led her across the grass and through a small stand of trees. Then he continued across a field dotted with flowers and divided by stone walls several feet high. Derek had not slowed his pace and Jennifer was breathing hard, but she could feel his strength surrounding her, protecting her, arousing her.

At last, they came to the stone ruins of what must have once been a small house. Only three walls remained, the walls crumbling and only a few feet tall. Yellow-and- white wildflowers grew next to the stones of the remaining walls. Finally, Derek stopped and turned to Jennifer. He released her hand and placed both of his hands on her face. His eyes were like fire as he looked at her.

"I won't share you, Jenny," he said hoarsely. "I won't share you with him or any man."

He kissed her urgently, desperately. Jennifer felt like she would explode just from his kiss and feeling his body pressed against hers. Her heart was thundering beneath her clothing. They were standing there, next to the old, abandoned stones, the gray sky above, the wind from the Scottish hillside blowing against them, whipping Derek's kilt against his legs and Jennifer's hair onto their faces. She felt a desperate need of him, and she welcomed it.

Derek stepped back and took her hand, gently pulling her down into the grass. He removed her jacket, and then his lips were on her neck as he unzipped the back of her dress, pushing the dress down to her waist. Jennifer's arms came around his neck as he buried his face in her chest. She inhaled the scent of his hair as he was kissing her, his lips demanding. For a second, Derek stopped, his eyes only inches away from hers. Jennifer looked into the dark of his eyes and shuddered, despite the warmth of her body in its aroused state. It was as though he had reached out and touched the very essence of her being—the seat of her soul—and bound it to his own. Then his lips were on her neck, her chest. She was acutely aware of her own mounting hunger. He kissed the lace of her bra, and she reached up to loosen it for him. When she felt his hands on her breasts she cried out, her breath coming in ragged gasps.

"Is the grass too rough?" he asked, his voice raw with desire.

She pushed her pelvis against his hardness in response to his question. He shifted his weight and moved her dress up above her hips. His hand glided on her thigh and to her panties. Then she felt his fingers slip inside the soft silk fabric. Derek groaned a deep, primal sound as he touched her delicate folds, moist and warm.

She remembered how he had been slow and purposeful the first time they made love, worshiping every inch of her body, testing it for responsiveness. That was at Cowden Hall, when they were lovers for one night. He was impatient now, though, desperate to claim her.

He removed the last obstacle of clothing and positioned himself above her. She clasped her arms around his neck, taking his fullness into the depth of her. This time, she moved with him in an age-old rhythm of their own, their passion spiraling upward, carrying them each in a blinding desire until, at last, Jennifer could ride it no longer and cried out as her body exploded in pleasure around him. She clung to him desperately as he continued to push into her until his entire body shuddered in release. He moaned, his face buried in her hair. His arms came around her, crushing her to him. She could hear a heart pounding, but she was unsure whether it was hers or his that she heard. Then she felt his warm breath upon her ear.

"I love you, Jenny McHugh," he whispered, his voice still strained with passion.

CHAPTER 13

"**A**re you cold?" Derek asked.

Jennifer was lying on the ground beside him, her head resting on his arm. Derek reached for his jacket. Her own jacket was beneath her, and her dress was still crumpled about her waist. A slight smile came to his lips as he placed his jacket over her chest.

"You blush very easily, Jenny McHugh," he said as he noticed the color rise in her face. "It's all right. We're alone," Derek said.

"What do we do now?" she asked, uncertainty in her voice.

"Well," Derek said with a smile, "I don't think we should return to Thornhill just yet. I've put my family in an awkward position." Jennifer tensed. "Don't worry. It's not the first scandal that Thornhill has seen in its history. Still, I think it might be wise to give my father a day or two before we return."

"A day or two!"

"Do you want to go back now?" he asked.

Jennifer sat up, clutching Derek's jacket to her chest.

"My clothes are a mess," she said absently. She looked at Derek. "I'm sorry. I'm feeling very confused at the moment."

"Let me help you dress," he said gently.

Derek quickly straightened his own clothes and then helped Jennifer with her dress. When at last they stood,

Jennifer looked down at her wrinkled clothing.

"I can't go back to Thornhill like this," she said.

"Come with me," Derek said as he held out his hand.

She didn't hesitate. She placed her hand in his, again feeling the warmth and security that it offered. They started walking in silence. Where would they go in their relationship now? He had said he loved her, hadn't he? What did that mean? Was that just passion talking? She realized now that she had been longing to hear those words from Derek, and now that he had spoken them, she felt even more insecure than before. She looked up as the hunting lodge came into view.

"I didn't realize we were this close," she said with surprise.

Derek smiled. "We can stay here. No one will bother us."

They entered the lodge and Jennifer looked around, remembering those early days and nights when she was here with Derek. They had an unusual relationship then. She had hardly known him, yet she had stayed here with him for several days.

Derek closed the door behind them. "I didn't eat any lunch today," he said. "Did you?"

"No, I didn't feel like eating," Jennifer replied.

"Well, it's almost time for dinner. I'll see what's in the kitchen."

Jennifer smiled. "I'll join you in a minute. I think I'll see if I can get the grass out of my hair."

She climbed the stone steps to the bedroom above. As she entered, its comforting silence surrounded her. She had loved this room the moment Derek had brought her to it, with its heavy bed draped in the Earl of Thornhill's tartan and a shield hanging above it. Derek had teasingly told her that it had been the secret hideaway of previous earls and their mistresses. Jennifer sat on the side of the bed. She could see her reflection in a small, oval mirror hanging on the wall, and she hardly recognized the image of the girl staring back at her with wild and windswept hair. She reached up to pull some dried grass from her hair.

"Leave it," Derek said.

Jennifer jumped slightly. Derek was standing in the doorway, staring at her, his eyes dark with intent.

"This is how I pictured you at night when I couldn't sleep," he said as he walked toward her, ". . . long, red hair, like fire, tossed about your face, wild and natural, the wind blowing it. Then I would dream that I was making love to you outside on the moors, just like today."

Jennifer's heart was pounding as Derek placed his hands on her face. She was surprised by the force of his kiss.

"I remember that first night when I brought you up to this room," he whispered. "God, Jenny, I wanted to make love to you then, and I think you would have let me. I was afraid, though; I was afraid of frightening you."

Derek kissed her again and then gently pushed her back on the bed. She could feel his desire as he pressed his body against her.

"You belong here, Jenny," he whispered urgently. "You belong at Thornhill. You belong with me."

"Where is she?" John Bracken demanded. He was standing at the door of Nina's cottage.

"I don't know," Nina replied.

John pushed Nina aside and strode angrily into the living room.

"She's not here," Nina said.

John ignored her and walked into each room, searching. At last, he returned to the living room.

"You know where she is, though. Tell me!" he demanded as he grabbed Nina's wrist.

"Let go of me, you bastard," Nina spat out. "Even if I did know where she was, I wouldn't tell you!"

For a second, Nina froze. There was a wild look in John's eyes and a depth of hatred that stunned her. Then,

Alison Blasdell

just as quickly, it was gone, and he released her.

"I'll find her," he said and turned toward the door.

"You leave her alone!" Nina shouted.

John turned a cold look upon her. "Tell Jennifer that I'm not leaving Scotland until we talk. If she ever expects to get that divorce, she's going to have to meet with me first."

Jennifer lay in Derek's arms as her body quieted, its hunger satiated. She smiled, remembering their lovemaking of a few minutes ago and feeling the warmth of his body next to her.

"How did you learn that?" she asked suddenly.

Derek propped himself up on one elbow.

"Learn what?" he asked.

"You know," Jennifer said, feeling herself blush.

Derek smiled. "Oh, that," he said, kissing her lightly.

"Have you made love to many women?" Jennifer asked hesitantly.

"No," Derek answered, "not all that many. I'm not going to lie to you, Jenny. I've had relationships with women in the past. It was never anything serious and no commitments were made, although I'd like to think that they still consider me a friend." Derek hesitated. "But perhaps more importantly, I've never slept with a woman without using protection, that is, up until today. I'm sorry. I was irresponsible."

The dreamy warmth she was feeling was shattered, replaced by cold practicality. She hadn't thought about consequences; she hadn't thought of anything other than desire. "I don't know what to say," she whispered. "I've never done this before."

Derek pulled her close. "I know that, Jenny."

"John is the only other man that I've. . . ."

Derek hesitated a moment.

"Jenny," he said gently, "are you using any kind of birth control?"

A thousand thoughts tumbled through her mind. Despite the intimacy she had just shared with him, she was uncertain of their relationship. She loved him, desperately. But what about Derek? What did she mean to him? It was *she* who had been irresponsible. She had reacted purely on emotion, passion, and need. And now there was the very real chance that she might have become pregnant. Her mounting anxious thoughts were interrupted by his voice.

Derek turned Jennifer until she was facing him. "Jenny," he said softly, "it's all right." He smiled slightly. "If it happens, it happens. I hadn't exactly planned on becoming a father yet, but then, I hadn't planned on falling in love, either." Derek's eyes held hers. "I love you, Jenny, and that is something that I have never said to another woman." Again, Derek smiled. "Ah, Jenny, you belong here with me."

She wanted to believe him, but insecurity invaded her thoughts. What did he want of her? "Here, in this room? As the mistress of the future Earl of Thornhill?" she ventured, unable to hide her uncertainty.

"No." He took a deep breath and closed his eyes. Then he opened them and looked at her. "I don't want to have an affair with you, Jenny," he said, his voice calm. "I want a lifetime with you. I want to marry you."

It was happening so fast—words of love from this man who had become the center of her world. How did one handle such joy, such happiness? But then, unwelcomed doubt washed over her, and she separated herself from him.

"Jenny, what is it?" he asked with concern.

"I never believed I could love someone as much as I love you," she began, her voice strained. "Sometimes it overwhelms me. My feelings for you run so deep, they frighten me."

"Frighten you? Jenny, I love you!"

"Why do you love me?" she asked bluntly.

"Why?" He shook his head, his confusion obvious. "How do I answer that?"

"We were brought together by these images of the past that I have. That's your passion, your interest. If they end? What then, Derek? What happens when I am just Jennifer again? Will you still want to spend your life with me then?"

Jennifer stopped when she saw the frown that came over Derek's face.

"Jenny, do you believe me to be that selfish and shallow? Do you think that my only interest in you lies in your visions of the past?" Derek demanded.

He stood up suddenly and walked to the window, his back to her as he gazed at the setting sun. She needed him back beside her, holding her, reassuring her.

"I love you," Jennifer whispered. "I'm just scared, that's all."

Derek turned to face her. "I know that. With everything that's been happening to you, now is probably not the time to ask you to consider a life with me. I want you to know this, though: even if you never have another vision, I can't think of a life more desirable than one spent with you. I want to marry you, Jenny."

"Are you sure, Derek? I told you, before these visions, I was very ordinary."

A strange smile came to Derek's face. "Jenny, I have a feeling that there is nothing ordinary about you. We'll just have to see, won't we?"

Jennifer ran across the room into Derek's arms. She felt his strength and warmth encircle her. Despite all the logical arguments she had posed, she knew that she could never walk away from him. Standing here, feeling his body pressed against hers was the most natural thing in the world to her. This is where she belonged.

The circle was there again, but this time, it was surrounding the burning sun. It was almost complete, the end point approaching the beginning. Jennifer felt a heavy sense of foreboding as she watched the end come closer to the beginning, completing the circle. Something awful was going to happen when the beginning met the end. She knew it. A sense of dread and fear overcame her. She cried out, and the sound of her own voice woke her from her dream.

She sat up in the bed. She could feel her heart pounding as her eyes darted around the room. Derek wasn't there. She threw the blanket off and stood up, searching among their discarded clothing for something to put on. She snatched Derek's shirt off the floor and slipped it on, her hands trembling as she tried to button it. Her eyes were drawn to the window and back to the recalcitrant buttons. She could see that it was morning, although the sky was gray.

Her fingers were shaking as fear spread its way into her body. She wasn't even aware that she was calling for Derek again. She gave up on the buttons and turned to run from the room. She got as far as the landing when Derek came bounding up the stairs, two at a time.

"Jenny! What is it?" Derek cried as Jennifer tumbled into his arms.

She was trembling as she buried her face in his neck.

"Derek, take me to Thornhill!"

"Thornhill? Why?"

"Please," she said, pulling her face back from him. "Please, can we go back to Thornhill?"

"Of course, but I don't understand. Why do you want to go to—"

"Now, Derek! Can we go now?"

He placed his arms on her shoulders. "Jenny, tell me what's happened. Why are you so upset?"

"I was dreaming. I saw the circle again," Jennifer said. "But it's almost complete. It's almost ended! Please, Derek, I'm scared!"

"Scared of what, Jenny?"

"I don't know!" she shouted. "Something awful! I have to get back to Thornhill. It's protected me in the past; I know it will again. Please, Derek," Jennifer pleaded.

Jennifer's breaths were coming in great gasps as Derek

crushed her to him.

"Okay, Jenny, we'll go. I'll help you dress, and then we'll walk back to Thornhill."

By the time Jennifer was dressed in her crumpled chemise and jacket, she had calmed down considerably. The fear and panic she had woken up with had subsided, but unconsciously, she found her eyes drawn to the window. As they were preparing to leave, Derek turned to her.

"Why do you keep looking out the window, Jenny?" he asked.

"I'm not sure. I think the circle was going around the sun, but the sun's not shining today. I don't know, Derek. I was so afraid when I woke up."

"Are you all right now?" he asked.

"Yes. I feel a little foolish," Jennifer said, avoiding Derek's gaze.

They were walking down the stairs together. When they reached the bottom, Jennifer paused.

"You were making breakfast when I woke up. Why don't we stay and eat here? There's no rush. I don't know what happened to me. I'm fine now." Jennifer grimaced and rubbed her hand across her forehead. "You must think I'm crazy. I'm sorry, Derek. I acted like a frightened child."

Derek placed his hand on Jennifer's face. He smiled slightly, his eyes warm. "No, I don't think you're crazy, although I must say I'm curious to know what *ordinary Jennifer* will be like."

"Oh," Jennifer moaned as she hid her face in her hands. She couldn't help but smile at Derek's teasing. When she removed her hands, she took his hand. "Come on; let's see what you were up to in the kitchen."

Derek didn't move as she pulled on his hand. Jennifer turned around.

"I think we should go to Thornhill," Derek said.

"But I told you, I'm fine. It was just a silly dream. I'm embarrassed about the way I acted, and I want to show you that I can be perfectly normal and adult like," Jennifer said, nodding her head to punctuate her statement.

"I know," Derek said softly, "but I think we should go back to Thornhill. Now," he said, gently but firmly.

Jennifer frowned.

Derek smiled suddenly. "My cooking is not as good as Clara's, and I'm hungry, madam. I ate very little yesterday, and I spent the entire night trying to satisfy a demanding lover."

Jennifer felt herself blush. He released her hands as he kissed her deeply.

"Come on, Jenny," he said as he broke away. He grabbed her hand. "Let's go before I change my mind."

They walked comfortably with each other across the meadow toward Thornhill. Derek didn't know what to expect when they reached Thornhill, but he was beginning to trust in Jenny's instincts—even if she had not yet learned to trust them herself. Her fear had been very real this morning, and Jenny did not strike him as the kind to react irrationally. It had taken great courage and a calm mind to have actively sought a historical basis for the visions she had experienced. This morning, she had pleaded with him to take her to Thornhill where she would be safe. That was exactly what Derek was going to do, even though Jenny now doubted the significance of her dream.

They spoke briefly about Derek's family. Derek's father would expect an explanation for his behavior yesterday.

"What must your father think of me?" Jennifer asked.

"I'll talk to him, Jenny. He'll understand. Please, don't worry," Derek said.

As they drew closer to Thornhill, Derek could feel Jennifer's anxiety returning. She frequently glanced at the sky, though she said nothing. He squeezed her hand in reassurance. When they reached the door of Thornhill, it was opened immediately, and Jeffrey stepped aside so that they could enter.

"Good morning, Lord Derek. Miss McHugh," he said.

"Good morning, Jeffrey. Where is everybody?"

"Your father and brother are in the dining room."

"Would you tell them that we will join them in a minute?"

Jeffrey bowed slightly and left.

"Derek, I look a fright. I can't go into the dining room like this. Besides, I would rather you talk to them first," Jennifer said.

"All right. I'll take you upstairs. I need to change, too."

Derek took Jennifer's hand and walked up the stairs. "This way," he said as he led her to his rooms.

"But, Derek," she began to protest. "I shouldn't be here in your room."

"This is exactly where you should be," he countered.

Derek closed the door behind her and turned. Taking her hand, he walked through the sitting room to the bedroom. He watched as she surveyed the room: the large bed draped in the Rannoch family tartan, the original, massive fireplace on the opposite wall, the thick, oriental carpets scattered on the floor, and tapestries on the walls.

"It's beautiful, Derek," she breathed.

"In here," Derek said as he opened another door, "is the bath. There are clean linens, soap, even a bathrobe on the back of the door," he said. "I'll change quickly and go talk with my father. Did you leave any clothes here?"

"No, I took everything back to Nina's," Jennifer answered.

Derek walked back into the bedroom and opened a large armoire. He removed pants and two shirts. He handed a shirt to Jennifer.

"This will have to do for the time being. I'll send someone over to Nina's to get your clothes."

Jennifer held up the shirt. Derek smiled.

"Of course, you'll have to remain here in my room until your clothes arrive," he said with a smile and then kissed her.

"What will your father and brother say about my staying in your room?" Jennifer asked.

"I'll handle that. Do you want me to have Clara bring some breakfast up to you?"

"No, I'm not really hungry."

"Are you sure?" Derek asked.

"Yes," Jennifer answered.

Derek kissed her again and then went into the bathroom. He emerged a few minutes later, dressed in clean clothes. Jennifer was lying on her side on his bed.

"Are you all right?" Derek asked with concern.

Jennifer smiled. "Yes, I'm just feeling tired. I didn't get much sleep last night," she said, her face coloring.

Derek sat down on the bed next to her. He reached for a blanket and spread it over her.

"I'll not be too long, and then I'll come back and join you," he said with a smile in his eyes. He leaned down and kissed her tenderly. He stopped suddenly when he heard barking out in the hall. Jennifer frowned and Derek laughed. He stood up and walked out of the bedroom into the sitting room. A moment later, two Irish wolfhounds came bounding into the bedroom. The female went immediately to where Jennifer lay on the bed and stretched her head to lick Jennifer's hand.

"Issy has found you again," Derek said, laughing, "and brought Bruce with her this time. I leave you in good hands. I'll be back as soon as I can."

While Derek met with his father and brother in the dining room, Jennifer tried to sleep. After half an hour, she got up. She was uncomfortable in her dress, and a bath sounded wonderful. She had to step around the dogs lying on the floor next to the bed. As she did, she stopped. The sudden cramping of her stomach surprised her. Again, she felt it knot, and then the burning liquid rose up into her mouth. She swallowed quickly as another wave of nausea assaulted her, and pain spread throughout her abdomen. She broke out in a cold sweat when her eyes focused on the floor. A shaft of sunlight from the window spread across the gray stone floor, bringing a sense of dread.

Jennifer didn't hear Issy start to bark, as the rushing sound filled her ears and the vertigo assaulted her. She stumbled out of the bedroom to the sitting room, swallowing the bile that rose to her mouth. She tried to call out to Derek but couldn't hear her own voice. She made her way out of the sitting room and to the steps. She didn't hear the dogs barking as they ran beside her. She had to find Derek, but instead of turning into the dining room, she found herself running blindly to the front door. She could barely stand upright as she opened it and stumbled outside. As if finely orchestrated, the gray clouds moved aside, and the bright-yellow sun, a perfect circle, poured its light on her. Jennifer made it down the steps and onto the drive when the final pain came. She doubled over and fell onto Issy, then slid down onto the pavement as the vortex engulfed her once again.

Derek was sitting in the dining room with his father and brother when he first heard the dogs bark. He looked up, a frown on his face.

"Brandon must have taken the dogs out," his father said in explanation.

It was then that a shaft of sunlight broke through the window. Derek froze, for at that same instant, he felt a strange, but familiar, change in the air. His eyes riveted to the dining table, where a pattern of circles repeated itself as the sun filtered through the lead glass of the windows.

"Jenny!" Derek screamed as he bolted from his chair.

His father and brother looked up in alarm as Derek raced from the dining room. He ran as far as the stairway when he heard the chilling, plaintive howl of a dog. He spun around and ran to the front door, his father and brother following him. She was there, lying on the pavement, her body still, and Issy and Bruce standing over her.

* * *

826 B.C.

Cela looked up as her mother approached.

"She sleeps?" Ega asked as she knelt down beside Cela and gazed at the nine-month-old infant nestled in Cela's arms.

"Yes. I wanted to feed her one last time," Cela said softly.

"Cela—"

"If you have come to counsel me not to go today, it is too late. Lodi and Cupa have already spoken to me." Cela squinted her eyes to look up at the sun, its warm rays reaching out to her. "Soon, it will be time," Cela said. "I have been here most of the night, hoping that the gods would answer me, that they would somehow help us. I heard nothing. Then this morning, I saw the people, tired and hungry, carrying their own children—*their own* children—to offer to the gods." A tear dropped down Cela's face as she looked at her sleeping daughter. "There is nothing that anyone can say to stop me. It must be done, Mother."

Ega reached out to touch her daughter. "I know," she said.

Cela looked up into her mother's eyes and saw her pain.

"I, too, have spent the night pleading with the gods," Ega said. "I had hoped that they would take me in your place. I had given up, until early this morning, just as the sun was rising. For a brief instant, I saw you moving through the sky toward the sun, and I realized then that the gods would accept none but their own—you, my child. I cried out to them, and they finally answered me. I saw peace for our people. I saw their bellies filled again and the children playing. I saw the Wise Ones studying again. I saw order once again restored to our people."

Cela squeezed her eyes shut. "You truly saw this, Mother?"

"Yes. It was as clear to me as any vision I have had."

Cela nodded her head in acceptance. "It is good then."

"There is one more thing, Daughter," Ega said, hesitating.

Cela detected something in her mother's voice and opened her eyes. "What is it?"

"You are not the only one to leave this life today."

Cela immediately clutched her infant to her. "Not my child!"

"No. Strangely, I saw nothing of the child." Again, Ega hesitated.

"What is it, Mother?"

"I saw Luc's head."

"What?!"

"I saw his head, separated from his body."

"How? How can that happen?" Cela asked, her voice anxious.

"I do not know."

"But—"

"Shhh, my child. The gods have decided."

Cela sat quietly, her mother beside her. At last, she looked up at her mother. "I have something to ask of you, Mother. Do not go to the sacrifices today. Take my child and hide her until the ceremony is finished. Pack food and clothing for a man and a babe, enough for a long journey. Then, when Dagga comes, give my child to him."

"To the warrior!"

"Yes. Tell him to take her far from here and never return."

"But, Cela, there will be peace afterward."

"Not for her," Cela said, looking down at the child. "I

know what happened to the People of the Sky. They were slain. They were killed by the very people they had helped. People like Luc became fearful of the powers they possessed and jealous of their gift of flight. They were all killed, or if some survived, they have not returned. They never will."

"The child?" Ega asked with amazement.

"I can feel it within her; the secret of the sky is there within her, too. She must never discover it. Never! Dagga must take her away from here and never let her move through the skies. Tell him, Mother. The child must not know of me. She must not know that she, too, is a Priestess of the Wise Ones and a Daughter of the Sky. Tell him all that I have said."

The tears were flowing down Cela's face and Ega's as well.

"Where is he?" Ega asked.

"I do not know," Cela answered. "Three nights ago, we spent the night together. I knew it would be the last time, but I could not tell him. He does not know that I am going to the ceremony today. He would try to stop me. I cannot even say good-bye to him, for he would know immediately. I do not know what duties he has been assigned. Mother, promise me! Promise you will do as I ask."

Ega swallowed, resigned. "I will do as you ask, and it will be as you say." She reached out and touched the head of her sleeping grandchild. "I understand now. That is why I did not see the child among us when order is restored."

They were both silent, and then Cela spoke. "Mother, please leave me now and wait for me in your hut. I would like a few more minutes with my child. Then I will bring her to you."

Cela's people had several permanent settlements that they inhabited as the seasons changed. Because of the excessive rains on the southern plains, the crops would not grow and the stored grain rotted. Cela's people desperately needed food. The Wise Ones brought the people back to the northeastern mountains in hopes of finding the wild sheep that inhabited this area.

The people had a settlement nestled in a protected valley in the mountains. However, all important ceremonies were held high up in the mountains to be nearer the gods. So it was that on this day, the sun was high in the sky when the priests and priestesses began chanting and following the age-old path that led up between the rocks and coarse shrubs to the mountain. Great fires had been lit along the ridge of the mountain. They would be kept burning through the day and night.

Cela walked with the priestesses, their hoods obscuring their faces. The children had already been gathered. They had been placed in a circle, the youngest being an infant not yet a week old. The oldest child was five years old. They were naked, and their bodies had been painted with the stain of dark berries. The large fires did not drive the chill off their bodies, though, and the older children shivered. Cela could see by their glassy eyes that they had been given the sleep plant to induce a drugged state. The plant was not native to the lands of Cela's people. It grew somewhere far to the south, beyond the great waters. Cela's people traded for plant root, which, when ground to a fine powder, could be mixed in liquid and consumed. But because of the large number of sacrifices Luc had ordered during his reign as High Priest, the supply of the precious root was almost gone.

Cela looked imploringly to the sky. *Hear me. I am Cela, daughter of the skies. Let this be the last time my people use the root for sacrifices. Let human offerings end with me.*

The priests and priestesses walked around the children three times, symbolizing the movement of the sun. Luc was there, standing by the fires. He was surrounded by four priests of the High Council. Behind them were a dozen guards. As Cela moved near them, she searched their faces frantically, breathing a sigh of relief when she did not see Dagga's face among the guards.

The chanting stopped, and the Wise Ones formed a semicircle facing the edge of the mountain. Luc began to speak the ritual of sacrifice, imploring the gods to accept the gifts of the people. Cela had not formulated a plan. Each time she had tried to think of how to stop Luc, her mind had clouded. Now, as she saw the time rapidly approach, she pleaded silently to the gods. *Show me what I am to do. I offer myself in their place. Please, hear me. Show me how to stop this destruction of life!*

It was too late, for Luc reached for a child, barely two years old. He held the child high above his head, preparing to walk to the edge and throw the child down to the gorge below.

"No!" Cela screamed. "You cannot do this!"

Luc stopped, still holding the child above his head. Cela stepped forward and pushed her hood down. Luc's eyes widened in surprise, and then a malevolent grin spread across his face. He turned toward the gorge.

"No!" Cela shouted as she started forward.

"Seize her," Luc ordered. "She will anger the gods!"

The guards looked uncomfortably at each other. They had received an order from the High Priest, but they were forbidden to touch one of the Wise Ones. Luc saw their hesitancy and, in a fury, turned quickly back to the gorge.

What would occur during the next few minutes would never be forgotten by those who witnessed the supernatural feat. Unlike other profound events in their history, however, this one would not be put into verse to be remembered for all time. It would never again be spoken of. It would be erased from the history of these ancient people.

"Nooooooo!" Cela screamed from the depth of her soul, and in that instant, the life forces soared through her, freeing her from the constraints of the ground. She was suddenly flying through the air. Some of the Wise Ones screamed; some stared wide-eyed in silence, their mouths open. Cela's white robe rippled as she soared, the sunlight casting a blinding glow upon her. Her long, red hair streamed behind her like fire. The Wise Ones in her path fell to the ground, feeling the powerful force of the gods as they directed the wind that carried Cela to the edge of the mountain. They watched in awe as Cela flew swiftly through the air. She descended to where Luc was standing and hurled her body into his, striking him in the chest, the force knocking them both down. Luc dropped the child, stunned. Cela looked up from where she lay to see the child dangerously close to the edge. She crawled a few steps and reached out, catching the child's leg and pulling it back. She rolled onto her back, clutching the child to her.

"Kill her!" Luc screamed as he struggled to stand.

The guards backed away and dropped to their knees, their eyes wide with fear as they stared at the priestess who had just flown through the air. Likewise, the priests and priestesses were staring, most rooted to where they had been standing, their shock evident on their faces.

"I said kill her!" Luc shouted.

He reached for a spear held in a guard's hands. In a blind rage of hatred and jealousy, he turned to Cela, who was still lying on the ground. In that instant, she thrust the child from her as Luc plunged the spear into her chest.

"Ahghh!" A bloodcurdling cry came from behind the priests and priestesses as a warrior ran up behind them. His strength was so great that several of them fell as he pushed them aside. In a gesture of strength and agility that came from a lifetime of battle, he removed his sword effortlessly as his powerful legs carried him forward.

Luc looked up to see Dagga bearing down on him. He screamed to his guards, but they remained immobile, their eyes on Cela, lying on the ground.

The move was almost graceful as Dagga raised the sword high in the air and propelled his body forward. Then the blade was slicing in an arc, the sunlight reflecting off of it as it came sweeping down, cutting cleanly into Luc's neck, completing the arc and coming out the other side. In horror, the Wise Ones watched as Luc's head rolled to the edge of the mountain and disappeared down into the gorge.

Dagga dropped his sword and knelt beside Cela. Her white robe was already soaked with her life's blood. As gently as he could, he slipped his arm under her head, cradling her against him. Cela opened her eyes. Her breathing was labored as the blood began to fill her lungs. With a supreme effort, she smiled slightly.

"It appears the gods have finally decided to accept my sacrifice," she whispered.

"You tempted them too often, Priestess," Dagga said, his voice strained.

"It is over? He is dead?" she asked.

"Yes. He is dead," Dagga answered.

"It is good," Cela said as a spasm of cough exploded in her. When she recovered, she weakly reached for Dagga's hand. "You must go now. You are in danger," she whispered, every word an extreme effort. "You have killed the High Priest. They cannot let you live."

"This life no longer interests me, Priestess," Dagga said, his throat constricting as tears flowed freely down his face. "I welcome death."

"No," Cela said, choking. "Please, you must go. Go to my mother. She is waiting for you in her hut. Take my child, Dagga. Take her far away from here."

Dagga squeezed his eyes shut.

"Please," Cela whispered. "She is in danger if she remains here. Do this for me, Dagga. She is your child. Promise me you will care for her as you have for me."

Dagga swallowed, the pain in his heart overwhelming. "How can I refuse you?" he finally asked, his heart breaking. "I will take the child."

Cela squeezed his hand slightly. "You have been with us all this time, and you still have not learned our ways," she gently admonished him. "Why do you grieve for me? Do you grieve when the sun sets? Do you not know that only one day has ended? Do you not know that the sun will rise again the next day and life will begin again? Only this body is ended. Life is not."

"If only I could be certain of that," Dagga said.

"Believe it," Cela said, "for it is true."

"You know this?"

"I know this, Dagga. I am a priestess of the Wise Ones, am I not?" Cela was silent a moment, the life quickly draining out of her. "I have tried to serve the gods well. Surely they will grant me one wish." Her eyes held Dagga's. "I will ask that I, Cela, Priestess of the Wise Ones, Daughter of the Skies, be granted another life with the warrior Dagga, but not in this time, in another time, and not as priestess and warrior, but as man and woman."

Dagga was having difficulty seeing and hastily wiped the tears from his eyes. "This is possible?"

"Yes, Dagga."

"As man and woman, not priestess and warrior. How, then, will I find you in this other life?" Dagga asked, his own heart tearing apart.

A slight smile came to Cela's lips. "I will find you."

Once again, her chest was racked with a violent coughing spasm, and then her eyes closed. Dagga watched as a stream of blood poured out of her mouth, taking her life with it.

✳ ✳ ✳

"Jenny!" Derek cried. He was kneeling beside her, holding her in his arms. His father and brother knelt beside him. "Something is wrong," Derek cried to his father. "This hasn't happened before!"

Jennifer had grown cold in Derek's arms. With horror, he watched as the rise and fall of her chest ceased. "She's stopped breathing!"

"I'll call a doctor!" Edward shouted as he began running to the house.

"Jenny! Jenny!" Derek screamed, shaking her shoulders.

There was no response. Jennifer's body was lifeless in his hands.

"No! Come back, Jenny!"

Derek quickly lay Jennifer down on the ground and positioned his mouth over hers. Grasping her chin and nose, he exhaled, forcing his breath into her lungs. Six times he breathed into her, but still she didn't move.

"Don't take her from me," he cried. "Please, Cela, bring her back. Bring her back. Jenny!"

Two more times he breathed into her cold, lifeless lips as he silently prayed. *Dear God, please help her. Don't let Jenny die. Please.* Tears filled his eyes as he was preparing to cover her mouth again when Jennifer suddenly inhaled sharply, the air rushing into her lungs.

"Jenny!"

He watched as, almost immediately, the color flowed back into her face and her hands grew warm. He didn't take his eyes off her as he watched her chest rise and fall evenly.

"Jenny," he said gently as he pulled her back into his arms. "It's all right. You're safe now." He could see her eyes move beneath the closed eyelids, so he continued to speak to her. "Easy, Jenny. You're coming back. Let it bring you back. You're safe. You're at Thornhill."

Edward ran toward them. "Dr. MacNeal is on his way."

"She's breathing again. I think she's going to be all right," Derek said as he continued to speak softly to Jennifer.

Jennifer suddenly gripped her stomach and moaned. She twisted to the side, out of his arms, and vomited onto the pavement. Her eyes were still closed as she drew her knees up to her chest and vomited again, her body violently racking with each heave of her stomach. Derek reached for her and cradled her trembling body in his arms.

"Relax, Jenny, relax. Just breathe deeply," Derek said as

he brushed her hair from her face. "You're safe. You're at Thornhill. I won't let anything happen to you." He continued talking as he absently wiped the traces of vomit from her face with his hand.

Edward and Harold were kneeling next to Derek. They watched as a single tear escaped from Jennifer's closed eyelids and cascaded down her face. It was a moment before she opened her eyes. Derek could see the depth of pain in her eyes as she struggled to speak.

"She's dead," Jennifer whispered. "Cela's dead. He killed her." Her body shuddered as a wave of tears flowed silently down her face.

"I know, Jenny," Derek said softly as he held her in his arms.

"I told you this wasn't necessary," Jennifer said when Shamus concluded his examination.

"They were worried about you," Shamus said. "Edward called."

"I'm fine."

"You've convinced me, Jennifer. There's nothing wrong with you physically, but Derek told me about this last episode. He said you stopped breathing. Your body was cold," Shamus said gravely. "Thank God Derek had the presence of mind to do mouth-to-mouth resuscitation. Who knows what could have happened this time."

Jennifer was silent. She was sitting up on Derek's bed. She was aware that Derek and his family were waiting in Derek's adjacent sitting room. She knitted her eyebrows together.

"I felt it," she said softly to Shamus. "I felt the spear go into her chest. I felt the pain, the ripping and tearing of flesh. Then it was hard to breathe; the blood was filling her lungs. I saw the hatred in Luc's eyes. It was as though it was me he stabbed, he killed." Jennifer paused. "It was always like that, though. I stepped inside of her each time I had one of the visions," she whispered.

Jennifer stood and walked to the window. "It's over now," she said, her back to Shamus. "There won't be any more visions. She's dead. So why doesn't everyone just get back to whatever it is he or she was doing? I'm fine. You said so yourself."

"Jennifer, this isn't exactly in my field, but you've had a profound experience."

Jennifer turned around. "Shamus, you're a very kind man, and I appreciate your concern, I do, but I would like to handle this myself. I want to be left alone. Please."

Shamus stood. "Nina is in London today. She'll want to know what happened. Will you call her?"

"You can tell her, Shamus. She'll be furious if you don't."

"I'm not comfortable with you being alone, and I'm going to tell Derek that."

Jennifer started to object when Shamus looked at her sternly. "No objections, Jennifer." Then his expression softened. "Will you promise to call me if you need anything?" Shamus asked.

"Yes, Shamus, I will . . . and thank you."

"All right. Shall I tell Derek he can come in?"

"Yes."

Derek, his brother, and father were waiting in the adjacent sitting room. Derek jumped to his feet when Shamus approached.

"Shamus?"

"Physically, Jennifer is fine, but she's had a profound shock. I don't need to tell you how unusual all of this is— the visions, an alternate reality, the violence. This connection she had with Cela . . . Derek, she said she felt the murder, as though it happened to her. Then to have stopped breathing, as if, for a second or two, she died with Cela." He shrugged his shoulders. "Jennifer is grieving for

Cela but also for herself. None of this is normal, so I wouldn't necessarily expect a normal grieving response. She was also, in her visions, the victim of violence."

They spoke for a few more minutes and then Shamus left. Derek turned to his brother and father.

"Go ahead, Son," Harold said, nodding to the closed bedroom door. "Edward and I will be downstairs if you need us."

Derek entered the bedroom and closed the door behind him. Jennifer was standing in the middle of the room, and to Derek, she seemed so small, so alone, so lost. He crossed the room to where she stood. He started to take her in his arms, but she stepped back out of his reach.

"I wish Edward would not have called Shamus. I wish people would not make such a fuss about this," Jennifer said.

"I'm sorry," Derek said. "Everyone is just concerned."

"Derek, you know how these episodes are. Why couldn't you have just told them that I would be okay?"

Jennifer started pacing, becoming more agitated. She glanced down at herself. "I don't even have any clothes to change into," she said.

"I'll send Clara over to Nina's to bring back some clothes for you. Ann can go with her."

"Ann? She's here, too?" she asked in exasperation.

"My father called her." Derek paused. "I thought I'd lost you, Jenny," he began.

Jennifer turned away from him. "I need to be alone, Derek."

Derek hesitated. "Jenny—"

"I seem to be upsetting everyone here. Just let me use your car, and I can drive back to Nina's. That would be best," she said as she started walking to the door.

"Jenny," Derek said as he touched her arm.

Jennifer jumped back immediately, putting distance between them. "Why can't anyone understand? I just want to be left alone!"

Derek dropped his arms to his side. "Jenny, please, just let me hold you. I love you," he said softly.

Those words appeared to have an effect on her, for he could see the tension in her body lessen. It was a moment before she spoke.

"I know you do," she finally said, "and I don't mean to be insensitive, but I need to be alone. I can't sort through all this with you or anyone else. Please, try to understand."

He looked into her eyes, her deep pain so obvious to him. "All right, Jenny," Derek said. "I'll leave you alone— for now. I'll send Clara for your clothes."

She nodded her head and then turned away from him. It was hard for him to leave her, but he realized that, at the moment, she was building a wall around herself, and instinct told him not to press her. There would be time. He would stay near.

For the next several days, Jennifer went through the motions of living. She spoke little and remained in Derek's rooms. She knew that she couldn't face Cela's death yet— not yet. For now, she encouraged the emptiness and coldness she felt settling inside of her.

Whenever Derek, his father, or his brother tried to speak with her, she became visibly agitated. She refused the comfort of Derek's touch, keeping a physical distance between them. The only time she left Derek's rooms was to walk the grounds of Thornhill, allowing only Issy to accompany her and always staying close to the massive gray stones of Thornhill. That was when she first heard it.

You must understand and accept.

Jennifer whirled around. "Who's there?"

Issy turned to look in the direction of the great house and barked. Then the Irish wolfhound positioned herself so close to Jennifer that her side was touching Jennifer's hip.

Ancient blood. Many lives.

"Who are you?" she asked as she turned around.

You know. You placed my stones.

Jennifer gasped and started to run as fast as she could, back to the safety of Derek's suite, the great hound at her side. The words were not sounds she was hearing with her ears, but words she was hearing in her head.

On the fourth day following Cela's death, there was a knock at the door as Clara entered Derek's rooms. "Excuse me, Miss McHugh," Clara said. "Lady Ann would like to see you."

"Clara, tell Lady Ann that I don't feel like—"

"Scottish men like to think of themselves as so rugged and independent," Ann said as she breezed into the room, "but they still feel the obligation to protect the fairer sex. And Rannoch men are the worst. You should hear my father and brothers! 'Ann, you should be resting. Ann, you shouldn't be driving in your condition. Ann, you shouldn't be climbing stairs. Robert, can't you make your wife stay home?' They're driving me crazy! You'd think I'd never had a baby before."

Ann laughed as she eased herself down upon the bed. "And you!" she continued. "They're positively beside themselves worrying over you. Derek calls Shamus MacNeal two and three times a day. Edward has refused to return to London. He, Derek, and my father take turns pacing at the bottom of the stairs, just in case you should emerge from these rooms. And I see Derek has taken to sleeping on the sofa in his sitting room, right outside your door." Ann smiled again, shaking her head. "Men." She placed her hand on her bulging abdomen. "Well, a walk will do me some good. Maybe it will hurry this baby along."

Ann pushed herself up from the bed. "Do you feel like walking? I would appreciate some feminine company."

Jennifer hesitated. Ann reached down, took Jennifer's hand in her own, and smiled at her. Ann had such a gentle way about her, and yet, Jennifer saw her calm assurance and determination. "Come," Ann said, "but let me warn you. They'll all be lined up at the bottom of the steps." She looked down at the wolfhounds lying beside the bed. "I knew Issy was with you, but how did Bruce, Angus, and Aillig end up here?"

Jennifer shrugged her shoulders. It was yesterday morning when she heard the voice while walking outside. She had run back inside the house, and as she ran up the stairs, Issy started barking and wouldn't stop. Jennifer reached the door to Derek's rooms and was opening it when the other three dogs appeared, pushing their way into the room with Jennifer. She tried to get them to leave, but like Issy, they walked into the bedroom and lay down. They hadn't left her side since then, except when Derek coaxed them out last night and early this morning for toileting and feeding, only for them to race back up to Jennifer. If he thought it strange that the four dogs insisted on staying with Jennifer, he didn't say anything.

"Well, no matter. I suppose they'll be coming with us," Ann said as she slipped her arm through Jennifer's. "Shall we?"

When they reached the top of the stairs, the three men were standing below. "What did I tell you? Three knights in shining armor," Ann whispered secretively to Jennifer.

"Ann, you shouldn't be climbing stairs!" Lord Harold admonished his daughter.

"Nonsense, Father," Ann replied. "Jennifer and I are going for a walk," she announced to the men.

Lord Harold stepped forward. "Are you feeling well enough for that, Jennifer?" he asked with concern.

"Would you like one of us to come with you?" Edward offered.

"That won't be necessary, Edward. We'll be on the grounds," Ann said firmly. "We won't be long."

Jennifer glanced at Derek who was standing across the room. She could fool the others, but she knew she couldn't fool him. Derek could see through her, and Jennifer wasn't

Alison Blasdell

ready to face that yet. The others were kind and their concern for Jennifer was genuine, but they had no connection to Cela. Derek was connected. To face him now meant that Jennifer had to face Cela's death. She just couldn't do that yet—not until she could begin to understand it. She walked with Ann out the door, the four great hounds bounding ahead of them.

The sky was gray again, and Jennifer was grateful for that. They walked first in the garden, and it was a while before Ann spoke. When she did, her voice was calm as she looked to Jennifer.

"Do you think your visions are over now?" she asked.

"Yes," Jennifer answered quietly.

Ann nodded as they walked.

"Someday, I would like to hear about her—your Cela," Ann said.

Jennifer stiffened.

"But later," Ann said. She smiled gently at Jennifer. "There will be time."

They walked on in silence, and then Ann bent down to smell one of the flowers.

"He loves you, you know," she said.

Jennifer knitted her brow.

"Derek loves you."

Ann didn't mention Cela or Derek any more. They walked around the grounds, Ann talking of inconsequential things until she tired and they returned to Thornhill. Ann held Jennifer's arm and guided her, not upstairs to Derek's bedroom, but into the family room.

The afternoon passed slowly for Jennifer. Robert, Ann's husband, arrived with the boys. While Derek was helping his nephews get their ponies ready to ride, Robert approached Jennifer. He was gentle and kind, like Ann, but Jennifer spoke little.

That evening, Ann and her family stayed for dinner. The boys, Andrew and Anthony, were allowed to join the adults. Although dinner was lively, Jennifer took advantage of the first opportunity to be by herself. Lord Harold and his family were going outside to sit in the garden while the boys played, taking advantage of the daylight. Jennifer slipped away and entered the closest room, the library.

It was quiet in the great house as Jennifer stood alone in the library. She and Derek had spent many hours together in this room, reviewing the details of Jennifer's visions. Derek had always been trying to find a tangible link between Cela's civilization and others. That was all over now. Cela was dead.

Jennifer walked slowly to the desk. Derek's notebook was laying on the desk next to a pile of papers. Gingerly, she touched the papers. They were the sketches Derek and she had made of the standing monuments and earth barrows. She could see them all, not as they were drawn on paper, but from the sky, just as Cela had seen them. The sketches began to blur as her eyes filled with tears. She swallowed, a painful constriction in her throat. She heard the door open, and then Derek walked up behind her and touched her arm.

"Jenny?" he said.

She didn't turn around but continued focusing on the sketches.

"Circles, always circles," she said in a strained voice as her fingers traced the patterns created by the stones. "I saw that circle. I saw it in my dream. I knew something terrible was going to happen. I knew it. I could see the circle coming to an end, but I didn't understand it. I didn't know that it was her life that was coming to an end. And there was nothing I could do about it. I couldn't stop it! I couldn't help her!" She reached both hands to the desk and, with a violent gesture, shoved the sketches off the desk, hurling them onto the floor.

"Jenny, stop," Derek said quietly.

She whirled around, her eyes blazing through her tears.

"Why, Derek? It's all over anyway! She's dead. I don't have any more information to give you." Jennifer reached for Derek's notebook. "You'll just have to be satisfied with this."

Jennifer shoved the notebook into Derek's chest and started to walk around him. Derek caught her arm, stopping her, just as Derek's father, sister, and brother entered the library, concern on their faces.

"Don't you understand? I have nothing more to tell you," Jennifer cried. "You always wanted more details. Well, there are no more details, unless you would like to know about this last one. Of course, that's it!" she accused hysterically. "You were especially interested in the sacrifices, weren't you? Would you like to know what they used to drug the babies and small children so they wouldn't squirm when they were thrown over the cliff, their bodies smashing into the gorge below? Food was scarce, but they still fed the children the traditional meal of burnt barley. That was always given to the victims before they were sacrificed. Did your Druids do that also, Derek?

"Would you like to know the words chanted by the Wise Ones at the time of the sacrifices? Give me that!" Jennifer demanded as she tore the notebook out of Derek's hands. She opened the pages, roughly turning them, some of them tearing in the process. "Let's see." She stopped suddenly. "The rest of this page is blank," she said, looking up at Derek. "The fertility ceremony. Were you waiting for more details? Go ahead, ask me!" she shouted angrily. "I can give you all the details you want. It was nothing more than rape, a brutal rape! I can even tell you what it felt like!"

"Jenny, stop this," Derek said, this time his voice firmer.

"Why? It's what you wanted to know. Or perhaps you would like to know what it's like to be killed, to feel a spear pierce through your chest, ripping you apart, to drown in your own blood, to die!"

"Jenny! That's enough!" Derek said, grabbing her forcefully.

"No! Let go of me!" Jennifer cried as she struck out at him.

Derek held her tightly as she fought and struggled until, at last, she collapsed against him, her pain finally released in a flood of uncontrolled grief, her body racked with tears. The very walls of Thornhill seemed to vibrate with her pain until, finally, the great house was silent.

"Why, Derek?" she cried when her body finally quieted. "Why did she have to die?"

"Jenny," Derek said softly, "she died almost three thousand years ago. I don't know why."

Jennifer frowned, her head resting on Derek's chest.

"But when I was in her world," she said, "it was real, it was the present. It was just a few days ago. I still don't understand why I had to see all of this. Why did this happen to me?"

"Ah, Jenny, we may never know the truth. You're an extraordinary woman, Jenny McHugh. Most of us can only dream about the past. A few, like me, spend our lives digging among the remains of ancient civilizations, trying to understand what has preceded us. But you, Jenny, you have an amazing gift." Derek pulled back from her slightly, his eyes shining. "You can go back. You saw the past, breathed it, felt it, lived it, and then returned with it all safely held here," he said, touching her head, "and here in your heart."

Derek and Jennifer were kneeling on the floor, his arms still around her. He reached over and picked up one of the sketches.

"Look at this," he said.

Jennifer shook her head, turning away from it as new tears fell from her eyes.

"Please, Jenny, look at it," he said again.

Jennifer slowly turned her head and wiped her eyes. It was a sketch of a megalithic monument, its stones in several circles, similar to Stonehenge.

"You saw the circle as ominous, coming to an end with Cela's death. But you said it yourself, Jenny, the circle was pervasive in Cela's culture. Why? What is a circle, Jenny?"

"What?"

"Tell me what a circle is."

"Derek, I don't want to think about circles or anything."

"What is a circle, Jenny?" Derek demanded.

"A round shape, like a ball," she said, unable to hide her irritation.

"No. Use what you learned from Cela. What is a circle, Jenny?" His voice was firm, commanding. Jennifer turned away.

"Derek, I don't care."

"A circle, Jenny!" Derek said roughly.

"A closed plane curve, every point of which is equidistant from a fixed point within the curve," she replied angrily.

"Symbolism?" Derek demanded.

"What?"

"Symbolism! Come on, Jenny, everything that Cela felt and knew is there, in your head, in your heart, in your *soul*! Why did they use the circle?"

Jennifer hesitated. "A circle has neither a beginning nor an ending. It is continuous. It is the symbol of life. It is unending, just as life is unending," she finished softly, her anger dissipating.

Derek held Jennifer there in the library while she cried until, at last, the remaining tension slipped away from her body and her breathing relaxed.

"I'm sorry if I hurt you by pushing you away these past few days," she said softly as Derek held her in his arms. "I needed to deal with Cela's death alone. You're too much a part of it all, and I needed to understand it.

"I'm acquainted with grief," she continued. "I lost my mother a year ago. But this was different. I could understand my mother's brain tumor. I was angry with God when He didn't save her, but I could understand how her death came about. How was I to understand losing someone who was already dead? The pain, the loss, the grief was just as real as what I experienced with my mother, but more complicated because I was inside of Cela, feeling her pain and loss as well. I needed to make some sense of it all."

He bent his lips to her ear. "I understand, Jenny. And no matter what, you can't push me away. I love you."

Was that true? Could she tell Derek about the voice she had heard in her head? *Ancient blood. Many lives. You know who we are. You placed us.* Did she dare? Did she dare tell him what she thought it was? She squeezed her eyes shut. There was no need. She hadn't heard it for a few days now. Perhaps it was over. Perhaps it had been her imagination.

"Would you like to come upstairs with me now?"

Jennifer pulled back slightly to see his face. "Yes," she said, feeling Derek's strength and love as he took her hand in his.

CHAPTER 14

It was the next morning, and the sun shone brightly as Derek made his way to the dining room at Thornhill. He overheard his father and brother talking as he approached.

"That might be, Edward, but I think we should discuss it with Derek," his father said.

"Discuss what, Father?" Derek asked as he entered the dining room with a smile on his face.

Edward sat back in his chair as Derek came around the table and sat down next to him. "You," Edward said, "and Jennifer."

Derek raised his eyebrows. "I see," he said as he poured a cup of coffee. He leaned back in his chair, savoring the taste of the rich brew. He smiled to himself. Jennifer was still asleep. They had spent most of the night talking and making love. He had held her close to him throughout the night, and even this morning, he had been reluctant to leave her side. He had been tempted to wake her this morning, but she was finally sleeping so peacefully, he decided to slip quietly out of bed and come downstairs alone for breakfast.

Clara entered with a tray of food. She looked around as though expecting another.

"Thank you, Clara," Derek said as she served him.

"Would you care for anything else?" Clara asked.

"No, thank you. This is fine. We have some things we would like to discuss now," Derek said, his meaning clear.

"Certainly, sir. Excuse me," Clara said and then left the

room.

Harold Rannoch raised his eyebrows at his son.

"Well, Father," Edward said with a smile, "I guess now is the time."

"So it would seem," Harold Rannoch said.

"What did you want to discuss, Father?" Derek asked.

"First, I want to know how Jennifer is feeling. Is she going to be all right?" Edward asked.

"Yes," Derek said. "She's fine. These past few days have been difficult, but," he said with a slight smile, "she's going to be all right." He paused and then looked up. "I've asked Jenny to marry me."

The room was silent for a moment, and then Lord Harold spoke.

"And what of her current husband?" he asked.

Derek sighed. "Jenny asked him for a divorce over a month ago, just after we went to Cumbria together. We had gone to several megaliths in the area and spent the night at Cowden Hall. The next morning, I found out she was married. I said some terrible things to her. I accused her of . . . well, that's not important. I'm not proud of how I behaved. I never expected to see her again.

"Her husband refused to give her a divorce, although she initiated the legal proceedings. I will tell you that Jenny has not been his wife for a long time, if indeed they ever really were man and wife," he added. "Her husband is a cold, self-centered man. Beyond that, it is for Jenny to tell you about that part of her life, not me."

The men were silent, and then Edward spoke. "I think we know the type of man Dr. Bracken is," Edward said with sarcasm. "So it is a matter of waiting until the divorce is final, and then you will marry?"

"Not exactly. She didn't accept my proposal," Derek said.

"What?" Lord Harold said.

"She says it's too soon and there's too much uncertainty. *If* her visions of the past are over, she's afraid that it won't be the same between us. She thinks I fell in love with her because of her link to the past, and if that is gone. . . ."

"What do you say?" Harold asked his son.

"It's true that her visions brought us together in the first place, but I love her. I love Jenny. If she never has another vision or experience again, I will be content to spend my life with her. I just have to convince her of that."

Edward looked at his brother. "There's something you're not telling us," Edward said.

Derek sat forward, staring into his cup. "Jenny hopes the visions are over. If they're not, she's afraid of what else may happen. She doesn't see how she can be a wife and, hopefully, a mother if she's going back and forth between the past and present. She says she can't consider marriage or a family—not if she is moving between realities. She said it's not fair to me or my family," he said pointedly and looked to his brother and father. "And there is something else that is troubling her, but I don't know what it is. She won't discuss it with me.

"Nothing like this ever happened to Jenny before she came here. Scotland and England were a trigger for something. I don't know. I've thought about it a lot. Reincarnation? Was Jenny actually Cela? Did something here uncover the memories of a previous life? Or is Jenny descended from Cela? Cela did have a daughter. Did Jenny just tap into the genetic memory passed down to her, inherited from Cela? Or is Jenny separate and independent from Cela and the past, and is she simply able to cross the boundaries of time within her mind? Whatever it is, I think it's just the beginning. I believe Cela and her civilization were just the first chapter. If that's so, then Jenny has another three thousand years of human experience waiting to be unveiled."

Both men stared at Derek.

"Lady Gwenivere?" Lord Harold asked.

Derek shrugged. "Probably. I never told Jenny about Lady Gwenivere. Jenny said it was brief, but she saw and felt everything Lady Gwenivere was feeling at that time, as though she was a part of her, just like it had been with Cela.

"I do know that it won't always be easy for her. There will be painful times like these past few days. Jenny is very sensitive, but she also has a great deal of strength. She doesn't even realize that. Still, I want to be with her if . . . *when* it happens. She'll need someone." Derek smiled. "And if I'm wrong and not another thing out of the ordinary ever happens, then I will look forward to a quiet life with her, doing the usual things that a man and wife do."

Edward seemed to be concentrating on what Derek was saying. "Somehow," Edward finally said, "I don't think your lives together will be quiet or ordinary in the conventional sense."

"Neither do I, which means that neither will yours," Derek said as he looked from his brother to his father. "Thornhill is my home. It will be Jenny's, too, and hopefully, we will raise our children here. I don't know if what has happened to Jenny will happen again, but I need to know—*she* will need to know—that she is welcome here and is a part of our family. If you have any reservations about her or about what has occurred and may occur again, we need to discuss those concerns now."

"It will certainly make life interesting," Edward mused, "but that's not what is important. What Father or I think is of secondary importance. The issue is you and Jenny, and I can see that you love her." Derek started to interrupt and Edward stopped him. "You want to know what I think?" Edward smiled. "Without sounding too melodramatic, I think you were meant for each other, and in terms of this becoming her home, well, who's to say that Jennifer's entitlement to Thornhill doesn't predate all of ours? I don't believe in coincidences, Derek. Jenny is connected to Scotland, to Thornhill, and to you."

Derek's face reflected his surprise. "That's very metaphysical for an economist," Derek teased his brother.

Edward laughed. "I've grown very fond of Jenny; I'm

actually quite attracted to her myself." Edward looked up to see a scowl appear on Derek's face. "In a brotherly way, of course," Edward added hastily and started laughing. "You have my approval and support, Brother. Now it seems that you need to convince her."

Derek acknowledged his brother's comment and then turned to his father.

"I think Jennifer is correct," Lord Harold began. "So much has happened to her and to you, Derek, in a relatively short period of time, and Jennifer is not free to marry you. I think she is being very sensible. I believe you both need some time before you consider marriage."

"Father? You object to the marriage?" Derek asked.

"Not at all. I've grown to love her, too, and I find the prospects of having her as a daughter to be delightful. And I agree with Edward—Jennifer and Thornhill are connected.

"My first meeting with her was such a strange occurrence. I was out walking with the dogs when they ran ahead and started barking. When I caught up with them, Jennifer was standing on the hill overlooking Thornhill. But that, in itself, was nothing unusual; it was the dogs. Jennifer was obviously frightened by them, but what she failed to notice was that they weren't barking at her. They had surrounded her and were facing outward, away from her. They'd formed a protective circle around her, and Issy was inside the circle, at her side. They were barking at me— warning *me*—and, I suspect, anyone else who approached her. They were of one mind to protect *her*." Lord Harold took a deep breath. "Quite frankly, it was unnerving, to say the least."

Derek listened, both fascinated and shocked by what his father said. "And you never told me," Derek accused.

"No, no one knows other than Brandon, who came looking for the dogs. There's a lot more going on here, Son, than just you falling in love with Jennifer. There's Cela, Lady Gwenivere, and Thornhill, and they're all connected to Jennifer. I don't pretend to understand, but I think you both need some time."

There was a knock at the door and Jeffrey entered. "Excuse me, sir," he said to Lord Harold, and then turned to Derek. "A Miss Bouvay is here to see Miss McHugh. I told her Miss McHugh has not come downstairs yet."

Derek smiled for the first time in several minutes. "That's okay, Jeffrey. Take Miss Bouvay upstairs. Miss McHugh will want to see her."

"Sir?" Jeffrey said, shifting slightly. "Upstairs?"

"Yes, Jeffrey, escort Miss Bouvay to my rooms. Miss McHugh is sleeping there."

Jeffrey nodded stiffly, his discomfort obvious, and left the room.

Edward looked down at his plate, pretending interest in the food there. He cleared his throat as he lifted his coffee. "We'll all be lucky if Jeffrey doesn't have a heart attack on the stairs," he said, trying to conceal the grin that appeared on his face.

"Yes, well," Lord Harold said in a voice seasoned from formal public speaking, "perhaps you should not wait too long to convince Jennifer to marry you. I'm not certain Jeffrey can withstand the shock of your impropriety."

Edward could contain himself no longer and burst out laughing as he slapped his brother on the back.

Several days later, Jennifer and Derek stood in the library. They were looking at a map that was spread out on the desk. Derek shook his head dubiously.

"I don't know, Jenny," he said. "There are no known prehistoric remains in that part of France. There are the cave drawings, yes, but not henges as you describe. That's a major wine-producing area. Are you certain you didn't make a mistake?"

There was a knock on the library door and Jeffrey entered.

"Sir, Lady Ann has arrived. Your father asked me to tell

you they are waiting in the dining room," Jeffrey said.

"Derek, we're keeping your family waiting," Jennifer said.

"We'll be right there," Derek said to Jeffrey, dismissing him.

"I know that area, Jenny," Derek began again.

Jennifer smiled at him. Each day, it became easier to talk about Cela. In fact, they had begun examining all of the drawings that Jennifer had made. Jennifer had found the work exciting, and the nights in Derek's arms surpassed her every dream. How was it possible to be so happy? To feel such love for someone and know it was returned?

Now she took his arm and gently led him out of the library as he continued talking.

"Wait," he said, and dashed back to the library. He returned carrying the map. "If it had been closer to the coast . . . ," he said, holding the map out as they walked.

They entered the dining room to find Lord Harold, Edward, Ann, and Robert Warrick already seated. Jennifer turned to greet them. Derek looked up quickly and then back at the map.

"You must have made a mistake," Derek insisted. "There are many megalithic remains in France. Carnac and Morbihan, in Brittany, are covered with them. But there aren't any in the area you indicate."

Jennifer looked at Derek's family, uncertain of what to say.

"What is Derek talking about?" Ann asked Edward.

Edward just smiled, watching his brother.

Lord Harold wore a patient look on his face.

Jennifer turned back to Derek.

"No, I didn't make a mistake," she whispered fervently. "It's right where I said it was."

"Look, Jenny, is it possible that you don't remember accurately? Maybe Cela made a mistake in her navigation."

"She wouldn't make a mistake like that," Jennifer said with confidence and turned to an empty chair at the table.

"I'm sorry, Jenny, but I think she did," Derek insisted as he moved to the chair next to her.

"No, she didn't," Jennifer replied.

"Jenny, I've looked at every possibility. Either you or Cela—"

"I know what I'm talking about. Cela would not make a mistake," Jennifer said, her voice firm and authoritative, "which means I'm not making a mistake. You're wrong."

"But," Derek began, placing the map on the table, obscuring the china and silver.

Jennifer took a deep breath and closed her eyes. "It was early spring," she began. "They counted by lunar months, so I would say it was the equivalent of our late March. At that time of the year, the earth's rotation is such that. . . ."

Derek's family listened intently as Jennifer's voice took on a different quality. She described the position of the constellations relative to the position of the earth at that time of year. She calculated in detail the degrees that mapped out the journey Cela had made, using the stars to guide her. When at last she opened her eyes, she looked down at the enlarged geophysical map of France.

"It's here," she said, pointing to a place on the map. "It's exactly thirty degrees to the south of the stones here—two rounded earth mounds, with stone lintel entryways," Jennifer said. "The mounds are clearly visible from the sky."

"And they cremated the remains of their victims there?" Derek asked.

"Yes."

Derek sighed. "All right, Jenny. No prehistoric remains have been detected in this area, but then, no one was really looking," Derek said with a smile. "There are aerial photographic techniques using computer enhancement that can reveal the slightest undulation in the ground surface. If we find something suspicious, then we can contact the Ministry of France to get permission to explore further. If the stones are under layers of earth, we can utilize sonographic waves to detect them. Magnetomety and soil resistivity can yield remarkable patterns of occluded ruins. We can obtain even more detailed images using LIDAR— pulsed laser light delivered from an airplane. The light reflected back is detected by a sensor and fed into a computer. The reconstructed images are amazing. Would you like to go to France with me?" he asked seductively.

"You believe me, then?" Jennifer asked.

"I believe you. You must be patient with me, Jenny. I've been trained in the scientific method, which neglects gifts such as yours. You're opening up a whole new world to me."

Jennifer and Derek both jumped slightly as they heard Harold Rannoch clear his throat. They both looked at the others seated at the table, as though seeing them for the first time.

"My apologies," Derek offered. "We were working—"

"Yes, so we heard," Lord Harold said, a smile in his eyes. Derek hastily folded the map.

"How did you do that?" Ann asked Jennifer.

"Do what?" Jennifer asked.

"All that with the stars," Ann said.

Jennifer shrugged her shoulders, still uncomfortable with the legacy that Cela had left. "Cela knew how to read the stars," she said shyly.

"Somehow," Edward offered, "I don't think too many meals are going to be 'ordinary' around here ever again." Edward smiled warmly at Jennifer.

"If you would like an outsider's perspective," Robert Warrick said, "there was never anything ordinary about Thornhill or its occupants."

"And just what does that mean?" Ann asked her husband with pretended indignation.

Jennifer smiled as Derek's family laughed together, feeling the love around the table, and she silently thanked God and Cela for leading her here to Derek.

Derek awoke to the sounds of Jennifer crying. She was tossing her head about on the pillow, and in the dim early morning light, he could see that her face was damp from her tears. She was mumbling something, but he couldn't understand her.

"Jenny, wake up," he said gently as he reached to pull her into his arms.

She opened her eyes and blinked. He could see her confusion as she looked about the darkened bedroom and back at him. Then her eyes cleared, and she reached for him. He could feel her heart racing against his chest as he held her tightly.

"What is it, Jenny? What's wrong?"

"I was dreaming," she said.

Derek was immediately attentive. He remembered the last time Jennifer had awakened after dreaming of the circles. She had been crying and so frightened. That was two weeks ago when he had brought her back to Thornhill, and she had the last terrifying vision that culminated in Cela's death and her near death.

"Was it like that last one?" he asked, pulling back from her so he could face her.

Jennifer shook her head. "No. No circles. I was dreaming about the day Cela died. I could see the children being sacrificed by throwing them over the edge of the mountains. I could feel Cela's sense of horror and helplessness, just before she flew to save the child. I kept dreaming it over and over again. I could feel her flying through the air as though I were flying. When I was a child, I used to dream I could fly like Cela did, but children weren't being thrown over a cliff," she added.

"I'm all right, Derek." She touched his face with affection. "You're leaving early this morning, aren't you?"

"Yes," he said. He could feel her relaxing in his arms, her dream gone now. "Are you sure you don't want to come to Edinburgh with me? I'm not certain I want to leave you alone now."

"I'm not alone; I'm at Thornhill. Nina is going to pick me up for lunch, and we're spending the day together."

Jennifer finished dressing and sat down on Derek's bed. She still had an hour before Nina would arrive. Derek had gone to his office in Edinburgh to begin making arrangements for a trip to France. He emphasized that the most they could hope for would be the discovery of another prehistoric site, most probably erected in the Neolithic or Bronze Age. He could not, at this time, publicly advance her theory of the primary purpose for the ancient megalithic formations: that they were used as maps for an ancient race of humans who could fly. That did not mean that he would not spend his life trying to find support, albeit circumstantial, for Jennifer's amazing revelation. Jennifer was just contemplating the life that could lie ahead for her at Derek's side when Jeffrey knocked at the door of the sitting room.

"Good morning, Jeffrey," Jennifer said.

"Good morning, ma'am," Jeffrey said. "There is a man here to see you."

"A man?" Jennifer said.

"Yes." Jeffrey hesitated. "He said he is your. . . ."

Jennifer knew immediately who it was. She stiffened.

"Where is he?" Jennifer asked.

"He is waiting in the sitting room," Jeffrey answered.

"Thank you," Jennifer said and started walking toward the stairs. "Is Lord Harold here?" Jennifer asked as Jeffrey walked beside her.

"Yes, ma'am. He is working in the library." Jeffrey hesitated and then spoke again. "Lord Harold does not know that Dr. Bracken is here."

Jennifer took a deep breath as she reached the bottom of the stairs. "Thank you, Jeffrey," she said. She crossed to the doors leading to the sitting room.

"Ma'am?" Jeffrey ventured.

Jennifer stopped and looked over at the butler.

"Would you perhaps like me to wait here in case you should need anything?" he asked.

Jennifer's heart softened at Jeffrey's kindness. She often wondered what he and Clara thought of her presence at Thornhill.

"No, that won't be necessary. Dr. Bracken won't be staying long." Jennifer smiled. "Jeffrey, thank you."

She opened the doors to find John standing before a window. He turned as she entered.

"John, what are you doing here?" Jennifer asked.

"We hadn't concluded our conversation when you left the party so abruptly," John said. "That was . . . what . . . two weeks ago? Have you been here all the time?"

Jennifer could see his jaw tensing.

"I don't think we have much more to say to one another," Jennifer said. "Surely our attorneys can handle the details. I've already told you that I want nothing from you."

"So you've indicated," John said. He looked around the room. "Now I understand your lack of interest in my money. You will really have no need of it as long as you are staying here, will you? Just what kind of an arrangement do you have with Lord Rannoch?"

Jennifer detected the irascibility in John's voice. She took a step backward. "I think you should leave, John," she said.

"I'm not going anywhere until we have this out!"

"Keep your voice down," Jennifer said.

"Oh, of course, Jennifer! I wouldn't want to embarrass you in front of your lover or his family—not like you humiliated me in front of hundreds of people," he snarled.

Jennifer closed her eyes briefly. "I'm sorry, John. I didn't mean for that to happen, but it's over. There's nothing I can do about it now."

"That's where you're wrong," John said as he advanced on her. "You will hear me out, or I swear to you, I will see that these divorce proceedings drag on for years."

Jennifer looked nervously toward the closed door. She

didn't want Derek's father to be drawn into this. His family had been so kind to her. If John didn't calm down, Lord Harold would surely hear him and come to investigate.

"John, what more could you possibly have to say?" Jennifer asked quietly.

"There's the small matter of one hundred million dollars," John spat out.

"I told you that I'm sorry about that, but that's out of my hands."

"I'll give you the divorce you want, Jennifer, but you're going to help me keep the money in that trust fund," John said loudly.

"John, please!" Jennifer whispered, her voice strained. "Keep your voice down. What can I possibly do about that money?"

"I have a few ideas," John said. "It will be a matter of you making a written statement admitting adultery. My father might consider that grounds for me to sue you for divorce and retain the trust fund. Those are my terms!"

"John, I can't make a decision about that this instant. I'll have to talk to my attorney."

"This is between you and me, Jennifer, and I'm not leaving until something is decided, one way or another. Perhaps we can see what your lover has to say about it when he returns," John said with rancor.

"No! John, I wouldn't even know how to begin to write such a statement."

"Then we'll discuss it. We can write it together."

"I'm not writing anything until I speak to Steven Cole."

"Fine. We'll call him together," John said.

"No, not here," Jennifer repeated. She couldn't imagine what would happen if Derek were to return early and find John here.

"Why not?" John demanded. "Are you afraid Lord Rannoch would be shocked to hear the details of our marriage? I don't give a damn if all of Scotland hears about it. I'm of a mind to drag your lover's whole family down in the process."

John was behaving irrationally. He was shouting. He would indeed create a scene if Derek's father came into the room. Jennifer was desperately trying to think of a solution. She had to get John away from Thornhill.

"John, Nina is picking me up soon. We're having lunch and then going shopping. I could meet you at Nina's later this afternoon. We can talk then," she said.

Jennifer could see John's eyes narrow.

"No," he said. "I'll drive you to Nina's now. We can talk on the way."

"John, I really—"

"Take it or leave it, Jennifer! You either come with me now and we settle this on the way to Nina's, or I'm staying right here."

"Damn you, John," Jennifer said with anger. She didn't trust John, but she had to get him away from Thornhill. "All right. I'll go with you, but first I'll let Nina know that we're coming," she said pointedly. "I'll tell her to expect us in a few minutes."

Jennifer spun around and walked to the door. John was beside her. She opened it and entered the hall. Almost immediately, Jeffrey appeared.

"Jeffrey, Dr. Bracken is going to drive me to Miss Bouvay's cottage. Would you please call her and tell her that we're on our way?"

"Of course, ma'am," he said, inclining his head slightly. "And shall I tell Lord Derek where he can find you when he returns?"

"Yes. Nina and I will be having lunch and then shopping. I'll be back by five."

Jeffrey nodded slightly as Jennifer and John turned to leave.

Once outside, Jennifer strode angrily to John's rented Jaguar. She slid into the seat, telling herself she would need to calm down in order to listen to John's proposal. She also had already decided that she would not sign anything until she called Steven Cole from Nina's house.

John slammed the gear shift into reverse and backed the car around. The tires squealed in protest as he pushed his foot down on the accelerator and drove away from Thornhill. Jennifer didn't speak but waited for John. When he did finally address her, she was surprised by the depth of his enmity toward her.

"How long have you been sleeping with him?" he asked savagely. "You don't have to answer that. I knew something was different when you returned home the last time. Was this all to get back at me? Because I have arrangements with professional women, you decided to sleep around in Europe. How many were there, Jennifer?"

"Professional women? Don't you mean prostitutes? And how dare you," Jennifer accused, "I never slept around. You were the one who was unfaithful to me. And on a regular basis! All the time we were married, I thought I did something wrong. You're disgusting!"

Jennifer thought she could discuss the divorce with John to hasten its happening, but she felt sick in his presence. She couldn't bear to sit close to him. "Pull over to the side of the road. I'll walk the rest of the way to Nina's," Jennifer said.

"The hell I will!" John said as he slammed his foot down on the accelerator.

Jennifer gripped the dashboard as fear seeped into her.

"I'll be damned if I'll let you steal my inheritance from me," John screamed.

"John, stop! You've passed Nina's!" Jennifer looked back over her shoulder as the car sped past Nina's cottage. "Please, John, stop. You're driving too fast for these roads."

John turned onto a narrow road leading up into the mountains.

"John, what do you want?" Jennifer pleaded. She had never seen him so angry. John was always calm, cold, and calculating. He abhorred emotional displays, which made him even more frightening now.

"John, please," she cried, tears springing to her eyes.

He glanced sharply at her, and for a moment, she thought she saw contrition in his eyes. Then he was back in control of himself.

"Relax, Jennifer. I'm not going to hurt you, but we are going to talk, and you will prepare that statement, admitting your adultery. Then you can return to your lover and you can both rot in hell for all I care."

Jennifer was stunned as John continued to drive dangerously fast up the narrow, winding road. She was afraid—afraid of John, even though he seemed to have calmed down. He was talking now in that superior, patronizing voice that she remembered so well. Suddenly, she felt a cold chill down her spine. She looked out the window, her eyes focusing on the mountains above.

"Where are we going?" she asked, a new fear gripping her.

He didn't answer as the Jaguar continued to steadily climb upward into The Highlands. John was talking, but Jennifer no longer heard him. Her heart was racing as a cold feeling of dread spread throughout her body.

"John, please. Don't go any farther. Don't go up there!"

John glanced at her. "What are you talking about?"

"Don't go there. I don't want to see that place!"

John glanced sideways at her. "For God's sake, Jennifer, you look like you've seen a ghost," he said with derision.

"Please, John. I can't go there, not to the top. It's too soon!" Images flooded her mind, causing her to gasp.

"What are you talking about?" John demanded.

"It's where they sacrificed the children. It's where she died. I was there! I saw it! Please, I don't want to go there," she begged.

"Have you gone crazy?" John demanded. He laughed suddenly. "Quite a switch. A few minutes ago, you were playing the lady of the manor."

"I'll sign whatever you want me to sign. Just stop the car now. Don't go to the top," she pleaded in a strangled voice.

"You're hallucinating again! You're still having those delusions," John snickered.

Jennifer was fighting against the rising nausea. It was hard to breathe. "John, I'm not hallucinating. They sacrificed the children on this mountain, and he killed Cela here. This is where she died."

"You're crazy!" John said as he looked at her. "I should have put you in an institution."

"John, stop! The car!" she screamed.

He jerked his head forward to see a car coming straight toward them. He slammed his foot down on the brake. A thunder of stones struck the bottom of the car as the wheels dug into the rocky road. John jerked the wheel to the left in an effort to miss the car. The sound was deafening as the car slammed into the side of John's Jaguar, throwing Jennifer's head into the passenger door. The Jaguar's center of gravity was much lower than that of the Land Rover they hit, and John's car hugged the ground while the Land Rover veered off to the side, spinning around.

When the Jaguar came to a stop, they both were thrust backward again, their heads hitting the leather pads of the seat. Before them, the Land Rover continued to spin. Jennifer climbed awkwardly out of the car as John ran around to join her. They stared, powerless, as the Land Rover spun toward the edge of the mountain, rocks and dust spitting from its whirling tires. Then the deafening sound of metal crunching against rock as the Land Rover slammed into boulders on the edge of the mountain and came to a stop. As it did, the door of the passenger side flew open, and the body of a child catapulted into the air.

"Nooo!" Jennifer screamed as she saw the child's body being hurled over the edge of the mountain. The realization of the child's imminent death pierced her very soul, and in that moment, as Jennifer watched in horror and helplessness, her soul remembered.

* * *

"Jenny? Can you hear me?" Derek pleaded.

"Shamus, why can't she wake up?" Derek asked desperately. "What's wrong?"

"There's no sign of serious injury, Derek. Just keep talking to her," Shamus answered.

"Jenny, please. Wake up," Derek said. He was standing next to Jennifer's hospital bed. She lay there, so pale, so still. He clasped his hands together and rested his forehead on his hands. "Please, God, help Jenny," he prayed. "Help her. And Cela, if you can hear me, help her find her way back to me."

Derek felt Ann's reassuring hand on his shoulder. "Amen," she whispered.

Derek was so grateful for his family. His father and brother were waiting in the hallway. They'd all come immediately when he called them.

"Lady Ann," Shamus said, "would you like to sit down?"

Derek turned to look at his sister. "Forgive me, Ann. I wasn't thinking." He turned to Shamus and, nodding his head in gratitude, accepted the chair he offered. Once he positioned the chair beside the bed, he solicitously took Ann's arm as she sat.

Ann smiled softly. "Thank you, Shamus, and please, call me 'Ann.'"

"May I get you something to drink?" Nina asked.

"You're very kind," Ann answered. "I'm fine. Perhaps you would like to sit with me?" she inquired of Nina, her voice warm and soothing.

Shamus placed a chair beside Ann and Nina sat down.

"Derek," Nina said.

Derek was searching Jennifer's face for signs she could hear him as he whispered to her. He felt Nina reach out, touching his arm. He tore his gaze away from Jennifer.

"Yes?" he said.

"Derek," Nina said softly but firmly, "I've known Jen all my life. She's sweet and kind and the nicest person I know, but make no mistake: she's tough. Underneath, she has a will of steel and the heart of a lion. She's going to be all right."

Ann reached for Nina's hand, squeezing it gently. Derek nodded his head to Nina, too overcome with emotion to speak. He turned back to Jennifer and took her hand in his.

"Jenny," he whispered, his lips by her ear. "Wake up. I've waited for you all of my life." He smiled sadly, wiping a tear from his eye. "I think I fell in love with you when I found you in the restoration room at the British Museum and you vomited on me . . . the first time."

Derek jerked his head up. Was he imagining it? He felt her squeeze his hand.

"Shamus!"

"Shamus went to talk to a nurse. What is it?" Nina asked as she jumped up from her chair.

"She squeezed my hand. There! She just did it again," Derek exclaimed.

"I'll get Shamus," Nina said as she ran to the door.

Derek watched as Jennifer's eyelids flickered briefly, and then she opened her eyes.

"Oh, Jenny!" he cried, hugging her to him.

It was a moment before Jennifer spoke.

"Derek?"

"Welcome back," Shamus said as he entered the room with Nina beside him.

"Shamus? Nina? What are you doing here?" Jennifer asked and then stopped as she surveyed her surroundings. "Where am I?"

"You're in the hospital," Derek said.

Derek could see Jennifer struggling to understand. "What am I doing in a hospital? Derek?" Jennifer asked with alarm.

"There was an accident," he began slowly as he gently

pushed her hair back from her face. "You were in the car with John."

"John?"

"Yes, he came to Thornhill after I left. You went with him in his car. Jeffrey was concerned, so he called both Nina and me to say that John was driving you to her cottage." Derek paused. "When you didn't arrive, Nina called me."

Jennifer frowned and rubbed her forehead absently. "John . . . he was very angry," she began hesitantly. "He didn't stop at Nina's but started driving up into the mountains. He was driving too fast." She closed her eyes, touched the side of her head, and grimaced.

"You've got a nasty bump on the side of your head. Shamus says it will be okay, though," Derek said.

Jennifer opened her eyes. "I asked him to stop. I didn't want to go up there. It's where Cela died."

Derek saw the tears beginning in her eyes, and he took both her hands in his. "Jenny, it's okay. You're safe now."

"No, Derek, there was another car. John tried to stop but we hit it, and the other car spun around and then. . . ." Jennifer's voice caught as she cried. "There was a child, a little girl. She was thrown from the car. Her body was thrown over the edge of the mountain and she died."

Jennifer flung her arms around Derek's neck and sobbed wildly.

"No," he said as he pulled back from her grip around his neck. He placed both hands on her shoulders and looked into her grief-stricken face as Shamus stepped forward.

"Jenny, the little girl is all right. She's alive," Derek said.

"No, I saw her," she cried.

"Jenny, she's unharmed," Derek repeated.

"It's true, Jennifer," Shamus said. "She wasn't injured. They brought her to the hospital with her mother. The little girl's mother was driving. The mother has a head injury, and we're watching her closely. We're hopeful she'll recover."

Jennifer wiped the tears from her eyes and frowned.

"But how can that be?" she asked. "Derek, I saw her. The little girl was thrown high into the air and over the edge. I saw it!"

"Maybe you're confused," Nina offered. "Who wouldn't be under the circumstances."

"No! I know what I saw. John and I both got out of the car when it stopped. The other car was still spinning, and then it hit a boulder. John was there. He saw it, too!"

A peculiar feeling came over Derek. "Jenny," he said, "what else do you remember?"

"What do you mean?"

"What happened next?" Derek asked.

Derek watched as Jennifer frowned, a look of confusion on her face. "I don't know," she said with some surprise. "The last thing I remember is seeing the child's body in the air, going over the cliff." Jennifer's eyes widened. "Derek, I can't remember anything else. I don't even know how I got here."

"It's all right, Jennifer," Shamus said soothingly. "Just relax. You've had quite an experience."

"But that doesn't make any sense. I remember everything up until then. I wasn't injured. Where's John? I want to talk to him," she said forcefully.

"He's downstairs. I believe the police are still questioning him," Nina offered.

"Derek, I need to talk to John," Jennifer said anxiously.

"Jenny," Derek said with a sigh, "John has admitted to driving too fast and not seeing the approaching car. He said he was able to stop and that you two got out of the car."

"Yes, I told you that. What is it, Derek?" Jennifer asked.

He didn't want to upset her further, but the peculiar feeling of a moment ago was getting stronger. Something was amiss. "Jenny, John said that the little girl was thrown just a few feet from the car. He said he ran over to check on the little girl and the woman inside of the car." Derek paused. "He said you just walked away from the accident."

"What!"

"He told the authorities that you acted strangely, and that he thinks you might have had a concussion. He said he asked you to help him with the woman, but you turned and walked away, leaving him alone with the woman and little girl.

"Two cars came along a few minutes later, and two men helped John extract the woman from her car. One man then drove the woman, child, and John to the hospital. The other man was following them when he happened to see you walking in the distance. When he stopped to offer you help, he said you fainted. He placed you in his car and brought you to the hospital."

"I couldn't have done that. Derek! I would never have walked away and left those people," Jennifer argued.

"No one is blaming you, Jennifer," Shamus said. "You were injured, too."

"But I wasn't! I didn't leave those people. And I saw that little girl's body go over the edge," she cried.

Jennifer sat up and threw her arms around Derek's neck. He held her tightly.

"Jenny, I'm just glad that you're okay," he murmured in her ear. "The child is all right, and Shamus thinks the mother will be, too."

"What about John?" Jennifer asked, still clinging to Derek.

"He wasn't injured."

Jennifer nodded her head and Derek released her. She sat back.

"When can I leave?" Jennifer asked.

Derek turned to Shamus.

"You had a concussion, but your scans are normal. You have a few scratches on your head and shoulder. They're minor. I'll start the proceedings now. Mind you, I want you to rest for the next several days, and I'll be over regularly to check on you," Shamus said.

Jennifer nodded and then looked back at Derek. "This doesn't make any sense, Derek," she said, tears forming again in her eyes. "I couldn't have walked away from those people. Never! And I saw that little girl's body go over the edge of the mountain."

"Shhh," Derek said, holding her in his arms. "You heard Shamus. You hit your head, and you need to rest."

Jennifer clung to Derek in silence, and then Shamus stepped forward.

"I'll be back in a few minutes," Shamus said. "I'll sign the papers for your discharge."

"Jenny," Derek said as he pulled back from her, "I want to talk to Shamus. I'll leave you with Nina and Ann. Is that all right?" Derek asked.

"We'll take care of her," Ann said reassuringly.

Nina turned to Shamus. "Can Jen get dressed?"

"I don't see why not," Shamus said.

"I'll be back," Derek said as he leaned over to kiss Jennifer. "I love you, Jenny."

Derek closed the door, and he and Shamus stepped into the hall.

"Is she really going to be all right?" Derek asked.

"Physically, she's fine," Shamus said. "The loss of memory disturbs me, but her tests are all normal. But then"—a peculiar look came to Shamus's face—"Jennifer's not like the rest of us, is she?"

Derek eyed Shamus MacNeal, all his senses heightened. "You heard the little girl's story, didn't you?" It wasn't a question but a statement as his eyes bored into Shamus's.

"Yes, I heard exactly what the child said," Shamus said softly.

"I'm going to find out what really happened up there," Derek said.

"How?"

"John Bracken!"

"He's already told the authorities—"

"I know what he said," Derek interrupted. "Now I'm going to find out the truth."

Derek hurried down to the administrator's office where he knew John had been taken. Only one policeman remained, and he was casually talking with another young woman. Derek identified himself and asked about John Bracken.

"Dr. Bracken has been released, Lord Rannoch," the officer said.

"What?"

The young man shrugged his shoulders. "He has accepted full responsibility for the accident, even made a very generous offer to the woman and child. The woman has regained consciousness, and the doctors say she is going to be fine. Dr. Bracken has gone back to his hotel."

Derek ran out to the parking lot. It was an hour's drive to Braemar. He had to find John Bracken before he left. It was fortunate that the early afternoon traffic was light, especially as he left the city and headed toward the small town of Braemar. When at last he reached the hotel, he was relieved to find that John had not yet left.

"This is a rather sudden departure, isn't it?" Derek said smoothly as he entered John's hotel room.

"What are you doing here?" John asked with surprise. "Get out! The authorities have released me. I'm free to go."

"I have a few questions that I would like to ask you before you go," Derek said.

"I've already answered the questions of the authorities and have accepted responsibility for the accident. I understand that the woman and child are doing well. There are no anticipated complications."

"Yes, so I understand. It's not the woman and child that I want to talk about. It's Jenny."

John's jaw tensed. "I don't intend to discuss my wife with you, Mr. Rannoch," John spat out. "Now, if you'll excuse me, I have a plane to catch."

"Not until we've talked," Derek said, stepping in front of John.

"Get out of my way," John demanded.

"Jenny doesn't seem to remember anything after your car stopped and you two got out. I thought you could tell me what happened." Derek said.

"I already told the authorities. She left."

"I don't think so," Derek said. "She wouldn't do that. She says she saw the child thrown from the car, high into the air and over the edge of the mountain. She would not have walked away."

"That's ridiculous. The child was there, by the mother. The men who came along and helped can attest to that," John said. Unconsciously, his eyes darted about the room, avoiding eye contact with Derek.

"I want to know what happened before the other car came," Derek said, advancing on John.

"Get out of my way," John said, picking up his suitcase. "I'm not going to tell you anything."

John started to step to the side when Derek grabbed him and jerked him around, slamming him into the wall, causing him to drop the suitcase. John's breath was knocked from him and he stood there, fear in his eyes. Derek released him and stepped back.

"Now tell me what happened," Derek said, his voice deadly calm.

"You're crazy, just like she is," John said, his voice rising. "She ought to be institutionalized. You should have seen her. We were driving up to the mountain and she started to panic, saying that she didn't want to go there. She started babbling about sacrifices, about children being thrown over the edge of the mountain, and someone dying. Then we saw the other car. I told the authorities what happened."

"But you didn't tell them the whole truth, did you?"

"I don't know what you're talking about. I'm leaving!"

John started to turn, and Derek seized him by the collar of his shirt. He pushed him back against the wall, but this time, he held him tightly, his hands pressing into John's neck.

"The little girl told an interesting story," Derek began, his face inches from John's. "According to the girl, the car was spinning around in circles, and she was pressed against the door. The door suddenly opened, and she said she remembers being thrown high into the air; then she was coming down out of the air, down into a deep crevice between two mountains. And then," Derek said, pushing his fist against John's neck, "she said she saw an angel—a lady angel with long, red hair, coming through the sky. She said the angel caught her and held her in her arms. Then the angel flew with her back up the side of the mountain and placed her down on the ground, next to her mother. She said the lady angel then turned and walked away."

Derek paused a moment. "Of course, then the girl saw her mother, not moving, blood all over her face, and she started crying. That's when the other cars arrived. The police ignored the little girl's story, assuming she was just hysterical." Derek looked deep into John's eyes. "She wasn't hysterical, was she?"

John didn't answer, but for the first time, Derek saw a cold fear in his eyes. It was not the fear of one man against another. It was not the fear of bodily harm. It was the fear of something unbelievable, unexplainable, and supernatural.

"I'll be damned," Derek whispered as he slowly released John's neck. "She did it. She really did it."

The enormity of what Derek had suspected hit him, and he stepped away from John. He turned, his own heart racing.

"She's crazy," John said, his voice weak and strained. "She's a freak!" he said, louder this time. "She ought to be locked up. I'm going to. . . ."

Derek whirled around and John jumped back, this time fearful for his life.

"I'll tell you what you're going to do. You're going to leave, and you're never going to return to Scotland." Derek advanced on John. "As soon as you get back to The States, you're going to notify your attorney that you want an immediate divorce—no conditions stipulated, just a quick divorce. You are never to contact Jennifer again. Never! And you will never breathe a word of what you saw up there on the mountain. Do you understand? Now get out of here," Derek commanded and turned to leave.

"You can have her," John spat out. "Maybe I should tell people what I saw. Maybe I should tell people what really happened, what she really did—*she flew through the air*," John shouted. "They'd haul her off to some laboratory. They'd lock her up. It's just what you two deserve. And you couldn't stop me once I'm in the United States."

Derek recognized the helpless hysteria in John's voice and turned to him. "You're a bigger fool than I thought, Dr. Bracken," Derek said as he walked back to where John was standing. "You don't have to worry about me. Think about it! What you saw was not humanly possible, was it?" He pushed John in the chest, forcing him back a step. "Are you foolish enough to go against a power such as that?" Derek whispered, a strange quality coming to his voice. "The little girl said it all, Dr. Bracken. Are you foolish enough to battle the *heavens*?"

Derek saw the stark fear in John's eyes and turned. This time he heard no reply as he walked out of the hotel room.

✳ ✳ ✳

"Are you sure you want to do this?" Derek asked again.

Jennifer laughed. "You've asked me that ten times since we left Thornhill. Yes, I want to do this and we're almost there," she said as she looked ahead.

They were driving in Derek's Land Rover up the mountain in The Highlands. They were going back to the site of the accident that had occurred a month before.

"I need to go back there. Maybe it will help," Jennifer

said. "John and I had been arguing. Then suddenly, I recognized this place. Cela's people had sacrificed children here. I think this is where she died. It was awful. I was so frightened. I begged him not to take me here."

Derek reached over and took her hand as they reached the top.

"Right here," Jennifer said. "We hit the other car here, and then our car slid about ten feet to the side," she said as she pointed.

Derek pulled off the road to the spot she had indicated and turned the motor off. He watched as Jennifer looked ahead.

"I can see it all so clearly," she said. "The other vehicle was spinning right there." She pointed and then reached for the door handle. "John and I both got out of the car."

"All right," Derek said. "Let's get out."

They both stepped out of the car, and Derek came around to where Jennifer was standing. She shook her head.

"The car was spinning around and then hit that boulder," she said as she pointed. "The door flew open and I saw the child. Her body was thrown into the air and over the edge right there," she said as she pointed to the edge of the cliff, "and then . . . nothing." She turned to Derek. "I remember everything up to that point, and then there's a thin film, like a curtain, that closes. I know the answer is there, right behind the curtain, but I can't see it."

Derek took her hand. "Does it frighten you, Jenny?" he asked. "Does this place or what happened here to Cela or to you and the little girl frighten you?"

"No," she said gently. "This place." She looked around. "I don't feel sad standing here. I feel good, very good." She paused, surprised at her own feelings. "That's strange, isn't it?"

Derek smiled. "Jenny, trust the good feeling. Trust yourself. You may never remember what happened here. Maybe you're not supposed to remember. Then again, if the time ever presents itself and you need to recall what happened, I have a feeling that the curtain will open and you will."

Jennifer looked at him. "You know, you've changed since we first met. You were so scientific then, and now you've become very philosophical."

Derek laughed. "You've got to admit that some very scientifically unexplainable things have happened to me since we met."

"I know. I wish I understood all of this," she said, looking around, the gray peaks of the mountains occluded by the gray sky, their very stark nature beautiful.

Derek looked at her. He loved her so much. He didn't know what he believed. Was Jennifer actually Cela in a previous life? Did he believe in reincarnation? Or was Jennifer descended from Cela? Had there once been a small percentage of human beings who had the ability to fly? What happened to them? Had they, as Cela said of the People of the Sky, been murdered by other human beings who had been frightened by such power, jealous of such ability? Did the trait reappear in a few people in the middle ages, such as Friar Joseph and the others that his research had uncovered? And once again, had those people been murdered because they possessed the secret of flight? Had this trait continued to be passed down to the descendants, where it laid quietly buried in the subconscious for thousands of years, surfacing in the minds of the descendants only at night when they dreamed, where it was safe. Had these people and their children finally learned to bury this incredible power in order to survive?

Derek searched Jennifer's face. "I don't know why you were able to see into the past, Jenny. We may never know that. But again, I would say to trust yourself. If it's important for you to understand, then the answer will come when you need it. In the meantime, I will be eternally grateful, for if you had not had the visions, I would have never found you. I love you, Jenny."

Jennifer smiled and threw her arms around Derek's neck.

TOUCH THE SKY

"You didn't find me, my love, I found you."

EPILOGUE

The little girl jumped out of her bed. The large, gray dog looked up from where it lay beside her bed. The girl ran across the room and opened the heavy door of her bedroom. The dog immediately stood and followed her out into the hall. The child's bare feet were silent as she crossed the ancient, gray stone floor to another door and opened it, her long, red hair tousled and flowing down her back.

"Mommy! Daddy!" she cried as she ran into the bedroom, the dog at her heels.

Derek sat up in bed just as the child hurled herself up onto the bed, laughing. He caught her in his arms.

"Daddy!" the little girl cried excitedly.

"Shhh," Derek said, pointing to Jennifer where she lay sleeping at his side. "Mommy is still sleeping."

"Mommy's a sleepyhead," the little girl giggled.

"Yes, she is," Derek agreed. He smiled as he settled his daughter on his lap. "Now," he said in a whisper as he kissed her on the head, "Tell me, little Lady Calista Rannoch, what has you so excited this morning?"

"Daddy, I had the best dream last night. I dreamed I could fly. I really could fly!"

SPECIAL LETTER TO MY READERS

Thank you for reading *Touch the Sky*, the first of three books in the Touch the Sky Series. I have always been fascinated with megaliths. When I gaze at a prehistoric stone formation or a crumbling castle, I easily step back in time, imagining the lives of people who once inhabited these sites. So, it was no surprise to me when, after visiting several of the megaliths and castles in the United Kingdom, I dreamed of the storyline of this book while sleeping.

In *Touch the Sky*, Jennifer sees an ancient race of people who could fly, and she meets and falls in love with Derek, an archaeologist who helps her accept her unusual ability to see into the past. Their story continues in *Daughter of the Sky*, where Jennifer again sees into the past—this time, the medieval world of King Henry VIII. But, more importantly, she is on a journey of self-discovery as she learns *what* she is—A Daughter of the Sky.

In the final book, Jennifer sees the Mongolian world of Genghis Khan. The power, implications, and expectations of a Daughter of the Sky are revealed.

I sincerely hope you enjoyed your time in Jennifer's world. I would love to hear your thoughts on *Touch the Sky*. You can write to me at alisonblasdellnovels@gmail.com or contact me at my website https://www.alisonblasdell.com.

Finally, reviews are crucial to an author. If you enjoyed *Touch the Sky*, please leave a review on my Amazon page.

Thank you, and best wishes,

Alison Blasdell

AUTHOR'S NOTE

Readers have asked me what is real in the book and what is the product of my imagination. Obviously, this is a work of fiction; however, in researching the background for this story, I uncovered some provocative facts.

The accounts of people flying, as documented in the sixteenth and seventeenth centuries, are factual. The Catholic Church did canonize Friar Joseph of Cupertino based, in part, on his demonstrated flying. So, also, are the written records of other people from various time periods apparently defying gravity and flying of their own volition. The writings from ancient Hebrew and Babylonian societies discuss The Shining Ones who came from the sky. Their arrival corresponded to amazing advances in civilization around 12,000 B.C. The 20,000-year gap in human cultural development (32,000-12,000 B.C.) is an anthropological mystery.

Britain and Europe are home to a myriad of Neolithic henges and stone megaliths. Archaeologists puzzle the purpose of these ancient structures. Some appear to predict the solstices and astronomical events; others are postulated to have had religious/spiritual significance. The purpose of the vast majority of these structures remains an enigma.

Finally, among those who, upon awakening, recall the nature of their dreams whilst sleeping, a small percentage of persons report the exhilarating experience of flying.

ACKNOWLEDGMENTS

I am grateful for the editing expertise of Joyce Mochrie, certified copy editor and proofreader. Thank you, Joyce, for your professionalism and graciousness.

Thank you to Amanda Gardner for her brilliant cover design. You are, indeed, a very talented graphic artist.

To my Beta Readers: Sandy Brewer, Vallie Gould, Gary Gould, Judy Smith, Scott Morton, Ed Smith, Raleigh Blasdell, and Grant Blasdell. Thank you for reading, critiquing, and encouraging. You're all amazing.

Alison Blasdell

THE CONFEDERATES' PHYSICIAN
A NOVEL BY ALISON BLASDELL

The year is 1863, and the United States is entering the third year of the Civil War. Young Samantha Carter, recently educated as a physician in Paris, defies her father, disguises herself as a boy, and runs away to enlist in the Union Medical Corps. On her way there, she is captured by a Confederate patrol. When the commanding officer, Major Ethan Winters-Hunt, discovers that the Yankee "boy" is a capable surgeon, he forces her to serve as a surgeon for the Confederate Army.

Samantha is unprepared for the horrors of battle and finds she must draw upon the strength and mysticism imbued in her as a child, running wild on the Western Frontier with the Lakota Indians. She must maintain her disguise under rigorous conditions. She is loyal to the Union, and yet she must save the lives of enemy soldiers.

As Ethan takes "Sam" from her first battlefield experience in Virginia to the defense of Atlanta, a tenuous friendship develops between them. Eventually, Samantha's identity as a young woman is discovered, and the friendship that Ethan and Samantha share turns into a passionate love that is severely tested by deceit and betrayal as the nation rages in war.

The Confederates' Physician is an epic love story that takes the reader back to the bloodiest time in American History—when families were torn apart, loyalties were tested, and innocence was lost.

Made in the USA
Las Vegas, NV
22 September 2023

77969749R00270